CONTENTS

PROLOGUE   1

1. CHAPTER 1   5
   A Misty Road

2. CHAPTER 2   12
   Oaths and Proclamations

3. CHAPTER 3   21
   Memories of Sand and Fire

4. CHAPTER 4   33
   Broken Promises

5. CHAPTER 5   39
   Simple Tea for a Simple Life

6. CHAPTER 6   50
   Nightmare

7. CHAPTER 7   58
   Circle

8. CHAPTER 8   68
   Sacrifices

9. CHAPTER 9   73
    Hero or Villain?

10. CHAPTER 10   81
    Magic and Murder

11. CHAPTER 11   94
    Gone in a Flash

12. CHAPTER 12   101
    Pactless

13. CHAPTER 13   112
    Trevils and Tribulations

14. CHAPTER 14   122
    Birthright

15. CHAPTER 15   128
    Cloaking

16. CHAPTER 16   150
    Piercing Light

17. CHAPTER 17   167
    Chaos Wrought

18. CHAPTER 18   174
    Destination

19. CHAPTER 19   188
    Lightbugs

20. CHAPTER 20   201
    Ruins

21. CHAPTER 21   208
    Hungry Eyes

22. CHAPTER 22   218
Scars

23. CHAPTER 23   223
Deal

24. CHAPTER 24   238
Stolen Name

25. CHAPTER 25   249
Suspicion

26. CHAPTER 26   256
Promises

27. CHAPTER 27   263
Hidden Home

28. CHAPTER 28   271
One-Hundred Percent

29. CHAPTER 29   282
Elven Queen

30. CHAPTER 30   288
Changes and Betrayal

31. CHAPTER 31   293
Cheating Death

32. CHAPTER 32   302
Lingering Hatred

33. CHAPTER 33   315
Illusion

34. CHAPTER 34   325
Black Flame

PROLOGUE

When a mage's talent manifests, it's the Spellbound Arch that first comes for you and when they arrive, they ask not but two simple questions.

The first: What did you destroy?

And the second: ...Who did you kill?

Journal Entry

Year: 830 E.B

I can not remember the days or times before. I cannot remember their faces nor the sounds of their voices. Nor of the clothes they wore, nor their smell.

Nor of the warmth of their touch. No, I remember nothing except the pain. The indignation. The burning.

My eyes focused as I squinted to block out the dazzling flame before me. An oddness assaulted my senses, like the smell of burning wood and others I couldn't recognize. They buffeted me. Bored into me. It made me sick. Pain... in my stomach, my head, my eyes, throat and nose. Pain in my ears, for I still could hear the unknown shrieking; but there was pain in my left-hand most of all. It hurt, more so than any words I write can describe.

I forced my eyes to focus as I glanced down to examine the source of that pain. I was on my knees, huddled in a muddy puddle with my left-arm sunk into the ground near to my elbow. Slowly, I removed that arm, and as the mangled mess came into view, I vomited red bile which coated the front of my ashen-covered dress. What was it? This thing? This... abomination? It wasn't me. It wasn't part of me. It certainly wasn't my own hand. But, despite my protests, when I commanded the ruined husk to close it obeyed. It was me. It was my hand; the blackened charred remnants of it.

I opened my mouth to scream, but I was wordless, soundless and silent. A breeze blew through my hair, fanning the flames of the still burning building in front of me as well as igniting the pain of my ruined flesh. I shoved it back into the ground, for I knew not what else to do. The muddy water cooled it, if only just.

Despite the heat of the flame in front of me, I felt cold. Chills ran down my spine and I wondered how long it would take the flame to either reach me or burn away. I couldn't find the strength nor will to care.

"By the hells, are you alright?"

Before I knew it, two strong arms grabbed and lifted me from the mud. I screamed and this time, sound came out, if only just. I felt myself being pulled away from the flame and into the darkness of the world beyond. The flame was the only place I knew. It was the only place I could remember. It was my solitude. My everything. Who was this other to deny me my only true home?

"Are you alright?" the stranger asked again. As I looked upon her figure, my eyes refused to focus. I could make out a multi-colored cloak, and shoulder length curly hair, but that was all.

As I opened my mouth to speak, only one word would come out. One word which encapsulated everything I felt in that moment. "W-W-Water..." "Water!" I heard the stranger snap her finger and before I knew it, a jug was placed to my lips, but it wasn't water she poured into my throat—it was life itself! The cooling refreshment seeped into my body, bringing a wellspring of new emotions. Tears of joy etched at the edge of my eyes, but my body wouldn't waste what precious little resources I had left.

The stranger laid me down to rest, but then I felt her fingers touch the skin, if you could call it that, of my left-hand. I tried to pull back, but the woman held firm.

I was growling like a wounded animal, but the woman said in a calming tone, "Easy... I can heal you. Fix you."

"Fix... me?" I croaked as a jolt of what felt like lightning coursed through my body. Suddenly, I felt tired. Exhausted. I laid my head back on a pile of small, cool rocks and it felt as comforting as anything I could remember, which was little. I glanced up and saw concern in the strangers eyes.

Before I could open my mouth to ask, the stranger said, "It'll be alright. You'll survive. You will survive. Tell me, what happened?"

Before I could, my mind drifted and I was no longer in that place. No, the place I went was warm and comforting. A place that smelled like fresh bread and butter. Smelled like spring flowers after a light-rain. A place that smelled of home.

When I awoke, I had been moved to the shade of a nearby tree. The stranger had set up a small fire with a cooking pot atop. The fire once again burned brilliantly in my eyes, and I squeezed my left-hand in reflexive response.

"You're awake," the stranger said. "I hate to do this now, and to someone so young... but I must, as it is my duty." She had stood until she lumbered above me. Kneeling, she stared into me with her sharp brown eyes. "What did you destroy?"

"I... I don't know."

"Who did you kill?"

"I... I don't know!"

The stranger rose, and glanced down the hillside. There, I noticed two hastily placed stones next to two mounds of dirt. "Remembering can be a curse, consider yourself lucky. My last question then, and this is from me alone... What is your name?"

"Kyra," I heard myself say.

"Surname?"

There was something at the edge of my lips, but when I opened my mouth to give it voice, nothing came out.

"No surname, eh?" The stranger said. Looking back at the stone slabs above the dirt mounds, two precarious ravens squealed back and forth between each other. Turning to me, the stranger reached down and ran her hand through my hair. "Black hair and the curiosity of ravens. "Ait Koqlu cot Oanq," or "From Stone and Ash." From the blood of ravens. Ait Ravenblood. Until we know more, you will be named Kyra Ait Ravenblood."

CHAPTER 1

A MISTY ROAD

Journal Entry

Year: 830 E.B

The days blended together as Lu'ce, my new master, whisked me away from near and far, with no seemingly concrete destination in mind. She had proclaimed something the day she had saved me, 'Ais koqlu cot Oanq.' 'From Stone and Ash' she had said it meant. For reasons beyond me, I couldn't get the saying out of my head. There was something about it. A beginning and an end. A hello and a goodbye. A birth and death. Reborn from the ashes of a previous life. Was I to be reborn? Looking at the remnants of my hand, I doubted I could. I will forever bear those scars.

The horse gave a slight neigh as the cart we rode lurched to the side. A few farmers, from the look of 'em, dirty and holding various tools of the trade, gave a rude gesture to our coachman. The man, sun-kissed and elderly, his eyes almost fully gray with age, paid them little mind.

Looking out across the dirt road, I could not help but notice a small flock of ravens with their black feathers and dark beady eyes staring at our coach from underneath the shade of a tree. Lu'ce glanced at me and grinned, pride filling her deep brown eyes.

"I sure know how to pick em', eh?" she had said.

"P-P-Pick what?" I had barely begun speaking again the day before, and Lu'ce had breathed a sigh of relief that I hadn't 'become a mute', as she so eloquently put.

"Why names, of course." Lu'ce had replied. "Ait Ravenblood. From the blood of ravens. Seeing how interesting they seem in you, and by the color of your own hair, I'd say I made the right choice."

"Why?" I had asked.

"Why... what?"

"Why are they interested?"

Master Lu'ce had scratched at her chin consideringly. "Rumor is that ravens can sense a person's resonance. Their latent abilities for wielding aethryis."

"Aethryis?"

Lu'ce sighed. "You really don't remember much, do you? Aethryis! Magic, as the commoners would say. And you—you must possess it in spades. Which is why what we do next is so important, and why I told you not to even try to reach for it... for now."

Master Lu'ce had explained previously that I was a mage and that when mages 'awaken' it wasn't always the prettiest sight. It can happen at anytime or in anyplace, but generally happens around people of my age or sometimes younger.

"You don't need to worry," I had said. "I'll never use magic again."

Master Lu'ce had stifled a laugh. "You say that now, but in a year you'll wonder how you ever lived without it. Mark my words on that. Still, I envy you a bit; the beginning, when your powers first come, is truly a wondrous time. You can use whatever order of aethryis you want, albeit muted. You're just a bottle of untapped potential."

"Order?"

"Order... a specific type. Take me, for example; I'm a Mystic. Or, as others would say, a healer. I can use aethryis to mend wounds."

I looked at my mangled hand; the skin was paper-thin and scarred. It did
not look like healing; it looked like butchery.
Master Lu'ce had frowned. "I'm sorry, but there is a limit to what I can do.
The sooner I can heal a wound, the better the healing takes. Your body... it
learns what its new form is like after a significant injury. Once it does, it is
very difficult to correct."
I had never thanked her for what she had done for me. Instead, I sulked, lost
in my misery as I bounced on the horse-driven cart on the dirt road with not
a home to return and not a destination to seek.

The train horn blew a loud bellow overhead, sending out a soft ringing echo through Kyra's ears. It resounded over and over in her mind, through the stone and metallic city around her, washing across the rain slick gutters, grates and buildings across all of Mistbreak, the city of sleepless nights.

Kyra stepped onto the platform as a flash of lightning brightened the dingy thoroughfare ahead as the train echoed the thunderous boom as its horn, signaling its departure. Accompanying the deep sounds was the soft humming of aethyris which propelled it forward across the tracks, leaving a small plume of white smoke in its wake which floated out across the populace of the bustling city like ocean foam against beached rocks.

She had finally made it: the place where the course of her life was to be set in stone. Or set in blood. It was a place where she could finally atone for her crime.

Looking around, it appeared Kyra was not the only one who was utterly lost in this jungle of brick and mortar. Wide-eyed young men and women stared onwards as helpless as lambs on slaughter day across the very city she had regarded so reverently in her dreams. But there would be nobody coming to help them. Just as there was nobody to help her. She shrugged and her mismatched cloak hugged her neck uncomfortably, dragging against her skin.

None could help her.

Mistbreak was a city shrouded in perpetual darkness. Thunderous clouds loomed overhead, and rain fell at an unremitting pace, which is the only reason, she suspected, that the city appeared to be so clean, despite the tremendous amount of creatures—the uncanny—who made it their home.

The mist, for which the city was named, made it troublesome to observe the people who inhabited it. It was quite impossible to make out the tiny shortcomings that made out each individual around her; human or otherwise. To witness what made each of them unique. In the mist, they all appeared as faceless apparitions to her. Wandering ghosts with no purpose. No meaning. That unnatural fog layer clung to her skin like a dank red clay. It made her nervous. Anxious and apprehensive. The hairs on her arms stood on end, as if sensing an unknown danger. Perhaps that was why tensions were said to be so high in the city? Perhaps this mist was mystical in nature? An *aethyrical* force. A powerful and evil one at that. One that prowled and prodded on the minds of the inhabitants here. Fed on them.

Or, perhaps, she was just uneasy about her first day.

It was then that Kyra noticed a crowd forming to her right. A mixture varying of both uncanny and humans. And, when she really concentrated, she could just make out what they all gawked at: there was a body lying alone in the middle of the thoroughfare.

"It's those bloody goblins," a dwarven man said with a deep, booming voice, wiping his giant red beard free of loose bread crumbs. His gauntlets clanked against his metal belt as he added, "Word is, they be gatherin' a force to the East."

"*Bah,*" a tall and muscular minotaur replied. "Superstitious nonsense. Prattle meant to pit us against one another. This here—this is obviously one of those damnable mages. I—"

The minotaurs' words died in his throat as, if summoned by the word itself, a group of cloaked figures descended upon them like the coming of a plague. *Mages,* dressed with their signature shifting magecloaks and silver-spun ringpacts on each of their fingers. They appeared from the mist, coordinated and deadly.

The onlookers fell silent as they quietly dispersed, leaving the mages to their work, but the minotaur mumbled something sinister under his breath as he reached down and grabbed a brown-cloth pack tied to a long stick which he set across his shoulders.

Distrust and animosity. It was so thick in the air. So palpable. Almost—Almost Kyra could almost taste it on her tongue.

She could think of no better place to serve her penance.

Forcing herself to look away, Kyra dared take the first steps towards what was to be her new home. Temporary or otherwise. It was then that an unfamiliar hand gripped at her wrist. Turning, she pulled her tightly gloved hand back with an audible gasp, asking, "What are you doing?"

A woman, slightly taller than she and appearing to be of similar age, stood with her mouth open and aghast. She had dark skin and short curly black hair with streaks of red and gold layered within. And her eyes... the left as bright blue as a glacier lit by moonlight and the right as green as a lush forest after a spring rain. She was a woman that beautiful women would consider beautiful themselves.

"*I'm so sorry!*" the woman said, thrusting her hands into her pockets as if to show she was 'disarmed.' "So terribly, terribly sorry. Truly, it's just..." She went silent for a time, her off-color eyes wandering out across the mist as if she searched for someone or something hidden in the crowded streets. When she failed to locate what she sought, her eyes focused back on her. "You look like you know where you're going." She clapped her hands in front of her in a mock prayer. "Apologies again. My name is Armeya. Armeya *Ais* Cane." She reached out a hand in greeting.

"Kyra," she replied. "Kyra *Ais* Ravenblood." Looking down at Armeya's hand, she grimaced, stepping back. "And I've never been to Mistbreak before. This is my first time. I—I can't help you."

Kyra turned to go, but Armeya planted a hand on her shoulder. "You are an adept at Dragrins, right?" she asked. "I mean, an adept to be?"

Nodding, Kyra tried again to step away, but the woman's arm held firm. Armeya was stronger than her slender figure would let on and she wondered if perhaps Armeya used aethryis to enhance that strength?

"Well then," Armeya said, "perhaps we should travel together? Safety in numbers? I'd rather not end up like," she glanced at the corpse, "*that!* To think, a murder done so openly—"

"No," Kyra replied curtly. "I'd prefer to find my own way. You should do the same. If we are to be adept mages, we need to be able to handle ourselves in all situations."

Armeya narrowed her multi-colored eyes. "One wrong turn down a dark alley could be your last," she warned. "You know, Mistbreak doesn't outright ban the travel of uncanny creatures on its streets, as you can plainly see. Nonsense, of course. It's savagery allowed to go unchecked. Worse, I've heard that problems with the *pactless* have become quite vexing of late. Truly, it would be safer for us adepts to travel together. Logical even. It's not like we're masters yet. We are still students at heart. Personally, I'd rather not end up as an aethyris-line before I've even received my own *ringpact.*"

Kyra searched around and, sure enough, mingled with amongst the mostly human crowd, she could make out various uncanny. A goblin or two. A gnomish. The centaur from before had seemingly found a few more of his kind and they stared hard at the mages with untrusting eyes. Some even hatefully. The mages themselves didn't seem to notice. Or, at least, pretended not to.

Then, of course, there were the elves. Not considered uncanny, a particularly cruel word when speaking of the 'others.' They had various ethereal skin tones and were dressed elegantly, in various bright colors, as they always seemed to. Both human and uncanny alike gave them a wide berth as they strode at the very center of the thoroughfare. The elves acted as if the gods themselves blessed the very land they tread upon. They were royalty indeed, and none dared to draw their ire.

Armeya smiled knowingly as she whispered, "You see... *unsafe.* So, new friend," the woman hooked her arm interlocked with her own. "*Let's go!*"

Kyra pulled away, but smirked at having lost the battle in this back-and-forth conversation. Master Lu'ce had once said that she should open up more. Make connections. Friends. 'Become whole.' She didn't agree with the woman's insistence, but Master Lu'ce had been a fine mentor and had never steered her wrong before.

"Fine," Kyra relented. "We can travel together... for now." Armeya smiled. "So, 'new friend'... do you happen to know where we are?"

Armeya scanned to the right, and then to the left, turning back the way they had come, and then turning forward. Grinning, she gave her nose a flick with the back of her thumb. "I've not a clue."

"*Great...*"

She shook her head, chose a random direction, and walked away into the sea of the masses.

"*Wait!*" Armeya cried out, reappearing behind her like a helplessly lost puppy, nipping at her feet with the promise that she would guide and protect her.

Kyra chuckled to herself. No chance of that. She couldn't even protect herself.

CHAPTER 2

OATHS AND PROCLAMATIONS

Journal Entry

Year: 830 E.B

"This will hurt," Master Lu'ce had warned me. "Bear it—embrace it! Pain is a part of who you are; a part of being a mage. Do not hide from it, nor shun it."

Naked and scared, two women whom I did not know had gripped me against a wooden board, my back left exposed to a third. Master Lu'ce had stood in front, doing her best to keep me calm and to draw my attention from them. But how could she? What were they doing to me? Why did I deserve this?

"We're ready," one of the women had said as I felt four small needle points press into the back of my neck. A warm tingle dripped down my neck and body. Blood... I was bleeding. I struggled against my captors, but Master Lu'ce reached out and grasped my shoulder, holding me firm.

"By the hells, just do it already," she said and as she did, the needle points became as daggers. One woman cursed as she rammed the device into the back of my neck. Pain shot throughout my entire body and I shuddered against it.

The world lurched and my senses betrayed me. I couldn't see. Couldn't taste.
Hear or feel.
I hadn't realized it at the time, but I was staggering and walking in circles.
The strange woman had released me, and vaguely I had the sense of some-
thing being pressed against my body. A towel perhaps? The next I knew, I
was waking, as if coming out of a dream. Fresh vomit laid beneath me and
Master Lu'ce stood above with pity in her eyes. I rolled out of the bile and
lifted my head; it felt weighed by anchors.
"It'll take time to get used to it," Master Lu'ce had said.
"What... What did you do to me?"
"Only what I must," she replied. "You must believe me. I did what I must."
Fresh pain radiated from the back of my neck and when I reached back, I felt
a strange metallic and square item embedded into my flesh. I pulled at it,
but a pain, like a shock, jolted my body.
"Don't," Master Lu'ce had warned. "You cannot remove it. Not now. Not
ever."
I traced the skin around the strange device and winced at the tenderness.
"What is it?" I had asked.
"Protection. From others; from yourself. It is called a magelock, and it is the
first step of many."
"'First of many'" I repeated. "With what goal?"
Master Lu'ce had smiled widely. "Why... to become a master mage in the
service of the Spellbound Arch, of course. The only path that remains to you
now. The only one that remains to us all."

Two tall, blackened metal gates, surrounded by a wall of red brick, stood clear and open, welcoming all the fresh faced students who stared emphatically at the sights surrounding them.

The courtyard of Dragrin's was well maintained. Well, indeed. Marble statues of men and women, unknown to her, shone in the unnatural light of aethyris-infused torches and the ghostly blue glow they gave off. The grass was amazingly green and verdant and as lush as a forest, despite the lack of sunlight in Mistbreak. It had been trimmed with the care only shown by a master groundskeeper. She suspected something magical in nature there as well as, no matter how many students trampled the stuff underfoot, the blades of grass sprung back as if reinforced with steel.

Armeya tugged on her arm, drawing her attention back towards her. "Are we just going to stand here all day?" she asked.

Kyra pulled free. This woman was about as clingy as they come, and her constant need for physical affirmation was grating on her every nerve. Perhaps she had been wrong to coddle the women's feelings for companionship. It was a farce, anyway. She wasn't here to make friends; she was here to atone.

"I'm taking it all in," Kyra said simply. "We're going to be here a long time. We're to be first year mages. Adepts. Remember your training as an apprentice? It is best practice to get a lay of the land quickly, so that you don't need to rely on others' knowledge to find your way around." She paused, seeing the woman's blank expression. "Didn't your master teach you any of this?"

Armeya frowned and her brow furrowed as lines of anger marred her otherwise perfect face. She said in a tauntingly sweet voice, "You know, if we are going to remain best friends, then you'll need to drop that serious act around me." The woman paused, chewing on her lip and studying her up and down as if she were a prize horse. Something to covet. A conquest. "*Hmm*, something tells me that this isn't an act at all. Something happened to you. Something bad. Pity." Snapping her fingers, Armeya gave her a quick wink. "I'll just need to break you of this rut, that's all."

"I'm not a dog," Kyra muttered under her breath. "And we are not 'best friends.' We're not even regular friends. If I'm moving too slow for you, and you want to go—*go!* I won't stop you. And I certainly won't be offended."

Armeya peered around the grounds of Dragrin's nervously, twiddling her fingers. The other young mages who shuffled around her grumbled their distaste that the pair of them stood awkwardly in their way in the middle of the walkway. Her eyes flashed a change of color for a moment as she said, "Fine, I'll leave you to it—for now. But don't you wander off too far. Best friends need to look after one another. Remember that."

"I told you, we aren't—"

Armeya suddenly disappeared into the crowd as easily as a mist breaks against the sun's dawn. Well, in all places besides the city of Mistbreak, of course. She stood in shocked silence. Whatever had she done to deserve that woman's incessant *friendship?*

"*Tsh,*" said an unknown voice. "That woman looks to be quite the handful."

Turning, Kyra was met with yet another unfamiliar face. Tall and thin, with pale skin and matching pale-blue eyes, this woman had a serious look about her—far more so than when compared with Armeya. She pushed a hand through her blond hair and she noticed that the woman was missing pieces of that hand. Specifically, three fingers, leaving just her thumb and an index on the left side.

"I wouldn't know," Kyra said, intrigued by the injury and holding her own gloved hand to her chest. "I've barely met the girl myself."

"And yet you both seem to get along so well." The woman cocked a mocking grin. "I guess that's just what it's like for outsiders like us. We're different, so we're drawn to each other like moths to an infused flame."

"That's one theory."

"And another?"

"... That some people are just clingy. No use explaining the unexplainable."

The woman chuckled. "Names Iona *Ais* Cracksman. '*Ais Koqlu cot Oanq.*' Pleasure to meet you..."

"Kyra *Ais*—"

"Iona, are you bothering your other adepts already?"

Kyra grit her teeth in frustration as yet another unknown interjected themselves into the conversation. This young man, with tanned skin, had an oddness about him. His hair looked silverish-blue, as the morning frost touched the grass, which contrasted his deep brown eyes. He held a hand out towards her. When she ignored it, he scratched at the back of his ear instead.

"This is Soren Frost," Iona said. "He was a self-proclaimed delinquent at our former apprenticeship. Personally, I think he's just starved for attention. Clearly his mommy didn't love him enough, probably why his family didn't bother training him them—"

Soren's eyes conveyed anger, but it disappeared in a flash, replaced with a casual grin. "*Prankster!*" he corrected. "Self-proclaimed *prankster*—not that you would know anything about fun, Iona. I remember you always being so serious. So lost in your books. And music." He leaned to whisper in her ear. "You know, we used to call her the bookkeeper at Talrose."

"Talrose?"

"Apprenticeship school, for those without a proper master. My... father was too busy to train me himself, so I was sent off."

Iona flushed red, and the lines of her jaw tightened. "Bookkeeper of Talrose, I'd forgotten that one. But let's not mingle words, Soren; that's one of the nicer names you and your ilk elected to call me. Care to repeat another?"

It was Soren's turn to blush, and he averted his eyes from Iona's baleful glare. "I don't know what you're talking 'bout," Soren said. "Perhaps your mind's fuzzy, being so clogged up with your novels all the time."

Speaking of fuzzy minds, her own head ached with an unknown pressure. It felt as if something was trying to push its way in. To dig for... something. But as if walking in on a mouse, the pain quietly slipped the moment she noticed it. Mistbreak... this place was said to play odd tricks on the mind. She would need to be careful.

Iona suddenly huffed and stomped away in a fit, but just before she disappeared into the crowd, she turned back, saying, "It was nice to meet you, Kyra. I hope we can chat again soon. '*Ais Koqlu cot Oanq.*'" And then she was gone, lost in a sea of unknown faces.

Soren stared at the crowd dejectedly. "She's always been that way. Alone. And speaking odd phrases with the old tongue like some sort of zealot. She said it's because her father... Well, that's not important. It's been a pleasure." As if summoned, Soren took off, disappearing himself into the crowd.

Suddenly, a large bell crashed, sending out a loud booming blast across the courtyard. With each strike, the crowd of students quickened and she, not wishing to be late on her first day, joined them in their frantic haste to get inside. It was as if being moved along by the waves of the ocean. There was a natural flow to it. A rhythm. If you moved too slowly, you would see yourself swept under. The only choice was to swim forward.

Inside, the narrow hallway opened up into an elaborate vestibule. The lights set on the walls shone the same eerie, ghostly blue as they had outside, leaving the room dim. The ceiling was most peculiar of all. It appeared to have been painted in a rather rustic style with bright colors of yellows, oranges, and greens with a scenery like a field of bright flowers on a sunny day. But, as time passed, so did the painting move. The sun began its descent on the other side of the ceiling and a moon, showing the same ghostly blue as the lights, took its place. The flowers, once gold and blooming, died with the change. In their place, there remained glowing white cotton flowers whose buds released, flowing across the canvas before it reset again in, presumably, the next day.

It was a cycle of life and death.

Kyra craved to study the aethyris of the canvas further, but the crowd surged forward once again, propelled by what she could only assume were masters of Dragrin's who waved their hands frantically in the air. She allowed herself to be carried away until she eventually found herself in a grand hall of sorts. Chandeliers set with metal chains hung high above the other students, who watched on at a grand stage where one individual that she couldn't yet make out stood reverently.

In her heart, she knew this to be Elder Reylar *Ais* Steelhand; the great and famous Steelhand mage. As they pushed forward, the other students gasped as they recognized him as well. The man was a hero. A living legend. A mage said to be so powerful that the utterance of his name could quell an entire orc rebellion without a single arrow fired. Not a drop of blood spilled. He had fought in the battle of Crystal Run and survived to tell the tale. Haggled with the hag of the Obsidian Mire.

And he was to be their mentor.

Kyra's heart fluttered at the very thought. It made the entire experience finally seem real. It made all her sacrifices with Master Lu'ce seem worth it. The only cost she struggled with was that of her own body. She glanced down and grimaced, squeezing her left hand tight.

It was worth it. It had to be.

Naturally, the adepts began forming lines and taking a resting stance with both hands neatly folded at their waists. Kyra followed suit, taking her place among them and folding her hands as well. Not long after, the doors of the grand hall squealed shut. Wood slammed against metal, letting out a creek as air rushed through her black hair, sending it swirling around her face.

When all was in place, Elder Reylar stepped to the front of the rostrum to address the hall. "Hello," he said. "And welcome to Dragrins, the Northern Outpost of the Spellbound Arch and, coincidentally, your new homes. As many of you are already aware, my name is Reylar *Ais* Steelhand, and I am this outpost's Elder. Each of you finds yourselves here because you have shown a will and the skill to wield aethyris at an advanced level. Perhaps even worthy to become bearers of ringpacts, and to provide services to those in need, for that is the ultimate goal of a mage: Service and Sacrifice."

Each student in the room echoed the Elder's voice, adding, "*Service and Sacrifice!*"

Elder Reylar paused, causing quite a few tongues to wag as a hushed murmur rose in the stuffy hall. He cleared his throat, commanding their attention. "But just because you've made it this far does not guarantee your time here will be pleasant or longstanding. We've a dozen or more first years who've yet to receive a ringpact. And some—some never will."

That proclamation sent another wave of gossip fluttering around the room. So loud it was deafening.

Reylars' voice rose above it all. "*Quiet!*" he commanded. The murmurs instantaneously died, and one could hear a pin drop as he added, "Just because you have made it this far does not mean success is guaranteed. That is up to the dwarven seers, for it is them and the deal that we mages established with them all those years ago who have sole authority to decide and create ringpacts... and their bearers. Each of you has spoken to them. Each has had their mind delved. Some of you have already received your answer. And some... required more time. It is unfortunate, and I do not relish the thought of what must be done." He waved his hand above an assortment of objects on a table next to the lectern. "But do so I will. That is the meaning of sacrifice. Now, let us begin... Nelly *Ais* Jarvest, please step forward."

A timid girl with light-brown hair raised a shaking hand from the depths of the crowd. Slowly, the other students backed away, leaving her isolated in the middle of the room. Her hand lowered to her side, and the shakiness was transferred to her knees. She looked as if she would flee from the room as everyone's eyes drilled into her.

She was as a wounded animal in a den of lions.

"Do not be afraid," Elder Reylar said, reaching out a hand which shined silvery-blue in the light. "Come forward."

Students slowly parted as Nelly made her way to the rostrum. The room remained quiet, all except Nelly's shoes, which squeaked irritably as she walked. The wooden steps up to Elder Reylar creaked from the additional weight until she stood in the presence of the Elder himself.

"Kneel," Elder Reylar proclaimed, and Nelly complied without hesitation. "Nelly *Ais* Jarvest, do you swear an oath upon this ringpact to preserve The Spellbound Arch? Do you swear to do what is necessary and what is demanded for the betterment of mages and others alike?"

Nelly was silent, and it was as if time stood still. Everyone held their breath, waiting impatiently for her answer. Then, she stared up at the Elder with a surprising amount of determination in her eyes as she said, "I do."

Elder Reylar reached to his lectern and lifted a small silver trinket. Circular and silver, it cast a magical light across the body of students. "Nelly Jarvest," he said, "I hereby declare you a Mage Adept of The Spellbound Arch to the order of Mystics, who seek to knit the wounds of those in peril." He gingerly slipped the ring around her finger and bade her stand.

There was a roaring of cheers as those of the same *Order* clapped wildly at the fresh addition to their ranks. Nelly stared out at them, smiling from ear to ear. Elder Reylar nodded, and Nelly walked down with newfound confidence. She survived the first trial and was now part of the Spellbound Arch. Her new family. Those near congratulated her by clapping her on the back until she, once again, was another faceless one in the crowd.

Kyra breathed out slowly, only then realizing she had been holding her breath.

Steady... she told herself. *Steady...*

Elder Reylar took his position back at the lectern. "Balsam *Ais* Tenerbris."

This calling and proclamation of oaths lasted for a time, with Elder Reylar announcing names, those adepts accepting their ringpacts and once again disappearing among the restless faces who either waited their turn or waited to get back to their own duties.

Kyra's mind wandered, and she could not help but think back to when she herself had met with a dwarven Seer.

CHAPTER 3

MEMORIES OF SAND AND FIRE

Journal Entry

Year: 837 E.B

I had inhaled the billowing black smoke from the furnaces of the dwarven mountain city of Goltirm. The heat was intense, and with every spray of molten metal that spewed out, sweat squeezed from my skin, pouring down my body only to sizzle in the air as it fell, evaporating as it met the earth at my feet.

How anyone or anything could live here was beyond my understanding. Beyond reason.

"Are you alright?" Master Lu'ce had asked, wiping her forehead with the back of her hand. She was tall and muscular. Elegance personified. Her hair was braided and blond with streaks of dark coursing through. When her hand fell to her side, it appeared absolutely soaked. "Blasted heat. I'll never get the smokey smell out of my hair."

I glanced at the woman; my teacher. My master. Even Master Lu'ce, ever stoic, couldn't keep a cool demeanor down here beneath the mountain.

"I'm fine," I had lied, trying and failing to halt my racing heart. "At least I will be once we leave." I held my hand to my chest, a habit Master Lu'ce had consistently chastised me about in the past. "I don't like the heat."

Master Lu'ce frowned. "Sorry, child, but you know we can't leave. Not yet. This rite is something that all mages must go through." She reached behind her own head, feeling at her magelock. "You know the only path forward is to have your mind delved by the dwarven seers. To let them see your secrets laid bare. To determine if you are worthy of receiving a ringpact. Worthy to be who you truly are."

I had brushed off her words. Worthy? I am worthy of nothing.

"I know, I know," I had said with complicity. "You've told me a hundred times already. Everyone has." I clenched my fist. "But I'm scared."

"There is no reason to be scared, child," Master Lu'ce had said soothingly. "And I want you to ponder something else. Distract yourself. If not this, then what other future lies before you? If you fail here, what is your alternative path?" She had softened her voice to a mere whisper. "I know your pain, child. I know it all too well. You've no family to return to. No home. At least, not one that wouldn't ostracize you because of your differences. We mages only know one family: each other."

I put on my strongest face, but beneath, I struggled to hold back tears. I appreciated that Master Lu'ce's words were said for my benefit, that she hadn't meant them to be insensitive, but they came off as cruel and unfeeling all the same.

Staring up, voice breaking, I had asked, "Tell me, what do I do?"

"Be brave!" Master Lu'ce had replied. "And pray to whatever deity you wish that the seer finds purpose in you. Now come, let's not keep them waiting."

Two dwarven guards met us at the city's gates. They stood stoically at the entrance to an immense wall of metal and stone. This wall led to the city proper, and, as far as I knew, was impenetrable, even by mages. Each guard walked forward in turn, hands reaching precariously to the swords at their hips.

One guard, beard braided down to his shins, had said, "State your business."

"We are here for the Rite of Dreamwalking," Master Lu'ce had replied, giving me a coy smile and a wink.

"Name." Master Lu'ce had opened her mouth to answer, but the guard raised a hand to cut her off. "From the girl."

I narrowed my eyes as I had said, "Kyra Ait Ravenblood."

The guard had nodded, as if they expected me. "Present magelock."

I had turned, moving my hair to one side to show the small metal chip embedded at the back of my neck. I had still remembered the time I had received it. That had been a dark day. When the only thing I thought capable of keeping me sane was stripped from me to but a whisper.

I longed to feel whole once again.

The guards had glanced towards one another, nodding as they did. Both turned and went to each side of the metal gate, which stood at least ten steps tall and thirty steps wide. One guard knocked elaborately, almost as if playing a tune. Then the second guard mimicked it, changing the rhythm ever so slightly. The hinges creaked as the gate opened. The sound of it screamed in my ears, sending pain radiating through my mind.

Master Lu'ce had appeared taken aback, the same as I, her hands going to her ears to block out the noise. After what felt like a lifetime, the door halted, falling silent, and the guards wordlessly prompted us forward into the city. Inside was a city within a city—as bustling a place as I had ever seen before. Traders, mostly dwarven, but with some other uncanny and humans mixed in as well, hawked their wares with a gusto. The crowd moved as if following some sort of dance. There was an order and purpose here that I didn't quite understand.

Master Lu'ce nudged me in the shoulder as she had said, "Not what you were expecting, eh?" I had shook my head. "Well you better get used to it. And quick. We need to make our way through this jungle."

Then, as if struck by lightning, I noticed something... different. Odd.

"Master Lu'ce," I had asked, "where are the children? I don't see any—"

My Master pressed a hand to her lips, stilling my question. "Shh," she had said, lowering her voice to nothing but a whisper. "Never mention children."

I had gently nudged her hand away. "Why?"

"Why indeed?"

Turning, I was met with the sight of an elderly dwarven woman whose fire-touched skin had far too many piercings of gold on her face and ears. The woman was short, quite a bit shorter than myself. This powerful woman appeared to be ancient.

"Please excuse me," I had said, "my name is—"

"Kyra Ait Ravenblood," the dwarven woman had replied. "And she is Lu'ce Ait Nox. You are both mages of the Spellbound Arch. She a master, and you, just an apprentice."

Master Lu'ce grinned, tapping her clenched fist to her heart. "It's an honor to see you again, Seer Helgeda."

"Enough of that," the dwarven woman had said. "You know how I detest false pleasantries."

Helgeda reached out, pulling Master Lu'ce into an embrace. It was odd to see the dwarven woman half Lu'ce's size handle her so easily. Master Lu'ce succumbed, kneeling a bit to wrap her arms around the dwarven woman.

"It's been too long, my friend," Master Lu'ce had said.

"It always is," Helgeda had replied. "But that is the nature of things. We have far too little time—and it's even worse for you humans. What, you only live to be around a century?"

Master Lu'ce snickered. "If they're lucky, maybe. For us mages, it's a little different—but not by much."

Helgeda had frowned, a look of genuine concern in her eyes. "That's a pity," she had said. "Truly. But what am I saying? At least your kind has no trouble ushering in the next generation. Which brings me back to Kyra's original question. You asked why you see no children here?"

I had nodded, not trusting my words after seeing the affection display between those two.

Helgeda got a sad look in her eyes. "It is because of the Mountain's Curse." It was then, at the edge of my senses, that I heard a soft sound, like the slow prattling of rain, the body of the torrent coming quickly behind it. I had placed a hand on my chin. "The Mountain's... Curse?"

"Aye, a terrible thing. Truly dreadful."

The rain now sounded like the crashing of drums and the torrent, the unison of a thousand voices crying out.

Master Lu'ce crossed her arms against her chest. "It's really no time for a history lesson—"

"History is all we have!" Helgeda had replied emphatically. "If the girl wishes to learn of our plight, then I am not one to shy away from telling it to her. Perhaps she will be the mage to finally make good on the pledge your ancestors proclaimed all those ages ago."

The sound was now in full fortissimo. The stone shook with its power, and the dwarven citizens all stopped in the streets, falling to their knees and staring towards the stone sky, illuminated by the light of a thousand small crystals. And then the sound receded, the stone settling and all resumed their day as if nothing had transpired. Reaching up, I dabbed at my eyes—tears, but I knew not for what I shed them, only that they needed to be shed.

I had opened my wavering mouth and said, "What was—"

Helgeda had turned her attention towards me completely, focusing her eyes as if she were attempting to drill through my head. To dissect what I was thinking. A nearby plume of fire and smoke lit the features of the seer's face for just a moment. Her face suggested she was far older than her body gave credence.

"Nevermind the call," Helgeda explained. "It is... unimportant, for now. The Mountain's Curse is the price my people have paid for our arrogance. A little over a thousand cycles have come and gone. Back when humans were still a growing folk, my ancestors dug the mountains of Exavar: the hills of the world. We held little regard for the ground. The earth and the soil. Nor the flow of energy between them. We cared only for the shiny treasures in our midst. The glittering gems. The silvery trinkets. But, like many things, it was never enough." Helgeda looked down at her fingers, rich with golden rings, and frowned. "In the end, we drove the mountains to enact its vengeance upon us. One day, inexplicably, our birthrate plummeted to but one in ten dwarven women being able to conceive. The rest, like me, are forced to watch as those select few bear the responsibility for all. And it has been that way ever since. The curse serves as the basis for the agreement between dwarven kind and the

Spellbound Arch. We create the ringpacts as a means for you mages to control your powers and, in exchange, the mages are to use such power to end our curse once and for all. So far however, only one side has made good on that ancient promise."

There was a silence between them as I considered the new information. Why hadn't Master Lu'ce taught me about such an important event? Perhaps she did not want the knowledge that mages are bound to dwarven kind to spread? Mages were supposed to be held in a higher regard. So powerful that they—we needed to chain ourselves. Only elves were said to stand above us in the social hierarchy. However, this still seemed like a rather important oversight, especially for Master Lu'ce.

"I'm sorry," I finally said, unsure of what else to say.

Helgeda had waved me off. "Ancient history. And not at all your fault, child. Some think that the curse should never be broken. That, in the end, it has strengthened us. Our people. But..." Helgeda placed a quivering hand on her own stomach, "those rarely know the pain of being infertile themselves. Of always hoping, but never knowing, until the countless ages of your body stare back at you in every reflection—a reflection of what you wanted, but have been ever denied."

Master Lu'ce put a hand to Helgeda's shoulder, squeezing lightly, and the seer returned the gesture. "I am fine, my friend. Let us finish what you came here to do. Please come to my home. I have little, but I've some tea to offer you. Don't let it be said that I am not a gracious host. Besides, I know how weak your human constitution is for the heat."

Master Lu'ce coughed, secretly wiping the sweat from her brow. "I know not of what you speak of, dear friend," she had said, smiling slyly. "But some tea would be lovely."

The walk to Helgeda's home was but a short way, and I soon found myself crossing my legs awkwardly on a stone slab that was supposedly a chair as Helgeda placed a cup on a nearby stone table in front of me, beckoning with the back of her hand for me to pick it up. Small puffs of steam wafted from the glass, and I could almost taste the honey in the air. A testament to the quality of the leaves used in the brew. Reaching out, the cup was warm to my hands,

*and, placing it to my lips, I let the warm tea run down my throat, soothing
me from the inside out. It tasted magnificent, and, somehow, the heat of it
made the heat of dwarven city seem less. More manageable, if that could be
believed.*

I couldn't help but smile.

"I'm glad you like it," Helgeda had said.

*The Seer's hut was small. Tiny, even compared to my own modest accommo-
dations on Master Lu'ce land. It was only just large enough for one woman
to live comfortably—even if she was of dwarven descent and thus took far
less space. Decorating the walls were various knickknacks of different colored
crystals and stones. They twinkled from the smallest glint of light that came
in through shuttered windows. The dwarven people are marvelous characters.
Some consider them uncanny, yes, but possessive of a mind that matched those
of humans and elves—despite what some textbooks would claim. Living deep
in the mountain, they built their homes straight into the stone—just as this
one was. The craftsmanship of it all never ceased to amaze me. These were the
descendants of the Builders. The cultivators. The true shepherds of the planet.*

The shepherds who'd abandoned their flock and their world.

*Master Lu'ce drained her own tea in one fell swoop, letting out a soft sigh of
satisfaction as she placed it back down on the slab. "So," she had said, drawing
attention to herself. "Are we ready? We've got a way to travel yet still, and I'd
hate to do so in the dark."*

Helgeda had grinned, the lines of her face like deep, jagged cracks in a cliff.

*"Are you not from the Order of the Mystics?" she had asked. "Surely you
can heal any harm that befouls you with that elegant ringpact of yours? My
people's gift to you, remember?" She smiled coyly.*

*"Ha-ha," Master Luce had laughed dryly. "Hilarious. Do you fancy yourself
a jester now? But come, I'm being serious. You know how much grief I get if
I'm late presenting my apprentice?"*

*"Much, I am sure. We both know you especially are kept on a short leash. I've
even heard rumors you've set more than one apprentice's clothes on fire during
your lessons."*

Master Lu'ce grimaced. "They had it coming," she replied. "Besides, I put them out... eventually. And no, Kyra's my one and only. I thought I was done taking in the lost, but her... well, she left an impression. I'm sure you'll see soon."

Helgeda had held a hand to her chin. "The world above is truly a mystery to simple dwarven folk like myself."

"Sure... simple." Master Lu'ce had coughed into her hand. "Let's go with that. Enough tea—enough pleasantries." She turned towards me. "Are you ready?"

Trying not to show how nervous I truly was, I had asked. "What do I need to do?"

"Nothing," Helgeda had replied. "Just finish your tea and relax."

Looking down, I noticed my cup was near empty. Oddly, I hadn't remember drinking so much. When my eyes came back to rest on the dwarven woman's face, it was distorted and wrong. Her eyes drifted apart, and it was as if I were spun around and around and then left to stand on my own.

Then it hit me, and I made my voice deep as I had asked, "You—You drugged me?"

"Not drugged... per se," Helgeda had replied. "It's all part of the ritual. To help open your mind to me. To bring down your defenses."

Master Lu'ce was standing nearby, and she placed a warm hand on my shoulder. "It's fine," she had said. "I'm here."

"Why aren't—"

"Why aren't I spinning as well?" Master Lu'ce had chuckled at my question. "Helgeda only added the powder to your tea. When you weren't looking, of course. Quite the nimble hands, that one. Surprising, I know. Amazing stuff, it is. Tasteless. Odorless. Nothing to give it away at all."

"Stop teasing her," Helgeda had said. "Can't you see you're scaring the poor thing?" The dwarven woman turned towards me with grandmotherly eyes. "I assure you child, it's nothing nefarious. Now, just relax, and let your mind drift in the clouds. Close your eyes. Go back—back to your dreams. Back to the dreams that haunt you in the night. The nightmares."

"I... I..."

Suddenly, it was as if my mind were no longer my own. As Helgeda had suggested, I floated, almost as if above my own body, looking down on the two of them, and myself, from a vantage. I kept going—higher and higher—until I left the depths of the mountain and found myself kneeling in a luscious field of white flowers. It went for as far as the eye can see on all sides. Over the hills and around rushing streams. This was a place of beauty, as if it were made for me. Just me. Beauty... far too grand. Nothing like this truly existed. The world was a dark and evil place. A place where the things you love burned.

Burned...

There was a spark, and suddenly the field lit with a hellish flame. Slight, at first, but the flames grew larger and larger until it encapsulated the land. I was paralyzed! Forced to stare the fire down and watch it smolder, reducing everything I loved to ash in its wake.

There it was: the source!

Realization dawned on me that this was not a new place at all. No, this was a place I remembered very well indeed. A blinding pain splintered through my head like the cracking of wood under the ax. The pain lept from my eyes to the back of my head, and a high-pitched ringing in my ears punctuated that misery as I plummeted back towards the earth.

At the center of the burned field of ash, I saw the thing I feared most:

A little girl.

The girl's clothes had been blackened and burned away from the flames. The skin of her left arm was charred, the flesh of it barely hanging on by loose scraps of skin. It was a scene I recognized, and one that I tried to pull away from with all her might before being vigorously flung into the girl.

It was me... it had always been me.

I felt it again. The loss. The grief. I wailed until my lungs begged for air and then I screamed some more. Each soft stroke of the breeze sent a radiating pain through my burned flesh and up my arm, and the pain in my head was as fresh as ever before.

"Why are you doing this to me?" I had screamed towards the sky and the void. I shrieked until I could take no more, collapsing to the ashy earth. My ruined

arm touched the soil and, driving it down into the dirt, I felt just the slightest
bit of cooling to ease my torment. It happened again. Again and again.
It always did.
That is where I remained, sobbing until my eyes bore no more tears. The white
flowers would grow no longer. Never again. I had killed them.
I had killed them all.

A bright light burned in my eyes, causing a sharp pain to radiate through my
skull. Groaning lightly to myself, I dared to open them.
At first, my vision was blurry, like looking through a fogged mirror of a
bathhouse. I was just able to make out indistinct outlines in the room. But
before long, my sight cleared, showing me the worried faces of Master Lu'ce
and Helgeda standing above me.
Somehow, during my sleep, I had fallen to the floor.
"She's coming too," Helgeda had said, visibly shaken.
Master Lu'ce ahd shook her head, the worry plain on her face. "That was...
intense. Are you alright, Kyra?"
"I'm fine," I had lied, slapping Master Lu'ce's hand away as the woman
reached out towards me.
Helgeda sighed, slumping into her chair like an elderly woman at the end
of a hard day. "You really aren't," she had said. Exhaustion played on the
woman's features, and the deep crags of her face appeared far darker than
they had been before. Carefully, she reached out and seized a pipe, which
already appeared to have some sort of plant crammed inside. Looking to
Master Lu'ce, and lifting the pipe forward, she asked, "Do you mind?"
Master Lu'ce had sighed, and pulled out a small metallic object, which she
struck with the edge of her finger. The object produced the smallest of flames
which caught the residues of the plant in Helgeda's pipe alight. Before long,

a white smoke filled the small hut, and I could feel the soothing effects of the herb as the icy grip of worry abandoned my wandering mind.

Helgeda had taken a deep drag from the pipe, held it in, and released it slowly as she placed the pipe back down on the stone slab table. "That was quite the unexpected turn."

I propped myself up, eager to hear what the dwarven woman had to say. "What was?"

My dream was fast fading, and, like holding a handful of fine sand, memories faded like grains sliding between my fingers, lost forever in a sea of dust and stone.

"I've had other mages have an intense reaction as well," Helgeda had explained, "but never one so intense that it flows back onto myself. There is a darkness in you, Kyra Ait Ravenblood, and I—I do not know what to do. I'll be honest, it petrifies me. What you're capable of. What you'd do if only you kn—"

"Does that mean she failed?" Master Lu'ce had interjected.

"No..." I had muttered under my breath, struggling not to fall into a pit of despair.

Helgeda crossed her arms. "Not necessarily," the woman had said. "Kyra has power, that much is certain, but what is unclear is if she can overcome her darkness. I will need to confer with the others on this. I cannot promise you an answer today, but you are free to go and continue with her training... for now. And the sooner you leave, the better. By the Builders, I need rest."

"You heard her," Master Lu'ce had said with a sudden harshness in her voice. "Let's leave her in peace."

I stood and had surprised myself that I could even manage it. Studying the tired dwarven woman one last time, I had said, "Thank you, Seer. I... I appreciate what you've done for me."

The dwarven woman waved me off, apparently too tired to continue the conversation as her eyes drifted between open and shut. Before I fully vacated the hut, I heard soft snoring sounds echoing between the stones.

Master Lu'ce turned to me with a cruelty that wasn't there before. "Let's go home," she had said. "While it still is your home."

I turned from her, the last bit of the sands from her memory spilling away.
"Home..." I had said sadly, knowing that one did not truly exist for me.
It would not be until I had a proper sleep that the experience would once again
plague me in my dreams. That I would remember what transpired. A fresh
scar on my mind. A bleeding ulcer on my soul.

CHAPTER 4

BROKEN PROMISES

Cheering shook Kyra from her daydream and she blinked away the tears that built up in the corner of her eyes as everything slowly came back into focus. Elder Reylar, still at his lectern, had announced yet another name. One that elicited cheers.

"*Salvator Skinner!*" he repeated.

Another rush of excitement came from within the crowd, and, as all others backed away, a fellow, short but muscular, with slicked-back brown hair, raised his hand with a gusto. Wasting no time, he forced his way through the crowd, not giving them time nor space to part in his frantic dash towards the lectern. As he went, he turned to address the other students, laughing and patting them on the back as if he were some sort of celebrity.

Elder Reylar frowned at the showmanship on display. It pleased her to see that. She had never been a fan of those who thought too highly of themselves. She looked forward to this newcomer being brought down a notch as she tried to hide her coy smirk.

Salvator approached the lectern with a grin that went from ear to ear. As he placed a foot on the steps, he proclaimed, "Salvator Skinner. At your service, Reylar."

Steelhands' frown deepened further still. "That's Elder to you," he said in a low tone that warned that this behavior would not be tolerated. "And wipe that ludicrous smile off your face. This isn't your mansion home in the country. There are no maids for you here. No mothers to coddle you and wipe up your spittle. No fathers to pay off those you insult."

Salvators' jovial attitude disappeared in an instant and in its place was a glint of anger, like the last light of a candle about to extinguish. "Let's just get on with it," he sneered. "I've got places to be."

Elder Reylar eyed him with all the calm of a raging storm. That is to say, with no restraint whatsoever. He shook his head again, but reached for his lectern all the same. "Kneel," he said.

Salvator, surprisingly, followed the order to the letter, but just as he had earned the slightest modicum of respect, he turned to face the crowd, hiding a pompous grin from Elder Reylar's sight. He was mocking him openly, for all to see.

Elder Reylar, however, was in a world of his own. Instead of rage in the lines of his old face, as he looked upon the trinkets before him, there was now a distant sadness. "I am sorry," he said genuinely, slipping some silvery object onto his thumb and waving his hand behind Salvator's head.

Directly above his magelock.

Salvator let out a scream of pain, his hands going towards the back of his neck as if he would rip the magelock from his flesh, if such a thing were even possible. If it was, she doubted it would be a very effective measure in controlling a mage's power.

"What did you do?" Salvator wailed. Over and over he cried out, asking the same question, but receiving no answer. Clutching at the bottom of Reylar's coat, some of the other masters came to his aid. Salvator stood, as if he would lash out at Reylar with the ferocity of a wild animal caught in a snare. "*Tell me!*" he repeated. "*What did you do?*"

"Only what needed to be done," Elder Reylar replied, barely meeting Salvator's eyes. "I've done what is expected of me. Nothing more—nothing less. The dwarven seers have found you unworthy of your gifts. Unworthy of receiving a ringpact. Unworthy of joining the Spellbound Arch. You know the terms of your power. If you cannot serve, then you are to be neutered. It is for the safety of all."

"*You've no right!*" Salvator protested, spittle trickling from his parted lips and gnashing teeth as he pleaded his case, his once neat brown hair now wild and flowing. "Do you know who I am? Who my family is?"

"I am aware," Elder Reylar said. "And that is the reason why we will help you in your transition. We are not here to cause you further distress, but to assist you in your dire need. And dire your need is, make no mistake about that."

"Help me?" Salvator laughed, as if consumed by madness. "You've ruined me. No—*you've killed me!* I-I-I can't feel it anymore. The light—the aethyris—it's gone! There is a void." He turned to the crowd, who had shoved their way back as far as the room would allow. "They'll kill you too. Mark my words. All of you. *All of you!*" He went back to his knees. "Please, I beg you, Elder. Restore my power. Don't make me live like this."

Elder Reylar truly looked gutted for the boy. It was a stark contrast to how they first started their conversation. Even she felt pity for him now.

"I take no pleasure in this," Elder Reylar said. "But please, go with the Masters. They will help you."

One master with a slender neck and long grayish-silvery hair placed a hand on Salvator's shoulder, but he quickly brushed it off.

Standing with shaking, weak knees, he spit in Reylar's face. "Fuck you, old man."

The master's hand gripped Salvator's shoulder firmer, but Elder Reylar warned her off. "Let him go," he said. "A little '*water*' has never hurt anyone."

The master nodded, releasing Salvator, who took only a moment before storming out a door in the back of the room, rather than face the looks of his bewildered peers. His curses could be heard echoing down the hall until, eventually, all fell silent once again. Order restored.

A panicked and haunted order.

Elder Reylar strode back to his lectern, wiping the spit from his face with a handkerchief, as if nothing at all had just transpired. Then, seeing the tone of the room, he decided to address the issue, saying, "Let this be a warning to you all. Your gift is only your own as long as you serve the betterment of all. To honor the pact of the Spellbound Arch. Those who cannot will live their lives forever severed from their power. Always just out of reach. So, now that everything has calmed, let us continue... *Kyra Ais Ravenblood!*"

Kyra's heart stopped; time slowed to a crawl. The eyes of her peers wandered the room, looking for the next adept to be... or the next victim. Then, to her horror, some of those eyes came to rest on her. Suddenly, she realized she had raised her hand high in the sky, as if she were issuing a challenge to the heavens above. Why had she done that? She wanted to run. To tear from this room. What if the seers hadn't chosen her? What if her life as a mage was to be cut short here? Now? Her time had come. *Her time.* Sink or swim. Home or no home. It all came down to what the dwarven seer Helgeda had decided. Her fate, left entirely in the hands of another. She hated it, but had to accept it. She would accept what was to come with her head raised high.

It was all she could do.

"Step forward," Elder Reylar commanded, and the world jerked back into rhythm.

Slowly, Kyra's peers parted to make a path for her to the Elder's lectern, their indiscrete whispering plagued her ears as she walked. Everything from judgments of her clothes to her hair... they were mercilessly tearing apart her character before she had spoken a word to them, but they didn't matter—none of them did. All that mattered was the ringpact and the one who currently held it.

Kyra's foot hit the wooden step and, looking down, she realized she had already reached her destination. The trip had seemed so short, but the steps ahead now seemed mountainous, and each step upwards was agonizing. Tedious beyond measure. At the top, she turned to Elder Reylar and blocked out the hundreds of other eyes that drilled tiny holes through her, trying to pry at her every secret.

Elder Reylar looked at her quizzically. "Are you alright?" he asked. "You're looking a bit... pale."

Kyra forced herself to match his gaze. "I'm fine..." she said. "Really... and I'm ready."

Elder Reylar grinned, the soft lines of his face showing that he wasn't the beast that everyone said he was. He was just a man. An old man. And he seemed... nice, but just under that mask of pleasantries were signs of a dark past. She knew them well, for she saw them every time she looked in a mirror.

"Eager?" Elder Reylar said. "Good, as long as you aren't *too* eager." He glanced towards the door Salvator had escaped through and then back to her.

"I'm not like that," Kyra replied. "Not like him, I mean. I have respect for the ringpact and our customs." She knew nothing could affect the decision of whether she received a ringpact or not now, but it never hurt to kiss a little ass, especially when it was *your* ass on the line.

"Let us hope not," Elder Reylar replied in a low whisper. "Although, I do feel for the boy. Let's hope for all of our sakes that he is the only one getting undesirable news today."

Kyra nodded, kneeling at the Elder's feet. Craning her head, she could now see the ringpacts all laid out—waiting for their owners to come forth. She couldn't help but wonder with untold anticipation which she would receive. To which order she would belong to.

Elder Reylar ran his hand over the tops of the rings, pausing between each as if he sensed for something in them. She wasn't quite sure why. Hadn't the dwarven seers created the rings specifically for each mage? Had each not already been assigned?

"Do you not know which is mine?" she dared to ask.

Elder Reylar smiled with that all knowing grin of a man well into his years. "The dwarves do not package them like a gift you send home to your parents," he explained. "They forge a ringpact for each student specifically, that is true, but this—this is the final test. The test to see if the ringpact itself accepts you. If it does, then when I wave my hand across it, It'll—" He froze, his hand trembling ever so slightly above the rings. The lectern itself shook, and then the floor, and she braced herself for fear of falling over. Small cracks appeared in the wood underneath her, and then, as if possessed, the quakes extended to Reylars' entire arm. He stepped back, going to one knee. He remained that way for a time until the trembling ceased, and he could stand on his own again.

None of the masters came to his aid this time, but all looked on in amazement.

Kyra moved to intercept him, but the Elder held out a hand. "Do not move," he said. "I'm fine—I'm fine. It's just... this power." He stood straighter, straightening his jacket. "That was quite unexpected. I've not felt a resonance that strong in quite some time."

"Resonance?"

"*Aye*," he replied. "It's a sort of connection between you and your ring-pact." Reylar's hand nimbly darted over the lectern, leaving a hole in the collection where a ringpact once was. "Give me your hand."

Kyra raised her shaking, sweat-soaked palm and, with little ceremony, Elder Reylar slipped the ringpact onto the ring finger of her right hand. It was a comfortable fit. One would say... a perfect fit.

"Congratulations," Elder Reylar said in a whisper. "You're one of us now." Returning to the lectern, he projected his voice strongly, adding, "Kyra Ais Ravenblood, I hereby declare you a mage of the Spellbound Arch to the Order of arcanists. May your magic dispel the lies of an unforgiving world. To cast light into the places where only darkness grows." He waved his hand, dismissing her, but gave her a slight grin and a nod as she stood to leave.

Cheers rang out in an instant, so loud her ears rang. She had done it—she was an adept mage of the Spellbound Arch. She finally belonged. She finally had a palace in the world. Tears rolled down her cheeks, and she felt relief and comfort for the first time in a very long while.

CHAPTER 5

SIMPLE TEA FOR A SIMPLE LIFE

Elder Reylar dismissed the students to their individual rooms as the ceremony came to its inevitable conclusion. In the end, ten students were deemed unworthy of receiving a ringpact and were subsequently sent off to... whatever they did with the dropouts. She was unsure. Likely sent back to their families to live out the rest of their menial lives. She paid them little mind. If it's one thing that Master Lu'ce had managed to drill into her, it is that the only person you can count on is yourself. And that's the way she would live her life: for herself.

A familiar voice called her name, and when she turned, she noticed Soren, his frosted hair a disheveled mess, matching his unkempt clothing, rushing towards her. He accidentally shoved past a group of gossipers, knocking one's tome to the floor. The woman yelled some choice curses towards him, but he didn't seem to hear her, or just didn't care as he continued on, a smile glued to his face like a kid on his birthday.

"Some people," Soren said, brushing off the front of his multicolored magecloak, attempting to straighten it. When he found the task impossible, he shrugged in a roguish way. "It's just rude to stand in the middle of a walkway, right?"

Kyra narrowed his eyes at him. "And some would say it's rude to run into them."

"But not you?"

She, being in an unusually pleasant disposition, glanced around the man and noticed that the woman he had run into was the one that she had heard gossiping about the style of her hair. And not particularly flattering comments at that. "In this case," she said, "I'd say you're correct. Quite rude of her indeed."

Soren's grin widened. "See, I knew it!" he said. "That we'd become fast friends, I mean." He glanced down at his own hands, as if he remembered something important. Then he held his right hand up to her, brandishing his newly gained ringpact, which was set on his middle finger. "Order of the Augmentors... I always knew I would be. I've always been a fighter, ever since I was just a little lad. Choosing to get into the thick of things. This just proves my instincts were right. And you," he whistled softly, "that *resonance!* But then designated as an arcanist? *An arcanist!* They act more as a support unit regularly. You know, dispelling magic. Tracking... the boring stuff."

Kyra sighed, her good mood already fast fading against this man's tide of emotions. "Boring, *eh?*"

Soren's face sank as he realized his insult. "Not that you're boring!" he amended. "It's just that *I* never got the hang of it, is all. Above my understanding. Far above. I'm more simple than that. Point me to a bad guy and let me go, fists flyin'."

Kyra, tired of the mundane chit-chat, turned to leave her new 'friend' behind. "I've got to get to my room," she lied. "Settle in. Unpack. Very nice meeting you."

"*Wait!*" Soren replied. "I just wanted to ask if you would like to have tea... with me."

"*Tea...*" she cocked her head. "Are you serious? When? Why?"

Soren glanced around nervously and then back towards her. "Now would be great."

"To reiterate, you want to have tea with me, right now?"

Soren nodded.

"I think I'd rather—"

"Kyra there you are!" Armeya emerged from a nearby group of other adepts who were zealously chatting with her. They seemed sad to see her pass and, when they turned their gazes from Armeya to her, they glowered with distaste, angrily turning to chat with each other while stealing the occasional baneful glance. "Are you heading to the dorms?" she asked. "Want to go together?"

"I would," Kyra replied. "But it seems Soren here wants to get—what was it again? Tea?"

"Oh, tea sounds wonderful!" Armeya had an air of excitement around her, and her off-colored eyes went bright with anticipation. She pushed back her black, curly hair which sat shoulder length and bounced neatly above her clean and pressed brown cloak. "Could I come as well?"

Soren crossed his arms. "Well, I mean—"

"Then it's settled." Armeya clapped her hands together. "Come on, let's go!"

"I suppose..."

"It's not too far, right?"

Soren looked utterly deflated by this point, but he put on a brave face. "I'll lead the way," he said. "And no, it's not too far."

As Soren had said, the walk wasn't too far, only a few streets from the main entrance of Dragrin's. They had spoken little on the way. Soren and Armeya mostly conversed about the weather and the various ways in which it would affect their hair. Vanity. Both of them were two sides of the same coin.

As Kyra approached a small shop at the corner of Avolin Street and Woodlan Road with Soren and Armeya in tow. Soren tapped his chest triumphantly, as if he'd just led them through the throes of a particularly bloody battle unscathed.

"Here we are," he said

Kyra scanned the area for any signage one expected of a business and found there to be none. "And where is here?" she asked.

"You know, I've heard of this place," Armeya replied. "Haven Teashop. Right?"

Soren grinned as he proudly said, "That's right. Have you been before?"

Armeya shook her head. "No," she admitted. "But I've read all about it. Many in the mage society circles consider it a prime location. Although... it is a bit elitist, ain't it? Are you sure they'll even serve us? Just some no-named adepts?"

Soren beamed proudly. "I've been here before. No worries there. Come on, before the tea gets cold."

Kyra followed the pair into the shop silently. Inside, it was a dark and dank environment, much the same as the outside. It had a wooden attire which was stained dark-red as opposed to the typical brick and the fresh smells of recently brewed tea filled her nose. Various leaves, roots, and mushrooms hung on neat strings tied to the open rafters on the roof.

Soren pushed ahead, choosing a table, and waving for them to follow his lead. She exchanged a glance with Armeya, who shrugged her shoulders, following. She too pulled out a chair and sat, resting her hands upon the dark wood.

"Nice ringpact," Soren said, turning his head down to admire his own. "But I prefer mine, thanks."

Armeya smirked. "I'd hope so," she said. "Yours looks so big that they shoulda' put it around your fat head."

"And what about yours?" Soren replied. "Thin and long—like your neck."

Armeya blushed, but then, after a moment, chuckled. Soren quickly joined in her laughter, but then his eyes went wide as he noticed something odd about her own ringpact. "Did yours just change shapes?" he asked. "Did it actually transform?"

Kyra peered downwards and realized that Soren was correct. Something was different. Changed. It had become slimmer, longer—more akin to Armeya's, but still not nearly as lengthy.

"You don't know?" Armeya said, peering at Soren.

"Know what?"

"About the different ringpacts? What makes each unique? Special?"

"... I know they help you focus your aethyris on a selected Order. Once worn, the ringpact will only allow you to use that specific type of aethyris, with exceptions, of course." Soren crossed his arms over his chest, turning his eyes from them to study the blank wall. "Those who bear gifts can often break through the limitations. Which reminds me—" Soren held out his hand and mist began to form around his fingers. Shards of ice suddenly clung to his skin, but as they did, he flicked them away with a look of disdain. "... Of course."

Armeya eyed him for a time before replying. "Each ringpact has a distinct shape or feature. Augmentor ringpacts are short and thick. Thaumaturges, like myself, have ringpacts that are long and thin. Arcanist ringpacts change shape, but always remain on one finger. Enchanter ringpacts are multiple rings tied together to symbolize the movement of aethryis from one state to another. And—"

"Alright, enough," Soren said. "I get it—I'll study up! But that's tutelage, so let *me* introduce you to something I know loads about... *Tea!*"

Armeya crossed her arms. "Fine then, Mr. Tea *expert*. Teach us! Teach us oh master of dirty water."

"*Dirty water!*" Soren replied in feigned outrage. He waved her off with the wave of his hand. "Nevermind, someone with your class wouldn't understand elegance if it bit her on the ass." Soren clapped his hands, hailing someone in the back. "Hey Katia, over here! We're thirsty."

Soon, a short woman strode up to the table wearing an off-white apron. In her hands, she carried a cup and a towel. Although, upon closer inspection, she found that the woman wasn't a woman at all, at least, not a human one. This creature had light, grayish skin which seemed to glow in the light of the nearby candles. And wings pulled close to her body that appeared to be transparent. One looked to have been clipped nearly completely off.

Soren coughed. "This is Katia Fang—"

"I can introduce myself," the woman said. "... Mr. Frost, and here I was just thinking to myself that you wouldn't be around as much now that you've become a mage adept at Dragrins. I'm *overwhelmed* with joy."

Kyra smirked secretly to herself.

"Ignore her," Soren replied. "She's got a bit of a chip on her shoulder. And a dry attitude to boot. Sylph are just like that."

"No," Katia amended. "We are just like that to *you!*"

"Sylph?" Kyra said, noticing Armeya was unusually quiet.

"As you can plainly see, I am a Sylphen woman." Katia waited for a moment, and when she turned, one of her wings shook, letting off a small glow of drifting dust which fell to the floor. "Is that a problem?"

"No, ma'am," Kyra muttered defensively. "I've just never seen one of... your kind, before."

Katia narrowed her eyes at Soren, and in those dark eyes, there was something of power hidden deep beneath.

"I'll have you know that I am a very agreeable person," she said. "But young Frost here... well, let's just say you two aren't the first young women he's brought to my establishment." Soren's face suddenly burned bright red. "Ah, so you do have *some* modesty," Katia added. "And some shame." The Sylphen woman turned to address her. "What do I call you, Miss..."

"Ravenblood," Kyra said. "Kyra Ais Ravenblood, but please, just call me Kyra."

Armeya crossed her arms. "And I'm Armeya Ais Cane," she muttered coldly.

"Kyra and Armeya," Katia replied, as if committing their names to memory. "Please, if you'll allow me just a moment of your time." She set down her cups and towel on the table and held out a hand.

"What's this for?" Kyra asked.

"Just indulge her," Soren replied, rolling his eyes. "Katia claims she can read a person's fate on their palms and see what tea suits them best. Utter horseshit if you ask me—"

"One more time," Katia warned, "and I'll send you home parched."

Soren looked as if he would protest, but, in the end, closed his mouth and took a long gulp, his eyes going back towards the back wall.

Armeya studied the woman defiantly before saying in a cold tone, "I'll take up the challenge." She placed her palm in Katia's open hand.

"Let's see here," Katia said, humming softly to herself as she ran the course of Armeya's hand. Armeya shot her a knowing glance, even winking her eye, but quickly shifted focus back as the woman added, "You've the rough hands of a farmer. Calloused, not so unlike your own personality. Oh, you hide it, though. The harsh edges—but you shouldn't. Calluses can be a sign of work and fortitude. You're stoic about your own troubles and have a desire to help others. As long as those others aren't too 'different' from yourself. You are also rigid, and when you should bend, you remain steadfast instead. It may break you in the end."

Armeya's coy smile disappeared, and she wrenched her hand back. "Don't act like you know me," she said with an unexpected indignation deep in her throat. "Uncanny bitch."

Katia simply smiled, ignoring her outburst. "I do not claim to know you," she said. "I only see... possibilities. About who you are. About what you'll become. Through that scouring, I've determined what can help you."

Armeya tucked her hands beneath the table. "And what is that? How can *you* help me?"

"With tea, of course!" Katia said gleefully. "Specifically, a deep-root tea. High in the mountains, there exists a tree with the roots as red as blood from which the tree gets the name *Bloodtouched Birch*. Luckily for you, I have some in stock."

"... And how exactly will this help?"

Katia shifted her hand through her ethereal white hair. "By finding the right flavor. The right aroma, heat, and texture, this tea will reveal to you exactly what you need."

"So, in other words, you have no idea. Is this all some sales technique?"

The Sylphen woman's lips parted as her grin widened. "Perhaps," she admitted. "Nevertheless, would you like to try?"

Armeya looked towards Soren with a look that could still a raging bull's heart.

"It's quite good," he said.

"Fine," Armeya replied. "One 'Bloodtouched' tea for me. Dreadful name." Armeya turned to her. "I did it, so it's your turn now. What about Kyra?"

Katia leaned forward, placing a hand out in front of her.

Kyra swallowed harshly. "I don't think I should—"

"Oh come on now," Armeya protested. "I did it! Just let her do her thing so we can get our tea and go back. I don't want to stay here any longer than I have to."

"*Fine...*" she conceded, with no small amount of hesitancy about the entire ordeal. She placed her quivering right hand into the Sylphen woman's waiting palm and held her left to her chest.

The master of tea rolled her fingers over and over the lines of her hand. At first, Katia smiled, as if this were just another day for her. As if this was a simple routine. Natural. But then, her features shifted, and something darker—something hidden—came to light.

"What is this?" Katia said, almost breathless, her chest suddenly rising faster and faster. "Why I—" her hands trembled, "*What is this?*"

Kyra struggled to pull away, but Katia's grip was like an iron vise. The pressure of Katia's nails on her skin felt like hot pokers. Burning, splintering heat. And that sensation brought back dark memories.

"You have a shadowy past," Katia said. "One shrouded in pain. A field of white stained red. A fire as cold as ice and as pitch as ash. You should not be... you should not—" Katia released her, taking a notable step back. The Sylphen woman stared in disbelief at her own shaking hands.

Soren glanced between the two of them. "Knock it off, Katia," he said. "Can't you see you're scaring her? Hells, you're scaring me!"

"Quiet Frost boy!" Katia replied. "I need time to think. Time..." She turned and disappeared into the back of the shop, a small wooden door slapping against the stopper.

"I'll just have my regular then," Soren yelled at her, but she gave no indication that she had heard him. Turning back towards her, he added, "Well, that was certainly strange. I've not seen anything like that. See, I knew there was something interesting about you, Kyra."

Kyra's own hands quivered, and she quickly hid them beneath the table. Playing it off with a chuckle, she said, "Yeah... strange." Secretly, she wondered just how much the tea master truly knew of her past. Not wishing to find out, she added, "I think I should really go—"

"It'll help," Soren interrupted in a serious tone. "I know it sounds like nonsense, but trust me, it'll help. It's helped me through some difficult times with my family. Some very difficult times."

The three sat in an uncomfortable silence for a time, not sure what to discuss after Katia's sudden outburst, when suddenly, the Sylphen woman appeared with three distinct cups. Placing one down in front of each of them, she said, "'The usual,' for the Frost boy. For Armeya, bloodtouched tea. And, for Kyra... dreamhaven tea."

"'*Dreamhaven*,'" Kyra repeated. "What's it taste like?"

Katia shrugged her shoulders. "Truthfully, I do not know," she admitted. "I simply read the palm and know that it is what you need. Now it is up to you now to figure out why it was chosen."

"This is a lot for just some simple tea."

"Try it," Soren said. He turned back to the tea master. "She doesn't mean it, Katia. Trust me, she'll be a believer after this."

Armeya went first, bringing the cup to her lips, where she suddenly paused. Everyone waited with an air of anticipation. A prospect of wonder... or of horror. She took that first gulp. In her eyes, you could see it: *Exaltation!* She quickly took another sip before saying, "It's superb!"

Soren smiled, lifting his own to sip on. "Told ya.'"

Katia simply nodded her head at a job done well.

All eyes then turned to Kyra, and she looked down at the liquid in her own cup. Steam wafted from the tea, filling her nose with a sweet scent that she just couldn't place. Something in her dreaded what was to come, but another part was filled with excitement—an excitement that only comes from the experience of new things. She lifted the tea to her mouth and drank delicately. Slowly. Deliberately.

It tasted awful.

She spit the stuff up, small drops of the tea splattering across the wooden table. "*What was that?*" she said, gasping.

"I already told you," Katia replied. "It's dreamhaven tea. Quite the rare leaf, I must say. Only found in a secret grove to the west. But don't you worry, I've ascertained a supplier with quick feet and even quicker hands."

"Why would I worry about supplies?" Kyra replied. "I never want to taste that again. It's dreadful. Truly horrible. A thing of nightmares."

"Oh please," Katia replied with a stern look. "You're beginning to remind me of the young Frost boy here. Enough with the melodrama. Something tells me you'll try it again. Everyone reacts this way at first. Go ahead, give it another attempt."

"No."

Katia looked at her pleadingly, and as she scanned the others, they mirrored the Sylphen woman.

Kyra sighed, staring down at the cup. Stomach acid burned into her throat, threatening to spill itself from her mouth just at the thought of that wretched taste again. "Fine," she relented. "I'll try again."

"And this time," Katia suggested. "Think of something pleasant. A fond memory. A secret lover. Perhaps those lovely white flowers... before they turned to ash."

Kyra shot the woman a sidelong glare before bringing the cup back to her lips. She did as Katia suggested, imagined the white flowers that she so often dreamed about. The tea had a bitter taste, burning her tongue yet again. But, after a moment, it suddenly became sweet. And sweeter and sweeter. It not only became the best tea she had ever drank, but something in a league of its own. She couldn't help herself as she downed the cup in one long gulp.

Soren whooped at her, clapping his hands, and Armeya patted her on the back as if she had done something truly noteworthy.

Kyra studied Katia's blank face as she asked, "Why did it taste differently this time?"

Katia said nothing, and the placid face she wore rapidly changed to dread. "Don't worry," she said. "It'll soon pass."

"What'll pass—"

A blinding pain seared its way through Kyra's head. Starting in the back of her eyes, it pushed its way through her mind and out through the back. It felt as if hot irons had skewered through her face, and it took everything in her not to scream in agony.

"Are you alright?" Armeya asked, reaching out, but her voice was now a distant thing. Not of this world. Not of this reality. At least, not *her* reality.

Kyra slammed her head against the table. She would do anything to stop the pain. Say anything. Memories flashed before her. An isolated thing that she had buried so long ago. The flowers were now red. The skin on her left hand had torn away. By fire or wind, she did not know. She writhed, pressing her palms to her head, willing with everything she had to make the pain stop.

And then it did.

As cold water soothes a burning wound, so did a refreshing pressure wash over her. It was over. The pain passed, and with it, the memories that had brought it on. When the room came too, she scowled up at Katia, and it took everything in her not to lunge at the woman.

"What did you do to me?" she asked in a warning tone, a premunition of violence yet to come.

"Nothing," Katia replied, crossing her arms across her chest. "I did nothing. I already told you, I read the palm, and it tells me what you need. Nothing more—nothing less. For whatever reason, you *needed* this to happen."

"*Centaur shit!*" Kyra replied, standing and shoving her chair back so hard it fell to the floor.

Armeya stood with her, putting a comforting arm around her shoulder.

"Come on, Kyra," she said. "Let's go. You never can trust an uncanny."

As Kyra turned her back on Katia, the Sylphen woman said, "I'll see you again soon... *Ais*. Ravenblood."

CHAPTER 6

NIGHTMARE

Journal Entry

Year: 830 E.B

I had just finished my errands for the day. Fresh bread, eggs, and a various assortment of dried meats were just some of the items I was tasked with acquiring. It had been a scolding, and the sun had still burned brightly overhead. I longed to return to the shade of my trees. To the spray of the cool water as I sat by the spring adorning Master Lu'ce's land.

"Move along," the shopkeeper had said. "Can't you see who's coming?"

As rude as the shopkeeper was, he had been right. Down the dirt-strewn street which housed a plethora of hawkers selling various wares, I had noticed a small entourage. Two tall individuals, shrouded in royal-purple cloaks were being followed by two plated guards and a middle-aged woman in a multicolored cloak.

The two purple-clad individuals radiated an aura about them; one that whispered of danger. I understood immediately what they were:

elvish!

Other shoppers hurriedly began clearing out of the space, giving the elvish entourage ample room. Why were they there? That place was named Harth's Wish and it had been just a small human settlement. There had been nothing of manors or balls here. Of anything of convenience at all. Still, there they had been all the same, as hard as it had been to believe.

I was lost in thought as the entourage had stopped before me. I had swallowed hard, but then the shopkeeper's surprisingly deft hand gripped my arm, pulling me into his stall.

"Sorry," he had said, addressing the two elven who now turned their gazes upon him. "The girl is a bit scatterbrained is all. Just not used to seeing one's such as yourselves."

"Sorry..." I had muttered, but there was a feeling quickly rising within me. Dread. Why had I felt it? I had done nothing to offend the group, so why did my body react as if I was in imminent danger?

The elvish said nothing as they moved past, and I had not dared to even meet their gazes at all, turning my head towards the ground in deference.

But the woman in their company, with the multicolored cloak—a mage cloak—caught my attention. She was middle-aged with blond hair. On her finger, she wore the ringpact, confirming my suspicions, but I couldn't tell which one from the quick glance. But what had surprised me most was the wear on her shaking hands. Her fingers had looked boney and scarred from overuse.

The woman had looked surprised as she saw me, and she opened her mouth to say something when the elvish man interrupted, saying, "Keep up!"

His voice had been like the shattering of glass in my ears. Like a mallet to the head. I had fallen back hard against the shopkeeper's stall, trying to right myself. What had that been? Had I been attacked? Looking down, my left-hand shook violently, and the old burn-scars had felt as fresh as ever.

The woman had fallen behind the elvish man, not daring to look back towards me nor voice her thoughts. As for myself, I stayed silent and still until the elvish entourage disappeared off in the distance. It was then and only then that I had finally taken a breath. The pain in my hand and head had quickly faded, but the remnants of the experience remained.

"This is me," Armeya said, standing in front of the door of her new quarters. She abruptly turned back once more to face her. "Listen... don't worry about what happened at the teashop. I'm sure we can find a different one around here in time. One without the creepy uncanny woman." An awkward silence that permeated between the two of them for a time before she turned the knob, putting one foot in the room. "Well... *bye!*" And in a flash, she disappeared from sight, the door clicking closed behind her.

Kyra stood, staring aimlessly down the hallway. She was lost in thought, with no true direction at all. Although she had put on a brave face for Armeya, what had transpired back at the teashop rattled her still. That uncanny woman... Katia; how much did she know of her past? She felt violated that a stranger was privy to such personal information. She felt strangely naked that the walls of her mind were so easily torn down and discarded, like yesterday's trash.

Another adept suddenly brushed up against her, forcing her gently into the wall. "S-S-Sorry 'bout that," the man said. "B-B-But y-you really shouldn't s-stand there."

The man was short and portly, and already wearing the traditional garb of a mage—a hand-spun, multicolored magecloak with an embroiled symbol on the chest. The magecloak, one of the symbols of a mage in service to the Spellbound Arch. Enchanted with runes from the days of the Builders, the cloaks were resistant to heat, cold, and a multitude of other elements, such as rot. They were a useful tool in a mages arsenal, but hardly spoken as such, being much less flashy than the ringpacts themselves.

"It's fine," Kyra said, paying the pudgy man little mind. "No harm done."

"T-That's a relief!" he replied, genuinely. He wiped a small bit of sweat from his forehead and then, with the same hand, he extended it out towards her. "N-Names Maxim."

Looking down at his sweaty palm, Kyra pressed herself even further on the wall away from him, but on that hand, she saw the true mark of a mage: a ringpact! Unlike her own, this was less of a ring and more of a metallic disk-like contraption. From the ring, set on his right-pinky finger, a rod traveled the course of his hand where the circular object rested in his palm. There was no mistaking it; this was the ringpact of a Mystic. A healer—just as her master was.

"Kyra," she finally said, drawing her eyes back to his pudgy face. "And I've really got to be going."

"Oh, y-you're right," he said. "I've a-agreed to meet up with an old friend. Y-Ymo Sangrey. You know, w-we've been friends for a long time. O-Once when I was an apprentice, I—"

"As I've said," Kyra interjected, "I've really got to be going. Pleasure meeting you, Maxim."

"Oh, t-the pleasure is mine," Maxim said excitedly. "And d-do be sure to not s-stand in any more hallways."

Kyra watched him go as she muttered under her breath, "I'll keep that in mind."

After a brief search, she found her own quarters and, presumably, a new roommate who awaited inside. That was what the situation was like—two adepts to share a room. It would be odd sharing. During her time with Master Lu'ce, she had her own quarters, as small and packed as they had been. As much as she detested the thought of meeting another person today, this confrontation was inevitable. She had always been slow to trust, and it had taken years before she was truly comfortable living with Master Lu'ce.

Best to suck it up and get it over with. No use complaining about what cannot be changed.

Kyra swallowed harshly, still tasting the sweet aftertaste of the tea on her lips. With a sigh, she pushed open the door to her room and stepped inside.

And yet, when she entered, things were not quite as she expected. This was not a room at all. In fact, this was not Dragrin's at all. Once again, she stood in a sea of white flowers, and there it was, off in the distance, as it always was: a quant wooden house.

Her old home.

Reaching down inside herself, Kyra could not trust her eyes to speak the truth about what her heart knew. Something was wrong. Very wrong. And in that wrongness, she lost her sense of reality, drifting back into a familiar nightmare. With the back of her hand, she gently brushed against the white pedals. They were soft and yet sturdy. The more she pressed, the stronger the flower withstood—until she could no longer move them at all.

Like a vice, vines entangled her feet, dragging her ankles under into the dirt. Kyra opened her mouth to scream, but knew that she couldn't. She'd never been able to before. Another vine had wrapped itself around her neck, strangling her. The vines ran the length of her legs; then her arms. And soon, the white flowers turned to ash, blowing away into the wind. Her mind pounded with a blinding headache, each rushed beat of her heart sending a wave of pain beside it.

A shadow of a figure appeared just before her head went under the dirt. Craning her neck to see, all the features of this unknown individual were shrouded in a black smoke that seemed to move with a mind of its own. This mysterious figure leaned down, and in a voice that was both masculine and feminine, whispered, "This is your fault. It was always your fault."

The vines around her neck loosened as she muttered, "... *I know.*"

"Then beg for forgiveness," the figure spoke. "*Beg!*"

"Please... forgive—"

A blinding pain shot through Kyra's head; this was wrong. Well, more wrong than usual. This was not how her nightmares normally went. Something was different. Changed.

Why?

"*Beg!*" the mysterious figure demanded. "*... Why won't you beg?*"

"Get," she said, willing the aethryis that ensnared her, like a perilous fog, to dissipate, "*out of my head!*"

Kyra woke and found herself on her knees in a plain old room. Far from a field of white flowers, this place was as simple as any she'd seen before. Spacious, with two beds and two dressers adorned on opposing sides of the room. In the center, a woman, her arms crossed, stared down at her with a look of pure contempt in her majestic features.

Elvish features.

"*Bah*," the elvish woman said, waving her hand wildly in the air. "To think my father would place me with a roommate at all, yet alone a human. Damn Adathin..." She stomped to the edge of one dresser, tapping her elegantly painted silver-painted fingernail against its wood framing. "Still, at least you appear to have some promise. And look at that ringpact; an arcanist! And a capable one at that. I'll tell you, girl, few can fend off one of my psionic attacks. Regardless, this... outrage cannot be tolerated. I'm the heir to a powerful house. I do not do... roommates. Don't get comfortable, you'll be leaving soon."

"What did you do to me?" Kyra asked, struggling to stand. Her body felt heavy, as if the power it took to dispel the mental attack had drained not only her mind, but her body as well.

Perhaps it had.

"You don't know?" the elvish woman said. "Do they let anybody become an adept nowadays?" The woman laughed to herself with a pompousness that suggested she saw herself as royalty among a commoner. "I'm elvish. It should be obvious. My name's Aluriel Mistwalker, if you must know. And it was psionics. A mental attack, and a weak one at that. I took a core memory, or, in this case, a nightmare, and turned it against you. Did my psionics really addle your mind that deeply?"

Like a fog clearing with the rising of the sun, so too did her mind. The nightmare faded back into its dark recess. Hidden deep and locked away. Memories from the day came flooding back like the breaking of the tide. The people she'd met. The ceremony. All of it washed away the doubt that stilled her muscles as she forced herself to rise.

"No," Kyra muttered in a contemptuous voice. "And I remember now. Is this how you greet everybody you meet? By dragging out their deepest fears? Is this some sick game to you?"

She knew she should hold her tongue. Master Lu'ce had warned her against tangling with elvish, but having to confront the one thing she feared most did not leave her in the mood to be modest, especially when it had not been the first time that day that someone had seen fit to intrude on her secrets.

"Only those whom I have no interest in actually meeting," Aluriel replied curtly. "As I've explained, I cannot leave this outrage unpunished. If I must punish someone, why not you? To think of someone like me—of elvish blood—not to mention my family's standing, to be 'squatting' with a peasant such as yourself. And a human too! The thought is too much to stand. Sickening. Insulting."

"Don't worry," Kyra replied. "The feeling is mutual."

Aluriel smiled, and her long, pointed ears stood straighter, as if perked up by something interesting. "Oh, you're a sharp-tongued one, aren't you? *Good!* At least they had the sense to not send some weak-willed ninny to *my* quarters."

Kyra rubbed the back of her neck, accidentally brushing against her magelock. "My master never could break me of it," she said. "What's the saying? ...I'm only human, after all."

"*Indeed...*" Aluriel studied her as a cat studies a mouse before a kill. "So then, human, what is your name?"

"Can't you just use your psionic abilities to pry it out?" Kyra asked. "Or are you afraid I'll break your influence... again?"

She just couldn't help herself. This elvish woman had frayed her last nerve.

Aluriel scowled, and there was a seething that went far beyond this simple altercation just below the surface of her features. Then, suddenly, she softened as she replied, "That would be rude of me, wouldn't it? Come, at the very least, we can be pleasant for the moment. And I would rather not simply refer to you as 'human.' Seems rather crass, don't you agree?"

"...It's Kyra Ais Ravenblood. And if we're through, I'd really like some sleep. Us humans don't get any special privileges. We need to make our appointments on time."

Aluriel motioned to one of the empty beds on the opposing side of the room from where she stood. "By all means," she said. "And it's a pleasure to meet you, Ravenblood... *Sweet dreams.*"

Kyra shuddered at the woman's tone, and, when she ultimately fell asleep, she dreamed of a field of white flowers burning to ash.

Just as she always did.

CHAPTER 7

CIRCLE

Journal Entry

Year: 833 E.B

I had shivered as I wrapped the remnants of a patchwork blanket snuggly around myself. It was cold, so much so that my appendages ached as the core of my body drew the heat away. It wasn't snowing, at least as of yet, but I knew with certainty that if it were to rain it would, and if it did... Well, I doubted I would have survived the night.

It had been two days since Master Lu'ce had left me out in the woods. Two days since she had demanded that I 'put my aethryis to the test.' Two days since I had last spoken to a human being. The Crescroft Woods is where she had taken me. Where she had abandoned me. You would think at this point that I would be amenable to loss, but I wasn't, and it stung all the more. First, I had heard the swift wind blow through the dead limbs of the trees in their winter states, sending a bone chilling crackling sound through the forest. Then I had felt it... the chill of death. I knew that if I did nothing, I would most certainly freeze to death. I knew nothing more certain than that.

*Gingerly, I had reached for the magelock at the back of my neck. The
metal device was freezing, and the surrounding skin burned with the chill.
Damnable device. All apprentices, like me, had their magelocks set to only
allow ten percent of their true power, give or take. I tried to draw in aethryis
from the air, at least enough to make a small light, perhaps even some
warmth. It was from the Arcanist order; a trick of the light. I'd had trouble
with that particular order, although Lu'ce had warned that it was common
for mages to take strongly to one order or another. I, however, seemed terrible
at all orders equally. Honestly, I couldn't see what Lu'ce had seen in me at
all. I must have been such a disappointment to her. Perhaps that's why I
was there, lost in the woods. Perhaps it was a punishment for being such a
worthless apprentice. Hells, I hadn't even been able to conjure a simple flame
in the entire three years I had been an apprentice. Lu'ce said it was a block
that I had to be rid of. That it not only affected my ability to conjure flames,
but to use all forms of aethryis as well.*

*Then it had clicked... this wasn't punishment, it was a test. A fatal one. If I
couldn't produce a flame to start a fire now, then I would surely die.*

*Using the last of my waning strength, I had picked the dead branches off the
ground as kindling and found dead and dried leaves scattered about. I dug
a hole in the dirt and placed it all inside. This was it, conjure a flame and
survive the night, then find my way out of this nightmare in the morning. I
drew in as much aethryis as I could, willing the smallest of flames to appear
at the tip of my extended finger... nothing. My left hand burned, as if it
were ablaze once more. I ignored the pain and tried again. And again. And
again...*

Nothing!

*"By the hells," I had cursed at the night sky. I couldn't do it. I couldn't. There
is a cold certainty when death comes for you. A calmness that breaks through
the storm. Once you know the end is inevitable, everything else becomes easy.
Slowly, I dropped the coverings from my shoulders, embracing it. Willing it
to come. In my vulnerability, my mind wandered away to a faraway place.*

*A forbidden place. A place that I once knew... and I saw a face shrouded
in the darkness of my mind. It was familiar and yet a stranger to my eyes.*

They were so big... or I was so small, and the stranger was doing something interesting. They had two sticks, and they were frantically rubbing them together. Faster and faster, the sticks swirled until there was smoke... then fire.

Fire!

I had reached out and grabbed two of the smoothest twigs I could. Putting one to the ground, I began spinning the other on top until, like I had seen. There was smoke; then fire. With hope returned, and the chill of death thwarted, I bundled myself back up, sitting as close as I dared to the flame. I would escape this nightmare once more, it seemed. One more night... it was all I could hope for.

It was all anyone could ever hope for.

Kyra frantically searched the corridors of Dragrin's, around a multitude of winding and turning hallways and stairs until she found the correct room for orientation. At least, she believed it to be, with all mage adepts like her standing outside.

Dragrin's was a large facility, and was used for more than just teaching. They hosted adepts, such as herself, teaching them, mentoring them, until they became master mages or flunked out, having their ringpact severed from their finger and their magic forever locked. A bleak prospect, but one that ensured all who made it this far worked their absolute hardest. Dragrin's also served as a base of operations for the Spellbound Arch in the North. As such, various circles with their members of master mages stayed here temporarily, seeking shelter. Rest and training as well, if needed. Adepts could even be expected to spar with a Master Mage if called upon. It was all for the betterment of the world. To protect order from both undue influences and themselves.

It filled her heart with excitement. Having a purpose. A road in life to follow... to not be abandoned and left alone.

Kyra had envisioned her first days at Dragrin's for years now. So far, it had not gone the way she expected—especially considering whom her new roommate was. But that was over for now. Now she could focus. Strive to be the best Arcanist she could be. The best Dragrin's had ever seen.

With renewed vigor, Kyra pushed through the crowd of gathered adepts and into the room.

As Kyra stepped inside, various objects immediately drew her attention. Vials of colorful liquids adjourned wooden shelves. Books, binding and pages frayed from frequent use lay bare on wooden tables barely fit to be called so due to the wear on age upon them. Similar to the great hall, a small lectern sat in the corner, with pages upon pages strewn across it in a jumbled mess. Feeling mischievous, she made her way over to those mysterious documents. A window to the outside lay just adjacent to the lectern, and she dared to glance out. It was dirty, and she doubted it had been cleaned in over a decade. She frowned at that as she ran her hand across the window seal. She grimaced, pulling her hand back. Looking down, black dust coated her gloved fingers.

Outside, other mages skirted about the grounds. From this vantage on the third floor, they looked like ants mindlessly going about their daily routine. Was this to be her life as well? Just another nameless face in a crowd? An adept mage of little rank? Sadness welled up from within. Arcanist's weren't exactly known for their many contributions to society, unlike augmentors, thaumaturges, and elven psionics. No, arcanist's were largely considered a support unit, even if they found themselves in scraps more often than not. It would be her job to divine truth from lies. Light from dark. But how could she do that when she so often lied to herself?

"What are you doing, *Ais*. Ravenblood?" someone asked, startling her.

Kyra dropped a scroll, one she'd not even realized she was holding. It went back and forth in the air until, eventually, it fell to the floor and, peering up, she saw Elder Reylar offering her a curious stare. His lips were straight and hard-set, something between chastisement and amusement.

"*Nothing!*" she said hastily. Perhaps too hurriedly, as Elder Reylar narrowed his eyes further. She added, "*Really!*"

"Nothing, eh..." Elder Reylar said, now trying to hide his grin behind his hand.

His name, apparently, wasn't just for show. Now that she had time to study his hands, she could clearly see that they were entirely made of metal. They moved so well—so human! Could aethryris do this? Or was there something else at play here?

"Well," he said. "You seem quite out of sorts for having been doing *nothing.*"

"I was just looking out the window," Kyra replied, turning and pointing outside. "It's just so—"

"Different?"

Kyra shook her head. "On the contrary," she explained. "It's similar... eerily so. Somehow, I thought things *would* be different here, but from what I've seen so far, and those I've spoken to, I fear little has changed."

Elder Reylar put a hand to his chin. "And that makes you fearful... about yourself?"

She nodded hesitantly.

"Change comes from within, child," he said. "It would be best if you learned that simple truth now, rather than later. Part of being a good mage, and especially a great arcanist, is to see things for what they are, and *not* what you expect them to be. Do you understand?"

Kyra nodded. "Yes, sir."

Elder Reylar relaxed his face, moving towards the lectern and straightening the papers. "No need to be so formal when it's just us speaking," he said. "Hells, if I had it my way, I'd always be referred to informally. But alas, not everything is as we would like it to be. It is another undisputed truth in the world. Yet another lesson for you, I suppose. Looks like I'm earning my Elder title today." He glanced down at her gloved hand. "Although, I suspect you understand that particular lesson better than most."

Kyra held her hand to her chest, muttering weakly, "I do."

"Ah, there she is!" a familiar voice said. Turning, she saw Soren, now dressed now in proper Mage clothing, with his multicolored magecloak tight-fitted against his muscular body. His silverish hair was long compared to other men, sitting around his shoulders in length. On the very edge of the right side of his breast, his shirt displayed the sigil of the augmentors: a silver embroiled shield.

"Ah, *Ais.* Frost," Elder Reylar said. "So glad you found the proper attire. Some of your previous preceptors warned me that you've had a bit of a rambunctious streak."

Soren smiled. "New home, new me."

"As is expected," Elder Reylar replied. "I wouldn't want to have to reach out to your family. I take this quite seriously. You should as well."

Soren grimaced at that, wordlessly hauling out a wooden chair which scraped loudly against the floor and planting himself into it.

Elder Reylar held a hand towards the seats. "You should sit as well, *Ais.* Ravenblood."

Nodding, Kyra found a chair as far from Soren as she could. Something in her was still bitter that the man had forced her into that tea shop the day before. She had wondered if he was in it with Katia. If it all had been just a mean spirited jest... but she seriously doubted it. The eyes the Sylphen woman gave her: they were full of pity and remorse. The woman had gained no amusement from what had happened.

Slowly, more and more of her peers made their way into the lecture room. Armeya clutched the seat next to her, smiling warmly, almost motherly, as she sat. Kyra returned the stare with a questioning look of her own.

"How did you sleep?" Armeya asked, likely just trying to break the awkward silence.

"*Fine...*" she lied.

Armeya clicked her tongue. "Doesn't sound fine. Not at all. You know, I heard a rumor you're being roomed with an elven. A powerful psionic at that. And not just any psionic, but Aluriel Mistwalker. A fucking Mistwalker—excuse my language. So... is it true?"

Kyra sighed, pressing her hands against her head to thwart off the oncoming migraine. "Word gets around here fast, doesn't it? ...Yes, she's to be my roommate, I suppose, but from how she explains it, I'll be forced out soon enough."

"And you best hope so," Iona replied, appearing suddenly and seizing the seat behind her. "Mistwalkers are trouble. Cut from the royalist of elvish cloth. You best not get on one's bad side. Although, from what I've heard, Aluriel isn't the only Mistwalker to worry about anymore."

Armeya turned, almost insulted that someone had interjected into their conversation. "And who are you?"

"Iona Cracksman."

"And your Order?"

Iona looked down at her hand and frowned. "... Enchanter."

"And you were speaking of another Mistwalker?" Armeya asked, curiously. "Where did you hear that little nugget of gossip?"

Iona smiled mischievously, hiding her hand beneath the wooden table. "I'd never reveal a source," she said, "but I hear that it's Aluriel's own brother. Younger brother. And rumor has it that the prodigal son falls very far from the family tree. Aluriel's the golden child, of course, and this one, whomever he is, is the runt of the collective litter."

"Best keep such rumors as that to yourself, *Ais.* Cracksman," Elder Reylar said so that all could hear, never moving from his lectern. "Secrets are worth more when they are kept secret. An Adept mage should know well enough already."

Iona went tight-lipped and hung her head low, as to not draw anymore of the Elder's ire. Soon, the room filled with the new mage adepts to the academy. Her peers. Classmates and brothers and sisters in arms. Individuals from all orders took their seats, waiting for whatever news was to befall them. She had to admit, there was an excitement in the air and she was not immune to its illustrious glamor.

When the room was near its capacity, and the seats nearly all taken, Armeya leaned over, whispering in her ear, "When do you think we're gonna—"

"Quiet!" Elden Reylar said, sparing Armeya a glance. "I'm sure some of you are wondering why we're meeting today instead of starting your first day of training. I am here to inform you, regretfully, that this cycle will be unlike any before. Typically, a mage would not be assigned a *Circle* until a full cycle after receiving their ringpact, but, as I've said, this time is different. You're all here to be assigned to a circle from which you will start regular patrols on the streets of Mistbreak. The first of which, for some, will be tonight."

There was a bustle as a panicked frustration resonated outwards.

One girl raised her hand before blurting out, "Why are we doing this? We've not trained for it." There was a shrill panic in her voice.

Another echoed her worry. "The uncanny will eat us alive. Surely you can't be serious."

Elder Reylar took on a stern look. "I've spoken my own concerns as well, but this comes from higher above. From the Spellbound Arch itself. Mistbreak... is on a dangerous path." The room was suddenly as silent as a moonless night. Not a sound could be heard, not even the breathing of air as Elder Reylar added, "Humans fear the uncanny, and that fear leads to frustration against the elvish. The elvish see this as a larger distraction from the pactless, whom they consider the true threat to peace. And we mages, we're in the middle of it all. I know you can see it—feel it! Their prying eyes upon you. Wishing you to save them from whatever perceived problems they have. The Spellbound Arch reluctantly asks for your help. Their various circles of master mages are stretched to breaking. Smaller tussles between locales are beneath the greater work they do, and so it will be up to us to help maintain order."

Elder Reylar said the words with confidence, and that confidence radiated throughout the room as more than one of her peers nodded their head in agreement, but there was something else—something deeper, hidden beneath that stalwart exterior. Regret. She did not believe that he trusted his own words.

Before Kyra knew it, she had raised her own hand, and Elder Reylar pointed to her. She stood, asking, "So we are to be both active mages and adept students? Won't that be dangerous? Both for our learning and our actual personhood?"

"You've always been a mage," Elder Reylar replied. "There is nothing you can do about that. As for it being dangerous... Yes, it will be. I won't lie; I suspect that some of you will not make it to your second year. It is regretful. Therefore, you'll need to be steadfast with your studying. Determined in your training. Humble in your friendships. And stalwart with your assigned circle. Each element will be required to survive. And not just in this place, but for what comes after. Now, to assign each of you to your designated circle."

Kyra sat, the weight of the moment sending a shock through her body. Armeya rested a hand on her shoulder, and she was surprised at how much she welcomed it.

"We'll start with Circle 1A," Elder Reylar said. "Circle name designated *Daemon*. Their augmentor will be Soren *Ais* Frost. Please, step forward."

Soren stood, and a nervous sweat crested his dark brow. He went to Elder Reylar and stood in front of him silently.

"Now then, a Mythic," Elder Reylar pointed forward, "Grimm." The timid, plump boy she'd met the night before stood, nervously shuffling to take his place next to Soren. Elder Reylar continued, adding, "For their enchanter, Iona *Ais* Cracksmans. And thaumaturge, Armeya *Ais* Cane."

The two women near her stood, shooting each other suspicious glares as they made their ways forward.

"And last, their arcanist... Kyra *Ais* Ravenblood."

She stood, silently taking her place among the rest. Armeya greeted her with a hearty smile and she tried not to pass out as she felt the eyes of everyone else in the room settling on her.

Elder Reylar cleared his throat. "As for your psionic and leader, he isn't—"

Suddenly, the door creaked open, and a figure came sauntering through. This individual was tall, with ashen hair pulled back into a long ponytail. His eyes were piercing golden, and his ears, long and pointed, jettisoning upwards.

"Nice of you to show," Elder Reylar said, with not a small amount of rebuke. Coughing into his hand, he added, "This is Adathin *Ais* Mistwalker, elven psionic and leader of Circle Daemon."

Adathin maintained his cool walk forward, eventually coming to stand before her. He had ethereal skin, which almost gleamed like the surface of the ocean at first light. He leaned down, so that he was face to face with her as he said in a deep voice, "I'm Adathin. It's a pleasure to meet you."

CHAPTER 8

SACRIFICES

Reylar *Ais* Steelhand... *Heh,* Steelhand, a name given to him as an honor which now felt more like a mockery. He peered down at his metallic hands with regret, loss, and sadness. It was just one of many sacrifices he had made in service of the Spellbound Arch and the Elvish Enclave mages were charged with serving.

And it wouldn't be the last he would sacrifice for them, nor the most costly.

"Are you certain that this is wise?" Reylar asked, pouring a dark liquid from a class decanter into two distinct glasses. A strong, pungent smell of alcohol wafted into his nose, which held notes of sweetness deep within. He swirled the two glasses around to infuse them with air before deftly sliding one across the deep-brown rustic table and bringing the other gingerly to his lips. He would never consider himself an alcoholic, but perhaps he drank too much. It wasn't his fault that the solace of drunkenness was the only thing capable of taking the edge off his mind. Capable of making him forget, if only just for a moment. For a brief breath in time. He drank deeply of the liquor, and felt the smooth, burning sensation move down his throat and settle in his chest, bringing with it the warmness and tenderness of life. It was something he so longed for, and that longing was worse whenever he thought of his dear wife.

His dead wife.

"Certain?" Lhoris said. "Wise?" The elvish man gave out a small chuckle. "That is not for me to decide. And certainly not *you*. We've orders, you and I. It's not our place to question them on whether they are wise or not. We simply comply, as is our duty."

Lhoris was a particularly tall and lanky elvish man. He had a dark ethereal tone, and a devilishly pointed nose to match his incredibly long and pointed ears. His hair was ashen and slicked back into a long, single-braided ponytail at the back. He drank deeply from his own glass and sighed out as the slightest edge of a smile cracked the corner of his thin lips.

That couldn't be right, Lhoris never smiled. Perhaps the drink was stronger than he had originally thought.

"Duty," Reylar said, setting his own cup to the table and pouring another finger. He laughed, contrasting the elvish man's seriousness and tone. "Unlike you, I've not yet mastered the art of 'obey' without reason. 'Do' without question. Call it yet another one of my human flaws. I've quite a few, if you haven't noticed."

"*Hmm,* yes," Lhoris replied. "You humans do have many of them, for certain. But please, do not waste *my* time on it. I've not the time nor the patience. I assume that you've not brought me here just to complain?"

"*Complain?*" Reylar said, letting his indignation fly freely. Perhaps it was the drink that made him so bold as he added, "We're sending children into a meat grinder. A slaughterhouse. Feeding them into it without so much as warning of the potential dangers. Of the Spellthief!"

Lhoris scoffed. "Spellthief. *Bah,* superstitious nonsense. You mages can be so dramatic. And the adepts children? Please spare me your false concerns."

"*Aye,*" Reylar replied, unwilling to back down. "They are still children. I know they are of legal age, but as mages, they are but helpless adolescents. They've just barely received their ringpacts. Their powers are still unfocused. It'll take time for them to warm up to their new strength. The newness of the aethyris in conjunction with the ringpact. And yet, your... 'Order,' would snuff the light out of so many before their time has come. How many lives do we potentially toss away? ... How many will die?"

"Again," Lhoris said, "being dramatic will not get you what you want. Besides, it is not my concern. Nor yours. Take solace that they've left the assigning of posts to you. Now, if you'll indulge me, I am curious... will you give the most dangerous assignments to those whom are weakest as a sacrificial ploy? A tactic to save your stronger pieces from 'the meat-grinder' as you say? Or will you risk them? Send only those whom you believe have the strength to prevail? I, for one, am glad I'm just here as your babysitter in that regard." Lhoris finished his drink and slid the glass forward, waving his hand, indicating he wished for another.

Reylar ground his teeth in frustration as he complied. This time, he did not swirl the glass, and he sincerely wished that the alcohol would go down bitterly in the man's throat as he returned the glass to him, sliding it across the table.

"I won't do it," Reylar proclaimed, more to himself than Lhoris. "I won't send the adepts to a certain death, no matter how strong I feel they may be." Suddenly, anger filled his heart, and he stepped closer, puffing out his chest dangerously. "And I do not sacrifice my own."

Lhoris looked upon him as if he were a dog who had just misbehaved. Bringing his sharp nose to the glass, he drank deeply of the contents, first with his nose, then with his mouth as he drained the entirety of it with one long gulp.

"You will do what you must," he said simply. "Or have you forgotten the deal? A life for a life. Or, in this case, many lives for one."

"You cannot hold her over my head forever," Reylar replied angrily, no longer caring about pretense or custom. This man outranked him in society by many scores, but he couldn't find it in him to care as he added, "She is not a piece on a game table. She is not something you can gamble with. She is my blood. *My* blood."

"We did not put her on the board," Lhoris said. "She put herself there. With her actions against the Spellbound Arch. With her continued rebellion. And you did nothing to stop her. You still do nothing. We could have ordered her squashed in a heartbeat, but we didn't. Out of respect and tolerance—for you. But make no mistake, her life is as a line of thread, and we, the scissors. Dangerously sharp. All around her. Circling her. Will you stay her from the snip or will you sacrifice her as well? Just as you did your wife."

Reylar couldn't help himself and he drew in aethyris from the ringpact and slammed his fist into the fine wooden table. Under his power, it splintered, cracking entirely in half. Even the floor beneath it couldn't withstand his fury as a portion caved downwards. He withdrew, staring at his hands. They were no longer his own. They hadn't been in a long time. Replaced with metal and animated through aethyris and builder runes of old. He could feel nothing in them. Not the cold of a chilled drink nor the warmth of his wife's flesh as she took her final breath. Not even the pain of stupidly punching a piece of furniture, as if throwing a fit could change a thing. His hands had been just another sacrifice, and he feared for what was to come.

He had so little left to give.

Lhoris felt woozy as he shut the wooden door of his quarters behind him. Finally he was free from that human stench, if only for just a moment.

"Damnable mages," he whispered to himself in his solitary. "Damnable Spellbound Arch. Damnable Elvish Conclave. Whores and peasants, the lot of them."

He breathed a sigh of relief that he had made it back to his lodgings in time. Drink, especially as strong as the kind the Elder provided, made him drop his walls. Made him fall prey to his inhibitions. He had secrets—too many to count. He couldn't afford to speak of them, for it was not only his life that was on the line, but perhaps the future of all elvish kind itself.

Lhoris moved to stand in front of his silver-spun mirror, basking in the beauty that was himself. Nobody had ever understood him. His intelligence—his ambitions. If they would just listen to him—if they would all just listen—then he could mend the chaos that inflicted the world, like an untreated wound covered in shit. But alas, they didn't understand. They never could. Sometimes when a limb is rotting away, black at its core, it is best to rend it away to save the whole. That was the mage problem—a plague that needed cleansing.

And yet here he was, cursed with the safeguarding of the very thing he hated. The very thing he despised with all his being.

He stared back into the mirror and pulled down his collar, revealing his own slender neck. He pressed a finger against a discoloration of the skin drawn in a thin line. It was lighter than the rest of his perfect skin. A blemish he could never be rid of. A testament to his loathing. Oh, what price would he pay to return the favor in kind? Anything. Everything. He would give it all to not feel this way anymore. To feel... whole again.

Suddenly the perfect being he saw in the mirror looked ugly and wrong. A doomed being. That's what he was: star-crossed and ill-fated. A husk and a shell of what he could be. Of what he was meant to be.

Almost he smashed that mirror. How dare it force him to confront such things. To make him contemplate such notions for even in thought, he betrayed that which was duty-bound—entrusted to him and him alone.

Lhoris reached down and felt a familiar circular object in his right pocket. Reaching inside, he gingerly circled the metallic object and closed his eyes, picturing a battlefield littered with them. Of the peace such a future would bring.

He couldn't help but grin like a fool.

There was a sudden knock at his door. His heart raced and he ripped his hand away from the circular object. He took one final look at himself in the mirror, tracing the old scar on his neck one last time before hiding it once again with a raised collar. He turned, straightened his coat, stepped forward and opened the door.

CHAPTER 9

HERO OR VILLAIN?

The Dimlight district was not the place Kyra had planned on being on this particular night, but fate, it seemed, had other plans for this juncture of her life. And for the life of her, she could not understand the Spellbound Arch's reasons for sending untrained, adept level mages, such as themselves, out on patrols. From the looks on the rest of the faces of those of her circle, they shared in her concerns.

"This is shit," Soren said, kicking a rock on the ground, which went skittering further into the darkened alleyway. He scoffed at the loss of his sole entertainment. "Pure centaur shit."

"C-C-Complaining won't help," Maxim replied. Surprising, the man had not made much of an effort to speak to the rest of them in the short time they had been on patrol. Hells, it had taken him most of that time to stop shaking after he had learned of their assignment for the night.

"Oh, and standing here will?" Soren replied with a certain air of regalness in his voice. As if conversing with Maxim was beneath him. "What are we even supposed to be doing? Looking for violent criminals? Uncanny? ...Prostitutes? We just received our ringpacts, what are we supposed to do? I don't know about all of you, but I've not even gotten used to the change of aethryis yet. It's strange... being only able to draw from one school of aethryis, even if it is much stronger than before."

Armeya, who had been content to watch the other two argue thus far, stood, imposing her presence upon them. The light from a nearby sign caused her off-color eyes to shine all the brighter and made her dark skin almost glow.

"Why are you complaining?" she asked. "Aren't you Soren *Ais* Frost? Son of Sepitus *Ais* Frost? Otherwise known as the Cryomancer?"

"Don't speak that name again," Soren replied dangerously, turning from the group. "*Bah,* if you want to waste your time here, suit yourself. As for me... well, this is the Dimlight District. I'm going to go find me some sort gambling parlor. Or something else that's entertaining."

Adathin, who'd been fine to simply observe the group fall into bickering between each other, made himself known. He stood tall, blocking Soren's way. "No, you won't," he said in an even tone. "Stay here... for now."

Adathin didn't threaten Soren. Not outwardly. But there was something in the man's eyes. Golden and glowing. They spoke of power and the threat that he would wield it against you. This elvish man was intimidating; much as his sister had been. But instead of cutting words, he let the immensity of his presence speak for him.

She had a hard time not being intimidated.

Soren ground his teeth, but, in the end, threw his arms up in defeat, sitting on an empty wooden box in the corner of the nearby alleyway. Adathin wandered away again, preferring to stand alone in the shadows just across the busy thoroughfare.

Iona hummed softly to herself, her blue eyes contrasting the red flames of the lamplights. Slowly, she kneeled down and withindrew a small string instrument from a black bag. It was made of a soft gray wood and had six silver strings running its length. Slowly, in the quiet, she began to strum. The melody was intoxicating, reverberating through her head as gently as a spring breeze resists summer's heat.

Then something peculiar happened, the noise shifted and spun, as if additional instruments joined the fray. Soon, she could hear the sound of a symphony backing Iona's soft strumming.

Iona held her chest high as she sang,

Ait' Koglu, Et' Koglu, from earth we live. Ait' Koglu, Et' Koglu, to earth we die.

A lovers quarrel, a widower made. His flesh, his power, he would trade. For what glimmer remains as hope should fade. Away, away, aught naught remains.

But yet ambitions desire shall lead him to the pyre. No more, oh please, no more.

Ait' Koglu, Et' Koglu, from earth we live. Ait' Koglu, Et' Koglu, to earth we die.

Iona's song died out as the woman shielded her face from the group. She sobbed softly to herself, but continued to strum wordlessly.

Armeya suddenly filled the void of conversation by nudging at her with an elbow as she said, "What do you think of him?" She glanced over at Adathin, trying not to make herself look suspicious or awkward as she did.

"Doesn't seem to be much of a leader," she replied, crossing her arms. "But, on the other hand, he seems better than his sister." She shook her head. "That woman is a thorn in my boots."

"You mean a pain in your ass..." Armeya chuckled. "And yeah, no kidding—she's elvish! They're all like that. Could be worse, though."

"What did you expect?" Iona chimed in, setting her instrument aside. The woman's eyes looked completely dry, and it surprised her that she had recovered so quickly. Iona faltered under her gaze as she added, "She's a

Mistwalker, through and through. But remember, so is Adathin. Elvish care only for themselves. Mistwalkers especially."

Kyra suddenly felt exhausted as she sighed in frustration and boredom. "If we're going to waste the night, then someone best speak to our new leader. At least one of us should get to know him better."

Iona and Armeya glanced at each other and then back to her. It was clear she had just been volunteered. It was her idea, after all.

"... *Fine,*" she muttered under her breath. In the past two days, she had been forced to be more sociable than the entire time she apprenticed for Master Lu'ce.

Trudging across the busy thoroughfare herself, she just barely avoided being trampled by at least two horses, a cart and a centaur who flipped her a rude gesture as she narrowly missed colliding with the uncanny's legs. But, as she turned to apologize, the centaur's eyes were inevitably drawn to the ring around her finger, and the uncanny moved on quickly after realizing that she was, indeed, a mage. An adept mage or a master mage, she did not think it mattered much in the eyes of the uncanny.

Is that what they think of us all? That we are to be feared? Hated?

She reached Adathin, leaning against the red-bricked wall he stood beside, and found that she had little to say. She stared at him silently for a long while, struggling with what was proper to even ask him. He was elvish. Royalty. And a Mistwalker at that. Royalty among royalty.

She best tread carefully.

Adathin scratched the back of his neck, some sort of nervous tick, as he said in a bashful tone, "Are you just going to keep staring at me like that? You're making me feel as if I have jelly smeared across my face... I don't, do I?"

"Sorry," Kyra replied, staring out at the multitude of denizens of the Dimlight District. "And no, you don't." Adathin let out an exhalation. "It's just, I'm trying to understand why you're standing over here alone. Surely it's an interesting tale. The brooding royal born who separates themselves from the others? Emphasis on the brooding." She spared Armeya and Iona a glance and both pretended not to know what was happening, grinning stupidly to each other. "Truth be told, I wish I could get them to leave me alone."

Adathin smiled with a hint of sadness on his face. "I'm hardly a brooding royal. Far from it. But hey, let's make it a game. Give me your best guess. Humor me. Since you seem to know so much, who am I? Really?"

Kyra narrowed her eyes, standing straighter as she put a hand to her chin. "Well, you've certainly got the air of royalty about you, that much is certain. Clothing is top-notch. Well maintained. From appearance... expensive." She waited to see if Adathin gave anything away, but his face was as stone. At the prospect of an interesting turn, she continued, adding, "And your stance: shoulders back. Tall. Proud." Again, he gave nothing away, continuing to smirk ever so slightly. Annoyed, she went for the killing blow. "Maybe your tale begins with your family. You know, I've already met your sister. She didn't seem to care much for me. Or humans, in general. I wonder if you share her sentiments? You see yourself above us. Better than us. That's why you shy away from us. You can't stand us."

Adathin's coy smile quickly turned to a sneer, and there was a long silence between them that was punctuated by the busy road of carts and horses they stood beside. Finally, his eyes turned back towards her, and there was danger in them. "And what would you know of her sentiments?" he asked. "Of our beliefs? Of mine? Do not speak about what you do not understand."

Suddenly angry, Kyra let slip her inhibitions as she said, "You know, when they told me you've fallen far from the Mistwalker tree, I expected to find someone different. Perhaps someone kind. But from what I've gathered so far, you seem to fit right in with them. You're a Mistwalker through and through. A prime example of an elvish man."

"*Enough!*" Adathin slammed his fist into the wall.

Kyra smiled coyly, unsure why or when she had become cruel. "Keep your temper. My life, and theirs, are, for better or worse, in your hands. Best not to kill us with rashness or hotheadedness." She turned and strode back towards the street, spinning just a few steps away, adding, "And sorry about upsetting you. Let's just think of this as a test. A similar one your sister put me through. I had to see what I was dealing with."

That was it. That's where her cruelty lay. She was getting back at his sister for how she had made her feel. But was that fair? To take her frustrations out on another?

Adathin's face suddenly calmed, and his eyes lifted ever so slightly. Playfully, he said, "And what is it you think you've seen? What are you dealing with?"

"You're not a hero," she said. "But perhaps you're not the villain either. I guess I'll just need to wait and see for myself. Not like I have much of a choice, *leader.*"

She did not remain as she turned from Adathin, cutting across the street far more gracefully than on her first attempt. On the other side, she was met with the bewildered faces of her classmates.

Before she could speak, Armeya accosted her, asking, "What did you say to him? He looked so angry for a moment. Furious even. And did he break his hand?"

Kyra waved her off. "It was nothing of importance."

"Tell that to him," Iona replied. "From the looks of it, he wanted to kill you where you stood. Hells, being a Mistwalker, he could probably get away with it. No, I *know* he could."

"Mistwalker or not, I'm not intimidated by him... or his sister."

Armeya's eyes went bright. "Ah, that's what this is about," she said accusingly. "You're still sore about what his sister did to you. While I admit, using psionics on you was extreme, you can't take it out on him."

Kyra shot her a dangerous look.

Armeya raised her hands in mock defeat. "I'm just saying."

"Best you both stop talking, look," Iona pointed, "here he comes."

Sure enough, as Kyra turned, Adathin crossed the street with a determined look on his face. Perhaps she had pushed him too far, and he came for retribution.

Adathin stepped to the entrance of the alleyway. "Soren, Maxim—to me!" At the call of their names, both men hurriedly returned to the mouth of the alleyway. Adathin nodded as he added, "I doubt this is what the Spellbound Arch meant when they charged us with this duty. I know that Elder Reylar said to stick to a major thoroughfare, but I can't help but feel that our time is wasted here. So we'll patrol—*actually patrol*. We will split into groups of two so that we can cover more ground. Kyra and Armeya, Soren and Maxim, and myself will be the three different groups."

"Wait, what about me?" Iona asked, a hint of anger showed on her furrowed brow.

"Enchanters aren't to be involved in patrol," Adathin replied. "They are to remain at a central base of operations. Lacking one, this will need to do." He pointed to the ground. "Here, in this case. If there are any enchantments that anyone needs, please do what you can. I know you've only just received your ringpact, and I can't expect much of you yet. Do you understand your assignment?"

Iona looked at the ground dejectedly. "I understand..."

Adathin nodded.

"Wait a moment," Kyra said. "And how are we supposed to communicate with one another? I'm sure you don't want us handling anything dangerous alone."

"*Like this.*"

Kyra jumped as Adathin's voice rattled in her head. "How did you do that?" she asked.

"We use psionic abilities for a multitude of tasks," Adathin explained openly for all to hear. "I can draw on memories. Make you see things that aren't there. Feel things that aren't real... *And address your mind directly.*"

A tingle ran up her back. Every time Adathin pressed his thoughts into her head, it felt like a violation of her being. Of her very core. Looking at the others, they reacted similarly, as each had their minds infiltrated by Adathin's psionics.

"If that's all," Adathin said, "Soren and Maxim will patrol the North. Kyra and Armeya, South. Meet here in two turns' time." And with that, the elvish man turned and walked off on his own, crossing the street with barely a bother as to whom was passing by.

Armeya shrugged her shoulders. "And you said he didn't intimidate you... What about now?"

"Now..." Kyra said, putting a hand against her chin. "Now I'm nervous that I made him upset."

CHAPTER 10
MAGIC AND MURDER

"So what did he say?" Armeya asked, her eyes flashing different colors for a brief moment. "Nevermind that, what did you say to him? Come on, it's just you and me now. Don't leave me in the dark." Her pestering was getting more and more persistent as the night dwindled on.

Mist, so common in the city, brought with it a cool chill which stuck to Kyra's skin. Try as she might, she couldn't shed it. Already, they had searched each alleyway they had come upon. Checked in with local shops, and nothing; not a whisper of disturbance. Despite the rumors of illicit dealings in Dimlight, this night was quiet, and she was thankful for it. As brave a face as she had put on, she would rather familiarize herself with her newfound aethryis before tackling anything more dangerous than a simple excursion.

"I said nothing," Kyra replied, hoping the woman would just drop it. "Except... Well I just compared him to his sister, that's all."

Armeya grimaced and clicked her tongue. "Wrong move there. Very wrong." Leaning close, she added in a whisper, "I heard that their sibling rivalry is a tale of legendary proportions. In fact, I'd heard that once, she challenged him to a battle of minds. A psionic duel."

Kyra stepped away, turning to look at Armeya. "A battle of minds?" she asked."Like chess or some other game of strategy?"

"*Shh,*" Armeya replied, shaking her head. "A little more discreet, *eh?*" She nodded, giving the woman a sour frown. Armeya continued, adding, "You could say it's a game of strategy, perhaps, but one that actually happens in the mind. You see, between psionics, when they infiltrate each other's heads, the one with the most willpower is victorious. While Aluriel is one year older than Adathin, *he* would have become the new head of the Mistwalker house once his father stepped down. An old tradition. A patriarchal one."

"You mean an ignorant one."

Armeya grinned. "Aye, as you say. Anyways, this didn't sit so well with Aluriel, as you can imagine. So, she challenged her brother outright for head of household. He tried to worm his way out of it, fearing he'd still her mind."

"*Still* her mind?"

"Do they not teach you a thing during your apprenticeship?"

"Not about the elvish and their customs," Kyra replied defensively. "Master Lu'ce taught me what I needed to survive. Both others and my... nevermind."

Armeya sighed. "Well, you had better brush up on them. And quick." She raised a hand and tapped on the side of her head. "Now, to still one's mind is to trap it in a specific state. Like a state of bewilderment. Or fear. Think of a halfwit that cannot even feed or bathe themselves. Their mind, constantly lost in the nether. That, except far far worse."

"And Aluriel challenged Adathin to a game with that sort of consequence? Well... what happened?"

"She won!"

Kyra scratched at her chin. "Then why is *he* not one of the lost you speak of?"

"That's the thing; there are rumors that Adathin let her win. It was never any secret that he detests who his father is. And that house politics held no interest for him. Much less the overall elvish politics. Some say he's an artist at heart. Others, that he's lazy. Either way, the contest ended with Aluriel the victor, but with Adathin of sound mind. Neither will say what exactly happened between them. This, as you can imagine, did not sit well with the rest of his family. Especially their father."

"I'd imagine..." Kyra continued scratching that particular itch. One not born of distress upon the skin, but instead, distress of the mind. "Well, that explains it," she concluded. "I inadvertently taunted him by saying that he didn't fall far from the Mistwalker tree. It must've struck a nerve."

"Must have," Armeya agreed. "And I'd bet that—"

A sudden sound of splintering wood from a nearby warehouse halted Armeya's tongue. Kyra stood still with Armeya right beside her, waiting. Then another sound, and footsteps; quick in pace.

"Should we check?" Armeya asked

"What do you think?" she asked. "Nothing else has happened so far tonight. I say we do."

Armeya grinned. "I was hoping you'd say that." She flicked her nose with her thumb. "Time to give these pretty new rings a test, aye?"

Kyra narrowed her eyes at the woman, but she was right; this would present an excellent opportunity to test what they are capable of. Stilling her racing heart, she nodded.

Stepping closer and closer to where the noise had come from, Kyra pressed her hand against the wood of the building. It was some type of warehouse. Unpainted, parts of the wood were rotting away with hardly any signs of repair. She'd have wagered it was abandoned if there hadn't been a lock and chains neatly wrapped around the handles to the double-wide swinging doors. And there was something off about the lock as well.

"Think it was just a rat?" Armeya asked.

"Awfully big to be a rat," she replied. "Guess we have no choice. Let's check inside."

"Thought you'd never ask." Armeya crossed her arms, craning her neck to look over the lock and chain. "How would they have gotten in?"

Kyra pointed up at an opened slit on the roof. "Possibly up there. But, wait a moment... should we tell the others first?"

"*Pfft, no!*" Armeya laughed, clearly a fake chuckle to hide her nerves. "It's probably nothing, but we've not found anything else so far. Let me see if I can open this." She clenched her hand and closed her eyes, and, after a moment, opened them again with an intense focus on the lock. Pointing a single finger at it, a bright light suddenly spewed from her finger, casting her shadow across the building.

When her eyes came to focus, Kyra realized what the light was. Fire. So hot it burned almost white at the tip. A familiar pain crept into her mind, originating from her hand. Trying her best not to scream at the woman, she asked, "Are you trying to burn the building down?"

Armeya ignored her, holding the flame against the chains which reflected the red smolder on its metallic surface. But, regardless of how long she held the magic to the chains, the metal did not bend. Did not break. Nor melt. Something held it together. Something... magical.

Armeya let the aethryis go, wheezing. "En... chanted. The damn lock is enchanted."

Kyra held a hand to the chain, gently prodding the edge.

"Careful!" Armeya added, pulling her back by the shoulder.. "It'll burn you."

"Unlikely." Kyra reached back out and snatched the entire chain with her hand and felt nothing but smooth metal. "Look—" She placed her thumb directly on the spot where Armeya had held the flame. "It's Freezing. This lock cannot conduct heat."

"Interesting," Armeya mused. "Well, since we can't exactly blow down the wall, I guess we'll just have to leave it as is."

Jiggling the chain, she tested the durability and found that it was quite stable. With an idea in her head, she said, "Not yet, let me try something else."

Arcanists... said to be masters of stealth and detection. Some of their many abilities included: Sight, concealment, and, luckily for her, lock-breaking. Abilities that were now hers to control and learn. Looking down at her ringpact, she noticed a shimmer. Aethryical potential. Raw and untapped. Leaning, she pressed her face close to the chain. Holding her breath, she tried to see—see the aethryis that held the chains steady.

... *Nothing.*

"How did you make that flame?" Kyra asked, not breaking her focus on the chains.

Armeya smirked. "It's a bit different than using aethryis from before the ringpact," she said. "Instead of commanding the aethryis around to my will, I needed to... bargain with the ringpact. To feed it some of that aethryis in return for access to our power. It had to be drawn—not through me—but through *it!*"

"Through it... Sounds like you're talking about a living thing."

Armeya nodded.

Kyra leaned back down, staring at the chain. She could practically taste the aethryis exuding from it. Holding her own ringpact up to it, she tried, as instructed, to pull the aethryis through the ring. The ringpact reacted almost immediately, sending waves of tingling pleasure through her arm. Then, like the light of dawn breaking through the clouds, she saw it. *Aethryis!* Infinite in its complexity, yet so easy to accept. As a commoner would say, magic in its purest form.

Strands of light circled continuously around the chain, connected by small strands that looked like it had been spun as a spider's web. If she could just focus, isolate the strand that bound, *and...* With a flick of her finger, she separated that strand, and the entire enchantment broke, the chains loosening in an instant, falling to the ground beside her.

Wiping sweat from her brow, Kyra said, "*There!*" The act had drained her far more than she cared to admit.

Armeya's mouth hung open. "*Amazing!*" Clicking her tongue, she added, "That's an arcanist for ya'. You know, that's some talent you've got there."

"You as well."

Armeya waved the comment off. "You do me too much honor," she replied. "I just made a little flame. Same as a wayward candle. But you... *Wow!*"

"It's not that impressive..." Kyra turned her head to hide her blush. Praise; she was not used to it. Quite the opposite, actually. "Now are we going to search the warehouse or not?"

Armeya, headstrong and daring, was already halfway through the door before she had even finished her sentence. Rolling her eyes, she followed the thaumaturge into the warehouse.

Inside, the smell of stale dust and mildew assaulted her nose and throat. The warehouse was stagnant, as if it had been sealed for quite some time. Then, suddenly, a metallic taste touched her tongue and made her want to empty her stomach. It was a familiar taste. One from her memories. And nightmares.

It was the taste of blood.

As Kyra stepped forward, not paying any attention to where she was heading, trying to locate the source of that gruesome smell, she ran directly into Armeya, who stood as still as a statue.

Touching her shoulder, she asked, "What's wrong?"

Circling the thaumaturge, she saw exactly what was the matter. There, in the middle of the room, in a pool of their own blood, an unknown human lay.

A corpse, fresh as the air riding the night wind.

Adathin moved like a ghoul fresh from the soil down the busy streets of the Dimlight District, each step punctuated by the soft reverberating of electrical signals that wafted off the various enchanted lights which lit the night.

Mages and their contraptions. They never ceased to amaze him... And annoy him.

It was no secret that the elvish, like himself, preferred a more... natural setting. Such as the genuine light of the moon. Or the soft glowing of the *brightpetals* that grew on the mother tree. But this world—this place—it was gray. Dark. Devoid of the beauty of nature and the bounties that nature brings.

Adathin had never experienced sitting under the warmth of twin suns nor the breeze that carried the chillness of the River of Tears, but he shared in the memories of the times before—before the 'modern' era. Times where the elvish had worked the land, trees and skies. That was in another place. Another time... Another world. Now, as terrible as it was to think, his people had become lazy. Complacent. The builders, elders of the dwarven, had made this world in *their* image. Of stone and metal. Then, just as the elvish had done, humans had migrated here and took it for themselves. Many other species, or uncanny, had come before his people had arrived on these strange shores. And when his people saw naught but strife, suffering and death, they took it upon themselves to rid the world of such barbarity, but at a cost. A cost that he now feared had changed them for all eternity.

So much of what they were was lost to time.

Adathin suddenly struck a wide-shouldered and red-furred minotaur. The uncanny man was tall, with thick black horns that curved not unlike a ram. His ax sat neatly on his hip, gleaming unnaturally in the magelight.

"Watch it human, I—" the minotaur spun and suddenly recognized him for what he was: elvish. In a softer tone, he muttered weak apologies.

Adathin waved the uncanny man off. "Do not worry, friend. It was my mistake."

They both knew it was a lie, but the Minotaur nodded and reverted to the conversation with his female companion. Was this uncanny woman considered beautiful? With her fur of rich brown and those enormous black eyes? He couldn't say, but, either way, the man seemed all too keen to continue chatting with her.

He left them in peace.

Was that to be the budding of something more? A relationship? Love, perhaps? Adathin chuckled to himself. Love was such a foreign concept to his people now, a contrast to the old times. So much now rested on the gains and loss of politics between the various elvish families. Nobody wed for simple love now. It was all calculated. Bartered. A transaction, same as going to any ole shop and buying a loaf of bread. His people lived such long lives, eventually dying and sharing their memories with each other and yet... they seemed to have learned nothing at all.

"Hey you!" a shrill voice cried out. "Yeah, you!"

Adathin spun, glancing about until he saw three shrouded figures in an alleyway nearby.

Trouble.

Adathin turned to step away, but the uncanny man from before, the minotaur, now stood behind him, imposing his colossal form upon him in a threatening manner. In the shadows, the man's fur no longer appeared to be that of a light red, but now rang dark... the color of blood.

"You heard 'em," the uncanny said, fingering the ax at his waist with his large fingers. "In ya' go. Move."

Adathin put his arms up defensively. "I'm going," he replied. At the mouth of the alley, the three figures parted, allowing him to venture in. He did so, asking, "I'm sure this is some sort of misunderstanding."

"The only misunderstanding is you strutting along here like you own the place," the man with the shrill voice said. "This is Dimlight, not the Upper Ward. You's were a fool comin' down here."

Assuming the man who had answered him was, in fact, the leader, Adathin replied, "Quite right you are, sir. Who am I to be 'strutting' on the streets that I presume *you* own? Foolish indeed."

"Aye," the man replied. "I do own these streets. My crew and I. And you see, we don't like it when the Arch and its little mages interrupt our business. We like it even less when you elvish parade yourselves around like uppity peacocks. So here's what we're gonna do: empty your pockets. All of 'em. Give me everything of value you have."

"Gladly," Adathin said, reaching inside.

The minotaur placed a firm hand on his shoulder and squeezed. It hurt, but only just.

"Slower," he warned.

Even slower, Adathin ruffled around his various pockets and pulled out everything of value. Some coins. From his coat, a thin and nicely bound book. A silver locket.

The shrouded man stepped forward, and he managed to catch a glimpse: he was human. Short and wiry, with thinning hair ending in a v-shaped widow's peak. And his nose... long and curved. The man reminded him of a rat more than one of his own species. Suddenly, the rat-man started tapping his various pockets, as if searching for something.

"What's this?" he asked, reaching in and pulling out a small, smoothed stone.

Adathin ground his teeth. "Return that," he warned. "You said to give you anything of value. That has value only to me. It is a stone. A simple stone."

"*Sure...*" the rat-man replied, obviously unbelieving of his words. "And I'm a giant gold dragon. You elf's are all liars and thieves."

Elf... a derogatory term used by feeble-minded idiots. Adathin could pity this man. It was obvious he hadn't the wit nor intellect to know when he was in danger. Genuine danger. But to allow him to steal his stone? Based on pity alone? No, that he could not abide.

"Last chance," Adathin said. "Return the stone and count yourself in the blessings of the gods or whatever it is you believe that it is *I* whom you robbed. Nobody else of my kind would give you the satisfaction. No other would show you such kindness."

"Rob?" the rat-man laughed, his nose wrinkling upwards. "No, we didn't *rob* you. Think of this as a... contribution to the ongoing work of the Dimlight District. A tax. And, of course, insurance for your continued well-being."

"And the stone?"

"Sorry, the tax includes the stone."

Adathin narrowed his eyes. There were four of them, and as he pried their minds, he sensed not a one had a lick of intelligence. He breathed easily, knowing he had nothing to fear from any of them. Suddenly, the minotaur gasped, stepping backwards from him and swatting frantically at nothing in the air.

"Help me," the minotaur said, panicked, his red fur standing on end like a riled up cat. "Get them off of me!"

"What are you talking about?" the rat-man replied, his compatriots fingering their makeshift weapons of hastily made shivs. "Hey you," he rounded on Adathin, "Stop it! Whatever you're doing, *stop it!*"

Adathin was suddenly so tired of pretense. He was elvish. Powerful. This abuse... he didn't need to take it from anyone. Let alone some common thugs.

"I wanted to stop," he said, "but you didn't listen. Why do they never listen?"

The rat-faced man's eyes went wide as he pried into his flesh. His head... His very mind. There, he found the man's uttermost secrets. His wishes. Desires. And that which he feared most.

He made that fear a reality.

The rat-faced man shrieked, dropping to the floor and scratching at his own eyes. He now truly looked like a rat caught in a snare, waiting for the moment when he would choose to gnaw his own leg off. As for his compatriots, he delved into the mind of the man still holding the shiv. The thug soon turned on the third, giving chase. Weak-minded fools. It was so easy to turn them against each other.

The minotaur suddenly took off running out of the alleyway and down the busy street as bewildered patrons of the Dimlight District looked on with worry and curiosity. As for the rat-faced man, he'd long abandoned his ill-gotten goods, as he writhed on the dirty and wet alleyway floor.

Adathin reached down and retrieved them. He had dealt with the entire group in less time than it took to put on his boots. He decided that he would pity them. Better that than to hate.

There was a nudge in his mind. Panic, but not from those around him. Distant. It was someone he knew... Armeya. She was calling out to him, but not intentionally. Something was wrong. Their connection wasn't perfect, but he was able to get a relative location from where she hailed. Looking down at the rat-faced man, he lifted the psionic spell. When the man looked up at him, it was as if he saw a *Daemon* in the flesh. The man turned and fled without saying another word. Hopefully, he had learned a lesson, but he had doubts. Human memories are fast fading. Fleeting things. What sends waves of terror today could be but a mild panic tomorrow.

Adathin sought Soren's and Maxim's minds, giving them the order to rally at Armeyas' location as soon as possible. He didn't wait for a response as he pocketed the stone safely back into his coat pocket and made his own way.

"What's your problem?" Soren had tried his best to make conversation with the man, but it seemed impossible. Every question, every proclamation, or joke, was met with little more than a nod or a shrug of his shoulders.

And he was sick of it.

"T-T-There's no p-problem," Maxim replied, averting his eyes. He seemed to cower slightly beneath him, like a small animal facing something much larger than itself.

Soren let out an exasperated sigh. "Did anyone ever tell you that you're—" He suddenly shut his mouth, wishing he had just let the matter drop.

Maxim, for the first time, raised his eyes to meet his own. There was defiance there—fire!

"D-D-Did anyone ever tell me... w-what?" he asked. "Finish that sentence."

Soren ground his teeth. How did he ever get stuck with this one? Even Kyra, as distant as she could be, was leaps and bounds above Maxim in terms of conversation. He studied the man, and his green eyes caught the magelight peculiarly. Were there tears there at the corners? His indignation died in his chest, leaving him feeling empty and guilty all at once.

"Sorry," he muttered like a scolded child. "Listen, I didn't mean anything by it. I'm just frustrated is all. I feel like a pawn on a chessboard. One who is about to be sacrificed."

"P-P-Pawn?" Maxim replied, his features brightening. "Do you play? C-C-Chess I mean?"

Soren cocked his head curiously. "Occasionally," he admitted. "My mother demanded... *wished* it of me. Said she'd not have a witless child. Only a talentless one."

"T-T-Then maybe we can play sometime?" Maxim seemed curiously excited at the prospect. "M-M-My brother and I u-used to play all the time." Then, suddenly, his eyes shifted downward, and his shoulders slumped.

"Brother, eh," Soren replied, hoping this was his *in* to having a proper conversation with the man. "You know, I've got some brothers. Sisters too. They can be quite a handful, huh?"

"I-I-I wouldn't know," Maxim replied. "N-Not anymore, at least."

It took little to get that hint. Maxim's brother was gone. Likely been for a while now.

"Sorry for your loss," Soren replied, knowing little of what else to say. "I know it is just words, but you and I... we're like family now. Whether or not we like it or whether we like each other. Look around," he flourished his arms outwards like some sort of showman, "enemies on all sides, and we, the only defense against the nefarious. Tell ya' what, since you're our Mystic and I our Augmentor, you can think of me as your shield. You heal me, keep me healthy, and I'll make sure nothing gets to you. I'll keep you safe."

Soren's words were meant to placate Maxim, but at the utterance of his Mystic calling, the man seemed even more distraught. He was impossible.

Suddenly, Soren's head exploded in awareness as he felt Adathin pierce his mind. The elvish man didn't seem to say anything, and wasn't subtle as he infiltrated his mind with vague references to where they should go. It seemed panicked. Something was wrong.

"Did you feel that?" Soren asked, rubbing at his temples gingerly.

Maxim nodded wordlessly as he began to run towards the place Adathin had indicated. For his size, the man could move.

Smiling, Soren focused and followed, excited that the night wouldn't be a total waste after all.

CHAPTER II
GONE IN A FLASH

Journal Entry

Year: 830 E.B

*"Faster!" Master Lu'ce had said, as she cracked her enchanted whip, narrow-
ly grazing the edge of my arm. It stung like the lick of fire as it seared flesh. I
had wanted me to cry out. To beg for her to stop. As I had done so many times
before. But no... not this time. I was getting stronger, and not just of body, but
of mind as well.*

*The lash came again and this time, and I had drawn aethryis into my body,
willing my skin to be as steel. I had heard the crack and felt no pain. I smiled
at my hard sought victory, but it was short-lived as the whip drew back and
lashed again, like a snake giving the mouse multiple doses of venom before
the eating began.*

*The second lash had hit me in the chest, knocking the air from my body, and
causing me to expel the aethryis I held. Pain flowed back into me, both fresh
and old. Master Lu'ce was a monster. And a powerful one at that. What
hope had I of ever catching up to her strength? But as cruel as my master can*

be, she is also kind. She had walked towards me and extended a helpful hand and I took it and she pulled me up, patting me on the back.

"Good job," Master Lu'ce had said. "Even taking one of my lashes is an impressive feat, especially for someone as young as yourself. You should be proud."

I had held my head dejectedly, as expected from a girl of my age.

Master Lu'ce had sighed in frustration. "And yet, you aren't. Proud I mean."

"No," I had admitted.

Master Lu'ce had fallen back on the green grass, laying down and staring up at the cloudless blue sky. I followed her lead, laying down myself. The grass was soft against my back, and it almost felt as if it could soothe the burning gashes on my arms and chest.

Master Lu'ce had looked over as if she remembered something important.

"Shit... let me fix those." She had reached out, and I felt the familiar cold metal of her mystic ringpact as it gently touched my skin. A soothing sensation had flowed through my body like water quenching a parched throat. Then the pain was gone. Evaporated. Gone to where, no one could say, not even the healer themselves. It was too bad the healing was only of the physical state and not for scars made of memories. Those were too often the most painful injuries of all.

I had breathed in with renewed vigor. My pain was gone, but the memory of it was still fresh. As I mentioned, Mystic healing does nothing for the mind. But just then, a loud thud hit the ground nearby. Craning my head, I turned to see a fallen bird squirming on the grass near some trees.

Master Lu'ce had clicked her tongue. "Poor thing."

I had rolled over, stumbling to my feet as I walked over. Before I could make it, a larger bird with sharp talons swooped down and landed nearby, as if to claim its kill. It gave me one sharp look with its beady eye before turning back to its meal as it began to peck, peck, peck.

"Should we do something?" I had asked.

Master Lu'ce hadn't moved as she replied, "Like what? The predator got its kill fair and square. Death... it waits for us all. It may take this form or another, but rest assured, it's there. Waiting. Does that bother you? Death I mean?"

Looking upon the prey, bloodied and broken, I couldn't help but think back to my old home. To the scorched bodies. How it had smelled. How the air had tasted of sulfur. This... This was not like that. This death had meaning. It would sustain the life of the predator. The remains would feed the grass and other wildlife would sustain themselves on that. Eventually, the predator themselves would die and that too would feed the everlasting system. It was then that I knew that death did not bother me at all. Not when that death was natural. When it was needed. No... what bothered me wasn't death, but death without purpose. Without meaning.

I would vow to never kill without purpose again, and to punish those who would. A childish promise, but in my mind, a victim's death would then have meaning.

I had never considered back then whether I deserved to be the hunter or the prey.

Armeya's face was as pale as a snow wolf's pelt, and she could tell the woman struggled to breathe with the air so thick of death. She tried to shift the woman, but it felt as if her feet were filled with lead.

"Armeya..." Kyra said calmly. After no response, she added in a harsher tone and shaking her, *"Armeya!"*

The thaumaturge snapped back, her off-colored eyes shifting from red to blue then brown and from herself to the corpse on the floor.

"Huh?" she whispered faintly. "Wha-Wha... What happened?"

"I don't know," Kyra admitted. "But this situation just got a lot more dangerous. Far too much so. I need you to reach out to Adathin. Tell him to come here. *Quickly!* But... don't mention the reason."

Armeya narrowed her eyes, some of that keen and wit returning. "Why?" she asked.

"Because others may be listening in. Other psionics. Their powers aren't exactly well known." Armeya didn't shift, obviously expecting more. "Also..." she admitted. "I'd like some time with the body. To search for clues. And I'd rather not disobey an order."

"To search... the body?" Armeya asked indignantly. "You're going to search the corpse?" She swallowed hard, adding in a whisper, "Are you sure they're even dead?"

Kyra glanced down at the remains. The blood, far too much spilled to survive, was still fresh. It was not quite hardened into one large scab on the floor as of yet. The signs of rigor mortis had only just begun to set in. From the angle, she could just make out the likely wound which did the poor fellow in.

And the smell. One never forgot the smell of death.

"I'm quite certain they are dead," Kyra said. "And now, I'm going to search the body. Among other things. I'm not—we're not going to get another opportunity like this to test our powers. Call out to Adathin and wait over there." She pointed to a wooden box in the room's corner. "Don't worry, I won't contaminate the crime scene."

Taking another haphazard look at the corpse, Armeya nodded her head as she turned and strode to the would-be chair. When she arrived, she sat, keeping her eyes decidedly away from the bloody scene, pretending as if she had not a care in the world, but the worry lines on her brow betrayed her.

Kyra returned her attention back to the matter at hand. Stepping towards the corpse, doing her best to avoid the blood, and kneeling down, two things drew her curiosity. Under the man's glossed over eyes, almost hidden beneath the contours of his face, was a nice, long red line from one corner of his neck to the other. Her guess, the likely death wound. On his right hand, two fingers ended in little stubs. Small pools of blood underneath demonstrated it wasn't an old injury. It was almost as if something feral had torn them off, but the peculiar concentration of aethryis around his hand spoke of a different story. This man was no ordinary human. He was a mage—like her. And now that she really could see his face, she realized she had seen him before.

"Armeya," Kyra said, standing. "He's a mage. An adept at Dragrin's. New... like us."

Armeya sighed out, placing her face in her hands. With bated breath, she replied, "I thought I knew him. Well, I don't *know* him, but I recognized him. I'd hoped... No, that's not important now. He's a thaumaturge—*was* a thaumaturge. Just like me."

Concentrating, Kyra followed a trail of aethryis, like a glowing mist encircling the body. A streak of it twisted away, twirling in the air towards a small window on the second floor of the warehouse leading out to the roof.

"Look," Kyra said, pointing at her discovery. "Our killer, most likely, escaped through there. Perhaps even chased the man here to kill him." Glancing back down, she noted that blood had sprayed away from the body, hitting some nearby crates. "No, I'm sure that's how it happened. Whomever it was, killed him up there, and shoved him down here."

"Can you just stop talking about it?" Armeya's words came light and panicked. She kept the rest of her notions to herself for now.

Turning her focus back on the body, Kyra noted his pale skin, and slight burns on the tips of his rigor mortised fingers. The way they curled... his death took time. Likely, he survived the throat slitting and the fall, slowly bleeding out in agony on the cold floor. It must have been excruciating. An awful way to die. Truly terrible.

Footsteps suddenly drew her to the rafters above. A burst of dust and debris fell from the wooden structure with every punctuated step. A hooded figure revealed themselves, looking down at the scene. From within the shadows of the clothing, Kyra just managed to make out shoulder length red hair. With little else, the mysterious figure turned and walked back towards the roof exit as quickly as they had come.

"*Wait!*" Kyra called out, making her way towards an old wooden ladder that went to the second floor. Turning to Armeya, she added, "Stay here and send help as soon as they arrive."

Armeya was on her feet in an instant.

"*No way!*" she protested. "How can you even think—" She was too late as Kyra was already halfway up the ladder. Reluctantly, Armeya added, "Don't get yourself killed."

Kyra had no intention of that, but there was something—some unknown force—spurring her forward. And she dared not fight against it. Before she knew it, her boots hit the rafters, and dust kicked into her face, choking her. Coughing out, wiping spittle from her chin, she found the narrow opening that led to the roof. Dashing forward, she nearly fell down to the ground as a wood board gave way, crashing a few moments later.

"*That almost hit me!*" She heard Armeya gasp from the ground floor.

Kyra pushed past, exiting the warehouse to the rooftops of the city of Mistbreak. On the roof, she saw lights dazzling, twinkling, expanding out into the infinite. There was seemingly no end to them, and, had she not been in a hurry, their beauty would have mesmerized her into stasis.

She moved on with a quick step, ignoring her own safety in favor of swiftness. More than once, she almost lost her footing, falling to the streets below, packed with both human and uncanny alike. Then, there, at the end of the building, staring down at the streets below, she saw the mysterious figure from before. They were slender and short, their robes hanging loosely at their ankles, revealing a pair of black boots. An outfit not unlike a battle mage's vestments.

"Who are you?" Kyra asked. "And why did you run?"

"I am the one they will not speak of. Not those who control this city, nor the ones at that 'school' of yours. I'm a lost one. Someone who has fallen so low that they now won't even recognize. And yet, I do not recognize you." Calmer, the shrouded individual added in almost a whisper, "You dabble in things you do not understand. Because of your ignorance, I will let you pass unharmed. But if you come for me—"

"Let *me* pass, 'unharmed?'" Kyra forced a nervous laugh, pretending to be unbothered, just as Master Lu'ce had taught her. "You seem to be confused about who's trapped here. Now, I do not know if you were the one who killed the man, but I intend to take you in for questioning. Don't make this harder than it has to be."

The mysterious figure laughed. "Funny," they said. "I was just about to say the same. You think you can do this alone? Even with that fancy ring of yours, I do not think that you will be a match for me."

"We'll see about that."

The mysterious figure reached down into their coat, pulling out an object that shined in the light. It was long, nimble, and metallic. A rapier. Middling in length and skinny, it was a weapon of precision. One that, Kyra suspected, the unknown fighter had much practice with.

"It's funny," the mysterious figure taunted, "how the whims of a head-strong girl are so easily dashed by the flashing of a weapon. At the threat of loss it presents."

Kyra ground her teeth, but an unusual presence stilled her feet. "You know nothing of loss," she muttered, taking a fighting stance Master Lu'ce had taught her, and that she had trained with for most of her life.

Instead of aiming the weapon at her, the mysterious figure raised the weapon high into the air. Clouds surged above the city and seemed to pulsate in anticipation of some cataclysmic event. Before Kyra could speak—before she could even breathe—a light, as bright as the sun itself, blinded her. She fell backward onto the floor of the rooftops, desperately trying to shield her eyes. The shattering of glass exploded in her ears, and the screams of the denizens that walked the streets below followed as a thunderous boom echoed throughout the city.

A ringing pain split her head, and as that noise cleared, she barely heard the horror below. Panic. Pure and unrelenting. It was a feeling she knew all too well. She forced her eyes to open and focus. Where the mysterious figure once was, there was now nothing but a blackened mark on the wood. They were gone. The likely killer had escaped.

She had let them escape.

CHAPTER 12

PACTLESS

Willow moved through the lair of the unwanted; the forgotten... the pactless. These were her people. This was her home.

"Willow," rang the tone of a familiar voice, setting the hair on her arm on edge.

Quistis appeared, holding her typical golden handled cane featuring depictions of a winged lizard. She was a tall woman, with slender arms and neck, with shoulder length blond hair off-setting her golden eyes.

"Didn't take you long to find me," Willow said. "It never seems to. Well... what is it then? Bear in mind that I'm not in the mood for any more bad news. Not now. Not tonight."

Quistis clicked her tongue, and her face shifted from subtle, soft feminine aspects to those expected of a masculine figure—hard set and angular.

"Well, prepare to be disappointed then," she said. "Sorry."

Willow pressed her fingers to her temple, rubbing in a circular motion and willing the ringing in her ears to give her a quiet rest.

"Go on then," she muttered. Secretly, she whispered a curse under her breath.

"As you know," Quistis said, "Dragrin's adopted more chattel into their fold. My father... no, nevermind." She took a moment to center her thoughts. "Of those, a few washed out—as is always to be expected. Well, it appears that one such young foal has found his way here. He wishes to speak to you. Demands it, really. Warning—hot headed this one. Pattering on about 'his family's' this, and 'unfair' that. I suspect you'll have quite the time with him."

"Enough," Willow replied. The ringing was only getting worse, and it was making her irritable. "Give me until half past the hour and show him where to meet me."

"Usual place?"

Willow nodded, her eyes going cross as she did. For comfort, she rubbed the small ring around her finger with her thumb. It was a gift... and a curse. One that forced others to seek her out. Never allowing her the peace she so desired. She couldn't help but wonder what she was still fighting for? The silliness of the world and its many rules. She longed for rest that she knew would never come. At least, not while she lived.

Quistis eyed her worriedly. "Let's give you the hour instead. Go on, draw yourself a bath. Take your time. You're filthy." Quistis leaned in, kissing her cheek. Her warm lips sent a wave of longing through her as she leaned into it, pressing her body into the woman. Leaning in, Quistis whispered, "Nobody will take you seriously if you look like an unwashed beggar. For better or worse, you're our leader. Act like it."

Willow smiled sadly, moving Quistis' face from her cheek with both her hands. Then she cupped the woman's face, leaning in and giving her a quick kiss on the lips. Breathlessly, she whispered, "Nobody takes us seriously, anyway. Not really. But that'll change... soon." She locked eyes with her love. "You have my word."

Quistis leaned in and kissed her again. "Remember, there is no need for you to hold this burden alone. I'll be there for you. Always."

Rising, Willow rolled her neck from side to side. Empty promises. Not lies—not really. She could tell that Quistis truly meant what she said. But, in the end, she knew her path would never allow her such peace. Peace to start a family. To retire from turmoil. To grow old and, eventually, die peacefully in her bed. But she would say nothing. It was an argument Quistis and she had already argued plenty of times before. Instead, she moved towards her private quarters, faking a smile, and hoping the water would wash the stains of her sins away.

They wouldn't. They never did.

Willow wrung moisture from her red hair, pulling the mid-length strands back with one hand, and running the length of it with the other. Willing aethryis to flow into her, she summoned heat, drying her loose strands, and being careful not to set the follicles aflame. It was a childish way to yield aethryis, but, then again, she couldn't afford to show any weakness. Even something as small as a string of awkward, wayward hair could lose her the confidence of her people. Lose her everything she's built. Always, she teetered on the precipice, waiting for the other shoe to drop.

She knew it would someday.

In her judgment room, set to appear just as the halls of the Archmages of the Spellbound Arch—those who wielded justice like a mallet and cried out a song of mercy—she sat, waiting until the door finally swung open, and the softest creaking of wood punctuated steps on the hardwood floor that approached her. Two guards, Enoch and Amon Payne, appeared. Twins, and both mages and pactless, having failed to gain a ringpact on the same day. They followed a rather disheveled looking young man with blond hair that clung to his head as if caked with mud. Then she realized, streaks of red ran in it. Blood. The lad's clothing was tattered. Ragged. It was as if he had slept on the streets for nights with not a bite to eat.

Likely, he had.

Enoch reached out, halting the young lad in mid-step. His dirty face came to rest upon her own washed and polished one. However, it was not the young man's clothing that interested her: it was his eyes. Bright and full of untapped potential. There was a sharpness in them. A wit of intelligence. An eagerness to learn. Or to find and wield power. It was always tricky determining which between the two. Tricky and dangerous.

"What is your name?" Willow asked, trying to press a tone of royalty. It was just another facade for the sake of everything she had built. She wasn't even sure why she bothered to keep it up. Sometimes she wished the place would come crashing down around her. There was nothing worse than waiting for the ax to fall. But, so far, her people had grown in both power and security. As much as she hated the deceit, it was best to keep appearances among those she did not know.

Or trust.

The young man broke his stare, but it returned shortly thereafter, and a fire burned in his words as he proclaimed, "My name is Salvator Skinner." The fire dimmed a bit as he continued, adding, "Well, just Salvator now. My surname is..."

Willow held up a hand, and the young man held his tongue. "I understand."

"I don't think you do," Salvator replied, an edge of arrogance in his words. "How could you? I've been thrown down. Cast aside. From my family—from my own father! He told me I am... unworthy. Unworthy to carry the family name now that I'm... He told me I'm a disappointment. So how can you possibly under—"

"*Stop!*" she demanded, a bit more harshly than she had originally intended. Adding in a softer tone, she added, "Believe me when I say that I understand. More than you can possibly know." She paused to give her words time to breathe until the young man seemed content to listen. "Do you think that I've not been reviled? Abandoned by those who once claimed they would protect me? Abandoned by those who claimed to love me through anything?" She bellowed a harsh laugh for dramatic effect. "I've felt their sting more than a battlefield of skewered corpses. You'll soon see that we all have."

Enoch and Amon nodded their heads in symmetry. Salvator mimicked them, nodding, and his pompous, ill-attitude was lost in a washing of pure regret.

Perhaps there was hope for the lad.

Willow shook her head, admonishing herself for bringing the young man even lower. Sometimes the feather worked better than the rod. "How about we start over?" she suggested. "First, let me introduce myself. I am Willow Ashen, leader of the Pactless of Mistbreak, for better or worse. And you—you are Salvator Skinner, son of Septimus Skinner, an Archmage Magistrate." She clicked her tongue. "Quite the pedigree."

Salvator looked dejectedly towards the ground.

Amon stepped forward. "She's talking to you—"

"What do I need to do?" Salvator asked suddenly. His question took her aback, but before she could inquire as to what he meant, he continued, adding, "Anything you need, I will do. Clean? Scrub latrines? Cook?"

"Preferably not in that order," Willow replied.

"It's not a joke!" Salvator blushed, but he tried to hide a coy smile at the edge of his lips. "This is my life we're talking about. *My* life. I won't be ridiculed."

"That was not my intention," Willow replied. Curiously, she asked, "Who do you think we are here? What is it you think we do?"

"I... I'm not entirely sure." Salvator held his left arm at his side with his right. "I know you help people. Mages like me... *Pactless.*"

"Does the title harm you so? *Pactless?*"

"It has always been taught to me that your kind are... wild. Like drug fiends. Addled by your unrestrained access to aethryis. Unfocused. Untrustworthy."

"... Dangerous?"

Salvator nodded. "Aye, my father said you are dangerous. He would tell me stories of what your kind has done before. Horrible things. Sickening."

"And what do you see now?" Willow asked. "Does my home give you that impression? Do I?"

Salvator took his time before eventually shaking his head in disagreement.

"The truth is, we are the true mages of the world," she explained. "Unbound by the agreement our ancestors made when they laid on the edge of extinction. An unfair and unwarranted leash around our necks. They claim we are dangerous, and they are just, but what right does any other have to trap a creature based solely upon their ability to harm? Young Salvator, we—*I* do not require you to do one single thing for your freedom. Not a thing. Here, we help train mages to harness their powers so that they do not harm themselves or others, if they wish it. Whether they stay is entirely their own choice. And theirs alone. Just as it is now yours."

Willow stood, stepping down from her raised highchair. She noticed the young man's face was scrunched—contorted, as if everything he had ever been taught about the pactless came crashing down around him. With little ceremony, she reached around his head, pressing the ring on her middle finger on the small metallic square device on the back of his neck. Willing aethryis to flow through her, she issued a simple command, and, just like that, knew that her work was done. She stepped back.

Salvator's eyes lit up as bright as the breaking of the dawn. His mouth hung open and, slowly, his dejected features turned into those of pure bliss. He looked down at his hands, and, suddenly, a bright blue flame appeared there.

Then he screamed.

Willow willed water from the moisture in the air, smothering Salvator's hands and catching him close as he collapsed to the floor.

"Take him to the infirmary," Willow demanded, and Amon lifted the young man into his arms without hesitation.

"*Wait!*" Salvator said, his voice shrill with both pain and excitement. Amon stopped mid-step and the young man's eyes locked onto hers. She saw a familiar determination deep in his soul as he added, "Thank you. Truly... Thank you. Can you... would you... teach me?"

Willow grinned and nodded. "Of course. Now shut up and rest. Heal. Try to resist the temptation to draw aethryis. For now, consider *that* your first lesson."

Salvator gave her a silent nod, and Amon swiftly took him away, disappearing through a wooden door, his footsteps clacking quickly down the hallway, which were quickly followed as his twin called for him to wait.

Willow had added another to her ranks. Another soul that she was responsible for. Another one, destined for the pyre.

Kyra stood on the rooftops overlooking Mistbreak feeling... defeated. Truly and utterly crushed. She had underestimated the mysterious figure. The killer. And worse of all, there was no one else to blame but herself. Ducking, she entered back into the warehouse from the second floor scaffolding and heard the ringing noise of angry voices arguing downstairs.

Great...

"There she is," an unfamiliar voice barked as she craned her neck to locate the source of the noise. Downstairs, where once there was once only Armeya and the body, now, a flood of people, some of which she recognized, and others, she not so much. They scoured the grounds, searching the warehouse for... something. And stranger still, the body that had been sprawled out on the floor had all but disappeared. Not even a drop of blood marked the stone floor where they had once laid.

"Girl," an unfamiliar elvish man said. "Get down here at once!"

Utterly confused as to why he was issuing her an order, she complied, slowly descending the same stairs she had used to get to the second floor. When she had both feet firmly on the ground, she saw the rest of her circle comforting Armeya, who appeared utterly confused by what had transpired. All except Adathin, who stoically viewed the scene as if he were painting a picture.

Approaching the elvish man who had called her, she asked, "Is Armeya alright?"

"Who?" the elvish man asked, looking back. Turning to acknowledge her, he gave a *humph* of disappointment. "Yes, yes, she'll be fine. Someone or something knocked her out stone cold. We would know more if you, an adept of inadequate skill, didn't go chasing a ghost in the night."

"A ghost?" Kyra replied, not bothering to hide her anger. A resentment she felt more in herself than this man. "I was chasing a killer!"

The elvish man scoffed. "A killer? Please. Who's been killed? The girl was muttering some similar nonsense before coming to her senses. I see no such evidence of a supposed murder. Perhaps the ringpacts are too much for you both. Perhaps we should consider—"

"Careful Lhoris," Elder Reylar said as he approached. "You have no authority over matters such as that. It is for the Spellbound Arch to decide if such measures are deemed appropriate. From what I see here, I would not even bother them with a hearing on the matter."

"Damnable Arch," Lhoris replied. Then, he went on with a softer tone, adding, "Our alliance won't always be there to protect you and your little band of rogues, Reylar." With that, he stepped away, pretending to look at something interesting in the room's corner and giving them the occasional sideways glance.

"Ignore him," Elder Reylar said, but his tone had a harsh undertone. Underneath that cool exterior, he was furious. She could feel it.

"What happened, Elder?" she asked, the situation making little to no sense to her. "Where is the body? The blood?" Then, as she remembered her place, she added, "On the roof! The killer is escaping! If we hurry, we can still—"

"There is no killer," Elder Reylar replied. "You were under the effects of a potent drug. Phantasmal leaf. Named for its ability to let you speak with the dead. Or what you perceive as such. Truth is, it can make you see whatever you wish to see. A dead loved one. A trinket. Riches."

"A dead body?"

"A chance to prove yourself," Elder Reylar corrected. "And likely your recalling of events affected what Armeya saw as well."

Something sounded wrong to her ears, and she decided to challenge the notion.

"No!" she said, not caring if she were to get in even more trouble than she already was. "I know what I saw. And Armeya, she saw the body first. Or we saw it at the same time. I... I..." The events in her head were getting fuzzy, and she nearly fell over when Elder Reylar reached out and grasped her by the arm.

"Good work stumbling upon this illegal operation," Elder Reylar said, changing up his tactic. "The drug is popular among many of the uncanny. Best we get it off the streets."

She grasped Reylars' arm with all her strength as she said, "I know what I saw."

Elder Reylar simply reached down and removed her hand, giving it a light tap as he did. He was strong. Much stronger than his old face would suggest.

"You're tired.," he said. "You need rest." Frowning as he glanced down, he seemed to notice at the same time as she did: she was bleeding. "Ask Maxim to heal that and you'll be escorted home for the night. We'll discuss this more in the morning."

"But the killer—"

"After a night's rest, you'll see things clearer."

As Reylar stepped away to speak with Lhoris, two other mages with sigils showing they were both Augmentors stepped forward to 'guard' her. She knew what it meant—she had caused trouble. Trouble for Dragrin's. Trouble for the city. Trouble for her circle.

Trouble seemed to follow her everywhere she went, but she would not be deterred.

"Armeya," she said, stalking towards the woman and trying not to sound desperate. "Tell them! Tell them what you saw. Tell them the truth." At that moment, Armeya looked like a child; hopeless and lost. She reached out, grabbing the woman by the collar, a small bit of blood smearing against the edge of her cheek. "Tell them!"

Soren stepped forward. "Easy. There is no reason to get so worked up."

Iona stepped between Armeya and her, like a protective sibling. "Back away," she warned.

Soren put a hand on Kyra's shoulder and added in a gentler tone, "We can talk about this later."

Kyra stepped back, utterly shocked. The eyes of all in the room, including those from her own circle, locked onto her with a mix of pity, contempt and anger.

Adathin finally broke his vow of silence as he said, "Let's go, Kyra." Before she could protest, he raised his hand, adding, "And that's an order."

Reylar barely glanced in their direction, but gave a nod as Adathin took charge. She couldn't do it anymore. Fight the tide. She was drained. Tired.

"Fine," she replied, dejectedly, letting Adathin lead her away. Turning up to look at him, she whispered, "I'm telling the truth. I know what I saw."

Adathin glanced down and gave her a coy smile. "I know... I know."

Lhoris slammed the door of his quarters behind him in a huff, barely able to breathe at all, his heart pounding heavily in his chest.

He forced three ragged breaths, each slower than the last.

Calm... he had to calm himself.

When his breathing steadied, he wiped sweat from his brow. He brushed strands of his hair and felt them to be greasy. He was a disgusting mess. How had he let his facade fade so much? He turned to peer at himself in the mirror and what stared back at him disgusted him to his core. How could this thing—this creature—possibly be him? Slowly and methodically, he began the painstaking process of grooming himself. First, he straightened his hair, using clean water brought to him by one of his few human servants he kept on hand. Then he dipped his hands in the water and pressed it against the back of his neck. It was cool, and he inhaled sharply at the pleasantness of it. He changed, throwing the sweat-strewn clothing into a small basket in the corner. He tugged on a tight undershirt and donned a royal blue jacket atop. Finally he began to recognize the one who stood in the mirror. At least he could breathe now. At least he could think.

And there was so much to think about.

A soft smile broke out on his chapped lips. A giddiness swelled from inside him. An eagerness. A longing. It had begun. It had finally begun.

CHAPTER 13
TREVILS AND TRIBULATIONS

Journal Entry

Year: 831 E.B

It was a mild spring day and once again, Master Lu'ce had gone into the nearby town of Goldcross for supplies: food, water and other medicinal items. As well as tobacco. Oh, how I hated the harsh smell of tobacco. That burning smell. It reminded me far too much of my past. Yet, whenever I broached the subject with Master Lu'ce, she adamantly refused the idea that she should ever stop. After a while, I had learned to not bother asking at all. It was a waste of breath.

Our little commune of mages, each with their own parcel of land, was unusually quiet. Disturbances of unrest within the uncanny community had been reported further to the South and, likely, any master mages had been sent to either investigate or deal with the said issues. This provided me with the rare opportunity of peace and quiet.

A stream cut through the parcel of land owned by Master Lu'ce, and I had always found it relaxing to sit nearby and listen to the water as it curved across the smooth stones at the bottom. There were fish too, tiny things not even worth the effort of catching, cooking and eating. Instead, I had taken to sharing the occasional piece of bread with the things, ripping off small portions and throwing them down into the clear azure water. They would wiggle and race and, with a quick bloop, the bread disappeared under the ripples in a silvery sheen.

It was peaceful; one of the few things in my life that was.

Master Lu'ce had returned later that evening, as the sun just plummeted behind the hills to the West. Curiously, however, she was not alone. Master Izrel Wynlam had accompanied her home with his own apprentice in tow. He was a short thing with light-blond hair and weary eyes. I had wondered if my own eyes looked similar to his. Weary and tired.

"Look at that," Master Izrel had said, his eyes running the length of my body up and down. "The girl's growing up fast. And her hair, still as dark as the day I met her. Not even this warm weather and sun could lighten it up, I see."

"I told you," Master Lu'ce bragged, "this one has the blood of ravens." they shared a laugh and, perhaps, they would share more later. This was not the first time Master Izrel had accompanied Master Lu'ce to her home. Far from it. He was also not the only one who would come to visit. One of the first spells I had learned was the minor manipulation of air as a means to block out sound. It had been... necessary, giving my masters tendencies and urges regarding men. But this was the first time I had ever met this man's apprentice. Sure, I had seen him around before, albeit briefly, but neither of us had seen any point in speaking to the other.

I liked that about him.

Master Izrel had coughed into his hands. "Excuse me, allow me to introduce my apprentice to you, Kyra. This is Norrix Ais Kilean, and I believe he is around the same age as you."

"Pleasure..." I had muttered under my breath, desperate for this introduction to be over.

Master Lu'ce squeezed my shoulder, perhaps a bit too strongly, her nails giving me the slightest of bites. "Now Kyra, these are our guests." I had muttered an apology and bowed my head. Master Lu'ce released her grip. "Good. Now then, Kyra, Izrel and I have decided that it may be time for you both to train with others besides ourselves. With peers. In that, you will now train with young Norrix here, as time and obligation will allow."

Norrix walked forward and extended his left hand. Seeing it, I reflexively pulled my own gloved hand back. He looked at me quizzically before offering me his right.

"Nice to meet you," he had said.

I looked again at his hand as if it were coated in poison. Sighing at what I knew Master Lu'ce expected, I reached out and shook it for the briefest of moments before pulling away as I had replied, "Nice to meet you as well."

Kyra awoke from troubled dreams. The mysterious figure she had met on the rooftops—the one who had summoned lightning; she couldn't stop thinking about them. Dreaming about them. Somehow, already, she had involved herself in things beyond her understanding. Like Master Lu'ce had told her so many times before, she had a knack for finding trouble.

And then there was the disappearance of the body.

She did not, could not, accept that both Armeya and she were somehow under the influence of some hallucinogenic drugs. To believe so would mean that she could no longer trust her own senses. And those were the only things she truly trusted these days.

As Master Lu'ce had once said, 'You're too clever for your own good. One day, that cleverness will get you into trouble. And on that day, you will find that the only one you can trust is yourself.' Her words rang far too true in her ears now. There was trouble brewing. Trouble in this city. This place. And she had nobody but herself to rely on.

Worse still, lessons began today.

Kyra pulled on her brand new multicolored mage robes, fitted specially for her from Mistbreaks' own local tailor. She had been surprised to find that the tailor was an uncanny. A fae, to be precise. One by the name of Elm

Silkheart. The fellow had been lanky and tall, with long fingers and even longer nails, which he somehow threaded glowing thread through. He had hovered his pale hands around and near her body, much to her distress, but, as he would explain, when he came close—close to his subject—he could detect the contours of their body. Knew exactly the likes and dislikes of their skin. She found the whole thing was rather ominous for her comfort, and when he had hovered near her left hand, she had reflectively pulled away, refusing to offer it up. Now, while the rest of her mage garments fit snugly against her body, the singular glove on her left hand did not quite fit as well as the right. Worse, it was an entirely unique color: stark white. It drew the eye's attention; something she did not wish for in the slightest.

Kyra wondered if this was one of those famous fae pranks she had read so much about.

Now the day was here, and she swiftly tucked her books under her arm and slammed the door to her room on the way out. Her roommate, the elvish woman Aluriel, Adathin's sister, had been gone when she awoke. In fact, she had been scarce since they had first met.

On the third floor, past two large wooden doors, lay a quaint entry way. Her destination. The subject: Historical Relevance. She pushed the doors open and held her breath.

Inside, she found Armeya and Soren already sitting together near the back, almost huddled into the corner with a rather large bookshelf perilously overhead. Each row had chairs and a long wooden desk to share. As much as she wanted to find a place to sit alone, Armeya waved her hands emphatically towards her, ushering her to sit with them. She reluctantly complied.

"First day, huh?" Soren said. He seemed nervous, which was not entirely within his character. "I've the jitters."

"I'd imagine yesterday was as much a first day as any get," Armeya replied. "I can't believe we ended up drugged." She had a far off look in her off-colored eyes, as if she herself didn't believe the words she expounded.

Kyra kept her mouth shut, as she still didn't believe the plausibility of such a thing happening. And she still had an unshaking feeling that they were being lied to. The thought still raced in her mind as it had done the night before, leaving her with nightmares quite unlike the normal ones that plagued her.

"Coin for your thoughts?" Armeya said, staring at her.

"I would rather just focus on what's in front of me," she replied. "No need to... think about the past." That was something she was surprisingly good at; shoving the various problems in her life to the back of her mind where they lingered and festered like an open wound.

"There is no need to be so serious," Soren said as he flicked his nose, grinning. "Ah, this is probably about the phantom you went chasing after. It's as Elder Reylar said, there was never anyone there. No need to be ashamed. We've all had bad drug nightmares."

Armeya turned balefully at him. "Have we now?"

Annoyed, she said, "And the lights shattering on the streets below? The lightning?"

"Coincidence," Soren replied. "A phylactery struck by lightning. It happens often enough. There was never an attack on you."

Kyra scoffed. "Coincidence. Sure..."

Armeya got that far off look in her off-colored eyes again. "Do you guys mind?" she said, flushing red. "Others are beginning to stare."

Turning, Kyra saw exactly what she meant. The thrill and excitement of the room had died, and the other adepts, whom had already taken their seats, stared at them as if they were pariahs.

"That's quite enough of that," someone said at the front of the room. "And yes, we could all hear you. I would like to assure everyone, there was a... misunderstanding. There was never an attack on any adepts here."

He was a tall and stout man whose disheveled desk, with its scattered papers and books, matched his person perfectly. His hair was undone, black and gray strands cut at odd lengths in no particular style. His magecloak was also a mess of stained and torn linen, with significant fraying at the bottom. Even his boots carried caked-on muck, which he stamped along the floor, flaking off bits and pieces as he went.

The master mage ran his gaze over the room as he said, "My name is Devdan Ais Trevils, and I will be teaching you the histories of the world and its many forthcomings and faults. You will learn the origins of mages, the pactless, elvish, and the Builders. Yes, even of the uncanny."

A student raised their hand.

"Yes," Master Trevils said, pointing.

The student stood, his light blond hair catching the light pecuniarily, causing it to almost sheen. He reminded her of a male peacock preening for a mate. And then she realized something... she knew him.

"Master," he said. "My name is Norrix *Ais* Killean and—"

"And?" Master Trevils interrupted. "We haven't got all day for introductions. You'll learn each other's names soon enough, and I need only remember the memorable ones. You, as of yet, are not memorable at all. At least, not in the ways you wish to be remembered."

Norrix ground his teeth. "Master Trevils," he continued, "I think I speak for everyone when I say that history is something that all of us should already know and have studied. I, for one, in apprenticeship, learned everything *I* needed to know. Why should we not focus on practical applications of aethryis instead?"

Master Trevils shoulders widened, and he turned to look out the window overlooking the courtyard below. "Does anyone else feel this way?" he asked. When no one answered, he turned, pointing at Kyra. "You, talkative one, do you agree?"

She pointed a finger to herself and mouthed, "*Me?*" Trevils nodded. "I... uh... no—no, I don't agree."

"Say it like you mean it!" Master Trevils replied forcefully. "Do you agree?"

"*No!*"

Trevils smiled a wicked grin. "There you have it, *Ais*. Killean. Not *all* are in agreement. Now, if you want to learn, sit. If you don't, you can help the kitchen staff clean during my lessons for all I care, since... 'practicality' is so important to you. Cleaning dishes will be about all you can do for the Spellbound Arch if you continue with this attitude."

Without a word, Norrix sat, but not before glaring balefully towards her. It was a look she remembered well from the past. It had not been the first time he had glared at her that way, and it certainly wouldn't be the last.

"Now, if there are no more distractions, let us begin. I—"

The door suddenly swung open and Iona stepped inside. She was breathless, and her hair a disheveled mess. Her clothing was almost as messy as Master Trevils'.

"Sorry," Iona muttered. "I—"

"Take. A. Seat," Master Trevils said, without even turning to address her. Instead, he picked up a long, metallic item and began writing into the air. Behind him, a board of blacked stone placed on the wall glowed, streaking white lines and copying whatever Master Trevils wrote into the air. "Those we call the Builders crafted this world. Long story short, the dwarvish are descendants of these folk. It is said they sculpted the mountains, the land, the sea and the sky. Old stories that hold no real relevance, I assure you... but they managed to do one spectacular thing. Does anyone know what it is?" This time, Trevils pointed at Iona. "You?"

Iona stopped just as she was about to take a seat opposite her own. Staring up, she said, "They opened the Rend."

"The Rend?" Master Trevils replied. "What is its true name?"

"Sorry," Iona apologized. "*The Dragonrend*... gateways to other worlds."

Master Trevils smiled. "*Aye,* portals to other worlds. To different times. Truth is, we know very little of the origins, but we do know one thing for sure: we humans, the elvish and all the uncanny... all except the dwarvish themselves, came from those portals. Came from other worlds and times. But for what purpose? That knowledge has been, unfortunately, lost. But while most know that a mage's oath is duty and sacrifice, secretly, we have another: to prevent the *Dragonrend* from ever opening again, through any means."

The rest of the lesson was a blur to her as she tried, and failed, to ignore Norrix's hateful stares. How had he come to become an adept at the same time as she? She hadn't remembered him during the ceremony. Albeit, she was quite distracted with her own turmoil.

"That's all for today," Master Trevils suddenly announced. As everyone stood, he cast a wide gaze across the room, adding, "Any arcanists are to wait and speak to me. All others, dismissed."

Iona shot her a contentious glare that all but said, 'Better you than me.'

"What do you think he wants?" Soren whispered. He put a hand on her shoulder as he mockingly added, "Be strong, little one. And if you think of breaking, remember what it is you fight for." He gave out a hearty chuckle as she slapped his hand away.

"*Ha-ha,*" she replied dryly.

Soren grinned coyly. "You wanna meet later for some tea?"

Surprisingly, she had wanted to give the shop another visit, despite how terribly it had gone the last time, but she suddenly felt as if the man was getting a bit too cozy. She couldn't have that. Muttering under her breath, she said, "No."

Soren blew into the air as if it were no concern. "Suit yourself. I'll just have to find something else to occupy my time. Or someone else."

Kyra rolled her eyes. "Please do."

"How about training instead?" Iona suggested, with not even a hint of jest in her tone. "Maybe Dragrins can do the impossible... teach you some discipline. How did the Cryomancers son fall so far from the family tree?"

"And what would you know of it?" Soren replied with a sudden anger deep in his voice. "You know what, I don't gotta take this. To the hells with you." With little ceremony, he straightened his magecloak in a white-knuckled heat and stalked out of the room.

Iona peered at his back, studying him curiously, like a cat getting ready to pounce. Turning, she said, "Guess I struck a nerve. Ah, well; what can you do? Anyway, good luck with the master." She stood, following the rest of the adepts out.

Even Armeya, during their conversation, had silently fled. Strange. Armeya didn't seem the strong, silent type. Maybe they could be best friends after all? Or, maybe, the turmoils of the night before still bothered her.

Master Trevils cleared his throat. "Anytime now, *Ais.* Ravenblood."

When Kyra turned, she noticed that two other students now stood near Master Trevils. One was Norrix, who had been earlier rebuked. The other was a woman she did not yet recognize. She stepped closer until she could hear the mumbled grumblings coming from Norrix.

"Now," Master Trevils said, "as you may or may not know, I have been appointed as the de-facto leader of all adept arcanists here at Dragrin's, despite my ill-regard for the post. Nevertheless, as it's already been decided, I take it very seriously that those under my care uphold themselves to the highest standards. The highest ideals." Turning towards her, she could feel his red-hot, piercing gaze, like a point of a blade pressed against her skin. "*Ais.* Ravenblood, it has come to my attention that you disregarded a direct order from the Elder by putting yourself in a potentially dangerous situation. A situation in which one from your own circle, including yourself, became drugged by phantasmal leaf." He clicked his tongue, and Norrix hurled a reprehensible grin at her. "Irresponsible and stupid. Incomprehensible behavior unbefitting of an adept who wields a ringpact."

"Master, I—"

"Do you wish to try and defend your actions?" Master Trevil asked. "How could you? I saw the look in the girl's eyes. Armeya... I learned her name whilst I was briefed on the situation. And you already know how much I detest learning the names of nobodies." He spared a glance to Norrix, who now crossed his arms, his lips going flat as if someone had sewn them shut. "Now the girl, Armeya, appears to be going through a tough time. All due to *your* reckless actions. You will make it right."

Kyra opened her mouth to protest again, but one look from Master Trevil caused her to rethink her tactic. "Yes, Master," she muttered, bearing her head down. "My actions were, as you say, 'irresponsible and stupid.' I will make it up to her. I'll—"

"I care not for the details," Master Trevil interrupted. "Only that order and tranquility are restored. You are an arcanist. Your job is to speak and show truth to those of your circle so that when the time comes, they may decide whatever action is appropriate." Master Trevil suddenly held out his hand, and a small orb of light drifted upwards, his Ringpact shining as brightly on his finger as the midday sun. Her head spun and the world alongside it. She teetered as a headache took hold, and it took everything not to fall to her knees. Master Trevil pretended not to notice as he added, "Truth is our light—our guidance. Without it, we are lost. Without it, your circle is lost. Be their beacon. Lead them not into danger, but into salvation." The orb of light suddenly winked out, and her headache faded just as quickly. "Practice your aethryis—all of you. We'll meet here every week for the time being. I expect results."

"Thank you, Master," Kyra muttered.

Norrix gave a false bow, and the timid girl followed suit. They both left her behind and, while she wished to ask Master Trevil more about what sort of power the ringpact granted her, she decided it would be best to clean up her own mess with Armeya first.

CHAPTER 14

BIRTHRIGHT

"Again!"

"No more," Salvator pleaded. "Please..."

"*I said again!*"

Willow called lightning to the tips of her fingers, hurling it at her obstinate student. It hit him in the chest, and she saw the shock rattle through his core. He fell to his knees, gasping for breath. She dropped, kneeling at his side.

"Breathe," she said, squeezing his shoulder. "Take in air and breathe out slowly. Deliberately."

Young Skinner did just as she instructed, taking a ragged inhale and shakily exhaling. When the man finally found his words, he said in as pompous a voice as any royal, "You dare strike me? Do you know who my—"

"Who your father is? Your family?" Willow smiled insincerely. "I do. You've told me. Many times, in fact. You've also told me how they've cast you out. They can't do anything worse to me than the Spellbound Arch has managed to thus far. Or do you think your family is more powerful? More... influential?"

Salvator glanced to the ground, knowing his threats had been utterly thwarted. It was troubling; the young man still didn't quite know what sort of situation he was in. Or, perhaps, he knew, but still refused to accept it. Perhaps he believed that if he mastered aethryis, he could get another chance at a ringpact. He wouldn't—it was a fool's dream. One that would get him killed if he pursued it too doggedly.

"Enough dawdling," Willow said, despising herself for what she had to do. When it came to unrestrained aethryis, only the strictest hand would do. A hand of steel. That thought caused a shudder to rattle through her. "Come. Stand. We haven't the time, nor I the patience."

Salvator, his clothing and dirty-blond hair a disheveled mess, protested, refusing to move as he mumbled, "I-I... I can't."

"You can," she replied. "And you will, or I'll walk out that door and shan't return. You may learn from someone else, if they'll have you. Albeit doubtful. Or learn from no one at all and harm yourself... again. Eventually, you'll get yourself caught. Or killed."

"*I understand!* Just... be quiet," Salvator relented, a small spark returning to his voice. He stood slowly, and with shaking knees. He brushed dust from his clothing and shook out his arms and legs. "You've made your point. I... I'm not used to this. Being spoken to this way. Treated this way."

"*Aye,*" Willow replied. "You're used to your servants. Used to those whom will kiss your ass for your father's approval or for access to your family's resources." Salvator continually nodded as she added, "You'll find none of that here. I can assure you of that."

Salvator held his head even lower. "I know..." His words reeked of desperation, as if speaking them out loud would somehow make him believe it himself. "*I know...*"

Willow knew she had to remain strong. Remain steadfast. She knew she had to be the leader that the pactless all believed her to be. What they all needed her to be. To be tough as Steel. Relentless as a storm. Unfeeling. Merciless... but she was none of those things. If they only knew the truth—they would hate her—despise her.

Willow squared her shoulders. She would be what they needed, and more. "Salvator, again!"

Salvator held steady, and he planted one foot back with his left hand extended forward. She followed his lead, placing one foot back, hand forward.

"When I signal you, I want you to make your body as tough as you can," she said. "As strong as a rock golem, and just as durable. Arrows should glance off your skin, swords should break against your arm, and you should wield the strength of ten men. This is the aethryis favored by the augmentors, and it should come the easiest of all with little chance of seriously harming yourself."

Salvator looked to concentrate, his face scrunching up as if he'd smelled something foul. She nodded, and then he lunged at her, flinging a wayward punch in her direction. Instead of ducking, she took it directly, slamming her forehead into his knuckles. There was a loud crunch and a snap as Salvator screamed in agony, falling back, clutching his now broken wrist with a white-knuckled fury.

"Oh, for the builders sake," Willow muttered, going down to one knee and taking his wrist in her hands. He struggled to pull back, but she held the augmentor's strength. He was but a babe fighting against its mother. "Stay still, I'll heal you." Taking a breath, she drew in power, letting aethryis flow into her. As always, it threatened to tear her limb from limb with its uncompromising ferocity. There was something about it. A primal sensation. A dreadful force. But when one masters themselves, they need not fear it. In this moment, it held no sway over her. Swiftly, she ripped the aethryis from the air and into herself, letting it flow into Salvator, whose wrist mended in but a single beat of her heart.

Salvator expelled air in a gasp, as if drenched by cool water. A soft spray of spittle struck her face, and his soft sobs of regret and terror swiftly changed into a seething of fury. Their exercises were done for the day. The man would not be receptive to anymore torment for a time. She had first bruised his mind, then his body, but this—this was his ego. He had been handled like a child. Told he wasn't special. Cast away. He needed time. They all needed time. New pactless recruits were always the same. Undisciplined. Told from very young that they were destined for greater things. They were like wild horses. They rode the wind and, when caged, fought their restraints until broken. But unlike horses, these lot needed to break so that they could realize they have never been free at all.

Salvator's indignation was short-lived, as fleeting as a midsummer breeze.

"I can't do it," he said solemnly. "My father is right. I'm nothing. I'll be nothing. I'm pathetic. A joke." Tears rolled down his face. "What should I do now?"

"*Hmm,*" Willow replied, choosing her words carefully. "Is that how you truly feel? Well, if you believe that you have nothing of worth, then you may go. Touch aethryis as you see fit, but I give you less than a decade before you do something you'll truly regret. Something foolish and damning. Either to yourself or a loved one. It's inevitable. Those who cannot master themselves let the world master them in return. And the world—the world is cruel. Crueler than any tyrant. Crueler than any human, elvish, or uncanny."

"Then tell me what I should do?" Salvator asked again, holding out his hand.

Willow reached down and grasped it, pulling him to a standing position. "First, you let go of what you think you were destined to be. That will be the toughest part of all, I think. After, you let go of everything you think you know. That is almost as tough as the first. But only then can you be remodeled into something new. Something better."

Salvator cocked a sly grin. "Something like you?"

"You don't want that," Quistis said, suddenly appearing from a darkened corner on the opposing side of the training room.

The training area was a spacious place in which smooth square stones were set in a giant square pattern. Wooden posts had been set to practice both martial prowess and aetherical magics upon.

Quistis' steps became louder as she came nearer. "As I said, you don't want that. And Willow certainly doesn't want that? Do you?"

Willow narrowed her eyes at Quistis. "No," she admitted. "I don't. What I want is for those who leave here to be better than me. More adapted to the life they must live. More stable. More free."

"Better than you?" Salvator replied, shocked. "How can we be? You're Willow Ais Ashen, leader of the pactless. I've heard the stories. Able to wield aethryis from all schools at a masterful level. I heard you even defeated the Cryomancer in one-on-one combat. How can anyone best that? How could anything?"

Willow turned to the side. "Stories and rumors, I assure you. Many things can defeat me. Many have." She suddenly felt very vulnerable as she scanned the exits of the training area, expecting an attack. "Far too many, in fact."

Quistis ran her hand from her shoulder down to her wrist. It sent a spark of longing coursing through her. Today, Quistis presented as masculine. Strong and as unmoving as a boulder. Where the day before she had worn a supple, rounded face, today it was squared and jagged. The peculiar aethryis she wielded even roughened her hands. She was glad for it. She needed someone to be strong for her today.

Salvator, apparently embarrassed, turned away from them both. But soon, he whispered under his breath, "How did you come to lead the pactless? What is this all for?"

"It's for—"

"She did it for me," Quistis interrupted.

Indignation flared in Willow as she said, "Quistis! What are you doing?"

Quistis used her strength to pull away. "I'm telling him the truth, as we should do for everyone." Turning back to Salvator, she added, "You want to know why Willow started the pactless? Do you want to know why she gave up everything she had ever hoped and dreamed? ... She did it for me. It was all for me."

"For you?" Salvator replied, obviously confused. "How so?"

Willow stomped her foot down hard. "I think that's enough—"

"The Spellbound Arch," Quistis cut in. "This world... it thinks it controls everything and everyone, but I've never fit into its narrow scope, no matter how much they hammered me. They insisted I was to be a nail. But why? Could I not be a screw? A peg? Could I not be the hammer itself? Or everything at once. *They* insisted I could not. The Willow you see before you is not the one you've been led to believe she is. She is kind, generous and understanding. She sacrificed everything so that people like us can be free."

"People like us?" Salvator replied.

"The unwanted," Quistis said. "The different. The forgotten. And, for that, she sacrificed everything."

Salvator turned to Willow, and she could barely meet his eyes as he asked, "What... What did you sacrifice?"

Willow found herself breathless. This proclamation went against everything she had cultivated about herself. Everything that she had led others to believe. What would the young man think of her if he saw the truth laid bare? What would they all think? Finally, she said in a weak voice, "I... I gave up my future position in the Spellbound Arch. My destiny."

"And what was to be your position?"

Quistis once again stepped in for her. "She was to be on the council itself. Groomed from birth to be one of the most powerful mages this world has ever known."

"A Councilwoman for the Spellbound Arch?" Salvator said in amazement. Soon, that admiration turned to outward dread. "...Who are you?"

She looked pitifully at Quistis, and couldn't bear the weight of her words as she said, "I'm Willow *Ais* Ashen, and I was once known formerly as Willow *Ais* Steelhand, daughter of Reylar *Ais* Steelhand." She held up a hand, showing the ring on her finger. "And this ring was to be my birthright. The ability to seal a mage's power via the magelock that each of us is implanted with. And the ability to release said power. But to preserve a future of free mages, I stole this power, just as the Spellbound Arch would steal yours. I gave up everything I'd ever been taught," she turned, taking Quistis' hands in hers, "for my love. So when I say you must give up what you were, what you are, and what you were to become... I know the cost. I've paid it... I still do."

CHAPTER 15

CLOAKING

Kyra stood at the doors of the peculiar teashop—Haven Teashop—owned and operated by the most interesting of patrons, a Sylvan uncanny named Katia. She glanced around for any form of signage and found none. Looking down, she scanned over the small note that her roommate, Aluriel, had given her.

"Here," Aluriel had said, "from my brother. Don't get used to it. I'm not a maid for either of you. Nor a serving lady. Or a postmaster." Then Aluriel had shoved the letter into her hands and stormed out of the room in a huff.

Carefully, she read over it again:

> *I believe you.*
> *Haven Teashop.*
> *Midday.*
> *— Adathin*

Kyra solemnly admitted that the man had such a way with words. Shaking her head, she carefully pushed the door open and stepped inside. Once again, the aromatics of various herbs and spices assaulted her senses. It wasn't nearly as bad this time around, but she wondered as to the mental effects some of these herbs may have on a person long-term. Did such a thing affect a sylvan? The uncanny as a whole? She shrugged her shoulders, taking a ley of the room. In the opposing corner, there was a space without much light where she saw Soren reading from a small notebook of sorts. He was alone. Multiple glasses were spilled out in front of him, and it seemed as if he were determined to run Katia out of stock all by his lonesome. Or perhaps it wasn't tea at all? Perhaps the man was drinking something stronger? The look in his eyes, destitute and lonely, suggested it was so.

There were other patrons as well. A dwarven man and woman, seemingly on a date of sorts, with how they looked longingly into each other's eyes. A discreet elvish woman who struggled to hide her identity with a loose cloak, but her ears, long and pointed, gave her away easily. She was sitting across from a human female. A friend? Perhaps more. It was against the law for elvish to engage romantically with humans, but all knew that it happened occasionally. Usually said events were kept quiet and pushed under the rug, so to speak.

Then she saw Armeya and Iona sitting across from each other at a small red-wood table. Katia herself spoke with them, and even she couldn't hear the words from their hushed conversation.

Finally, her eyes met her intended target. The reason she'd been summoned. Adathin. The elvish man sat alone with a seat across from him, already hauled out for her arrival. His ethereal skin caught the light of the nearby candle peculiarly, giving him a sort of ghostly glow. And his eyes, yellow and piercing, seemed to carry a hint of red in them today.

Noticing her arrival, Adathin raised a hand and stood, reaching out and drawing the chair out for her even further than it already had been. With a quick step, she moved across the teashop, running a soft, gloved hand over the various wooden furniture. She sat, and Adathin followed suit.

There was a silence that lingered between them for a long time. Or, at least, she felt it was lengthy. Perhaps it was just her nerves. Ever since the events at the warehouse, she'd had trouble trusting her own senses. It would be a problem for anyone, but she—she was an Arcanist. One whose mission was to seek truth. Reveal secrets. If she could not be trusted, then who could?

Finally, Adathin broke the lingering silence. "Kyra," he said. "I'm glad you could join me. It's a pleasure."

"The pleasure is mine," Kyra replied formally. "Now, regarding your letter, I—"

Adathin suddenly broke out in a mirthful laugh. "'The pleasure is mine?'" he repeated mockingly. "Really now? Is that how you actually feel? Is that how you speak to everyone?"

Kyra fought to keep the red from her face. She couldn't decide whether she was more embarrassed or furious by the man's openness.

"No," she replied, coldly. "It isn't how I normally speak. It isn't how I feel. But we humans are supposedly 'beneath' your kind. The elvish. Your sister reminds me of it regularly, as did my former master."

It was Adathin's turn to go red in the face, and he fidgeted with his fingers like a child. "Sorry," he muttered under his breath. "I meant no offense. It just struck me as humorous considering our talk in the Dimlight District. You cared not for formalities then. I'll be honest, it was refreshing."

"Different settings require a different tack," she replied. "We were working together. Your choices could have gotten me killed."

"And instead, it seemed your own choices almost got *you* killed when you went chasing ghosts in the night. And on the rooftops, no less. As daring as any heroine in a story, I must say."

Kyra laughed mockingly. "Hardly. I've had training from one of the strongest mages in the world: Lu'ce Nox. No 'ghost' could best me."

"And yet..."

She huffed in frustration. "*They cheated!* They summoned lightning to blind me and fled like a coward."

Adathin raised his shoulders and cocked an eyebrow. "That sounds like losing to me."

She went to stand, but she instead turned back and whispered, "I thought we were here to discuss what happened, not for me to be berated. Believe me, I've already heard enough from the other masters and Reylar. Not to mention his elvish advisor, Lhoris. That man is insufferable. Besides, it was just phantasmal leaf, was it not? Everything I saw was just an illusion." She stood, clutching her gloved left hand to her chest. "This was a mistake. We shouldn't be talking about this. Let it go."

"*Sit!*" Adathin said, not aggressively, but with a stern voice. "As my letter stated plainly, I believe you. I... I don't believe it was a drug."

Kyra reluctantly sat, narrowing her eyes at the elvish man. "Why? Why do you believe me when no others do?"

Adathin sighed loudly. "It's hard to explain."

"Try me."

"Very well," Adathin replied, taking a deep, shuddering breath. "While there *was* phantasmal leaf in those crates, the effects of it only really take effect when its smoke is inhaled by the user, but there was no smoke. No fire of any sort. Then there was this... this feeling. A feeling of something dreadful. Something wrong. I had it the moment I stepped inside that warehouse. Almost I couldn't bring myself to look upon the supposed scene of the crime. It was as if something warded me away from it. It felt like... psionic aethryis. Elvish magic."

"But... would you be able to tell? To be able to see the deception? To break the illusion?"

"Yes, normally I could, but there are some psionics out there, like my father, for example, who are so powerful and skilled that they can mask their use. Able to place layers of illusions on top of one another, shrouding their lies with more lies until it's quite impossible to know what the truth is."

"So... you think your father did this?"

Adathin's eyes went wide, and he barked a sudden laugh. "No," he said. "By the hells, no. He wouldn't be seen in a place like the Dimlight District. Nor would there be a need to hide himself or his actions if he did. If he needed to slay a man, human or mage, he would do it out in the open for all to see."

"Then who?" she asked. "And who even was the person I found? Armeya said she recognized him as a student."

"Who indeed," Adathin said. "I've been hearing rumors. Whispers. Some speak of goblin schemes and others of the pactless. That mysterious person you mentioned, you said they summoned lightning... Willow Ashen, leader of the pactless, is said to have a special affinity for its use. It is her *calling*."

Calling... an ability unique to humans, and not just mages. What would be commonly referred to as a gift, it is something peculiar that falls outside of one's typical aetherical school. Armeya, for instance, could change her eye color. She had noticed her doing so on occasion. Soren's father, the Cryomancer, had a gift for ice-based aethryis. Soren himself may also share that calling, as said gifts are typically genetic.

A sudden sound of breaking glass stilled her thoughts. Searching for the source of the noise, she found Armeya standing with Iona clutching her shoulders and urging calm into her.

"No," Armeya screamed, as beastly as any predator on the attack. "He's here. He's right here! Do you not see him?" She turned, grabbing Iona's magecloak and dragging her close. "Tell me you see him."

Iona slowly and calmly removed Armeya's hands and set them at her side. "I don't," she admitted in a motherly tone. "But that's ok. This was a bad idea from the start. Let's get you back to Dragrin's. Back to your room. Your bed. You need rest as the rest of the drugs flush out from your system."

Armeya suddenly looked tired as her eyes drooped. Very tired. The woman appeared as if she hadn't slept in weeks. "Ok," she conceded, and the two stepped past them with hardly a glance in their direction.

Kyra reached out, but Adathin placed a hand atop hers and urged her to quiet.

Katia then appeared by their side. "Strange times," the sylvan woman said. "That poor girl. Something is so clearly bothering her. Something sinister. Dare I say, evil."

Evil... such a childish word. This world was full of variations of gray, and to pretend otherwise was living a fantasy.

"What did she want?" Kyra asked. "Why was she here?"

Katia ran over her with a cool gaze, her wings fluttering ever so slightly, leaving a cloud of glowing dust hanging in the air like floating drops of snowflakes. "She wanted to try some bloodtouched tea."

Kyra's head ached at the mention of the accursed stuff. "Why?" she asked. "She saw what it did to me. Why would she want to try it too?"

Katia shrugged her shoulders. "She mentioned that there was something she desired to see. Something she *needed* to see."

"And Iona?"

"Here for support, I think. Too bad Armeya went manic; that was the last of the tea I have. Whatever she is searching for, she'll need to find another way. Enough prattling though, I'm not in the business of giving away other people's burdens. Now then, is there anything else I can get you two?"

"Just some regular tea," Adathin said. "With some honey."

Katia narrowed her eyes. "I serve nothing here that is 'regular.' At least not the way you mean. But I understand, I'll get you a delicate blend." Katia turned her gaze towards her. "And you?"

"Water," she replied. "Just water."

Katia smiled knowingly and calmly sauntered away. As she disappeared behind a wooden door, the woman softly hummed something to herself.

Adathin crossed his hands and his eyes turned serious. "Truth be told, there is one more reason I believe you."

Kyra's back straightened. "And why is that?"

Adathin appeared uncomfortable, but he seemed to set his jaw as he said, "This has not been made public yet, but there *is* a missing student. Went missing yesterday in the evening. A thaumaturge mage named Freed Gallok."

"... Freed Gallok," she mimicked, committing the name to memory.

Adathin shuddered, his face turning to shock. "What's wrong?" he asked, suddenly.

"What's wrong—" Her voice caught as she repeated his question, the words dying in her throat. Reaching up, she felt tears flowing freely down her cheeks. It was odd. She was suddenly full of regret and sorrow, but she could not for the life of her figure out why.

Freed Gallok... who are you?

Journal Entry

Year: 831 E.B

It had been late into fall, and the day had a certain chill about it. Norrix and I had taken it upon ourselves to train together. Master Lu'ce and Master Izrel had looked pleased at the prospect, and I assumed they were even more pleased that they could share the day in pleasure together.
Norrix had wanted to train his augmentation skills—the power to enhance one's own body. He seemed to favor that particular school, shying away from enchanting and mystic styles most of all. That was common. Both enchanting and mystic were Orders that were less taught and more often gifted by the threads of fate. Sure, both could be taught in some ways, as Master Lu'ce had instructed her, but there was never an ease to it. That is, unless you had a specific knack for it.
I hadn't the knack for any particular Order of manifesting aethryis. Nor had I any gift beyond the scope of regular uses of aethryis. None whatsoever.
"Are you paying attention?" Norrix had asked, standing in a fighter's stance, one foot in front of the other and fists balled. Despite the chill, sweat had poured down his brow, falling steadily to the mulching and dead leaves beneath his feet.

I shook my head clear. I had been daydreaming again. Getting lost in my own thoughts, as I so often did. Master Lu'ce had reprimanded me constantly for it.

Norrix had tapped his foot impatiently. "Are you ready?"

Drawing in aethryis, I had steeled my body. At least, the best I could. "Ready," I had answered, taking my own stance, which was very similar to Norrix's. I suspected that Master Lu'ce and Master Izrel had been trained by the same Master themselves, but I had never asked.

Norrix launched himself forward, but before we could come to blows, he stopped. We had both heard the sounds of wailing coming from inside a collection of nearby trees which headed into a greater part of a forest which lined the edge of Master Lu'ce's property.

"Did you hear that?" Norrix had asked.

"Yes," I had replied, nodding as I did. "Should we check it out?"

Norrix hadn't waited for me to ask as he was already ten steps ahead, jogging along towards the trees. Before we arrived, a girl with brown hair and a drab gray traveling tunic, which almost touched the top of her brown boots, appeared from the treeline. She appeared out of breath, and she stumbled more than once into the grass, glancing over her shoulder every few steps. Upon noticing the two of us, she had opened her mouth to scream, but instead, she stopped in her tracks and examined us.

The girl was deciding if we were friend or foe.

"It's ok," I had said with as sweet a voice as I could muster. "We won't hurt you."

The look in the girl's eyes said she didn't believe me, but a moment later, heavy trudging echoed from the woods and she sprinted towards me in a dead heat, slipping past Norrix, who had offered a calming hand.

"What is it?" I had asked in astonishment.

"R-R-Ruffians!" the girl had replied.

As if her words summoned them, two boys exited from inside the wooded area. Each boy, one tall and stocky, the other short and skinny, wore well-embroidered vests of dark blue. Each one was smiling widely, while turning towards each other and then forward again. It looked as if they were playing a game with each other. Which game however, I could not say.

"Who are you?" Norrix had asked.

"None of your business," the tall boy had replied, giving Norrix a sneer.

"Yeah, none of your business," the short boy added, mimicking his friend.

"You're on the land of Master Lu'ce Ais Nox," Norrix had said. "Leave. Now!"

The taller of the boys spat on the ground, and his mannerisms said that he thought less about us than the remnants of his vile spittle. "And if we don't?" he had warned, violence imminent in his gait.

Norrix rose to the challenge, standing taller and wider. The boy had exuded confidence and yet I found the entire ordeal foolish, unnecessary and crude. Turning to the frightened girl, I leaned down and had asked, "Who are they to you?"

"M-M-My cousin," she had replied in a soft voice more befitting a mouse than a person. "And his friend."

An anger, deep and unseated, suddenly filled my chest. It burned and broiled beneath my skin. I stepped forward, trying to keep anger from my voice as I had asked, "Why do you torment your own family?"

The taller boy had sneered at me with all the contempt he could summon. "What is it to you, filth?" His gaze suddenly swung down to my ungloved hand and his face turned from a sneer into a look of utter disgust. "...Freak."

Norrix had apparently had enough, and he launched himself forward without another word, fists flying.

When all was said and done, there had been little of a fight at all. Norrix had been the victor, standing over the two boys, who had each received a whooping from him. Both boys' faces had been bruised, their eyes quickly swelling shut, and blood trickled from the edges of their mouths as they breathed in grated, rasping breaths.

"Cousin!" the girl had shrieked as she broke free from my friendly hand, running towards the boys with all due haste. When she arrived, she knelt beside them and wept, squealing apology after apology.

"What is going on here?"

When I turned, I saw Master Lu'ce and Master Izrel stomping in the grass towards us. They had looked... displeased.

The taller boy quickly stood and took on an affronted face. "This one—he attacked me!"

"Us!" the smaller boy had said.

Master Lu'ce was on me now, gripping the back of my cloak and pulling hard. Master Izrel had gone to his own apprentice and was holding him similarly.

"Liar!" Norrix growled like a chained animal. "Liars!"

The taller boy stood straighter, and had replied in a regal tongue. "I do not lie, commoner. I have no need for it."

"And yet you do it all the same," Norrix had replied.

"Enough!" Master Izrel had commanded, drawing all attention to himself. Sighing, he added in a solemn voice, "Go, you three. Go! Tell your parents I'll come and address this personally at my earliest convenience."

The taller boy narrowed his eyes. "But sir, he attacked—"

Master Izrel gave the boy a stare that could silence a volcano mid-eruption. The taller boy had swallowed hard and turned, heading back into the trees whence they had come.

"Good," Norrix had said.

"Good?" Master Izrel had replied, throwing his apprentice to the grassy mound. "Good, you say? And what happens if that young man's family demands restitution for your actions? You—You interfered with a family affair. You used aethryis against them as an apprentice—no, don't deny it, I saw their bruises."

Norrix took the verbal berating, but kept glancing at me as if I would save him.

I hadn't.

Finally, when Master Izrel had his fill, he had marched Norrix off Master Lu'ce's property with an apologetic nod.

I turned to address Master Lu'ce, but her eyes had drilled into me as if I had been caught with my hand in the cookie jar. "Do you know why Norrix is being treated as such?"

I did, or, at least, I thought I did.

*"He used aethryis unaccompanied as an apprentice. That is against the rules
the Spellbound Arch has set for us."*

*"That's only part of it," Master Lu'ce had replied. "The other... culpability.
Norrix could have killed those boys by accident. Or maimed them for life.
Even if he did not, he interfered in a family affair."*

"But the girl—"

*"The girl was not in any genuine danger. It was not his place. Nor I. Nor
yours."*

"But she asked for help," I had protested.

*"Aye, she likely did," Master Lu'ce had replied. "And help was given, but at a
cost. Norrix will pay some price for it, and the girl will probably turn a blind
eye to him. Culpability. Accountability. Liability. We are all responsible for
our own actions, little one. Sometimes the hardest thing to do is to do nothing
at all. You will live a long life. Far longer than most ordinary humans, noble
or not. Do not sacrifice yourself for the nameless ones without cause."*

*Master Lu'ce had never said what she meant by 'nameless ones' and I—I had
never asked.*

Freed Gallok... the name had been spinning in Kyra's head ever since
Adathin had told her it the day before. It was burned into her brain. It
even invaded her dreams as she went over and over the scene she so clearly
remembered. It wasn't a drug-addled illusion, as suggested. No, it couldn't
be. She refused to accept that.

The mist hung like a heavy sheet over the city that day. Thick and
stale, and Kyra could swear she tasted something metallic at the tip of her
tongue. The stuffiness of it filled her nose. The city-folk of Mistbreak had
long said that when the mist was extra dense, it meant that death loomed
just around the corner. Superstitious nonsense, of course. Death was a
constant part of city life. Of life in general. Especially nowadays. But with

how the fog glued to her skin, making it crawl with dread, she was quickly becoming a believer in the supernatural.

Just as a gentle spray of rain fell atop her head, she forced open a side entrance that led into the main hall of Dragrin's. The dormitories were separate from the primary structure itself, and she was only now starting to become acquainted with the grounds as a whole. The bones of the building were old. Ancient. Every scratch—every nook—told a story. A tragedy. A ballad. For example, near a bust of an old, deceased elder, she made out two initials carved into the not-so delicate wood. *'J.R'* and *'S.T'* had been scribbled with what she assumed was a dull knife and then encompassed. A pact of eternal love. She pondered whether that love survived the trials and tribulations which were expected of all mages. *Could* it survive? It was not uncommon for mages to wed—to even have children—but it was no secret that a mage's life was also controlled by the Spellbound Arch, which, in turn, was controlled by the Elvish Conclave. It was the price that all mages paid, even her, for bringing the world to the brink of calamity. The price of blood. So how could one give their life in devotion to another when their life was already spent?

Kyra peered at that marking for a long time before the distant noise of laughing and gossip broke the spell. And the time. She was going to be late for lessons if she daydreamed any longer.

As she arrived at the correct room, on the first floor, marked by a silver placard, she found there to be a crowd of her peers huddled outside. Try as she might, she could not breach the mob. Worse, she could hear arguing coming from inside.

"Come on then," the voice of a man said, violence etched in every syllable. "Show us how strong the Cryomancers son truly is."

Cryomancer... son... It didn't take her long to make the connection. *Soren!* As if summoned by her very thoughts, she heard Soren's voice, low, distant, and breathless. "You got me. How's about we call it a draw, eh?"

Another voice suddenly attempted to reason. A familiar one at that. "S-S-Stop it!" the voice said in a stuttering fashion.

Maxim.

"*N-N-No!*" the angry voice replied mockingly. "You're a Mystic, right? Just heal Frost here after I give him a proper beating. Shouldn't be too hard, eh?"

Then the sounds of fists flying and grunting became clear. Soren gasped out, and then she heard the shuffling of wood as something was knocked to the floor. She was furious, but she didn't understand why. This was none of her business. She had no place getting involved. Yet... an anger filled her like a flood. Primal and dark. She was like a dam cracking under the pressure. She grit her teeth so hard that they ached. But why... Why did she care? *Why?* It made no logical sense. It went against everything Master Lu'ce had taught her.

Finally, she'd had enough as she yelled, "*Move!*" A light suddenly exploded outwards from her hand, casting out a wave which made everyone around her stumble back. Seizing the brief opportunity, she pushed inside to witness Soren knocked flat on his ass with a brown-haired, burly fellow standing over him. The man had a shocked expression, which Soren also shared. They both stared at her in wild amazement, and, when she looked down, she realized that light was streaming from her palms. Aethryis seemed to pour from her now, and she willed herself to calm, releasing it.

"What is going on?" she asked, directing her questions towards the bigger man.

Soren vaulted upwards, patting himself free of dust as if nothing awkward had transpired. "Nothing," he said, giving her a wink. "I was just horsing around with ole Zadock here. We're... old friends."

Zadok spit on the floor. "Yeah... *friends.*" The man looked her up and down with his bright green eyes and dark sunken features. "And who are you to even ask? You think you're special? *Hah,* you're an arcanist. A lowly arcanist. A pathetic bitch." He stepped forward threateningly and added with a whisper, "Do you really want to test me?"

Before she could react, Soren stepped in the way, grabbing Zadok's hand. The man grunted and tried to pull away, but Soren's grip was as iron. He did not flinch; did not quiver. Then Zadok screamed and pried at Soren's hand like a wild animal caught in a snare.

"Never threaten her again," Soren warned. There was no jest in his tone. No childhood antics. This was something new to her eyes. Someone new. "Threaten no one from my circle again. If you do, I'll show you why my family holds the title of *Frost*." Slowly, he released the man.

Zadok stumbled back, gripping at his wrist. She could see it, they all could, the sheen of ice which surrounded the skin where Soren had gripped him.

"Take your title and shove it up your ass," Zadok replied, making a swift exit, shoving past the crowd of wide-eyed spectators who murmured incomprehensibly.

Looking down, she saw a similar layer of ice surrounding Soren's hand. He must have noticed it as well, because he laughed and casually shook it until the small pieces of ice fell away and dissipated as nothing but drops of water on the floor.

"Sorry," Soren said. "But this is something you'll need to get used to if you hang around me. People always think they're so tough. They like to challenge me as if I was my... father." Sighing, he added, "Sorry again to be such a burden."

Soren's words rang strongly in her ears. There was a familiar pain there. Old pains from his past. Same as hers. Or similar, at least. Perhaps she could ease it. Shoulder some of his burden.

"It's alright," she replied. "I know how you feel. Truly, I do."

Soren forced a laugh. "You don't... but thanks for saying so anyway." Before she could respond, he turned to address Maxim. "And you! Try not to provoke others on my account. Remember what I told you, I'm *your* shield. Stay firmly behind me and restore me if needed. That's your role. Mine... Mine is to get hit."

Maxim smiled coyly, his face going red as he nodded wordlessly.

"Now what's this?" A tall and slender woman stepped inside, pushing the gawking adepts out of the way. "Ah, I see that some have decided to get a head start on lessons today. I'll make this clear for all in attendance: dueling is not forbidden at Dragrin's. In fact, as adept mages, dueling will be required as you work your way towards mastery. But duels are elegant affairs. Duels have rules. They are *not* backdoor brawls at some unnamed tavern. If you wish to settle a difference, approach any master and issue the challenge against your fellow mage. You will not be turned away. All challenges will be accepted. Now, *Ais.* Frost, as your reputation seems to have preceded you, you'll have the honors of cleaning up this mess. Oh, and for introductions... I'm Silvia Deerling, and I'll be your master of Martial Combat." That attracted everyone's full attention. "Discipline," she continued. "Discipline. Honor. Integrity. These are just some of the qualities that will be expected of you all. But those alone will not make you worthy of your ringpact. Far from it."

Kyra felt the tight band wrapped around her finger, like a parasite leaching from her. It was a symbiotic thing. The ringpact fed from her and barred to but one Order of aethryis, but she wasn't sure what she received from it in return.

Master Deerling struck her lectern with her palm. "Attention when your betters are speaking." She peered out around the room and then motioned to a section of the room which had been cleared. "There are times when a physical confrontation is inevitable. I would have you all prepared for those times." She moved to an empty space in the room. "I will face each of you, one on one. If you should land a single solid hit on me, I shall lend my name to you receiving the rank of master. You may use aethryis, but you must strike me physically. Now, let us begin."

The entire room of adepts stood frozen, waiting for any brave enough to step forward.

"That's enough for today," Master Silvia Deerling declared as a blue flame, which danced gracefully in her hand, dissipated into the air. "It's quite apparent to me that many of you are still struggling with your ringpacts.

You must succumb to control. Be dominated to dominate. Submit to defy. Learn this; sooner rather than later. When you understand, the ringpact will obey you. *Dismissed!*" She swiftly turned her back on the class, scribbling something in a small notebook, scowling the entire time.

Torturous. The entire lesson had been utterly maddening. And worse, not a single adept had landed a strike on Master Deerling.

Kyra stared dejectedly down at her own ringpact. Such a simple thing to behold. Nothing but bent metal, but so utterly important. Aethryis no longer obeyed her as it once had. Now she had to plead with her ringpact. She had to be *allowed* magic by it. Beg for it. It was infuriating, and judging by the faces of her peers, downtrodden and pitiful, they would likely agree with her sentiments.

Sighing, she wiped cool sweat from her brow and rubbed it across her magecloak. That earned her a stern glare out of the corner of Master Deerling's cold eyes, but the woman said nothing as she swiftly fell back to her notes, making a quick swish with her pen. Was it another mark against her? Was the woman to be her enemy, perhaps? She wasn't so sure. Making mistakes here was as easy as breathing, it seemed.

Soren approached, heaving heavily as he dropped a wayward arm on her shoulder. "*Phew,* that was exhausting." His voice quivered, and his eyes drooped. "How's about another round of tea? On me?"

"Can you think of nothing else but tea?" she asked, shuffling away from him and letting his arm slide off.

Soren eyed her curiously and then replied with a yawn, "*Nah,* not really. If I try to become anything more than a nuisance, then everyone comes rushing in to serve me as a means to please my father." He made a mocking gesture with his hands. "The Cryomancer... *Pfft.* Being a deadbeat and a delinquent is the only way I get any peace and quiet."

"Then why are you here at all?" She purposefully eyed each individual wall of the room as she did a small twirl. "Why are you at Dragrin's, I mean? Why live this life? The life of a mage? Surely there are more 'peaceful' options."

Soren pursed his lips and placed a hand against his chin, his ice-chilled eyes wandering as he seemed to search for the words. Finally, he said, "Because, what else would I do?" His answer prompted her to ask more questions, but he continued before she could, adding, "If not this, then my family would require me to move home. Even if I refused, there would be plenty of wayward mages and other sorts who'd come for me as a means to either help or hurt my father. It has nothing to do with me, of course. Being at Dragrin's isn't only what was expected of me, but it's also the only place I can truly be me... at least for the time being. For just a moment longer. Be happy Kyra, you're free! Free to choose. Free to travel. Explore... *Love!* It's a lot more than I can say for myself. Now, if you'll excuse me, I'm parched."

With that, Soren straightened his magecloak and tiptoed by, melding into the small crowd of students heading for the door. As she followed, a sudden burst of pain exploded into her head, sending her reeling into a nearby bookcase. She just barely managed to catch herself from falling flat on the floor.

"What's going on?" Master Deerling demanded, now glaring intently in her direction. When the woman discerned it was her, her eyes seemed to soften a tad. "Why am I not surprised? One of the troublemakers is also nothing but a clumsy mess."

"I just slipped," she lied. "Sorry, Master."

Master Deerling waved a dismissive hand. "Fine, fine—just go! And pick up any of the books that fell." She muttered more under her breath that she couldn't quite hear.

Kyra placed each book back on the shelf and even straightened others, which had not been her fault. Quickly, she fled the room, just in time too, as another jolt of pain rattled her. She barely managed to catch herself on a nearby wall.

"... *Kyra,*" a voice hailed distantly in her mind. "*Kyra!*"

"A-A-Adathin?" She had said the words out loud to nobody in partic-ular. A few of her peers stared curiously at her and then moved away as if she were nothing but a beggar in the streets. In her mind, she asked, "*What are you doing?*"

"Meet me in the library," Adathin replied. *"Hurry, we may not have much time."*

The library... lucky for her, it was but a short distance away, just off of Hawkson Hall, named after Zada Hawkson, the first elder of Dragrin's. She rounded the corner and saw the entrance; it was a tall wooden doorway, inlaid with silver etchings in the runic language of the Builders. She had often been told stories of such runes from Master Lu'ce. She said they were magical in nature. Different from the aethryis they now used. Each rune could be a gift or a curse, or often, both. But there was supposedly nothing better at protecting old relics, which many considered books to be.

Just outside the library, she saw Adathin donning his own magecloak and hiding from someone inside. She hurried to his side, asking, "What's this about?" A sudden sense of anger rose in her chest. "I'm not some dog to be summoned on command. Nor your servant." Her face went red as she realized how close her words felt to what Aluriel had conveyed to her the previous day.

"Apologies," Adathin replied, not even bothering to glance in her direction. "But this is important, and time was of the essence. Quick, conceal us with your light."

She stood shocked for a time before asking, "... *Excuse me?*"

Adathin subsequently spun to address her. "Your aethryis," he explained. "Arcanist's aethryis! You can bend light to your will, can you not? It's supposedly the basic principle of being an Arcanist. Can you not camouflage us so that we may enter the library unseen?"

She stepped beside him, walking towards the entryway. "Why cannot we just—" She felt warm hands suddenly grasp her as Adathin pulled her into an embrace, spinning her away from the entrance and pinning her against a nearby wall. Breathlessly, she said, *"How dare you!"*

"Shh," Adathin replied, putting a finger to his lips. Then, directly into her mind, he added, *"Trust me and be silent."*

He was so close to her now. So very close. His body was pressed against hers, and she could feel the rising and falling of his chest. Hells, she could feel his heart beating at a thunderous rate just below his clothing. He was nervous. Scared. And that made her ten times more frightened herself. Realizing that his one hand gripped her gloved left, she shifted, tugging free. Then she heard it—off in the distance. Voices speaking in hushed tones. But every once in a while, anger would course through, causing the voice of one to become louder before being shushed by the other.

"We are to spy?" Kyra asked, and Adathin simply nodded. She groaned as she added formally, "If this is what is demanded of my circle's leader, then I'll try." Just as she had done with the lock a few days earlier, she pulled in aethryis from the ringpact. She had wielded aethryis hundreds of times before while training with Master Lu'ce, but that was before the ringpact. Now, instead of herself being the target and source of the aethryis, she had to draw it in through the trinket. The ringpact fought her, not knowing what she asked. It was like training an animal who did not understand what it was you expected of them. Slowly, she fed the image of what she wanted into the ringpact, as if it were conscious. Then—*understanding!* The space around Adathin and her shimmered, and his eyes mirrored a brilliant yellow, almost golden, as they shone all the brighter.

"You did it!" Adathin said excitedly, but quickly hushed his own voice. "Sorry."

She *had* done it. A cloaking. She had seen it done before—even practiced it when she was a child—but she could never get it quite right. This particular casting came easier now with the ringpact. It was almost as if the trinket wanted her to succeed. The ringpact just needed to be shown the proper way. Shown how to work with her and not against. Perhaps they weren't as bad as she had initially thought. Perhaps this was their true purpose. A focus, of sorts.

"We'll need to stay close," Adathin whispered, wrapping his arms tightly around her, his back going straight as an arrow. "Sorry again for the discomfort, but this is the only way."

Reluctantly, she wrapped her arms just above his stomach, trying to calm her beating heart as she replied, "You're right, I can barely make the space of the concealment this large. Let's move. Slowly." She didn't see it, but more felt his approval as they walked lock-stepped into the library.

"Why are we here in the view and earshot of all?" Lhoris asked.

Reylar sighed; why did it have to be this man? Lhoris had always been so full of himself. Even when compared to other elvish men. They're like peacocks; preening and squawking among themselves about who had the brighter feathers. It was beginning to grate on his every nerve.

Lhoris, his elvish advisor, had come from a lesser family, one with many kin. He was a distant middle, far from first-born and heir, but not even the youngest, to be showered in praise and gifts. No, the elvish man's only hope for relevance was to throw himself into the service of the Elvish Council in hopes they would bestow upon him the title and purpose he so desperately wished for, but was denied by his own family. Instead, they had saddled him with this role. A role the man so obviously detested—an advisory to a fellowship of mages. Hardly the prominence the man had wished for, and yet, Lhoris still found a way to blame everyone but himself for his bad fortune. This was to be another one of those times.

"Lhoris," Reylar said, forcing himself and his tone to calm. "I wished to brush up on some reading and found that this would be an appropriate meeting site. I assure you, none are prying. Why would they? We keep no secrets."

Lhoris narrowed his eyes. "No secret, eh?" The man smiled. "Why not your office?"

He forced a smile in return. "Truth be told, I'm running out of expensive spirits to offer you. Here, I'm not obligated to share my trove."

The elvish man took on a dangerous look. "You waste my time, Elder. Please tell me you've made headway in finding your long-lost adept? Not that I see why finding him is so urgent at all. Mages wash out all the time. Abandon their posts. *It's human nature.*"

Straight to the point, as always. Lhoris was not one for small talk, and even less so when speaking to humans whom he considered beneath him. Clutching his hands tight and wishing he could still feel anything from the wrist down, he replied, "That adept's name is Freed Gallok. And I've nothing to report, but I wanted to offer another theory."

Lhoris smiled, but his eyes were full of fury. "Theory?" he mused. "You drag me from my work to offer me a theory? You have a job to do: find the boy. Dead or alive, I care not. The Spellbound Arch has decreed it since you made such a fuss, and now it must be done. It is not your place to offer theories, but to offer solutions. To obey your betters."

Reylar shook his head. "Perhaps we've gotten off on the wrong foot," he offered as an olive branch, "here—*look!*" He leaned over a small table, placing a hand on the single book that lay there, already open to a specific page, and pushed it to the other side where Lhoris sat.

The elvish man's green eyes scanned the pages hurriedly, and as he did, the lines of his face deepened. His scowl etched even sharper into his face. "What is this?" he asked, slamming the book closed. "What are you trying to say? Speak plainly."

Just then, he noticed a shimmer in the corner of his eyes. A small sheen in the air. A curious thing. Turning back, he replied in a soft tone, "What I am trying to say is that we were wrong. The effects of phantasmal leaf can only be experienced through the inhalation of the drug. Inhalation via smoke. It's written clear as the day is bright on the very page I showed you."

"And?" Lhoris' patience was clearly at the breaking point.

"And there was no smoke to be seen in that warehouse. No lingering odor of burning. Even now, at the edge of my mind, I feel something is... wrong. Something peculiar. You feel it too, don't you?" Lhoris went tight-lipped, and he added, "I thought so. With a missing mage and seemingly no clues, we must retrace our steps. Mage adept Cane claims she saw a body. Adept Ravenblood as well. And there is only one thing that I can think of that could have hidden the body from our collective sights."

Lhoris' expression went to shock and awe. "You can't be suggesting—"

He held up his hand. "Suggesting or not, I can see no other way. This reeks of psionics. Elvish magic."

"Preposterous," Lhoris replied, waving a hand through the air as if trying to cut it in two. "How dare you accuse the elvish of wanton murder."

"I never said that... I merely stated that I believe psionics were used to hide the evidence. For what purpose? I do not know." He paused as he heard a soft gasp coming from the space of shimmering air. He narrowed his eyes and then nodded in that direction. "We should revisit the crime scene. Perhaps take the mages who saw it firsthand. Kyra and Armeya. The Mistwalker kin as well."

"*No,*" Lhoris replied sharply. "We will not use adepts in this. I'll contact the Elvish Conclave and the Spellbound Arch for further instructions. You will put this from mind. *Far* from mind."

It was his turn to be angry. Throwing a chair towards the shimmering air, making sure not to be too forceful, he declared, "These are my students. *Mine!* I will not abandon them. Not on your order. Not on the Elvish Conclave's order... not even on the order of the Spellbound Arch itself. I have a charge. A duty."

Lhoris stood and put his hand to his head, mimicking a headache. "Enough with the dramatics... Fine, I will notify you of any other developments. I will push for action. Is that all?"

He turned back to the shimmering air. "That is all. Dismissed."

CHAPTER 16

PIERCING LIGHT

"So, how did I do?" Salvator smirked in his pompous way. No matter how many times Willow had mocked him for it, warned him against it, and berated him, the man just couldn't seem to shake the air of nobility he thought was rightfully his.

It would be his downfall.

"That was... acceptable," she admitted, though she was reluctant to say anything more that would potentially inflate Salvator's head further. It was truly in the man's best interest. She had been training with the man for the better part of a week and already it was a wonder he could fit through doorways with how massive his ego was. "Although," she added, "I'd say your footwork needs work. You're heavy on one side and you lean awkwardly into every strike."

Salvator grinned even wider, as if her comment had been expected. "You know, you can just accept that I was perfect... because I was." She narrowed her eyes at him, and he frowned. "When are you going to give me some jobs? Missions? Tasks? I tire of this. Enough with the training. I won't hurt myself now. I promise."

Willow scratched at her chin, eyeing Quistis, who returned her a simple smile.

"What I'm curious about is why you are so eager to help at all?" Willow queried. "What is it you want? *Really* want?" Salvator turned and there was a flush on his cheeks, a reddening of his face and eyes. He tried to hide the blush, and the unspoken answer was revealed. "You seek recognition," she concluded, nodding to herself. "To be known. Loved. Perhaps even feared. I know your type. I know what awaits them—"

"*To be seen!*" Salvator interrupted, his anxiety turning to anger at the knife's edge of derision. "We deserve to be seen. To be heard."

"We?"

"... I—*I* deserve to be seen."

The truth was finally out in the open. Salvator's truth.

Willow turned and set her rapier tip-side down on a nearby pillar as she leaned against it. "You know that glory does not await you here. That ship has sailed. Sunk to the bottom of an endless sea. A crushing ocean of despair." She pointed at his chest. "It died when your ringpact forsook you. What you do now, what we all do, is considered immoral. Dangerous. Illegal."

"What I do?" Salvator replied, still angry as he threw his blunted practice sword to the ground. "Immoral to be who I am? Illegal to be what I cannot change? I can't help it. None of us can."

Willow nodded, turning a sharp eye towards Quistis, who held her hands wrapped around her chest. Turning back to Salvator, she said, "It would be best to learn this now: just because you are born a certain way, doesn't mean you'll be allowed to live it. It is the nature of the world. The law."

Salvator kicked his practice sword, and it went spinning across the training floor. "It's not fair!"

"No, it is not," Willow agreed. "But fair has little to do with it. The world doesn't care. People don't care. Your safety, and everyone else's who is under my protection, is all that *I* care about. It's the only thing I can afford to care for. That, and your freedom to choose a life for yourself, for if you are not free, then you are a slave, and that is something I will never tolerate."

Willow's magelock itched against the back of her neck. The ultimate source of injustice. A mage's invisible chains.

"*Choose...*" Salvator repeated her words back to her, and a small flicker of hope rose in his eyes. "If I'm free to choose, then I would choose not to remain invisible. I want to be seen and heard. To shine as bright as a star on a moonless night."

Quistis chuckled, adding their own voice to the conversation. "I see you've been reading some of the books I've provided you. Let's see, that one is from 'Tempresses' Autumn Fury.' A classic, if I do say so myself."

Salvator turned towards Quistis. "Aye," he admitted. "Who knew the written word could carry such weight? Those books, they've... helped. Helped me get through some of the darker nights. The lonely ones."

Willow snorted. "That, and a heavy drink, if I am to believe the rumors. I've also heard you've become quite close with the brothers Enoch and Amon. Troublemakers, those two. Brutes... the perfect company for you, really. But alas, even brutes have their proper places."

"Hey, don't judge them by their looks." A small fire seemed to rise in Salvator. "They're sharp as a knife... in their own ways."

Salvator's defense of the brothers surprised her, although she would not show it. Quistis shot her a knowing glare, and she knew that this sudden change of heart had likely come from her.

Nodding, Willow said, "Right you are, *Ais*. Skinner. And as I've said before... choice. If you want to help us, you're free to do so. Despite what the mages and elvish think of us, we keep the peace around here in the Dimlight District. Mages rarely come here at all, and the constables of Mistbreak even less so. It is up to us to keep order, for if it is to break down, there would be a reckoning. In that, I've heard... whispers of a new crime lord. One who's been making a ruckus in the district. An uncanny. A goblin known as Tarx. Find the Goblin and drive them out of the district, preferably away from the city as a whole." She thought back to the dead adept mage. "Steps have already been taken."

Salvator's interest seemed piqued. He almost looked giddy, and about to hop with anticipation. "And if the goblin won't leave? What then?"

Willow narrowed her eyes. "If they won't leave, then you'll have a fight on your hands, I would imagine. Take the brothers with you—you may need them. Brutes have their uses." Salvator turned to leave, but she hastily added, "And remember, *Ais*. Skinner, calm the storm, and ride the winds. Do not let yourself be swept away in the aethryis, for I won't be able to save you. No one will."

Journal Entry

Year: 835 E.B

Master Lu'ce spun, and her whip wound tight against my neck. I had gasped and struggled, trying desperately to continue to hold the short sword in my wavering hands.

I failed.

My blade had struck the soft dirt and let out the mutest of rings as a few autumn leaves of red and yellow colors drifted away in the gust of wind. With whatever strength I had left, I had grasped at the binding around my neck. Metal—heated metal—as if it had just come from the forge; that is what it felt like.

Master Lu'ce had clicked her tongue. "Not the short sword, then." To my relief, the noose had loosened as her whip fell to the wayside. I had gasped frantically at the air, my throat burning as if I breathed in acrid flames. Before I could speak, Master Lu'ce had pressed her hand against the wedge of my face and a cooling spread throughout my body, like a spray of mist as waves crash against rocks on the ocean. It was exhilarating and exhausting, and it had not been the first healing I had received that day.

Lashing Lu'ce Ais Nox, a specialized mystic who fought more like an aug-mentor, wielding her enchanted whip which she nicknamed Cerberus. I had heard the whispers in the taverns we visited. In the towns we passed. Stories, both old and new, of a woman who could fell one-hundred goblins while simultaneously healing the sick and the needy. I had looked up to her. Worshiped her. But not for her strength or her kindness. Not even for the sacrifices she has made to raise me. No, I worshiped her because she knew exactly who she was. She didn't shroud or hide it from the world. She was a killer with a heart of gold, and while I had no wish to kill, I wished I knew who I was. Who I truly was.

"Pick another weapon," Master Lu'ce had commanded, her annoyance as plain as a white rose in a bouquet of red. "And think this time, think."

Master Lu'ce had laid out a multitude of weapons on the grass near the stream under an old tree. The tree was near barren of leaves, most laid out like a blanket for the weapons to rest on. I had leaned down and picked up the short sword, carefully setting it back in its place. I was never good at fighting with fists or weapons. In that way, Master Lu'ce and I differed greatly. My strengths lay in my use of aethryis itself, and, despite my attempts at skipping any martial training, Master Lu'ce would not allow it. No matter how strong my aethryis control became.

I considered my options: A mace? No, too impractical, and would require greater strength on my part. A flail? A little more range, but no. Greatsword? How strong had this woman thought I was? True, I could augment my body with aethryis, but Master Lu'ce had warned against that at a basic level. A truly good mage fighter could draw and release aethryis in-between heartbeats if needed. I had no such control. Not yet. Finally, my gaze had come upon a spear. This particular spear was old, the wood cracked and splintered in various parts. The head itself appeared to be a rusty dagger hastily tied off with some rope. Hesitantly, I picked it up.

Master Lu'ce hummed softly to herself as she had said, "Hmm, a spear. A safe weapon, as far as close-ranged weapons go. It gives you a reach advantage. A good choice, I would say."

I would smile at Master Lu'ce's kind words, but she had laid out some benefits for each failed weapon I had chosen. Still, I rolled the haft in my hand over and over, getting the proper feel. The proper grip. More than once, a piece of wood splintered away and bit into my skin, leaving small remnants of itself behind. I found the balance and aimed it forward.

Master Lu'ce had stood straighter, rolling her whip and cracking it on the ground before pulling it back into a neat circle in her awaiting hand. I knew the way Master Lu'ce attacked. The way she fought. Her movements. Her strengths. Her weaknesses... or so I had thought.

I had dashed forward, putting all my weight and remaining stamina into this one attack. No fancy flourish, no fuss, a mad dash aimed for her chest.

I just needed to strike her—to tap her, to be claimed the victor. Lu'ce had stepped to the side, her left, as I knew she would. The whip came unfurrowed and, with a flick of her wrist, launched forward in an arcing motion. I had to time it perfectly. Master Lu'ce twisted, and I had seen it coming.

I had ducked, and the whip flew overhead as I had flourished the spear, wrapping the whip as I did and pulling, forcing Master Lu'ce to lose her weapon or be forced closer. There was a glint of surprise in Master Lu'ce's eyes as she came, just as I had expected. I had her now. I had aimed the spear back towards her as she came into range and thrust it forward. There it was—I could see it...

Victory!

And then the spear stopped a mere breath from the woman's chest.

"Close," Master Lu'ce had said, pride in her voice. "But still not enough." She flicked her wrist, and the whip shuddered with vibrations as it continued its spin. The very tail-end had lashed against my ribs and with one last pull, my body lifted off the ground as I was tossed aside like a rag-doll.

It was still not enough. It was never enough.

Kyra trailed Adathin by a step, and Armeya right behind her; both her companions shared the same stoic look. She feared she appeared the same: they all looked as if they trudged towards the gallows. There was fear beneath each of them. Behind them. Like a wave. Ripe. Almost she could taste it in the air. Their collective strain. Like a clinging sweat.

She held her magecloak tight around her, bracing herself for whatever may come. Truth. They needed to find the truth.

The doors of the warehouse were slightly ajar when they arrived. Looking down, it appeared that someone or something had cut the lock. That in itself was not surprising. After she had broken the protections on her previous visit, the lock had been left as no more than simple looped metal. Any manner of ruffians or vagrants could use the place to hide out in.

"Careful," Adathin suggested, his tone low and full of worry. Then he added in her mind, "*Someone is here. I feel them. Sense them.*"

Kyra agreed with a nod as Armeya pressed up close against her back, whispering, "Someone's here, aren't they?"

She didn't respond.

Adathin dragged the door ajar, letting out the softest of creaking wood. The silver clasps on the door's edges scraped metal on metal, punctuating their arrival. There was little to be done about it. The building had not been well maintained. Rust coagulated on everything it could touch, and the smell of old rat piss and shit hung musky in the choking air.

"*Stay close,*" Adathin projected in thought.

A purple glow enveloped his hand and then, suddenly, a long, intricate blade basked in that same glow appeared into his eager hand. He grasped it firmly before the blade fell.

Surprised, Kyra gasped, asking, "What is that?" Then she amended in a whisper, "*Sorry...*"

Adathin smirked coyly. "You should really learn more about my people. This blade is a psionic weapon. One made from my own mind."

"Psionic weapon? Is it an illusion? Will it even cut?"

"*Oh, it'll cut,*" Adathin sent proudly. "*It's as sharp as my will and requires no maintenance... It's the perfect weapon.*"

"Perfect for assassination." Her thought came too quickly, and she was unable to shield it in time.

Adathin frowned.

Armeya pressed forward. "I want to see this done, so we leave. The sooner the better. Excuse me."

Kyra had never heard Armeya be so formal before. Nor so impatient. She had been so cheery a few days ago. So carefree. A ripe thorn in her side. This change was disturbing in its own right. Perhaps even more so than the current predicament they found themselves in. She followed Armeya with Adathin right behind.

Inside, most of the boxes that once cluttered the area had been removed. Kyra had heard rumors of mages from other circles chatting about the task. That the Spellbound Arch trusted no others to remove the contraband that was inside. Still, even without the illicit cargo, the warehouse was plenty crowded. Trash littered the space, and she could hardly take a step without trudging into a piece of rubbish or two. It was disgusting, but this was the job. A mage's job. The ones that no bards would speak of in their retelling of deeds long done. The dirty parts.

A scratching sound drew her ears, and light burst from her hand as she placed her palm forward towards the source, just as a small mouse skittered out from under an old newspaper. It had made a den for itself. A nest. It was wide and looked to be just about to pop. Pregnant. She suddenly felt awful about intruding on the creature's home.

"Rather skittish, aren't ya'?"

Kyra's breath caught as she whirled her light upwards to the balcony above the stairs, where she had previously seen the presumed killer. There, three hooded figures stood. Two were burly and one skinny. Each staring down at their group, their faces shrouded in darkness.

"Who are you?" Adathin asked, leveling his purple glowing sword forward, the tip aimed straight at the skinny man's chest. "I am the leader of this circle of mages. You will identify yourselves. *Now!*"

There was soft laughter that started low and only grew and grew. Then, the skinny man threw his hood back, revealing a familiar face. One she had seen not too long ago.

Salvator Ais Skinner.

"*You?*" Kyra whispered to herself, rubbing her thumb against her ringpact absently.

"Oh, you remember who I am, do you?" Salvator sneered at them as if they were insects about to be crushed underneath his boots. "Pathetic."

Adathin lowered his weapon, stepping forward. "You are one of the banished, aren't you? Deemed... unfit to receive the ringpact?" He laughed, but it felt forced. "And you call us pathetic."

Salvator spit at the dusty wood beneath him. "'Unworthy.'" He spoke the word with such disdain, as if its very existence enraged him. "There was nothing unworthy about me, nor any of us. I've joined the pactless. They are my friends. My family. My purpose. I'll never turn myself over to you—"

"We aren't here for you." Adathin spun away, as if Salvator was of no consequence. "We're here on official business and you're disrupting a crime scene. See your way out, please." He glanced back over his shoulder. "And tell your leader that if she did this, we'll come for her soon enough."

Salvator snorted. "Interrupting a crime scene? What crime?"

"Oh, she'll know. Now, begone pest."

There was a loud bang as Salvator struck the railing. "Cocky, elf," he replied. "But we'll see if you still are soon enough."

Adathin turned back and held his gaze. "Meaning?"

Salvator rolled his neck from side to side, and Kyra could hear echoing cracks as he did so. "Get ready. I've been meaning to test myself against those ringpacts. I'll show you how a true, unbound mage fights."

With little warning, all three jumped from the second floor to the first. As they struck, air shot from beneath their feet, sending all manner of dust and debris spiraling into the air. They each chose a target. Salvator, as the leader of this ragtag group, took Adathin for himself. Armeya, who had narrowly missed being crushed by one big lout, was now cornered against a wall. And she... Well, the last fellow, as big as the second, rounded on her with violence in his dark eyes.

A reddish light brightened the warehouse as Armeya threw a ball of scorching fire forward towards her would-be assailant. The man was quick—far too quick for his size as he dodged. Armeya cried out as his fist struck her in the gut. She toppled, doubling over.

"*Armeya*—" Kyra's cry was cut short as her own assailant swung a wild haymaker. She ducked, shuffling towards Armeya and leaving Adathin alone with Salvator on the other side of the warehouse.

Those two looked engaged in a back and forth. Adathin swung his purple sword gracefully, each swing deliberate and weighted. Salvator, for as boisterous as he's had, seemed to be quite the capable fighter himself, easily avoiding the blade. He fought weaponless, and with each weaponless strike that landed on Adathin, she could see him shift ever more uncomfortably.

Kyra had little more time to think as her assailant bore down on her now, more fiercely than before. Instinctually, she tried to launch her own ball of fire, just as Armeya had done—but nothing happened. Nothing. Cursing to herself, she knew her mistake immediately. The ringpact: she was locked out of that power. A thaumaturges power. No matter how hard she fought, it would never come. She felt like a chained dog.

Shooting Kyra a coy smile, as if he knew her plan, her assailant summoned a small flame in his hand and then whipped it at her. It was far less powerful than Armeya's had been, but despite that, as she blocked it, she felt a familiar heat lick at her skin, singing it. She would not scream—she would not... *could* not.

Armeya, however, did. Her assailant caught her by the arm and, by the way he twisted, it looked broken. Still, the man continued twisting, causing Armeya's screams to become wails of agony.

"*Stop!*" Kyra yelled as her assailant's fist struck her in the head. Blackness threatened to take hold. Threatened to pull her into its inky dark. She fought it. With everything she had, she fought. Armeya was in trouble. Adathin as well. Why oh why was she an Arcanist? So useless in fights. Bound to be a support for others. How could she protect them? Her circle?

As misery took root, her ringpact resonated. It echoed with power. Echoed with her will. Her desires. It whispered tales of forbidden knowledge. Pacts of old. And then she knew—knew she could protect them.

She could fight.

A spear as long as her arms exploded outwards from her extended hand. It narrowly grazed her assailant's face as he skirted away, his eyes wide with shock. It was unlike any spear she had ever seen. Glowing brightly, with an ornate beauty that defied logic.

It was a spear of pure light. Swirling, weightless and ethereal.

Before her assailant could react, Kyra grasped the weapon and thrust it forward, catching him in the shoulder. She could hear the soft sizzle as the skin around the tip of the spear burned. The man grunted uncomfortably as he reached the haft, pushing the spear backward and away from his body. The entire spear was made of light but corporeal, and as the man grasped it, she could hear his flesh burn against it. Still, she could do little against his inhuman strength. As the spear cleared his shoulder, she flourished, swiping right and sending a neat line across the edge of his nose. He fell back, holding his injured left-arm uselessly as a small trail of blood ran from the cut down his face.

The others had desisted from their fighting, staring at her in a sort of awe. All except Armeya, who leaned heavily against boxes. It seemed about the only thing she could do to remain upright.

Salvator clicked his tongue. "You put on quite the show," he said. "Perhaps we underestimated who the real threat is here." He turned and gave Adathin a coy grin. Then Salvator clutched at his head, as if he would rip out his own hair.

"Real threat?" Adathin seethed. "Do you think yourself stronger? In possession of a will harder than my own?"

Salvator grunted, staggering back into one of his mates, who came to check on him. Suddenly, he recovered, shaking his head as he said, "Let's go. Leave it to an elf to use trickery rather than fight fairly." Adathin snorted, but made no move to stop him. Salvator spat, "Until next time."

The three pactless strolled away towards the warehouse door, which hung open. She spun her weapon as they moved past, trailing behind them. Once they were gone, she dropped it and it sizzled away into nothingness as she moved to Armeya's side.

"Is it over?" Armeya asked, the words coming out low and breathless.

Kyra glanced at the door. "For now," she said. "But I think they'll be a problem again.." Kneeling, she asked, "Can you walk?"

Armeya groaned, rolling her shoulder back and forth. "Y–Y-Yeah," she replied. "Just need to—" With a pop, her arm straightened, and she let out a sigh of pure relief. "Just a dislocated shoulder. It happens; an old injury. Common when you work on a farm. Don't look too worried about me."

Kyra helped her stand. "I'm not worried." Rolling her eyes, she asked, "You worked on a farm?"

Armeya chuckled. "Yeah, as a kid. My parents own one. A rather large one at that. I miss it sometimes. The animals. The freshness of the air. It's different from this place. From the city. It feels so hard to breathe here sometimes."

Kyra held her hand to her chest. "You can say that again." Adathin had moved to the middle of the warehouse, surveying the scene. She helped Armeya to her feet. "Are you up to this?"

Armeya got a wide, foreign look in her eyes, and then, suddenly, those eyes came to rest in the center of the room. She crossed her arm across her chest for support. "Yes, I'll be fine."

"Look at this," Adathin said, kneeling. Kyra trailed over, with Armeya lagging closely behind. At the center of the warehouse, there was a reddish smear plastered on the floor.

"Is that... blood?" she asked.

"Seems so," Adathin replied. "Smells like blood too."

Adathin was right. There was a metallic tang that hung in the air like a rotted carcass.

Kyra kneeled and tried to imagine how the body had been before. "Here," she said, drawing an outline in the air. "He'd been laid out like this." Pointing up, she added, "Obviously, he'd been pushed from the rafters up top. When I made that connection last time, that's when I noticed the mysterious figure up above and gave chase."

Adathin nodded. "The fall explains the patterns of blood. The way it fans out."

Armeya kneeled as well. "And he was still alive when he struck. Look—" she pointed to weak lines of red in the stone. It was as if someone had tried to scribble something out. "Freed tried to write something before..."

Adathin stood. "Before someone or something finished him."

They all nodded together.

Adathin walked away, leaning on a nearby post. She followed, wishing to be away from the old smell of death.

"What could have done this?" she asked.

"Anything really." Adathin stared fiercely at the scene with his yellowish-golden eyes. "Doesn't take much to push someone from a roof. But... It's the hiding that concerns me most. I was here: there was no blood before. No smell of death. So either this happened afterwards, which we know it didn't, or..."

"Or our memories have been altered. All our memories, simultaneously. Elder Reylar included."

Adathin nodded. "It's the only thing that makes sense, but even that explanation doesn't cover it. There is something about this. Something even I cannot fathom."

"So... what do we do now?"

"Notin'!" replied an unknown voice.

Kyra spun to greet this newcomer, and Adathin's purple sword reappeared in his hand in a flash of light.

Out of the shadows approached a short fellow; far too short to be human or elvish. From their skinny disposition, it couldn't be one of the dwarven, either. Step after step until they came into the light. Green skin, long ears, and a sharp nose. It was a goblin. Male, if she had to guess. This one had gray eyes, well, eye, as one looked to have been violently removed, punctuated by a large scar. He gnashed his sharp teeth and looked to be picking at his gums with the pointed edge of a dagger, which looked as long as a short sword in his small hands.

"What do you want, you uncanny prick?" Armeya asked. Kyra noticed a deep-seated anger seemed to build from inside the woman, and her face contorted in unreleased fury.

"Prick?" The goblin laughed, and others still in shadow echoed him. "Quite the balls on ye', lass. Maybe ye' don't know the situation you's find yerselves in? I'll educate ye'. This is my place. *Mine!*"

Adathin's arm looked tense as he squeezed his sword tighter. "Yours?" he said condescendingly. "Uncanny cannot own property; not in Mistbreak, anyway. So tell me uncanny, what's your name?"

The goblin man seemed to spit the word, "Tarx. And don't ye' forget it."

"... Just Tarx?"

"We've no need fer' two names, elf, but if you want my warband, you can have it: Grimsbane. And if you're looking for our leader, well... bad news, 'fraid, you won't live long enough for it to matter." Tarx whistled, and figures moved in the shadows behind him. "Time to join yer' dead mage friend, I'm 'fraid. Meet the family."

Several more goblins poured in from seemingly everywhere. The rafters were full of them, as well as the first floor. They were surrounded. Utterly trapped, like rats in a cage.

"Stay behind me," Adathin said, dismissing the sword. When she gave him a curious look, he added, "It would do us little use against so many."

"Can't you frighten them off?" Armeya asked, rising panic in her voice. "Uncanny are stupid and weak-willed. Use it against them. Your psionics."

A cold sweat seemed to break on Adathin's forehead. Turning, Kyra said, "I think he's already trying. It isn't working."

"... It's not," Adathin confirmed, lowering his head and breathing harshly. "Something is... blocking me. I can't sense them. At least, when I try, all I get is a garbled mess of their thoughts all flung at me at once. It's overwhelming, and I cannot pick out a single target."

Armeya reached up with her good arm and summoned a flow of air, tearing at a support beam and causing a few rafters to fall, sending a spray of broken wood and falling goblins.

"Kill 'em!" Tarx demanded, pointing at Armeya. "Start with that thaumaturge bitch. Then the elf. Keep the dark-haired one; the Boss'll have some questions."

The goblins moved slowly, pressing in from all directions. Despite the attempt, Armeya's actions had done little to dissuade them. Desperately, she tried to re-summon her spear of light, like she had done before, but she was tapped out. Tired. Whatever force had compelled her and made it possible seemed to have fled her just as quickly as it had come.

Perfect timing.

Then the sounds of screaming goblins assaulted her ears. High-pitched and squealing. The breaking of bones and the guttural sounds of death punctuated it. Turning, she saw something odd: Soren Frost, wielding a sword made of ice, had barged his way in through the front door, breaking through all manner of goblins in his way like a wayward log barrels through a rapid river.

"Time to go," Soren announced, breathless.

Kyra turned and ran—ran with all the strength her legs had, only stopping briefly to make sure Armeya followed. Outside on the streets of Dimlight, a crowd had formed to see what had caused the ruckus. Wide-eyed human men, women, and even uncanny alike gawked in unison. It was quite the spectacle she imagined. A few wayward mages running for their lives from a wild pack of goblins. A bard would get a drink thrown at their head if they tried to spin up such an absurd accusation.

Adathin grabbed her shoulder, pulling her. "Can't stop now, keep running!"

They pushed through the crowd, and she could hear the faint whispers of a furious goblin screaming for their heads. Slowly, the voice became but a quiet buzz as they reached the outskirts of Dimlight. They ran headlong into some constables, and Adathin stopped to explain the situation to them. More and more constables arrived, heading into Dimlight to begin the search. The constables didn't have the magic of mages, but they were reliable enough, and many even wielded enchanted weapons and armor. She didn't need to worry. They were safe... for now.

Kyra leaned over for support, wheezing. From the looks of it, they all did. Even Maxim, whom she had not even seen before, was now with them, sharing in their misery.

Maxim, upon seeing Armeya's arm, rushed to her side. He pulled out a small vial of a dark liquid and prompted her to drink while saying, "H-H-Here." Armeya eyed the foul-looking stuff, and with a gulp, downed the whole vial. The look on her face said it all. It must've tasted horribly. "S-S-Sorry."

Soren stretched his back and rolled his shoulders, letting his long blade of ice turn into water, which splashed to the ground. "What in the hells were you all playing at? You go off gallivanting alone without us?" Soren turned to Adathin, clearly unwilling to let this slide. "Well?"

Adathin flushed. He had obviously not expected to be challenged so openly. "I... er, well..." He bowed his head in defeat. "I-I'm sorry. Time was of the essence. I-I should've... well... you know."

Soren glared angrily. "What I know is that you didn't trust us. It looks to me that you only trust Kyra. Trust her enough to speak to her, at least. I'm your augmentor. Your fighter. Your shield. You point in a direction and say go, and I will force my way through. You say to hold the line and I will damn well hold it. Remember that next time you try to pick a fight with a goblin warband—" He suddenly tumbled over, clutching at his side.

She rushed to his side. "What's happened, what—" Then she saw it: red spilling from under his shirt. She raised it gently, and he squirmed. When it was clear of his flesh, all became known: Soren had been stabbed.

"*Hmm,*" Soren said. "I didn't notice that. Heated blood must've blocked out the pain."

Adathin leaned down. "How bad is it?"

Soren coughed a laugh. "I feel it now; doesn't feel great, I'll tell ya' that. Maxim, would you mind using some of your mystic aethryis to fix me up?"

Maxim went white-faced and cold as he said, "I-I-I can't. S-S-Sorry."

Iona suddenly showed her face as if appearing from the mist itself. Taking a brisk glance at the situation, she pulled a small white cloth from her pouch, which held a glowing red rune engraved into it. "Here," she said. "This will stave off the worst of the pain. It won't heal you, but it'll slow the bleeding and begin the body's natural healing process."

"*Ugh,* thanks," Soren muttered. "Look at that, Iona Ais Cracksman, taking care of me. Never thought I'd live to see the day. Never thought I'd—" Soren suddenly got a far off look on his face, as if he didn't recognize the woman who stood in front of him.

Iona narrowed her eyes and Soren shuddered, his lucidity returning.

"You may still not," Iona said, cracking a small smile. "You're just lucky I was around. Try to remember that."

Adathin helped Soren to his feet, and they all started the shameful walk back towards Dragrin's. Beaten and broken, it was a long and silent trip.

CHAPTER 17
CHAOS WROUGHT

Willow entered the audience chamber, with its low ceilings and small windows, barely illuminating the space with the help of dim mage lights. It was her audience chamber, like it or not. It was a space where she had to confront the tough decisions. The deadly ones. She hated it. Despised it with all her being. Some had taken to calling it 'The Pactless Court,' though she found that term silly. Her decisions revolved around what the pactless group would do, but she wielded no authority over those who did not desire it. Nevertheless, if referring to it as her court made the others more attentive, she wouldn't correct them. They had to listen to her. They had to—for their sakes.

"Salvator," Willow said, not concealing the deep-rooted anger she felt. "Are you happy now? Proud? Do you feel seen? Heard?" Salvatore hung his head low, and the twins averted their eyes from her baleful glare. "You two, dismissed. I'll deal with you both later."

As if escaping the hangman's noose, the twins skirted from the room, leaving Willow and Salvator alone, and the air grew heavier as the sounds of their footsteps became quieter.

"I asked you a question," Willow repeated, seething. "*Speak!*"

Salvator's face was red hot. Burning. He fidgeted with his hands as he replied, "I-I... I'm not sorry!"

Salvator's words surprised her. She had expected a plea for mercy. An apology, of sorts. Maybe some groveling. Yet, even now, she could see strength returning to the young man. His eyes locked onto hers; piercing and broken eyes.

"They aren't better than us," Salvator said. "I proved it—I fought them. We did... and we won. *We won!*"

Willow flicked her thumb against the arm of her seat. "Did you now?" she asked. "You won? Really? You showed them all! Showed them they were wrong about you?" She forced a laugh. "But you didn't, did you? All you did was prove them right. Proved yourself unfit for a ringpact. It's pathetic. They were adepts. Amateurs. Barely attuned to their ringpacts, which limit them until they become more acquainted. They had no business there, and regretfully, neither did you."

"I fought the elvish man!"

"And he took pity on you." Willow stood, circling her ward. "I know of the Mistwalkers, although not this Adathin you spoke of. They are a powerful and noble family. Their psionic abilities are top-tier. The only reason you remain unharmed is because that 'elvish man' took pity on you. He did not see you as an adequate threat."

"That's nonsense," Salvator retorted angrily. "I felt his magic in my mind and my thoughts, but my will won over."

"Not possible."

"Or..." Salvator trailed off for a moment, then added, "N-No, I'm sure it was because of my own willpower."

"Explain," Willow said, trying to hide her curiosity. "What causes you to hesitate?"

Salvator sat and leaned back into the fine wooden chair, its soft brown wood creaking against the strain. "I felt his presence in my head, like small needles. No, not needles, fingers. It was as if he pulled at the very fabric of thought. And then... nothing. Poof, he was gone. We... I decided it was best for us to leave. Besides, I saw no sign of any goblins there, like you said. The place was empty, besides *them*."

Willow sighed, pressing her fingers to her temples. "Tarx showed up afterwards."

Salvator stood up as quickly as a cat, and his chair fell to the floor with a clack. "He did? What happened?"

"Nearly killed them—the ones you fought. If my information is right, around fifteen goblins showed. Perhaps more. You lot were lucky." Willow swallowed hard. "I was lucky. I... I'm sorry. I shouldn't have sent you three alone. It's just... you reminded me of someone."

"... Who?"

Willow laughed, genuinely this time. "Me. That stubbornness—that drive—I knew you needed to do something worthwhile, so I sent you after a lowly goblin. But he was anything but lowly. There are strange forces at work here. First, the dead mage, and now a goblin warband. Something is coming. Coming to upset the delicate balance."

Salvator righted the chair and gave her a coy smile. "And that's a bad thing? A dead mage, I mean. The elvish man mentioned that. He thought that perhaps you..."

"Perhaps I... what?" Salvator raised his shoulders in a nonchalant fashion.

She ground her teeth in frustration. "A dead mage is bad business for all. The balance between the uncanny and mages is what keeps us, the unwanted and outcasts, safe. When that balance is threatened, those in power seek to correct it."

"And..."

Willow turned as Quistis entered, wearing a grave look as she said, "And when those in power seek to correct something they perceive as wrong, it is the innocents that suffer. When a correction happens, it is almost always an overcorrection. In the end, it is we who would suffer most of all."

"Get him inside and lay him on the bed!" Adathin exclaimed, pushing through a crowd of gawking adepts.

Kyra clung tightly to Soren's legs, assisting in lifting him up and gently placing him on the thin padding. The white mattress was instantly stained red from the leaking of blood from Soren's wound. The infirmary at Dragrin's was spacious, filled with adepts who stared wide-eyed at the commotion she and her circle caused—the chaos they wrought. Although Soren appeared in good spirits, joking jovially among his peers, she sensed it was all a facade. The color on his face and the deep lines of pain on his brow revealed that something was truly wrong.

Master Michlas *Ais* Aracan suddenly appeared, shooing everyone away from the bed. "Get back, get back! Give the boy some room to breathe." Master Aracan, a man of at least seventy, had light-gray hair that contrasted with his darker complexion. His eyes shone the lightest blue, resembling a flash of lightning in a dark sky. His back was slanted, and he walked with a slight limp in his gait. It didn't appear to be caused by age. Mages didn't age the same as regular humans, but looked to be from an old injury.

"He's been wounded," Adathin explained, forcing back a few onlookers who crowded to get a glimpse. "By a goblin's blade."

The master ran a hand through his long beard. "And this?" He dabbed at the cloth wrapped around Soren's midsection with his crooked fingers. "Are these Builder runes? Interesting."

Iona pushed forward. "It's mine," she said. "I always carry it with me. It has been useful in the past."

"*Hmm*, useful indeed, I've no doubts." Master Aracan seemed to consider the situation before placing his hand on Soren's exposed stomach. "This may hurt."

"I can take it—" Soren suddenly reached out, gripping Adathin's wrist. The man spasmed as she braced, holding his legs with all her strength. He thrashed, and then suddenly relaxed.

Master Aracan shook his head. "This is bad. Dreadful, really. You—" he pointed an accusatory finger at her, "what happened? Speak. *Now!*"

"He, uh, we... I mean..."

"They tried to play detective." Turning, she saw the crowd of her peers part to allow for a surly faced elvish man to pass. Lhoris wore the scowl he so often wore of late, and his fierce golden eyes seemed to pierce straight through to her core. He came to rest in front of her and reached down, gripping her wrist and pulling her arm up with a twisting motion. "You insolent, disobedient children."

Lhoris twisted harder.

Kyra now stood on the tips of her toes, but she refused to cry out. To give voice to the pain she felt. Refused to give the man any ammunition or satisfaction in his aggression.

Adathin intercepted, reaching out and clutching Lhoris by the collar. "Let her go," he seethed, deep and low, like the growl of an animal about to lash out.

Lhoris eyed Adathin critically, but eventually let her arm free. He stepped back and straightened his shirt as if he was the one inconvenienced. "You've done it now, Mistwalker. Now we see that the wayward son—the family's lone wolf—is nothing but a black sheep." Lhoris stood straighter, sneering devilishly. "The Spellbound Arch will hear of this. The Elvish High Council as well. Oh, mark my words. I'll even send a courtesy letter to your father. I'm sure he'll be thrilled to learn about all you've done here."

With that, Lhoris turned on his heel and stalked away.

"And what have you done, prick?" Adathin muttered under his breath. Lhoris ignored him and stepped outside the room, turning just for a moment to smile gleefully at the scene.

"My, oh my," Master Aracan said. "Now I'm *really* interested."

"We encountered some goblins in the Dimlight District," Adathin said. "We were trapped, and Soren freed us. Fought off a few on the way out. They stabbed him for his trouble. It was my fault. My fault he was wounded. My fault we were in danger at all."

"Danger is all part of a mage's calling. And, fault or not, it matters little." Master Aracan hummed softly to himself. "I can't heal this wound. No mystic can. That blade that pierced him was poisoned. See here, the lines of black." He traced Soren's wound. "It's from a plant known as magebane. Rare, expensive, and illegal. It's hard to imagine some lowly goblin just having the plant lying about." Master Aracan shrugged his shoulders. "Well, in any case, I'll keep *Ais.* Frost here under observation while I send for the requisite supplies."

Maxim pushed his way forward through a gawking group of whispering students. "W-W-What are his chances?"

Master Aracan eyed him dangerously, stepping away from Soren, who groaned in pain, but seemed desperate to keep on a straight face for the other adepts, who now clambered to his side to ask him a multitude of questions.

"If you must know," Master Aracan said. "His chances are around fifty-fifty. Without the proper healing herbs, even rarer than the magebane itself, then healing is completely up to him. To his body and its natural immunities. The magebane reacts with latent aethryis in a victim's body. It attacks it, like a disease. It'll feed on him until either he overcomes it, or succumbs to it. It's as simple as that. Death is the worst case scenario. There is also a chance he will be free of the burden of magehood entirely, reduced to being a regular human, unable to draw aethryis ever again. Best we can do is make him comfortable while we wait to see which."

The news shuddered Kyra to her core. Never able to draw aethryis again... somehow that sounded worse than death.

Armeya gasped. "And there is nothing *we* can do? Can we not find said healing herbs?"

Master Aracan shook his head. "I've no sense of where to even look. As I've said, the herbs are rare. You can ask around, if you must, but don't be discouraged if you find nothing. His fate is no longer in our hands."

"Healing herbs... Master, how long does Soren have?" Adathin asked.

Master Aracan took on a considering look on his face. "Five days before the poison fully takes hold. A few more as it ravages him and after... we'll just need to see."

Turning to Soren, Adathin said, "Don't worry, I'll save you." Then the man forced his way through the crowd of adepts towards the exit.

Soren coughed. "Appreciate it, leader," he called to Adathin's back. His eyes suddenly rolled, and he closed them. It looked as if he had finally passed out.

Kyra turned to witness the startled looks of Maxim, Armeya, and Iona. She shared in their shock. After a moment of silence, she gave each a small, knowing nod—nothing needed to be said between them. Turning, she followed Adathin, and the others were quick on her heels.

CHAPTER 18

DESTINATION

Journal Entry

Year: 831 E.B

The weather had been blisteringly hot that summer season. So hot, in fact, that I took to wearing far more revealing clothes than I normally would have liked. Despite that, I wore my singular glove—my shame. I hid my scars because of cowardice.

And I remain the same coward to this very day.

In the market, Master Lu'ce had snatched a young man by the back of the collar. As she did, various brightly colored fruits fell out from beneath his drab, holey and unwashed brown shirt. The fruit struck the ground, some break opening, spilling their innards to the thirst of the dirt below, which ate it eagerly.

A rather large man had come lumbering up, clearly exhausted and out of breath, each gasp coming labored and hard. "T-T-Thank ye'," he had said. "Been tryin' to catch this one fer' a while now."

Master Lu'ce had looked at the man and then back at the boy. He was skinny, nearly skin and bones, and his hair was sandy brown, with flecks of actual sand strewn about. It was obvious he hadn't bathed in days, at the very least. Perhaps longer. I had wished to step away as his scent pierced the shroud of my nostrils, forcing its way in. Yes, the boy clearly had needed a long perfumed bath.

"Why?" Master Lu'ce had finally asked after taking in the situation.

"Why?" the man had replied. "Theft, of course. I thought you knew, given that you caught him for me."

Master Lu'ce shrugged. "Just a guess, to be honest. I have a knack for sussing out trouble. And this one," she looked at the boy whom she still held firm, "this one is trouble."

"Let me go!" the boy had demanded, struggling and squirming in Master Lu'ce's grip. I had recoiled, for I knew that once my master had her grip on you, there was no escape. I had learned that painful lesson many times before.

"No, I don't believe I will," Master Lu'ce had said, turning back to the heavy-set man. "So, what did he steal, and why?"

"Some fruit, as you can see," the man had said. "Likely some cheese as well, although the sand-scrubs that frequent here may be the culprit as well, I suppose. As for the why, because he's a thief! Always has been, like his father before him. Bless the Builders that man is gone. Too bad he couldn't have taken his spoiled acorn with 'em."

Master Lu'ce had raised her hand, demanding silence. Turning to the boy, she had asked, "Is this true? Did you steal from this man? Are you nothing but a thief?"

"No!"

Master Lu'ce had given him a leveled glance.

"... Yes, I stole from him."

"Why?"

The larger-set man stammered as he said, "W-W-Why does it matter? The law is the law!"

Master Lu'ce glared at him before asking again, "Why?"

"He doesn't sell to me!" the boy had said. "Even if I scrounge up the money, he won't sell. None of them will. I... I take odd jobs out on the farms. Stable work here. Harvest there. Those are the good months. The farmers and ranchers

typically feed me, but in-between seasons, or when I can't find work, they want me gone, so they starve me out. They try to charge ten-times more than anyone else, if they sell at all. All because of my father."

Master Lu'ce had clicked her tongue. "Tsk, tsk, Ait. Merchant. Naughty, naughty. Sins of the father leaves the entire world with nothing but murderers and thieves. Is it true what the boy says? Do you and the others refuse to offer a fair price for goods?"

The merchant had taken a long step back, clearly feeling the situation turning. "That's our right!" he had protested. "We've no obligation to coddle nor care for the boy. His own father didn't even want him. It'd be better if—"

"Careful merchant," Master Lu'ce had said, bringing her gleaming ringpact into full scope. "Choose those next words wisely."

As the merchant's eyes came to rest on the ringpact, realizations set in...

Mage! He bowed his head low. "Apologies to you and the Spellbound Arch," he had muttered.

Master Lu'ce had finally drawn her attention to me as she asked, "Kyra, what do you think should be done?"

I looked over at the boy, and he shied away from my glance. He was a coward through and through. I didn't hate him for it. Far from it. We were cut from the same cloth.

"The law is clear," I had said. "And it's as the merchant says, they are under no legal obligations."

Master Lu'ce had sighed, taking her free hand and resting it on her forehead. "Such a bland answer. So black and white. Kyra, how many times have I told you? The world is various shades of gray. I'll show you." she released the boy, quickly reached into her pocket and shoved a small sack of coins into his quivering palms. "Take the unbroken fruit and leave the rest for the birds." The boy looked at her and then back at the merchant before he found what little courage he had as he briskly picked up two apples and an orange, leaving the few other pieces. "Take it and leave this place. That's more than enough for a train or carriage ride into a proper city. You can find work there. Permanent work. Start a life. Have a family. I recommend you not follow in the footsteps as the one who sired you and keep to the honest path."

The skinny boy with the sandy hair nodded with a glint in his eye as he walked away.

The merchant found his voice as he said, "But some has to pay—"

"I will," Master Lu'ce had replied. "Here," she pulled out a single coin, rolling it between her gloved fingers. I could sense the aethryis in the air from the enchantment on the gloves she wore. The coin came to rest on her thumb as she casually aimed forward and flicked it. The coin had clanged loudly, reverberating in the air, and I could barely see its bright form flash before my eyes as it struck the merchant in the stomach. The man doubled over, the coin and him falling to the burning dirt.

Master Lu'ce turned away as if nothing had just transpired and I had followed closely behind.

"What is right by law is not always what is right," Master Lu'ce had said. "You would do well to remember that."

Kyra caught up with Adathin just outside Haven Teashop. She had previously lost him in the fog and the crowds, but his mention of herbs... she knew this had to be the place he had stormed off to.

"It's my fault," Adathin muttered under his breath, not even turning to acknowledge her. "This is why I never wished to be a leader. Not of a circle of mages, nor of my own House. I never wanted others to rely on me."

The tone of deep-rooted sadness was unmistakable. It was a feeling she knew all too well. Not knowing exactly what to say or how to act. Remembering old lessons with her master, she placed a single hand on his shoulder comfortingly. "Let's just get some tea and figure out what to do next." Truthfully, she had no clue what they could do at all.

Adathin smiled with sadness in his green eyes. "Well, if anyone has the healing herbs we need, it would be Katia. This is as good a place as any to start my search."

"Our search," she corrected, and he smiled. She doubted they would find anything here. Magebane was rare—rarer than rare. And its counter was supposedly even rarer. She didn't even know its name, just that it existed. She squeezed Adathin's shoulder harder. "Let's just go in and sit. We'll... figure something out." She had little hope of that.

Adathin nudged the door open, and she followed, noticing the entire place was filled to the brim with people. It seemed as though the tea shop had been occupied by all manner of folk, from centaurs, dwarven, human, elvish, and yes, even some goblins all shared the tiny space. It was hard to hear anything other than the passionately mixed voices of the patrons. It was even harder to breathe. Luckily, two elvish, a man and a woman, stood and exited the teashop in a huff, muttering something about not receiving their refreshments in a timely manner.

She claimed the table and chairs before anyone else could. She expected the other patrons to stare at them. A female mage and an elvish man alone... but none did. It was as if they were invisible. A strong waft of a potent plant which hung overhead caused her nose to crinkle. It was then that she noticed Adathin studying her. He suddenly burst out in a laugh, and she couldn't help but reciprocate. It was a strange feeling. Laughter. The muscles in her face were... unused to the strain. Quickly, she hid the smile behind her gloved hand, trying not to look too embarrassed.

"Fancy seeing the two of you here," Katia said, her one wing as luscious as ever. Where had she even come from? Her mouth went suddenly smooth as she glanced between the two of them. "In fact, you two seem to be getting along well. Quite well, I must say."

Adathin sputtered. "No-no... no, but I'm glad you're here. We simply required your... unique expertise." His eyes suddenly trailed far off. Distant. "It's someone from our circle. He's been... stabbed by a goblin's blade." He peered at the group of goblins in the corner and a nervous sweat broke out on his forehead as he whispered, "One poisoned by magebane."

"*Magebane...*" Katia's eyes became sharp at knives in the night, and her tone paired. "Nasty little weed. Well, for mages anyhow. Who was this unfortunate soul?"

Adathin went mute and Kyra strengthened her resolve as she replied, "...Soren."

Katia dropped the glass she was holding, and as it shattered against the wooden floor. All eyes in the teashop were drawn towards them. Katia spun and shot a warning look at them all, and the patrons returned silently to their own business. "*Frost-boy...*" she said somberly. Shaking her head as if to snap herself out of a trance, she added, "He's always been too eager to prove himself. Too restless and foolhardy. I told him it'd be the death of him. I warned that boy so many, many times. If he thinks—"

Adathin interrupted, replying, "We were hoping you could help us. And sorry, time is of the essence."

"Help you," Katia replied. "How—"

"Don't start without us!" Iona, Armeya, and Maxim bursted into the teashop, each wheezing breathlessly as if they had run the entire way from Dragrin's. Perhaps they had.

"You left us," Iona said, straining and leaning on a wooden beam. "You didn't say where you were heading."

"Y-Y-Yeah!" Maxim replied. "We j-j-just wanna h-help."

Armeya nodded to their words, and they all encircled the small table. Adathin rose and offered his seat to Armeya, who declined. Since everyone else stood, she did so as well, sliding her chair back in as she did. They must have looked foolish to others, each with hard-set eyes and determined faces.

"It looks like you have assembled quite the entourage," Katia said. "You'll need it if you want to help young Frost-boy."

Adathin tapped his foot eagerly. "So you'll help us? I would be in your debt."

Katia straightened her long dress, her wings fluttering ever so slightly. "A debt owed by a Mistwalker... interesting." Her eyes ran over the length of her shop, and at the corner of her mouth there was a tug of a smile. Her eyes came back down to rest on Adathin. "Help will depend on what your definition of the word is. If anything, I can guide you to what you need... roughly. It's a plant... named evarch, otherwise known as a moonwillow. Its healing properties are legendary, almost as legendary as its rarity. But I can assure you, it exists." She shifted her dress to show an old scar on her body, jagged and deep, with black lines etched from the center. Whatever blade had made those cuts must have been forged from the essence of malice and hate. "I was once on the cusp of life and death. Teetering the line. My mate at the time, Citrun, searched and found the evarch. He used the entire plant, boiled it and served it to me before he... died."

Kyra glanced at the others who held shocked expressions on their faces as she asked, "He died?"

Katia nodded.

"It was a noble sacrifice," Adathin said.

Katia's eyes went dark as she replied, "It was a stupid sacrifice. I told him there was enough for the both of us. *I told him!* But no, he wouldn't listen. He insisted I take the entire dose for myself. I... I..." She trailed off as soft tears glistened in the corner of her eyes and her one wing seemed to sag with regret and loss. "I still miss him still. That stupid man..."

That was also an emotion she knew all too well. That frustration to mask the sadness. Anger to mask the pain.

Katia stood straighter. "Enough of my musings. What's done is done. If what you say is true about Frost-boy, you'll need to leave. *Now!* Luckily, the herb isn't too far a journey. About half a day's ride north from the town of Oldrock. If I'm not mistaken, the train runs straight through the town. Lucky." Adathin smiled, and he obviously was trying to hide his excitement. "Take horses north for half a day until you come to Northbell Woods. Then, follow the *lightbugs;* they'll lead you straight to an old temple, if your desires are genuine. The temple was made to worship those who heal. At its peak, only under the light of the moon, shall your prize await. Hurry, Frost-boy has about a week's time before the poison erodes his magic. Eventually, it'll drain him completely and after... Well, only luck can determine his fate then. Unless..."

"Unless we have the moonwillow." she replied.

Katia nodded. "Unless you have the moonwillow."

Adathin glanced around, staring into each of their eyes. His people. His circle. None turned from him. Determination; everyone wore it plain on their faces. When his eyes finally came to rest on hers, a wide smile blossomed on his face as he said, "We have our destination and our mission. Come, let's prepare for the journey."

Journal Entry
Year: 833 E.B

It was a battlefield, not a small skirmish, as it had been described. The Spellbound Arch had a way of... bending the truth. It never sat right with me. The deception. The lies.

Until...

As always, Master Lu'ce had been as an unbreakable force against the Spellbound Arch's enemies. This time, it had been a group of kobolds, crazed from the chemicals that lay deep in the earth and lashing out at a nearby settlement. This one hadn't even a name yet, being occupied by only a few human settlers whom had struck out on their own with the promise of riches dancing in their heads.

Fools, the lot of them. They had so much already. Health and family. Things I had no longer had. Things I couldn't even remember ever having. How could they not see how rich they were? How could they have been so blind?

"Where is she?" A disgruntled man had asked. His face and body were littered with deep scars, but he didn't even seem to notice the pain. The physical pain anyway, for there was something much more pressing to him... his daughter was still missing.

I had found his daughter in the attack's aftermath. The father had called it right—the girl had been inseparable from a small wooden horse she had always carried; it was the only thing I could use to identify the body, ravaged and damaged as it was. Kobolds were not carnivorous by nature, but crazed on deep-earth fumes, they could no longer reason what was proper. There was no cure for their ailment either, only peace in oblivion.

I had felt for the father—I really had. I've also known what it is to lose. What it feels like. I could still see it there in his eyes, beneath the fear... hope. I had not wished to kill it, but truth was the only comfort I could provide.

"We found her," I had said, keeping my voice calm and steady, despite my racing heart. "She was— "

Master Lu'ce had silenced me with a glance. Her face forbade me from speaking further. I swallowed hard.

"She was..." the father had replied, waiting on those next words.

"She is gone," Master Lu'ce had replied matter-of-factly.

The hope flickered out of the father's eyes. His last hope. His wife... his son... and now his daughter—gone! He was alone now. Truly alone. As I was. As I am.

"How?" the father had asked, barely able to contain himself. "Was it... quick? Painless?"

Thinking back to the corpse, I had known without a doubt that the girl had suffered.

"It was painless," Master Lu'ce had said, giving her another glance that told me to remain quiet. "She succumbed to the fumes of the mines quickly. She likely didn't even know what happened as she slipped peacefully into rest."

The girl's body had not been in the caves at all, but just outside. We hadn't even gone into the mines below for risk of exposure ourselves. Instead, we had burned the kobolds out and Master Lu'ce had struck them down with her whip like the rabid animals they were.

"Her body," the father had said. "When can she be returned to me? I—I must bury her next to her mother. Yes... t-t-that's what she would want."

"She'll be returned as ashes, I'm afraid," Master Lu'ce had replied. "We cannot risk the toxic gasses infecting any others. I am... sorry for your loss. We will be as respectful as we can with her."

The father winced at that, but nodded and accepted that it needed to be done. He walked away, his heart full of grief, and as he did, I turned to Master

Lu'ce and asked, "Why did you lie to him? His daughter met a cruel fate. A terrible end."

Master Lu'ce looked back at me and, surprisingly, smiled. "The truth, unlike so many tell you, does not always bring peace, nor closure. A lie, told with the right intentions, is sometimes better than a cruel truth."

A lie could be better than a cruel truth. I wanted to doubt Master Lu'ce's words. I really did. But what she said rang true. I solemnly wondered what my life would be if I never knew the truth of my own sins. To be blissfully unaware of the chaos I had created with my own hands.

Kyra wasted no time, hastily stuffing a small bag with the essentials for her journey: a deep-pocketed coat and other crucial items. Fall's chill was beginning to settle in, and heading north promised a further drop in temperature.

The door to her quarters banged open and promptly slammed shut, jolting her attention. Aluriel marched purposefully toward her, an unmistakable anger etched on the elven woman's face. Before she could react, Aluriel seized her by the front of her magecloak, pulling her so close that the lingering scent of wine on the woman's breath filled her nostrils and strands of her tousled hair brushed against her nose.

"What do you think you're doing?" Aluriel demanded in an accusatory tone. The woman's grip loosened on her magecloak, and Kyra instinctively stepped back, uncertain of how to respond.

"I-I..." Kyra stammered, her mind instantly going blank. What had she done to this woman?

Aluriel sighed condescendingly. "Typical Human; only thinking of yourself and never of the consequences. I suppose I shouldn't blame you, you're just acting within your true nature and—" she tapped her head dismissively, "well, I'm trailing off. Adathin, my brother... how did you manipulate him into this foolhardy plan to find some moon herb or the like? You are causing genuine problems for him, I hope you know. And his problems ultimately become *my* problems."

Kyra struggled to control her rising anger, but failed as she retorted, "I've not tricked him into anything." Softening her tone a tad, she added, "Adathin cares for his circle, and for the mages he leads. Unlike you."

An understanding seemed to blossom in Aluriel's eyes. It was an unwelcome revelation.

"My brother? Lead? *Ha!*" Aluriel offered a coy smile. "But I see it now... you've taken a fancy to him. My brother, I mean. How could I've been so blind?" She waved a finger teasingly. "*Tsk, tsk,* naughty, naughty."

"How—How dare you!"

"How dare I?" Aluriel said dangerously. "No, how dare you!" The woman circled her like a cat stalking prey. "Such relationships, as you know, are immoral, and worse, illegal. A human and an elvish; the mere idea makes my stomach churn. Your kind is only a small step above those damnable uncanny. Listen," she strode ever closer, "abandon any thoughts of Adathin. Nothing can come of it. Nothing *will* come of it. Even my foolish brother would never fall for a lesser being like yourself. Any feelings you believe to be genuine are only projections. Give them up or we'll be forced to revisit this conversation. I won't be so understanding a second time. Oh, and one last thing, Elder Reylar wishes to speak with you. This is the last message you'll hear from me. Have a *pleasant* trip."

With that, Aluriel stalked back out of the room, as if carried by the wind, doing her best to mimic a goddess made of flesh and bone.

The mention of Elder Reylar made her breath catch. Kyra swallowed hard. Nothing good could come from this.

She knocked on the door of Elder Reylar's quarters three times, each rap more firm than the last. The door, made of darkened wood—perhaps walnut—was thick, not hollow. It made a deep sound. Faintly, a voice from the other side of the door beckoned her to enter.

She turned the latch and pushed the door clear, revealing a humble yet fanciful arrangement of furniture. To her right, a small work desk with cubbies filled with decanters of liquors of various colors and sizes. To her left, a long table, likely made from the same wood as the door, with a few chairs at its edge arranged formally.

"Please, *Ais.* Ravenblood, take a seat."

Kyra spun around to find Elder Reylar seated and scribbling behind the work desk. How had she not noticed him before? He was a bear of a man, broad-shouldered, with a rough, untamed beard of dark-brown with layers of gray throughout. He extended a hand, pointing to the open seat opposite him.

Taking the seat as instructed, Kyra crossed her arms and leaned on the table, but a stern look from Elder Reylar caused her to flinch back. She decided to hold her hands by her side instead.

"What did you call me for, Elder?" Kyra asked

"I believe you know why you're here," he replied, snatching a decanter behind him with a light-colored liquid inside. "Do you partake?"

She narrowed her eyes. "That's prohibited for adepts by the Spellbound Arch... sir."

Elder Reylar laughed. "So it is. So it is." He poured himself a finger into an awaiting glass, took a sip, and wiped excess liquid from his beard as he sighed heavily. "Disobeying an order to let the incident go from Dimlight. Starting a brawl with one of the pactless. Openly fighting a horde of goblins in full view of other citizens of our fair city." He clicked his tongue. "For one who is so concerned with rules, you lot sure relish in breaking them." He pointed back to the empty glass in front of her. "Last chance. Are you sure?"

Kyra gulped. "N-No, sir... but one thing, the pactless started the fight with us. It was that man, Salvator."

Elder Reylar's eyes widened. "The Skinner kid? *Bah,* what were you thinking, Willow?"

"Sir?"

Elder Reylar finished his drink, setting it lightly on the table. "I shouldn't have said that. Put it from your mind. Besides, we're here to talk about you and your circle."

"Sir, with all due respect, perhaps you should have this conversation with Adathin. I wouldn't feel comfortable undermining him."

Elder Reylar stroked his beard. "Loyal then? Good to see. Perhaps I should have spoken to Adathin, but I've decided to speak with you instead. I know what you lot have planned. Soren *Ais* Frost... he comes from a prominent family himself. His loss of magic would send waves through the adepts that I'd best avoid. His death even more so. So, this trip of yours, I permit it. Hells, I'll even excuse any lessons you miss as a favor from me to you, but I would have you do one more thing for me."

Kyra stood straighter. "Anything, sir."

Elder Reylar smiled. "I know of the treasure you seek, but I would ask for something else. Nothing spectacular, but when you're in those Builders' ruins, please look out for a special ore."

Intrigued, she asked, "An ore? Like a rock? What does it do? What does it look like?"

"'What does it do?'" Elder Reylar mimicked. "This is a fair question, but one I won't answer. As for what it looks like, the ore itself has a soft, red glow. It may be tricky to find, hidden in the shadow of the ruins as it is, but I implore you, please find it. Bring me back a single cluster, and, if possible, do not share this information with anyone else."

"Not even with Adathin?"

"Especially not." She must have gotten an uneasy look on her face, because the elder soon added, "I know I ask for a lot. And I know it may be tough to lie to—"

She raised her hand to silence him. "I understand. There are times when the truth is not worth speaking. That the lie is for the best of all. It will be done."

Elder Reylar smiled wider. "You know, I've spoken to your mentor, Master Lu'ce before. Fine woman—even finer mage. And it appears that she is a fine teacher as well."

Kyra nodded. "She is the best."

"*Hmm.*" Elder Reylar returned to his seat, pouring himself another finger of liquor. "*The best...* we'll just have to see about that."

CHAPTER 19

LIGHTBUGS

The train screeched to a grinding halt, letting out a blaring of its horns and the roar of its engines as they were slowly shut down. She had arrived. Her trip had been a relatively short one, only around half a day's time. During it, Kyra had ridden out of the perpetual bleak fog of Mistbreak and into the sun. The brilliant, blinding sun! It was the first she had seen of it in months, and she scarcely remembered what it looked or even felt like.

She had sat alone; Adathin as well. Iona and Maxim had oddly seated together, sharing an occasional laugh between each other, as if they were old friends. Armeya had disappeared into another cart entirely, and Soren's absence from the group was sorely noted. She found herself missing the man's ability to make light of any situation. For the first time, she could feel the collective mood—it was not pleasant.

Kyra rose, shouldered a small bag, and brushed past an elderly couple. They had been gawking at the scenery the entire way, pointing out each and every tree, rock, or cloud that reminded them of something from their youth. It was sweet at first, but their insistence on drawing everyone into their reminiscence had grated on her nerves. The others of her circle looked to agree as nobody would meet the couple's eyes as they walked past, exiting the train. She followed closely behind.

Kyra stepped into the light. The sun. *Heat!* It felt like it had been an eternity since she had felt actual sunlight on her skin. Usually, she was not one for the sun nor warmth, but after being deprived of it for many months, it was a breath of fresh air. The smell of warm bread on a winter chilled morning. Refreshing. Utterly rejuvenating.

There was another thing that caught her attention. Even though the plume of smoke leftover from the train lingered in the air, there was a sense of cleanliness about the place. It was something that she had never attributed to Mistbreak, and something she just realized she missed when she had lived with Master Lu'ce.

Looking out over the small village of Oldrock, Kyra couldn't help but be brought back to her childhood home. Well, what had been her home before she had destroyed it. It had been so long ago now. She clutched her gloved hand to her chest. Perhaps she was supposed to have grown up in a place like this, instead of as a ward to a master mage. Grown up as an admirer of warmth and sunlight. A child of fertile earth. Perhaps she was supposed to have married a simple farmer. To have become a simple wife. To have raised children. All of those avenues had slammed firmly in her face the day she incinerated her own family's homestead. Family included. No, she put the thought clearly from her mind. She was a mage, and nothing about what had happened would have changed that. Her destination always led to here. Always.

Adathin's hand suddenly came to rest on her shoulder, and she jumped with a start. He eyed her curiously as he muttered softly, "Just checking on you. You seem... out of it. Are you alright?"

Kyra brushed him off. "I'm fine. It—I mean this place... it reminds me of something. A memory better left forgotten."

Adathin nodded in understanding.

Iona shot her a stern expression. "We all have 'em. I don't think there's a mage alive that doesn't have regrets. Secrets they'd rather not share. Best not to wallow in them. Especially now." A smile crept onto her face. "Come, let's see the mayor of this *blossoming* city."

Maxim nodded to Iona's words and followed her as she went.

"Shall we?" Adathin said, holding out a hand to help her down a small ledge.

What did the man expect from her? That she would reach for it? That she would go skipping daintily through the countryside with him? Aluriel had made it quite clear that he thought of her as a lesser. Perhaps something akin to a pet. All of the elvish people did. It was a lesson she had learned long ago when living with Master Lu'ce, but that she had somehow forgotten.

Kyra walked by without an acknowledgement. There was something about Adathin's presence now that irritated her. She couldn't place it, but she could feel his eyes following her. She refused to give him the satisfaction of turning back. There was a grumble from behind as Adathin stalked forward like a chastised child sent to his room by his parents. She couldn't find it in herself to care. If he could fool with her feelings, then she could return the favor.

As she stepped off the platform, the sun's rays played daintily in her eyes, casting a warm glow on Oldrock's quaint surroundings. The air held a mixture of village scents—freshly baked bread, earthy fields, and the distant, misty flow of a nearby river. The sound of chirping birds filled her ears, creating a contrast to the industrial clangor of Mistbreak.

The townsfolk of Oldrock glanced at them with a mix of curiosity and caution. The elderly couple from the train continued their animated discussion about the similarities between Oldrock and other places they had previously been, blissfully unaware of the indifferent gazes they received.

Kyra hesitated for a moment, taking in the picturesque scene. The village, with its simplicity and warmth, tugged at the edges of her memories. Yet, she pushed those thoughts away; they were there with purpose.

Noble purpose.

Kyra inquired with a few of the village patrons about the location of the mayor's residence. The inhabitants of Oldrock, all human, regarded her with suspicion, some even with outright derision. Hushed whispers about mages causing trouble reached her ears more than once. The palpable distrust lingered, but reluctantly, they pointed her in the right direction... eventually.

She knocked on the mayor's door, and a small plume of dust fell into her hair as it cracked open. Shaking herself off, she pushed open the door and entered. Inside, Maxim sat on a small stool near a roaring fire; she speculated about who would light a fire in the middle of the day until she spotted a small cook-pot hanging from metal rods above it. The aroma of cooked meat filled the air—beef, seasoned with various herbs and spices, no doubt. Her stomach grumbled, and she secretly hoped that the mayor would offer her a bowl. Master Lu'ce had always said her appetite was of legendary proportions and that she should never shy from a free meal.

Iona and Adathin stood side by side, engaged in conversation with the mayor—an elderly woman with gray hair almost as long as her entire body. The tips of her hair hovered just above the floorboards, prompting her to wonder silently about the time it must take her to clean and dry it daily. The woman tried to stand straight, but age had not been kind and her body groaned in agony. She seemed stuck in a perpetual slump.

"Ma'am," Adathin said, pleadingly. "I assure you, we mean you no harm. Nor that of your people. We seek a special herb to help a friend, nothing more. The actions of previous mages do not concern us, nor define us."

The mayor chewed on her lip for a time before coming back with a crooked smile that made her seem like a witch from a child's tale. "Doesn't concern ya'?" she said with a heavy accent. "That sums it up right, mages are always looking out for themselves. They care not for us normal folk. We only feed and clothe ya', we do. Where do ya' think you get your meat from? A city? *Bah*." The woman flailed her arms in exasperation. "Uppity mages. Uppity elves."

Adathin looked to be at his wit's end as Armeya chimed in to save him. Stooping down to the woman's level, she said, "Back problems, eh?"

The mayor narrowed her heavy-set eyes. "Yeah, what of it?"

"My parents own a ranch," Armeya said. "I worked on it myself for many years, until my magic came, that is. I know what sorts of injuries happen. I know what people like you do for us. What you sacrifice for us. Forgive my friends; they don't know our ways and lack the proper manners. City folk, am I right?"

The mayor smiled, revealing herself to be a sweet elderly woman, and not a wild witch of the woodlands. "Oh, child," she said. "It warms my heart to see one of our own in a magecloak. You understand. Truly, you do; look at those calloused hands. Come, come, you all look tired. Here, eat."

Maxim perked up at the mention of food, but Adathin replied, "Sorry, ma'am, we don't have the time—"

"As I said, rude." Armeya cut-in, quickly hurrying to the cook-pot and serving a hearty helping into a bowl, handing it over to Adathin. He stared defiantly at it before finally accepting his fate.

"Thank you," Adathin mumbled softly.

The mayor beamed in delight. "That's better. Now eat, all of you."

One by one, they took turns getting their own bowls of stew. As expected, thick chunks of beef floated in a deep brown broth, accompanied by various vegetables and spices. As she ate, sprigs of sweet and savory herbs clung to her teeth. She drank deeply of the warm broth until nothing remained in the bowl. It was delicious. A hearty home cooked meal made with love. She couldn't remember when it was the last time she had eaten one.

As she ate, the mayor wasted no time sharing local gossip and problems the small town faced—ranging from a lack of rain to landslides and fires. Then she spoke of the uncanny they had recently dealt with. Oldrock kept a small militia to handle any sort of banditry, but goblin packs had taken to raiding their grain stores. Then, overtime, more. Despite their efforts, nothing was seemingly safe from pillage.

Armeya listened intently, nodding to the woman's every word. After all was said and done, the mayor agreed to lend them a few horses and provide food and water free of charge. Armeya had proven to be a shrewd negotiator, but still, Adathin insisted on paying the mayor for her troubles. He had pulled out a small sack and handed it to her. She bowed generously and then, when she peeked inside, she nearly dropped it, her mouth going slack. The mayor insisted it was far too much, but when Armeya glanced at the money sack for herself, her expression nearly matched the mayors.

"Are you sure you can't stay?" the mayor asked, almost pleading now. As quick as she had been to anger, she seemed equally quick to friendship.

"We can't," Adathin replied. "We have a task to do and I want to see it done. Quickly and quietly."

They quickly said their goodbyes, and she mounted her newly borrowed horse, a white mare with brown spots. She had ridden in the past before, but not extensively, making the experience rather uncomfortable for her. When each member of their circle was mounted, Adathin called for movement, and the townsfolk, who had gathered to see the commotion, parted before them as they headed north.

"*Whoa!*" Kyra exclaimed in the drawn-out manner, the way Master Lu'ce had taught her during her youth. Her horse, a white mare with brown spots, neighed and swung its head from side to side. The ride had been uncomfortable; the beast disregarded her commands the entire way, and the only reason she reached her destination was because the horse had naturally followed the others of its herd.

Armeya had seemed quite comfortable on her mount, even going so far as to show off by having the horse twirl around in a flourish. Everyone else seemed comfortable except her. Even Maxim, usually shy, now whispered to his horse with no stutter at all. Iona had pulled out her string instrument and had sung to them for most of the ride. Her songs were all melancholy, of past stories of love and loss. War and its aftermath. '*Ait' Koglu, Et' Koglu, from earth we live.*' That phrase came up frequently during her songs. There was something about it. Something foreign. Sinister.

The tall trees at the edge of a forest now lay before them—the Northbell Woods, as they were called. It was said to be a gathering spot for all manner of creatures, uncanny included. The mayor's warnings had been about goblins, but Katia herself admitted that even her people had a stronghold somewhere out in these woods. They were vast—far larger than any city could be. If a tribe or warband of uncanny hid out here, it would be virtually impossible to find them by accident. The trees themselves were still lush, despite the encroaching fall. The leaves had just begun their turn from green to red, and soon, brown. There were no paths to lead them, only sprawling deer trails heading in all different directions. That, and the fresh footprints of something that walked on two legs. Small, with pointed toes: goblins, most likely.

Iona kneeled low, running a hand over the prints. "Look here. Goblin tracks. Fresh."

Adathin nodded. "I suspected as much. If the goblins are pillaging Oldrock on the regular, then their camp must be relatively close by. It can't be out in the open, but the edge of a forest is perfect. This'll be more dangerous than we initially thought. We can't let ourselves be caught."

"We won't," Iona assured him.

Kyra wasn't so sure.

"*We* won't," Adathin agreed. "Because you all are to return to Oldrock and wait for me."

Kyra wore a shocked expression, and it was unsurprising to see that everyone shared it. "You can't go alone," she said, bewilderment marring her words.

"Soren is my responsibility. *Mine!* This was all because I couldn't leave well enough alone. Think of it as an atonement. I will risk no one else from my circle." Adathin locked eyes with her. "I won't!"

"I refuse to obey that order." Kyra jumped from her horse and stood her ground in the mud. "I'm coming with you."

"I as well," Armeya chimed in.

"M-M-Me too!" Maxim said.

Iona stood and brushed off her magecloak. "You already know I'm in."

Adathin sighed, and his shoulders slumped. He knew he was thoroughly outmatched, but he suddenly glanced up and said, "No, Iona. No. You aren't a fighter. There is little use for an enchanter where we are going.

And we need someone to bring back the horses and to get help if we don't return. That, I leave up to you."

Iona looked shocked at first, then she ground her teeth furiously. "Can't fight? Really?" She turned and slammed her fist into a tree, causing it to shake and crack, scattering bark and causing leaves to fall overhead. "Can't fight, my arse."

Amazing! Iona had a gift. Something beyond the confines of her calling. Beyond the confines of the ringpact. Many mages had them, but some did not. It seemed that Iona's talent was strength based on the augmentor's calling. Perhaps she *could* fight. Perhaps...

Adathin, however, looked undeterred as he replied, "It is our way. Enchanters are not to fight, but to support if needed. You aren't needed. Go back, as I've ordered."

Iona looked like she would challenge Adathin right then and there. There was a palpable tension in the air that could be cut with a knife. A cackling of electricity laced with fury and frustration. Then, suddenly, Iona's face calmed, as if she had come to a sudden realization. "As you command, leader," she muttered defiantly. Turning, she grabbed a rope and began tying the horses together.

Adathin gave a nod and turned to address the rest of them. "If you're to come, we'll need to proceed with caution. Move with purpose and silence. We are here for the moonwillow; nothing more, nothing less. The comings and goings of the uncanny out here are none of our concern. Nor the problems they cause."

Armeya planted her feet. "But the goblins—"

"Not our concern," Adathin repeated. "If we discover anything, we'll tell Elder Reylar when we return. Now, let's move. Iona—" It was too late as Iona had already straddled her horse, leading the others away and back towards Oldrock.

"Y-Y-You made her mad," Maxim whispered under his breath.

"That I did," Adathin agreed. He sighed, adding, "But it's for the best—she'll get hurt. It's not an enchanter's place to fight at the front.

Never has, and never will be. Come, she'll be fine. We've wasted enough time. Soren is waiting for us."

They had wasted most of the day, and by the time they had made their way even a fraction into the dense thicket of the forest, night had fallen. It was dark, and the clouds overhead ensured it would be a moonless night. Kyra fumbled around, seeking any signs of loose sticks or leaves; the temperature was rapidly decreasing, and they needed to make a fire as quickly as possible.

"So..." Adathin said, lifting a small branch in his arms. "Want to talk about it?"

She sighed, exasperated and tired from the day's ride. "Talk about what?" she asked, not really interested in speaking, but not wanting to cause anymore of a rift by not.

Adathin dropped the sticks. "About this—the attitude. What happened? I thought we were getting along. Did I do something wrong? Say something upsetting?"

"I don't want to talk about it—"

"I need to know," Adathin declared firmly. "I'm the leader of this circle. I-I need to know."

"Fine," she replied, her anger boiling over to the breaking point. "Your sister said—"

"C-C-Can you guys stop?" Maxim strolled between the two of them, picking up some of their dropped branches.

"Yeah," Armeya chimed in. "Not the time, nor the place. Have your little spat when we aren't knee-deep in a dark forest with a goblin warband potentially at our backs. That would be great, thanks."

Adathin's bit his lip. "... *Fine!*"

Kyra turned away from him. "... *Fine!*"

"*Thank you*," Armeya said, exacerbated. Then she tripped on a root and narrowly avoided falling on her face. A small chuckle crept from her throat, and before she knew it, they were all laughing together, the tension drifting away into that starless night.

Back at their makeshift camp, the small fire they managed burned a light red, and the small sizzling of meat brought pangs of hunger to her stomach. Before long, Maxim pulled a stick off the spit and handed it to her. He had sprinkled something from his bag on the meat, some kind of spice or rub.

"H-H-Here," Maxim said as she took it.

Taking a bite, Kyra's mouth was filled with the rich juices of the meat. She hadn't even been sure which animal it had originally come from, but that spice mixture Maxim had put on it, a combination of salty, sweet, and savory, made her mouth water for more. Reluctantly, she waited until everyone had their own before she placed more on a stick and set it over the fire to char.

"*So...*" Armeya said, taking a bite of meat from her own stick. As she tasted it, her eyes sparkled with delight. "*This is good, Maxim!* Really good! Oh, my..."

Maxim smiled as he ate silently to himself.

"What were you going to say?" Adathin asked.

"Ah, yes. So... how are you taking to the ringpacts? Maxim and Kyra, I mean."

"D-D-Different," Maxim said.

"Agreed," she replied. "The feeling of using aethryis is different now. Not worse, not better... just different. Every time I think I hate the ringpact, I discover something new about it."

"Like that spear you made? The one made of light?"

"Yeah... like the spear."

Adathin chimed in, adding, "I've been meaning to ask about that. That spear reminds me of my own psionic weapon, but I am curious about something: why a spear? Could it not be a sword or something else?"

Kyra set the stick down at her side and took the other from the fire. She held it out, aimed at the sky. "A spear is what I've always been comfortable with. Master Lu'ce trained me in all manner of martial weapons, but I never took to any other more than the spear. She said it must be something from earlier in my childhood, but truthfully, I can't remember what exactly."

"Can't remember?" Armeya asked. "Isn't that strange?"

Kyra shuddered, as if a particularly cool breeze had washed over her. It hadn't. The line of questions had become close. Too close to her heart. Too close to her secrets.

Armeya, undeterred, peered down at her gloved hand. "And what about that? The glove; you always seem to be wearing it."

Kyra dropped the stick and held her gloved hand close to her chest. "*I-I-I.*"

Armeya's demeanor turned from general curiosity to shock as she replied, "I didn't mean to offend you."

Kyra stood, turned her back on the group as her heart thundered. "I need some air." Hurriedly, she ran into the woods, stopping to catch her breath not too far from the light of the fire. She was upset, but not stupid. To go gallivanting into the night alone would be almost certain death. She leaned against a nearby tree and slid down. It was all she could do to keep her knees from buckling. No matter how hard she tried, she just couldn't escape it; her past. The burned flesh on her hand was a testament to her sin. One that she couldn't hide, not with the fanciest of gloves. They could see through it—she knew they could. Silently, she wondered if they would still consider her a friend if they knew what she was. What she did. If they truly knew her. If they knew what she had done to her family. The ones she had cherished. She laughed out loud for no reason in particular. Look at her now, completely reliant on what others thought of her. Of what her circle thought. Master Lu'ce said it would happen one day: that she would find people to care about, and that they would be her greatest strength and greatest weakness.

Her master had been right. She always was.

A sudden shuffling of leaves from behind startled her. She wiped her eyes free of any loose tears and saw the faint outline of Adathin as she turned.

Adathin settled on a nearby stump of an old tree that the wind had blown over after rot had routed out its very core. She felt much like the tree as he asked, "Are you alright?"

Kyra forced her shaky breath to be steady. Master Lu'ce had taught her manual breathing techniques to help with her... episodes she had once had. She had believed herself free of them, but even now she could feel the unrelenting panic threatening to overwhelm both her reason and logic.

"I'm fine," she said. "It's just... those questions are a little too close for comfort."

"You want to talk about it?" Adathin asked. "We're your circle... Hells, we may as well be your family."

"... I have no family. Not anymore."

Adathin sighed. "But you could, if you would let us—" Suddenly, small specks of light sprung from under some nearby bushes. Glittering and hovering in the dark night, there was a slight buzzing to their ascent. Lightbugs, just as Katia had said. Adathin's green eyes flared with renewed vigor as he called out, "Come here, everyone. *Hurry!*" Soon, the others came trampling through the woods, and they stopped in awe as they saw the floating lights. Adathin turned to each of them. "These are our guides. Our guiding lights."

Once the spell of the lightbugs beauty broke, Armeya put a hand to her chin, asking, "And how exactly will we tell them where we need to go? They are pretty, though."

"I... *hmm.*" Adathin seemed like he was at a loss for words.

Kyra's ringpact suddenly resonated with her, as if trying to tell her something important. She stood, holding her hand out to the lightbugs. "I think my ringpact is trying to tell me something." A surge of power swelled within her. "Wait... something's happening!"

A small orb of light suddenly flickered into existence in her open palm. It hung in the air for but a moment before traveling outwards. As it passed close to the lightbugs, they encircled it, smothering the light. They devoured it. Fed on it. When they were done, the lightbugs buzzed louder than before, and their light, but a flicker before, was now a raging inferno.

They circled her over and over and then suddenly zipped off into the woods, leaving a light trail in their stead.

Armeya turned to her. "Do we follow?"

Kyra shrugged her shoulders.

Adathin's bright golden eyes lit up with excitement. "Smother the fire quickly. *We follow!*"

CHAPTER 20

RUINS

"Get to the storage and start packing. Come on, quick now. Quick!" Willow was shouting various orders at her merry band of pactless, and they rushed to get it done. There were around nineteen of them at the moment, but more were out in the city, gathering information. She had to know what was coming.

She had to know.

"You should just let me go speak with him," Quistis suggested.

Willow set her jaw sternly. It had been an argument they'd had many times before. Too many times for her to recall. "No. Nothing good could come from talking with—with talking with Reylar. *Nothing!*"

Quistis swiftly embraced her, taking her by surprise. Her warm body was like ointment to her own wounded soul. She leaned in and whispered, "He isn't as bad a man as you think."

"And you weren't his star pupil," Willow replied.

"No... *I* wasn't." Quistis got a far-off look; a familiar one. It was typical when they discussed both of their times at Dragrins—especially when they discussed Reylar. "That was in the past—this is the now. We can't afford to be frightened of him any longer. Frightened of what he may or may not do. Frightened of the elvish or the Spellbound Arch. We need to live, Willow. *Live!* All of us. Together."

Willow placed both hands on Quistis' shoulders. She had to make her understand. She just had to. "And we will... in time. We just need more time. To make contacts. To broker deals. To—To curry favor."

Quistis' eyes rolled. "There will never be enough time. Not enough time for them, for me... *for you*." She lowered her head, whipping it around exhaustedly. "We'll... we'll talk later, ok?"

Willow nodded sadly. "Later than... I love you." Quistis nodded but did not speak the words back. She was in trouble, and she knew it, but there was nothing to be done about it now. She had to prepare for the worst. With an open goblin attack in the Dimlight District and whisperings of more to come, the Spellbound Arch was sure to respond with force. There would be mages here—powerful ones. Where she and her pactless were merely a thorn in the side of the Spellbound Arch, some wayward mage and their circle may look to make a name for themselves by arresting the lot of them. Or by wiping them out entirely.

The thought sent a chill up her spine.

Salvator wandered through the door with a disheveled look on his face. He had been quite unhappy to have been told to stay within the compound after his fiasco, but she wouldn't let his hotheadedness cause any more trouble for them. She wouldn't make that mistake again.

Willow called out to him. "You can help in the armory if that's more suited to your tastes."

"*Tastes...*" Salvator grumbled something inauspicious under his breath. "No, none of this is suited to my *taste*. Not one bit. I've proved that we are stronger than the mages at Dragrin's. That we can fight them. I say let them come—let them try to take what is ours. We'll be ready."

Willow set down the medicinal equipment she was packing and stared at the intolerable man. "So you want war? If so, you're free to leave anytime you like. Go fight your vendetta somewhere else where it won't get my people killed. It'll get you killed as well. I won't stand by while all my hard work goes up in smoke because of a rash and careless wretch of a man."

"So you're fine if I die alone, where nobody will hear or know?"

"Now you're getting it. If I don't know, I can hold out hope that you went out in the world and gained some humility. That you survived both the world and survived yourself." She forced a laugh to relieve the tension. "No chance of that, I'm sure."

Salvator looked unamused. "Our people... our people are tired of running!"

There were, surprisingly, a few others who echoed his sentiments, but did not stop to challenge her openly. She had just about enough of this cocky upstart. It took all she had not to blast him away with her lightning. "This is not the time nor the place for this. Either help us or leave. Your choice."

"I'll help," Salvator replied. "But first, I have a message for you, if you even care. It's from Quistis. She said that she went to meet an old friend and that you'd understand. Looked right pissed with you, I must say."

Willow dropped the small bundling of blankets she had picked up. "Repeat that... What did she tell you? Exactly."

Salvator eyed her curiously. "Quistis said that she went to meet an old friend. Big deal. Why's it matter?"

Willow turned and fled from the room, running as fast as her legs would carry her. She heard Salvator yell something from behind her, but his words faded underneath the beating of her heart. What was Quistis doing? Why had it come to this?

Why?

Kyra trailed the mesmerizing lightbugs as they danced through the dark thicket of plants and trees. Lost in the dense foliage, not a trail was visible beneath the mud and mulched leaves. The forest air turned musty, filled with the scent of dampness and decomposition. Wherever the lightbugs were leading them, it was an uncharted path.

"How much longer do you think?" Armeya asked. A sudden breeze made her shift uncomfortably, and she tightened her magecloak snugly around her. She mirrored the action. The magecloaks were not just for fashion or recognition; it was crafted from the clothing of the builders, complete with runes that offered protection from both the heat and the chill.

The lightbugs abruptly halted, twirling before disappearing into the night sky, plunging them back into darkness.

"*Great...*" Adathin muttered. "Now what do we do?"

All eyes turned to her; she was their arcanist. Their source of light. Of truth. Channeling aethryis through the ringpact, she summoned a brilliant light which exploded outwards, forming a small ball of swirling luminescence above her palm. It twirled and looked almost misty in form, like you could reach out and touch the vapors.

"*Pretty,*" Armeya said, her off-colored eyes glittering in the rays.

Kyra, despite her inner turmoil, had to acknowledge the beauty she and her aethryis could create. Adathin prompted her to lead, and she nodded. "Follow close," she muttered, hoping her aethryis wouldn't fade away. As they moved around her to make a singular unit, their collective heat and the pressure of the situation caused her to sweat. She had no idea where she was leading them. What if she led them into a wild animal's maw? A trap? An entire goblin warband? Panic swelled within her, and before she could succumb, Adathin placed a comforting hand on her shoulder.

"I trust you," he said, simply.

Trust—perhaps a fool's trust was what she needed. Calming herself, she pressed forward.

Through the thicket of mud and sticks they walked, being careful as to not lose each other. Suddenly, she walked headfirst into a large oak, which earned the laughter of her circle. She shared in it. If a potential untimely death wasn't the time for laughter, then she could think of no other time. In fact, it was strange how easily the feelings of joy came to her now. Dragrin's had changed her. Or, perhaps, those of her circle had. It was different than how it had been with Master Lu'ce when she was an apprentice. She had never had peers who were equal to her, only a pseudo guardian who, for better or worse, knew all her secrets. Here, with them, she could be who she wanted to be. Who she pretended to be.

They walked for a time before Maxim called out at his discovery of a white stone pillar, confirming they found the ruins. She had, somehow, led them successfully through the forest, though their return remained yet uncertain.

"Come on," she said, following the remnants of the structure. Soon, she found solid footing, and her circle broke off as the pathway widened to allow the ease of travel.

Armeya ran her hand across the stone. "It's so smooth... as if it were carved just yesterday. Wait, look here," she pointed, "Old runes. Builder runes. The Builders made this place. If so, why is it so disheveled?"

"Builders' runes don't protect something forever," she said. "It requires a continual upkeep of magic provided by enchanters. This deep in the woods, the place was long ago abandoned. I doubt any enchanters would make the trip here on a whim, if the Spellbound Arch even knows this place exists at all."

"Perhaps we should have kept Iona around."

"Perhaps," Adathin admitted. "Or perhaps not. Either way, we can't change the situation we are in now. Let's stick together as a group and—" Soft footsteps interrupted him. "*Quiet,*" he projected into her mind.

Kyra found herself being dragged behind a pillar with Adathin by her side as she dispelled her orb of light. Armeya and Maxim had slinked back into the dark of the forest just as light shone from deeper within the ruins corridors. The shadows of two figures cast outwards, cresting across the stone pillar she hid behind. A low murmuring became louder as two individuals, carrying torches, stepped into view.

Goblins.

"Oy, Suih," said one goblin, "Why is it we got patrol duty and no raidin'? Did ye' piss off da' boss man again, eh?"

Suih turned, and Kyra could just make out the loose feminine features of the goblin woman. Shorter than her compatriot, Suih had long, black nails and a hairstyle that rivaled the nape of a wolf in hunt of a dark-green coloring.

"What'cha mean, Ciek?" Suih replied. "Dis' is because you let a pig escape earlier. Cost Crezz his breakfast it did."

The goblin man gnashed his teeth, his light-green skin and long tattered ears flustered as he twisted his neck in disgust.

"You's wanna go? I promise nobody'a miss ya'."

Suih's fingers edged the hilt of a knife in her waistband, but then she burst out into laughter. "You always were the jokesta', Ciek. Come on, den', let's finish up here and get back to da' drinkin'."

The two goblins laughed together and soon moved on, leaving the cobbled walkway open and dark once more.

"*Call the others back,*" Kyra suggested in a whisper, but as she turned, she saw Adathin's face as white as if he'd seen a specter. "What's wrong?"

"I... can't," Adathin replied. "I can't even sense them. It's like what happened back in the warehouse. Something is blocking me. Blocking my psionics."

Kyra noticed a cluster of softly glowing red ores jettisoning from the stone nearby. She had seen something like it before... It looked like that goblin's dagger back in the warehouse. Her heart caught in her chest with a sudden realization: was this why Reylar had asked her to find the ore? Did it block psionic magic? If so, why would he want an object like that? Elven protection? So many questions filled her mind, but at the distant sounds of the stomping of feet, she pulled herself together.

"We'll need to figure it out later," she said. "Hurry, let's pass inside. I'm sure Armeya and Maxim will catch up to us soon."

Adathin appeared bothered, but he must have seen the wisdom in her words as he nodded and let himself be led down the cobbled road.

Without the guidance of her light, she could hardly see an arm's length in front of her own nose. They stepped crouched, walking on the balls of their feet to make the least amount of noise possible. This was crazy; an insane mission. They should turn back now. Turn back and let fate decide for Soren... but she knew they wouldn't. She knew Adathin wouldn't abandon this foolish task so easily. Hells, she suspected the man would head straight into the goblins' camp for even the chance to undo a perceived mistake. In truth, the responsibility was never his. Soren knew the danger. She and the others knew. Nobody blamed him for anything. But, like most things in life, an individual is their own harshest critic. Glancing at her own gloved hand, she chastised herself as a hypocrite.

Adathin's hand grasped her wrist. "Here," he said, pulling her in another direction. In her absence of mind, she had walked straight past the stairway entrance of the ruins. "I think this is the way."

Kyra swallowed hard. It felt as if they went into the belly of the beast. The hairs on her arms stood straight, as if sensing unseen danger. "Only one way to find out," she said solemnly.

Only one way.

CHAPTER 21

HUNGRY EYES

Armeya heard distant footsteps echo out across the cobblestones and, in a pure panicked instinct, she seized Maxim and dragged him into a nearby treeline. Pressing him against the wood, she covered his mouth as he tried to protest. After a moment, realization filled his eyes as he too heard the approaching noises.

"*Goblins,*" Armeya whispered quietly into his ear.

Maxim set his eyes as he replied, "W-W-What about Kyra? A-Adathin?"

Armeya peeked around the corner and spotted the two of them hiding behind the ruins of a stone pillar. They were far closer than Maxim and she were to goblins on the cobbled walkway ahead. No matter how hard she tried, she couldn't make out what was said between the two goblins. Turning back to Maxim, she whispered, "*We'll wait for them to move on, then join the others. We—*"

A hushed sound came from deeper in the forest, catching her attention. Scanning behind, Armeya saw nothing but empty darkness. Squinting, she could barely make out two orbs flashing in the perpetual dark; it was some sort of animal. A low growl soon followed.

"What do you smell, boy?" a voice echoed from deep in those shadowed woods. "Intruders?"

The growling continued, accompanied by the sounds of scraping feet on dirt and rustling leaves. Maxim pulled at her cloak in panic, but dared not speak.

Armeya had to act quickly. Clenching her hands together, she reached for aethryis, drawing it from the ringpact as she had been practicing. The aethryis came easier to her this time. It was a blessing when she needed it most. She thought about summoning flame to burn them away, but an overt use of aethryis would attract unwanted attention, so she decided against it. She so longed to incinerate that goblin and its pet beast, but she couldn't endanger the others for her ill-begotten vengeance. She would risk her own life, not others. It was an oath she made to herself and her former master. To her mother as well.

Reconstructing the aethryis into a strand of air, she sent it whirling outward, floating it through the leaves and thicket away from them. At its destination, she detonated the air, sending leaves flying skyward to fall down like snow petals.

"What was that?" the goblin exclaimed, and she heard the faint rustling as they and their beast stalked away.

"We need to move," Armeya whispered to Maxim.

"B-B-But what about Adathin? K-Kyra?"

"We can't risk going to them now. We'll be seen. Caught. Let's head deeper into the forest. Come on."

Maxim hesitated, so she tugged on the man's magecloak and forced him to move. Armeya sent another strand of air out, drawing the goblin even further away. Whether that second false trail of aethryis worked, she didn't know, but she continued guiding Maxim in the opposing direction, away from the ruins and deeper into the forest. They would wait out any goblin patrol and, hopefully, find a way back to meet Adathin and Kyra.

Pulling her magecloak close for comfort, Armeya couldn't help but pray for their safety.

Kyra rushed ahead, swiftly turning around a corner and pressing her back against the hard stone, which emanated a strange warmth. The interior of the ruin seemed notably warmer to her. In fact, contrasting with the gloomy forest outside, it was downright cozy. She had heard the goblin and its beast in the forest, but something else had distracted them. Armeya and Maxim, she wondered? Good, Adathin and she would have been spotted if the goblin had moved but a few more steps. She strained to listen for any signs of Armeya or Maxim's capture, but no screams reached her ears. No pleas for help. Just the sound of wind rustling through the night woods. She could only hope that those two had found a hiding place until morning.

Adathin slipped around the same corner, narrowly avoiding a collision with her. Despite the apologetic glance he shot her way, she refrained from speaking. They just stood there in silence for quite some time, as each gust of wind played through the corridors like a flute, creating a haunting vibrato in the forgotten halls. It was eerily beautiful, yet every note sent a shiver up her spine. She hadn't anticipated her life as a mage being this eventful, at least not so expeditiously. Judging by Adathin's pale face, he likely shared in her sentiments.

"It seems safe," Adathin finally said, distancing himself from the stone walls and attempting to garner his bearings in the middle of the dark corridor.

"*Safe...* I don't think you know the meaning of the word." Kyra hid her evasive smile. "But I take your meaning. The goblins patrol outside, but not in here. Why do you think that is?"

Adathin rubbed his chin, and his long ears twitched. "It can't be anything good, that's for certain."

Kyra sighed. "Thought so, but what can we do now? Go back? Try to find Armeya and Maxim? No chance of that, I think. Not in this darkness."

To worsen their situation, rain began softly pattering on the cobbled stone just outside the ruins' entrance. "*Great...*"

Adathin, surprisingly, smiled. "Actually, that may be beneficial for them. It'll make the patrols uncomfortable. The trails slick with mud. It'll wash out their scent and, most importantly, it'll douse any non-aetherical fire. The goblins will be blind. Even blinder than they already are."

"That's one less thing to worry about. I suppose we should get on with it? Find what we came here for and worry about locating those two in the morning." A sudden realization dawned on her. "Wait, can't you just reach out to them? Into their minds, I mean? Ask them if they are ok?"

Adathin got that haunting look about him; one he had been burdened with so often of late.

Kyra narrowed her eyes. "I take that as a no?"

"I'm being blocked again," Adathin replied, clearly frustrated. "I can hardly sense you from where you stand now. Armeya and Maxim? They could be dead for all I know, and I couldn't even tell—" She frowned, and he corrected himself, adding, "I'm sure they're fine. I'm just..."

Kyra held up a hand. "I know—I know. We're tired. Both of us. And it feels like we've hardly had time to breathe these last few days."

Adathin let his arm dangle uselessly at his side. "Ever since the warehouse incident. And we are still no closer to finding Freed's killer. It's all so—"

"Frustrating?"

"I was going to say infuriating." Adathin laughed. "But misplaced anger won't help Soren, nor anyone else. Let's move on and find this 'moonwillow.' Would you mind?"

Kyra then noticed how dark it actually was just further down into the ruins. She could hardly see an arm's length in front of her own nose. Drawing aethryis inward, she formed a small floating orb of light. Working with the ringpact was getting easier and easier by the moment, and she was grateful for it. Having to struggle to use even the most basic aethryis didn't bode well for their continued survival. She willed the orb of light forward, and followed close behind, similar to how they had followed the lightbugs. Adathin stayed close as well, but not too close. A small bit of hesitation lingered between them, likely stemming from their recent disagreement at Oldrock. She contemplated addressing it, but decided against it. No, now was not the time to pick at a fresh wound.

"Is it just my imagination, or did you seem irritated by me back in Oldrock?" Adathin suddenly asked.

This man! It was as if he could read her mind... perhaps he could. That gave her pause as she replied, "No, why would you think that?"

"General demeanor," Adathin said. "Something seemed off about you. Different. Unusual."

Kyra couldn't help but let her anger boil over when she said, "Nothing is off, nor different. Your sister made it very clear where you and I stand, that's all. She couldn't have made it any clearer, in fact."

Adathin grumbled under his breath. "*Ugh,* my sister sticking her nose where it doesn't belong once again. She's exactly like my father, always pushing where they are unwanted. What did she say to you? Exactly what did she say?"

It took everything Kyra had to control her anger now. "Aluriel merely reminded me of my place in the world. Yours as well. It was my mistake, really; I should've never thought that things could be different between us."

Adathin narrowed his eyes, and his cheeks flushed red. "Different between us? How do you mean?"

"Don't play coy," she replied. "The late-night talks. The tea. The covert operation... you needed a friend. And, hard as it is to admit, so did I."

"A... friend?"

"Yes, a friend." She stared at him with white-hot fury. "And I thought you were my friend until your sister reminded me that we could be no such thing. Not now. Not ever."

"But... why? Why could we not be... friends?"

"The difference between us. Humans and elvish are not partners, but merely acquaintances. We aren't equal. If anything, humans are servants of the elvish. And these," she lifted her hand to show him her ringpact, then she reached back and touched the magelock on her neck, "these are our chains. Ones that we now willingly place upon ourselves. You—you are free. Free to use your talents. Your power. Free to live your life as you see fit. Simply put, I am not. Never was. Never will be."

"*I...*" Adathin looked struck, as if she had run him through with a knife. Then his eyes went keen as he replied, "I'm not free either. I'm not free to choose my standing in the world. Nor to choose my occupation. I'm not even free to love, but I'll be damned if I'm not free to choose who my friends are." He stared deep into her eyes now, intent and direct. "And we *are* friends. Whether or not you admit it, we are. And because we are friends, I will tell you a secret."

Adathin's words stunned her as she replied, "N-N-No... you don't need to, I—"

Adathin held up a hand. "Everyone knows the story. The record of how I lost my birthright during a mind-duel with Aluriel. How I lost my right to lead House Mistwalker to my sister. What if I told you that I didn't lose it? Or, more so, I lost on purpose."

Kyra paused, leaning against the edge of the stony hall. "And why would you do that? Lose purposefully?"

Adathin seethed as he replied in a low, dark voice. "Because I hate him. My father, I mean. I... I'll never be him. And if I were expected to lead House Mistwalker, I'd have no choice. Aluriel... She's a lot more alike to him than I could ever be. So, one day, she and I struck a deal. I'd lose a duel to her, and she would spare my mind, against traditions. Win-Win. She gets to lead the House as she's always wanted, and I get out as I've always wanted."

"Then how and why did you get stuck leading a group of mages at Dragrin's? I thought that was only for the lower caste of elvish."

Adathin snickered. "Aye, it's considered low work. Those without a House or influence typically take it on, as part of the ancient deal between the humans, dwarves and elvish. Aluriel is here as payment to the Spellbound Arch. She'll work with the mages until she is called back into the Elven Council's fold. Me, I'm here as punishment. Punishment for being weak. For being cowardly. It's a sort of... excommunication. A debt. I must work with the mages until I am deemed worthy to rejoin my family. But little do they know, I have no intention of returning. Ever."

Kyra had been wrong. Wrong about everything, it seemed. Truly, Adathin was unlike any other elvish she had ever met. Perhaps they could be friends. *Perhaps...*

A sound caught her attention off in the distance. Low at first, but getting louder by the moment. Adathin seemed to hear it too, and a purple-glowing sword fell into his awaiting hand. She followed suit, summoning her spear of light. It spun outward, lighting the way forward, and that's when she saw eyes. Not two, not four... but eight. Eight glowing red eyes.

Hungry eyes.

Adathin leveled his blade forward as the creature suddenly stopped, just outside the reach of her light. "Step back. Slowly," he said.

Kyra's feet felt frozen to the ground as panic, deep and primal, welled from within her chest. Horrified to her very soul. Something about the creature's visage made her skin crawl. A soft scraping and low clattering brought her back to the here and now. She stepped back as quickly as she dared.

Adathin followed, keeping his purple blade extended out as far as he could. She could see it in his gait—he was as terrified as well.

Then there was a scuttling of dozens of tiny feet as the creature, unwilling to let them leave, broke into the light. It had four long mandibles with four eyes on each side of its face. It was long and with a carapace that looked like armored plated pieces across its whole body—a body which housed no less than twenty legs. It looked like a worm, and a monstrous one at that. No, not quite a worm, but something far more savage.

A monstrous centipede.

The creature's eyes fixated on her, and it opened its maw and roared, but instead of a deep guttural noise, it sounded as if millions of insects screamed their resentment in unison. The sounds bounced off the stone, echoing and vibrating until it physically struck her. She held her hands to her ears and screamed, but she couldn't even hear her own voice as she was drowned out.

The centipede-like creature lifted its body, easily eclipsing them until it hovered just a hand beneath the roof of the ruins.

"Run," Adathin yelled. "*Run!*"

Kyra spun and abandoned all reason, pushing her legs to obey and flee. The creature cocked its head as if curious, and then it began its pursuit. Instead of traveling on the floor, the creature instead dug its feet into the edges of the wall as it gave chase. It was fast—too fast for her to elude. As its sharp-looking mandibles came to close in around her, the creature suddenly shrieked as one of the mandibles broke off, landing to the side. A dark-green ooze spurted from the creature's missing limb, and it chittered in rage. Adathin stood between her and the creature now, his purple blade covered in that green ooze, sizzling softly until it slid off the tip.

"Don't stop," he said, as he began swiping furiously forward, driving the creature back. "Keep moving, I'll catch up."

Kyra ran for the exit, but just as she was about to step through, an orb of green spittle nearly struck her, landing in front of the entrance. It hissed and sizzled on the stone and soon melted into it.

Acid.

More skittering of legs, and the creature fell in front of her, blocking the only known exit. It seemed completely unaffected by its own acidic vomit.

"What now?" Kyra asked, jabbing at the creature with the edge of her light spear. The creature seemed entirely unbothered as the spear glanced off its armored carapace. Glancing back, she saw Adathin slowly recovering. Apparently, the centipede had crushed him against the wall in its frantic attempt to block the exit. He now stood, rushing back to her side.

"It seems we'll need to fight," Adathin said. "Can you?"

"Do I have much of a choice?" Kyra asked as the creature lashed out. Adathin swiped his sword, blocking one of the legs, but then its long tail wrapped around, swatting him like a common insect, which sent him flying back, sliding across the floor.

Once again, she stood face to face, alone with the creature. It seemed to be focused on her and her alone. Deep in those red eyes, she saw...

understanding. A deep resentment. Hate. Looking down, she recognized the creature wasn't staring at her, but at her spear of light.

Then an idea came to her.

Kyra dispelled the spear and, instead, summoned a globe of light. Then another. And another. Soon, the room was filled with them, and the creature, frantic from the illumination, attacked each one by one. As each was devoured, she dispelled it and summoned even more. Slowly, she backed away.

"Are you okay?" Kyra asked, not daring to glance down to check on the man.

"*Ugh,* I'll be fine," Adathin replied. "So that's it, huh? Your light. Now we can make our escape."

Hesitantly, Kyra shook her head. "We still have a duty, and I mean to see it through. *We* will see it through. The moonwillow; we must retrieve it."

"But—"

"We can do this."

Adathin chuckled. "You're either very brave or very stupid. And I am more so for agreeing. Can you keep it busy?"

"For a time," Kyra replied. "I'll summon a few more, and then we make a break for it. The creature seemed to come from the left corridor. Perhaps it's guarding something?"

"As good a lead as any," Adathin agreed. "Are you ready?"

Three

Two

One

Kyra broke away from the aethryis, feeding each orb a little more to hold their form for just a moment longer. While the creature was distracted, she turned and fled, Adathin at her heel. He seemed determined to place himself between her and the creature. Was it true then? Did he truly value her as an equal? Was this his way of showing it? Too much was happening to focus on that just now. First, they needed to survive.

CHAPTER 22

SCARS

"Do-D-Do you know w-where we are going?" Maxim asked, his breath coming ragged and shallow.

Armeya glanced around, pretending to know their destination—in truth, she had not a clue. Not even an inkling. She dared not summon fire to light their way, and every wayward brush of a tree limb or rustling of leaves sounded like the march of a thousand goblin feet to her ears. Panic gripped at her, and she knew she had to regain control soon or lose herself to panic. Forcing her breaths to slow, she said, "Of course I do." A beam of moonlight broke through the dark clouds above, revealing a route directly ahead. "See, a path. We'll follow it and find somewhere to lie low for the night. We'll be fine, trust me."

"I-I-I trust you," Maxim stammered, and she could see in his eyes that the man truly did. She smiled, despite her worries. Their little circle of mages was truly coming together now. There was a certain trust between them. A goodwill. She could feel it and it reminded her of home. And like home, it was filled with reliable folk. She felt honored to have found people whom she could consider friends.

Maxim let out a sudden scream, and she twisted to the sound. "What's wrong—" Her words were cut as something heavy struck her in the head, and blackness quickly consumed every waking thought. Groggily, she fought the void, but it came on nonetheless. She had let her guard down, and now the price was to be paid.

Kyra straightened her magecloak, and then her disheveled black hair as she rested beside a stone pillar. The night sky was a swirling river of black clouds and scant rays of moonlight that broke through like the silver of spawning trout. They had found a place where the ruins had collapsed, succumbing to the elements. The air outside was fresh, a welcome relief from the musky, heavy air of the ruins. They would be safe outside; at least, that is what she hoped. Safe from that creature... at least for a time. Adathin and she would wait until the morning to continue onwards.

And worst of all, she was still worried about Armeya and Maxim's safety.

Adathin settled in beside her, pulling his own magecloak snuggly around his body. He cut a splendid figure—slender, with muscular undertones. His light-golden eyes met hers, his skin reflected the faint moonlight in that ethereal elvish way. His long ears fluttered nervously.

"What?" Adathin asked, scratching behind his ears as if to play it off as just an itch, but she had been privy to his tick: his ears always gave a twitch when he was nervous.

"Nothing," Kyra replied, pretending not to notice as she settled into her depressed disposition. "Just... how did it all go so wrong? And not just this either. My adept training was supposed to be different. Hells, my life was supposed to be different. I keep thinking I'll see a way forward—a path to peace... yet it always just eludes me."

Adathin grumbled something to himself before saying, "It's just the way of the world. Trials and tribulations. The world tests us, and we have the chance to become better. Harder. Those who learn from their inevitable failures become stronger, and those who learn nothing, weaker. So we'll continue to learn. To adapt. To overcome."

Kyra chuckled. "Wonderful speech, but is that how you really feel?"

Adathin turned from her, his eyes fixated on a plain pile of rubble. "I... I don't know. It's just something my mother told me once, when we were still speaking. I've lived by those words... it's the only thing that's given me the courage to push on."

Kyra looked down at her gloved hands, running the tips of her right across the palm of her left. She could feel it even beneath the gloves—the malformation. The disfigurement.

Her penance.

"Why do you do that?" Adathin asked. "Hide it, I mean."

She wanted a distraction; to change the conversation, but there was a feeling deep inside, resonating with something Master Lu'ce had once told her. 'You'll need to trust someone sometime.' *Trust...* Perhaps this was that time. Perhaps she could share some of her burden. "I... this is what it means to be a mage."

"Meaning?"

Kyra steeled her heart as she gripped the glove, slowly removing it. She dared not even look at the hand herself—she hadn't for years. Then the words he had said gave her a small amount of courage, and she dared glance. In the small rays of moonlight, she saw it—the remnants of her hand. It still had both general form and function, but the skin was tight and scarred. Burned. A blackened mess in various shades. The scarring was vast, and even the healed skin seemed paper-thin. It was a hideous thing to behold. Grotesque. Surely Adathin would turn from her with sickness in his stomach and mind. Nobody could accept this. *Nobody.*

Suddenly, she felt warmth rush into her hand. It startled her, and she barely managed to stop herself from jumping back. Adathin's hand was now held firmly against her own. It had been so long since she had touched anything with her bare skin. And to touch another? *Never!* She had never—could never. Adathin shifted, tightening his grip around her decrepit hand, staring at her as if peering into her very soul. His warmth permeated her skin, and she felt years of tightness in the muscle fade away like water sliding from a leaf. She did not hold the tears back. She dared not try. She let them flow wild and free. Beside it all—the warmth and the touch—she could see it in Adathin's eyes... *acceptance.* Understanding and affirmation. She was accepted. *He* had accepted her.

A skittering sound drew her attention as Adathin withdrew his hand, standing before she could even react. It was a good thing he did because a moment later, the creature, the centipede-like monster, burst from the entrance to the ruins proper, its eight red eyes filled with death.

It didn't hesitate as it charged, but Adathin blocked its path, his purple sword materializing into his hands as the centipede struck with its razor-like mandible. It slid off Adathin's sword, lighting up the night with sparks as carapace met blade.

Kyra found her feet and moved, diving behind a stone pillar as her weightless spear of light materialized in her hands. She spun around, and as the creature was about to crash down on Adathin, she stabbed forward, piercing the monster in one of its red eyes. The eye exploded, sending green blood spewing across the otherwise white stone of the ruins.

The creature skittered in pain as it turned its attention back to her. Adathin used the distraction and slammed his own blade into the creature's side. The armor-like carapace deflected his attack, but Adathin was relentless as he struck no fewer than a dozen more times in a fury. Kyra matched his pace, stabbing forward to his beat. They were synced now. A singular unit. They bore down on the monster, pushing it back until they came to stand side by side. She spared him a glance, and he was smiling ear to ear—the man was actually smiling! In that moment of realization, she knew she would follow him into the hells and back again.

The creature spun and slapped Adathin with its long tail. He flew back, striking the wall, his sword falling to the ground and disappearing into nothingness.

"Adathin—" Kyra cried, only to be interrupted by the loud roar of the creature. It gnashed its mandibles together as it focused fully on her now. She backed away until her back pressed against rough stone. To her right was the open entrance back into the ruins. She could make a break for it—to draw it away. To her left, stairs led to the upper portion of the ruins where a tower had once stood, now open to the frigid night air. Suddenly, she heard the scraping of metal and saw that Adathin had recovered. The man didn't attack the creature directly, but, instead, cut away at a piece of the remaining tower. His purple blade was in his hand again, and it was, as he had told her before, impossibly sharp. With but three strikes, he cleaved the stone from under a broken walkway up above, causing the rocks to crumble and break, falling down.

Kyra wouldn't make it to the ruins now as the rocks fell, slamming against the creature's body as it skittered and howled in indignation. She was in a dangerous position, too close to the furious monster as it spun around, trying to avoid falling debris. She went up the stairs, avoiding stepping on the multiple broken staircases. Up top, looking down, the creature lay amongst the debris. Then she saw it: *opportunity!* The rocks had severely damaged one of the armored carapaces. It was open now, and she could see green blood oozing from the wound. Looking down, she gripped her spear of light firmly in her hand, and then leaped atop the creature. As she came down, she slammed the tip of her spear into the open wound, using all her strength to drive it in further.

The creature reared up straight, and she held onto her spear with all her might as the creature thrashed wildly around. It skittered and screamed in agony, its remaining red eyes going wild with fury. Eventually, the monster slammed back to the ground, and as she regained her footing, standing atop the beast, she gripped the spear in both hands and plunged it through the monster and into the ground below. With a twist, she detached the armored section and ripped the monster's head clean off from the rest of its body.

The creature fell silent as its many legs still spasmed as if the ground still laid under them as it attempted to run. The brain was gone, but the body still cried out to flee until it too fell still.

She looked at Adathin, who beamed with both shock and pride at her. She couldn't help but return the man's gesture.

CHAPTER 23

DEAL

Armeya felt a gentle swaying as her body rocked back and forth. Grunts and indistinct words punctuated her ears, accompanied by an angry voice whose demands felt strangely familiar to her, like a memory lost to time. She reached for it, but it slipped through her fingers like fine sand... Then a splash of cold water abruptly brought her back to reality.

Opening her eyes to a blinding light, she initially thought it was morning with the sun casting its tormenting rays on the outward mountains. However, as her eyes focused, she realized the clouds had cleared, revealing a night sky adorned with stars—thousands, if not millions, of them, all as bright as she had ever seen before. Even the land she came from, her parents' humble ranch, could not produce such a dazzling sight. It was breathtaking, and with a sinking heart, she realized she couldn't recall seeing even a glimpse of them since arriving in Mistbreak.

Another splash of cold water struck her, sending a shiver up her spine. Glancing down, Armeya saw goblins leering dangerously at her, treating her like an object of lust or an impending dinner—quite the strange combination.

"*Get away from her!*" Maxim protested from a nearby cage, free of his usual speech impediment. She craned her neck, struggling with the movement, and spotted Maxim who appeared relatively unharmed. Gingerly touching the back of her head where she had been struck, just above her magelock, she felt barely dried blood. She hadn't been unconscious for long, and the night was still hers. Glancing around, she saw no signs of Kyra or Adathin. Hope flickered—hope that they were still safe, though the overwhelming number of goblins still gave her pause to the prospect.

"Oy, look at this one," a goblin remarked. The uncanny's teeth cut oddly, and she could smell a sickening odor wafting from them. Beasts, the lot of them. "Those eyes! Why dey different colors? That normal?"

"More normal than you—you uncanny prick," Armeya muttered, struggling to control her anger. This place, filled with their filth, was stifling. She despised goblins—uncanny creatures she considered barely sentient. They were always ready to betray their betters. To stick a knife in their backs. Her previous experiences with them on her family's ranch involved raiding livestock and murdering ranch hands, for they knew no other way. They were slaves to their primal instincts, and she hated them for it.

"I said, let us go!" Maxim yelled, still free of his usual stutter. She wondered if it was his anger or conviction that cured him.

"Maxim," Armeya said, her voice low. Each word she spoke brought a fresh and sharp pain to her head. Seeing the sinister smiles on the goblins' faces, she added, "Don't scream. Don't give them the satisfaction. They crave it. They *need* it."

"*Armeya!*" Maxim exclaimed excitedly, as if he had expected her to be dead. "A-A-Are you okay? W-What do you mean?"

The three goblins nearest them laughed.

"They'll want to know what we know," Armeya replied. "And they'll do anything to get that information. *Anything...*"

Maxim looked dejectedly upwards towards the sky. A goblin suddenly kicked her wooden cage, rattling it. When she turned to glare at the creature, he said with a wide grin, "Boss wants to see ya'."

Oh, how she loathed them all.

The goblin reached forward to undo the ties of knotted rope that held her cage shut. Should she kill him? Set him ablaze? No, there were too many, and she needed to play for time. Time for Adathin and Kyra to seek help. Time for Iona to realize their tardiness. She just needed more time.

Armeya's cage rattled open, and the goblin pulled her out. Her knees were weak, and as she stepped down, she gave way, crashing into the muck. Cheers erupted among the goblins as they laughed and jeered at her. Almost losing her composure, she barely kept from lashing out at them.

Another goblin did the same with Maxim, pushing him forward until he stood next to her. "Oy," the goblin said. "Why's ya' so big?"

"I-I-I..."

"Ignore them," Armeya said. "They'll try to provoke you to attack. They want to rough you up a little first. It's all a game to them. A bit of sport. Don't play it, no matter what."

"... Ok."

The goblin frowned and then turned on her. "Oy, it's not nice to interrupt our bit a fun. But no worry, we's is gonna have lots O' fun later."

Armeya smiled as the goblin came close. Leaning down, as if she were going to say something in return, she instead spat in the goblin's face. Another chorus of laughter spilled from the others, but that one wiped the spittle away with one hand and then struck her in the stomach with the other. It hurt, but she barely kept from doubling over as another goblin tugged at her magecloak.

"Come on then, boss is waitin'."

Armeya let herself be led and as she walked, she got to see more of their surroundings. This wasn't just a ragtag encampment; it was more akin to a small village. Huts were built into the canopies of trees, walkways made of lumber, and pens for raising animals. Society! On one hand, it sickened her to see so many uncanny in one location. On the other hand, she was amazed that they had managed to create this much in such a harsh environment.

Maxim and she were forced to walk through slush and mud, her boots soaked through to her stockings below. The wetness burned at her skin, but she forced herself to remain straight-backed and calm; undaunted. She would not show weakness—she was a mage, and these animals would not cow her.

Eventually, the two of them were shoved into a hut that stood a bit taller and was nicer than the others. It featured fanciful adornments outside, such as animal skulls and fur skins draped in a strange pattern. It was a crude imitation of proper society, but an imitation nonetheless. However, the interior was vastly different; candles burned lightly on proper wooden furniture, including a desk, chairs, a table, and even a bed. Now these are the amenities that she would expect from proper lodging. A sick realization startled her that this 'boss' goblin might not be the same as the others. This level of coordination—the strategic theft from Oldrock with no casualties—these indicated a careful approach, not characteristic of goblins. She wondered if it could be another type of uncanny entirely—perhaps even a human or one of the elvish.

To her surprise, a tiny figure adorned in a crown of thorns, wearing a robe fit for royalty, approached. This goblin, unlike any she had seen before, held a deftly carved walking stick adorned with a red-glowing rock at the tip. Most concerning was the intelligence behind the deep black eyes. Despite her initial doubts, the leader was indeed a goblin, but unlike any she had encountered before. She just had a feeling that this man that stood before her now was different.

The goblin leader spoke in as regal a voice as she had ever heard before, saying, "Apologies for the rough hospitalities. No matter how often I tell my brethren, they seem to have issues overcoming their... baser urges. No excuses, ugliness is just that: ugly." He flourished his robe with the twist of his tiny wrist. "May I offer you something to drink? Tea? Perhaps something with more... bite?"

Armeya held her chin high, refusing to be taken in by the show. A pig in lipstick is still a pig, she reminded herself. "No—"

"*W-W-Water!*" Maxim croaked.

The goblin nodded and turned, pouring water from a gray jug into two metal cups that seemed dark and rusted with age. Maxim eagerly drained the entire glass the moment it was placed into his quivering hands.

"As I said, baser urges," the goblin remarked, shaking his head. "I feel truly awful about how we have come to meet, but let me try to make amends. My name is Kri'ed'suld, but many here just call me Kri'ed."

"Or Boss Man," Armeya replied.

Kri'ed smiled, and it appeared genuine, despite his absurdly large incisors. "Ah, that famous human wit," he said. "Oh, how I've missed it. It's one of many things I've missed about the civilized world. The fine clothing. The food—*Oh, the food!* Candies and chocolates. *Spices!* Warm coffee on a cold winter dawning. Hells, anything other than drab, burned meat." He grimaced. "You can hardly imagine the pains of being forced to live out here."

Armeya narrowed her eyes; this was not quite what she expected. The goblin poured himself a drink from a separate glass decanter. The liquid was dark and smelled of alcohol. Cheap alcohol, but alcohol nonetheless.

"Forgive me," Kri'ed said, "but this is as fine a medicine for what ails me as any other I can find."

Armeya pulled her magecloak close as she asked, "What do you want from us? Our death? Coin? Something worse?"

Kri'ed sputtered, and the dark liquor dribbled down his age-etched green face. "Death? By the Builders, no. If I wanted you dead, I would hardly be wasting my time speaking with you now, would I? As for coin... not exactly, but you could say that what I want has similar value. Or, at least, could be seen as valuable."

"Then what?"

Kri'ed smiled. "We'll get to that, but first—*sit, sit!*" He took the lead and sat in a purple plush chair. When neither of them moved to follow, he continued as if they had, adding, "As you wish. No... we do not need coin in exchange for your release. Demanding so would be illogical. It'll bring The Spellbound Arch down on us like... well, like flies on shit, excuse the language. I require something else. Something more. *Something...* that will imply a great deal of trust between both our parties."

Armeya laughed, despite her nervousness. "Trust? You want us to trust you? Never. You're just uncanny scum."

Kri'ed's smile slid from his face, leaving a deep-rooted scowl in its place. "*Uncanny.*" The word came out dangerously. "A horrid label for those deemed unfit to even be granted the name of their own species. Instead, you would lump us into one group and deem us outsiders, but we *aren't! I am not!* We have just as much right to life as anyone else. The right to respect."

"Respect?" Armeya repeated tauntingly. "*You* want respect? Don't make me laugh. I know your kind; I've seen uncanny like you countless times before. When I worked on my family's ranch, I saw your kind raid and pillage—kill and steal without empathy or remorse."

"And is your kind any different?" Kri'ed squeezed the glowing-red handle of his walking stick so tightly that his veins throbbed. "You take and kill. Steal and rape the land of its resources. Your Spellbound Arch acts as the sword hand of the Elven Conclave who serves nobody but themselves. *We* steal? *We* kill? Talk to the elven lords you serve now if you want to hold anyone to account."

Armeya was dumbfounded and, as she opened her mouth to retort, she found that she could not. This goblin Kri'ed spoke truth. He was right! Their entire civilization was based on inequality, and she was but a cog in that machine. An unwitting defender of it. She shook her head to straighten her thoughts. No, she couldn't let his words dissuade her. He obviously wanted something. Something important. Perhaps she could leverage it to her advantage. Perhaps they could make it out alive.

"I ask again," she said, "What do you want?"

Kri'ed's hand loosened on his walking stick. "For you to deliver a message, that is all."

"And what will we get in return? Our freedom, I suppose."

"That," Kri'ed replied, "and something else. It is my understanding that someone, or something, has been killing mages."

Armeya's breath caught, and for a moment, she was transported back to that warehouse. She saw the corpse on the floor and the smell of blood churned her stomach as bile ran into her mouth. Then she was back, and she wiped cold sweat from her face. "*Who—Who told you that?*"

Kri'ed waved his hand dismissively. "Unimportant, but what *is* important is that I know who it is. Would you like to know?"

"... *Yes!*"

"Then do we have a deal?" Kri'ed stood and walked to stand in front of her. He stared up at her, and her own surprised expression reflected in his dark eyes back at her. She could see that he knew he had won. He reached out and opened his hand, his long, untrimmed black fingernails dancing dangerously in front of her. "Deal?" he asked again.

Armeya spared a glance at Maxim, who seemed to be sweating profusely. He would be of no help here. She turned back to Kri'ed and stared at the goblin's crinkled old hand as if it were a dagger. Freedom and knowledge for the deliverance of a simple message. She couldn't hope to get better terms than this. Reaching out, she shook his hand, whispering, "Deal."

Morning had arrived, and Kyra kneeled by an open flame, rubbing her hands together to ward off the morning chill. Her gaze fell upon her glove which laid on the ground beside her and she felt awkward as her hand experienced anything other than the snug confinement of the glove's cloth. With a pang of regret, she dragged the glove back over her scarred flesh, concealing it once more. Just because Adathin said he understood didn't mean others would. Yet, even knowing there was someone—anyone who did—filled her with a sensation she had long since lost:

Hope.

They had set camp for the night and finding the moonwillow had been easier than she had expected. It glowed with a light-blue light, not so different from the moon itself. Adathin had packed it away safely in a glass bottle he had brought and they slept under a canopy of dense trees. It was uncomfortable, but not the worst place she had been forced to sleep before.

Now, in the morning sun, Adathin emerged from the treeline, carrying something bright in his hand. Grinning slyly, he handed her a handful of berries and, with a proud voice, said, "Here!"

"You're a regular ole mountaineer," Kyra replied, putting a playful note in her voice. "Far from the stuck-up elven lord I thought I was afflicted with."

Adathin hid a grin. "Oh no, I assure you, I am the same stuck-up elven lord you believed me to be. But I have layers. *Layers!*"

"Clearly."

Kyra chuckled, and they shared a meager laugh together. She tried to recall a time when she was as close to anyone as she was to Adathin now. Only Master Lu'ce had come to mind. And perhaps Norrix as well, once upon a time. As she stood and scratched at the back of her neck, just at the edge of her magelock, the severity of their situation crept in: they needed to find Maxim and Armeya. Why hadn't they followed? What had stopped them? Goblins? Or perhaps more terrifying creatures of the night?

Adathin mirrored her thoughts as he asked, "Do you think they're alright?"

Kyra wished to lie to spare his feelings, but she respected him too much for that. With a gulp, she said, "I-I don't know. All reasoning tells me they would have found us if they were alright. *But...*"

"But you *hope* they are alright?"

Kyra nodded silently. "Hope... perhaps that's all we have to grasp onto these days. Hope that we make the right choices. Hope that those choices do not harm the ones we serve. The ones we care for. The ones we lo—" She turned, hiding her burning face. What was she doing? What was she saying? Self-judgement plagued her; how had she ever thought that the man before her had considered her a lesser being? Less than a day ago, she had felt that way, but now those concerns seemed so silly. So childish.

Adathin straightened his magecloak. "Are you ready?"

Kyra kicked dirt over the fire until it extinguished, sending a rising swirl of white smoke into the air. "I'm ready."

The entrance to the ruins was nearby, and it revealed more in the daylight than they had seen the night before. Old runes were deftly etched into the walls, now devoid of magic, making them bland and inert. Still, she had never seen runes such as those before. And so intricate as well. Why had they been carved? What did they say? Mean?

The morning sun had also exposed the dilapidated state of the ruins themselves. Scatterings of pulverized stone were cast out all around them, and despite the broken eggs they had found in the slain creatures' nest, they encountered no other evidence of lingering danger. Another one of her worries slid away.

Exiting the ruins, they retraced their steps from the previous night. The trip was brisk without danger barring their way and with light to guide them. Kyra pointed to where she had last seen Armeya and Maxim as she said, "They were hiding behind these trees... I think."

Distinct footprints in the mud confirmed the two's presence, leading away from the ruins and deeper into the forest. Interlaced with goblin and paw prints, they followed the trail until they found an outline of someone's body in the mud. Whose it belonged to remained uncertain, but there was no sign of a struggle or drag marks. Perhaps Maxim or Armeya were knocked out and carried away? Or killed. But the lack of blood gave her a small glimmer of renewed optimism. There were more goblin footprints up ahead, and a single set of human prints led away, confirming her theory.

Kyra stopped abruptly as she turned to Adathin. "I believe they were ambushed in the forest, and one fell. The goblins carried that one and marched the other beside. I can't imagine Armeya would have been led quietly along, so we should assume she was the one being carried. Also, Maxim seems to leave deeper prints in the mud than she. If we follow the trail, we'll find them. Whatever remains of them, anyway."

Adathin frowned as he replied, "My conscience is about to get a lot heavier, it seems."

"Perhaps—"

"Please, don't," Adathin said. "I know the odds of finding the two of them in one piece. Of finding them alive. I dreamed of it. Nightmares, really. Goblins aren't the most hospitable hosts in the best of times. For prisoners... Perhaps we should just turn back and leave."

"Leave?" Kyra replied, unable to hold the shock from her tone. Adathin turned his head from her as she added, "We can't leave. They'll..."

"Facts are facts," Adathin replied. "They're probably dead already. And what are we to do if they aren't? Fight an entire goblin warband alone? I still can't use my damnable psionics. There is something in these woods that bars me from it. I feel so blind. So helpless."

"Like the rest of us, then?"

Adathin hung his head low. "Yes, I suppose... but you at least have your aethryis. Your arcanist magic."

The man seemed helpless. So distraught. So full of fear and regret. It was her turn. Her turn to lead him. To pull him out of the dark, no matter what they found. She placed a comforting hand on his shoulder as she said, "We need to do this... for them. Believe in what I am. I'm an arcanist! Just like the library, I'll conceal us, and we'll slip right through. If they're gone, at least we can tell their families the truth. If not, then we'll regroup and reassess."

Adathin looked as if he would protest, but when he looked into her eyes, she forced him to see her determination. Eventually, he relented with a nod and she turned back to the tracks with renewed purpose.

Following the trail proved to be quite the laborious task; mud sloshed around their feet and then solidified, leaving a hardened surface caked against their skin. Animals had traversed over the muck and grime, making the tracks of Maxim and Armeya's capturers difficult to discern. Just as her hope dwindled, distant sounds reached her ears—the rhythmic echoes of wood being chopped, voices orchestrating labor, and the assorted noises of animals followed. As she approached, a makeshift village unfolded before her—a crude settlement, yet there was no denying its existence. Temporary housing, arranged haphazardly, hinted at the transience of the place.

Goblins were buzzing in abundance, bustling around the place in the hundreds. They toiled on lumber, tanned hide, and tended to animals; a field behind the village even boasted some crops.

Adathin voiced the astonishment they both felt. "What is this? Are they... farming?"

Kyra nodded. "That's what it looks like. Goblin farmers... now I've seen everything."

A rustle of twigs from behind prompted her to swift action. She grasped Adathin, pulling him close, and raised an invisibility barrier around them. A goblin holding a chained wolf suddenly appeared from the brush, seemingly following the same tracks they had been. Unlike the others that came before, their tracks were far less prominent, possibly overshadowed by the hardened earth. The wolf, however, driven by scent, crept ever closer.

"Stay close to me," Kyra whispered. "I think I have an idea."

Slowly, she moved them out in the open towards the goblin village. Her plan was simple—to blend in with the various smells of animals and confuse the wolf and its handler. She moved as quickly as she could while maintaining focus and keeping the shield up. There was also the hassle of the parade of goblins that strode to and from, some getting so close to them she could have reached out and plucked the tip of their pointed ears. Her plan worked as the wolf, enticed by the aroma of cooked meat, swiftly led the handler away. Finally, they took refuge near a chicken coop, concealed by the clucking hens.

"Did you see them?" Kyra asked.

Adathin shook his head as he replied, "No, but I saw some hanging cages. Empty—" A pair of passing goblins stilled their conversation.

"Can ye' believe boss man won't let us kill em?" One goblin said.

The other spit contemptuously in the dirt. "Proud and proper, the boss man is. He dresses like em'. Talks like em'. Even lives in da' big house like em'. Fixin' to think he's one of em'."

"Oy," the first warned. "Talk like that'll get us both gutted."

The goblins' conversation trailed off as the two walked away to continue whatever menial tasks they had been performing.

"Has to be *them*," Adathin said. "The big house," he pointed, "over there! It's the biggest building I can see, if these hovels can be called such."

Kyra nodded wordlessly and led the way towards the building, maintaining the invisibility barrier that protected them. Adathin remained close, though his panicked breathing gave her worry. At the big tent-like structure, a straw-fastened door barred their way. She nuzzled it open, and was surprised to find a rather pleasant interior with the pleasant smell of flowered perfume. The Elder of Oldrock had told her of goblin raids. Perhaps they had also stolen some furniture as well.

A creak of wood drew her attention to a seemingly asleep goblin in a wooden rocking chair. The goblin was old, with thin white hair on his head and a clean-shaven face. Next to the chair was a cane with an oddly shaped red-glowing ore on top. Adathin eyed the stone as if it were a lethal poison.

"I can smell you in this cramped space," the goblin man said suddenly without even opening his eyes. "You reek of blood. Acidic blood at that." His eyes popped open in surprise and shock. "You killed *Ak'zo!*"

They were caught, and she reluctantly let the barrier drop. The goblin man's eyes narrowed as she came into view.

"Who's Ak'zo?" Kyra asked, stuck between conversation and killing the goblin as quickly as she could. Looks like Adathin was in the same dilemma as she, his purple blade forming in his hand, but his feet still leaded to the ground.

"The creature of Salshys, or what you refer to as the Builders' Ruins. An enormous creature with sword-like mandibles, skittering legs, more than one can count. And, above all, acidic blood, which it spits as a projectile arsenal. Marvelous creature... and quite dangerous."

"Quite," Adathin replied. "And yes, we killed it... what does that mean to you?"

The elderly goblin's eyes lit up in delight. "*Excellent!* Truly exquisite work. And to answer your question, it means everything to me. Mages and their elvish handlers seem to be just as capable as I've read."

Kyra narrowed her eyes. "He isn't my handler—"

"Do you know what this means?" the goblin man replied, ignoring her protests. He stood, nearly prancing, and began rummaging through some loose books on a nearby table. Glancing around, Kyra noticed other pieces of red ore were scattered about the room, which looked oddly similar to the ore that stood at the head of the cane.

The old goblin suddenly glanced back, asking, "Would you mind handing me that?"

She complied, handing the goblin his cane. He frantically searched through a particular publication, muttering all the while to himself. Seizing the opportunity, she drew in a hint of magic and created a small invisible barrier around her hand, using it to pluck one of the ores from a nearby shelf. Hastily, she wedged it into her pocket. The goblin man warily turned to look at her, but continued into his reading as if he hadn't noticed.

"Where are they?" Adathin asked suddenly. "Where are our companions?"

"Companions?" The elderly goblin man gave him a curious glance before realization set in. "Ah, the other mages; of course, of course. They left this morning, back to Oldrock they went. Quite the pair, them. That thaumaturge, Armeya, has a glare that could kill a raging gargantuan. The boy, however, was rather pleasant. Already forgot his name, though. Funny that. He taught me how to properly prepare a roasted pig and what spices to enhance the flavors with. Even had a tonic to ease this nasty ache in my feet. Quite knowledgeable."

Adathin breathed out, and she could visibly see the stress leave his body. "So they're alive?" he asked.

"Quite so. Now... What are you two doing here? If I'm not mistaken, you have to get back and help a friend?"

Adathin's mouth hung open, and he appeared stunned. "I... I suppose so," he said. "Well, if they really aren't here, then we'll take our leave. That is, if there won't be any trouble?"

"No trouble from us. Have a safe trip back."

"But—"

The elderly goblin man became somewhat angry as he replied, "My kin won't harm you, I can assure you of that! However, I do hope we'll all see each other again very soon, but for now, I need to plan a brief trip to the ruins. So much to study and so little time. I thank you again for taking care of Ak'zo. Troublesome creature, to say the least. Cost me a good thirty or so, killing all the offspring that emerged from that place."

"So that's what happened to the eggs," Kyra whispered, more to herself than to anyone else. Then curiosity got the better of her as she asked, "You protected this place? Your... home? But you're goblins? You don't keep permanent homes. Why?"

"We protected Oldrock too," the old goblin replied. "We need their supplies, and they need to not be dead. Mutually beneficial. The supplies were, as you would say it, payment for services rendered. Just as you've already taken *your* payment for services rendered." He gave her a knowing smile.

Adathin glanced between the two of them, ears twitching. "What does *that* mean?"

Kyra pressed her hand firmly against the small piece of hidden ore. "I haven't the faintest... I think we should go."

"You should. As I've already said, safe trip." The elderly goblin man, not bothering to even acknowledge their exit, was still shoving his nose into each and every book he could find.

Outside, the other goblins, at least twenty or so, stood watching the entrance of the tent. They were waiting. Someone had obviously raised an alarm. Surprisingly, all parted as Adathin and she walked towards them and out to the edge of the camp. One goblin even stepped forward and pointed them in the direction to get back to Oldrock. The goblin said it would take them until nightfall before scampering away and leaving them at the edge of the forest alone. Armeya and Maxim were safe, if the elderly goblin man was to be trusted. Considering he could have easily ended their lives there and then, she found she trusted him, if only just. All that, and they had the moonwillow. A day's journey back, half a day's train ride home, and no enemies in between—it appeared they had succeeded in their foolhardy mission, after all.

CHAPTER 24

STOLEN NAME

Soren struggled helplessly against the crisp sheets of his hospital bed, now marred by the sticky remnants of his breakfast. It was hard to admit, but the false bravado he had maintained thus far was crumbling away to ash in front of his very eyes. He could feel his aethryis dissipating; the channels on his body closing to its touch. The prospect of becoming just a mere human frightened him, and yet, it also brought about a grim sense of relief. Perhaps without aethryis, he could lead the simple life he had always fantasized about. Away from the complexities of elvish politics and mage intrigue. Away from his family and the problems they brought alongside them.

However, there was something deep and primal that urged him to fight on.

Under the guidance of Master Aracan, mystics brought him more fresh linens and lifted him while others changed them beneath him. It was degrading. Utterly humiliating. How would he ever live this down? Surely, the rumors of the weak and pathetic Soren Frost had already circled around and webbed their way around the ears of his peers. He would have no respect from either the masters nor his fellow adepts. And without respect, he was nothing at all. It was the only gift his familial relations had given him. The only thing his name commanded.

Turning dejectedly, Soren stared off into the nothingness. It was all he could think to do. But then, suddenly, a familiar voice broke his veiled thoughts, unexpected and entirely unwanted.

"Hello, son," the voice said, low and cool.

Refusing to turn, he whispered under his breath, "*Mother...* To what do I owe the pleasure?"

"*Tsk-tsk,*" his mother replied as she strolled from the entrance of the infirmary to the edge of his bed. She moved with a certain serpentine grace, and he couldn't help but wonder how long it would take before she sunk in her fangs. "Is that any way to treat your poor, dear mother?"

Soren caught a few glances from his peers, their eyes fixed on him expectantly. *Great...* Now, in addition to being the pathetically weak Soren Frost, who couldn't even handle getting nicked by a goblin blade, he's also disrespectful to his own mother. If the others of his circle ever found themselves in a tight spot again, he vowed not to stick his neck out for them. They couldn't possibly be worth all this trouble.

Like the dawn claiming the sky, a sudden burst of pain from his wound cleared his head. His mother looked down at him with annoyance as he asked, "You never answered... What are you doing here?"

"Why... checking on my son, of course—"

"Cut the shit," Soren whispered, seething and hoping no prying ears could hear his disrespectful words. "What are you *really* doing here?"

His mother sat on the edge of the bed and her flowing glacial hair flicked him lightly against his face. It seemed an intentional slight, as she wouldn't dare raise her hand to him in the presence of so many. She pressed back, leaning against his wound. The pain was intense, but as he shifted, she shifted with him, forcing pressure onto it.

He grinned and took the pain, like he had done so many times before.

"Appearances," she said. "My idiot son played the hero, and now I have to play the part of the grieving mother. It's quite exhausting, I must say. Oh, the pains I put up with for this family."

"Or you can just leave," Soren suggested. "I assure you, I wouldn't mind."

His mother forced a laugh. "Not a chance. I'm here, and so we'll make the best of it. You'll show me what you've learned, Three."

Three... Now that was a name he hadn't heard in a long time. An infuriating nickname, but her mocking wouldn't break him. Not this time.

Soren gritted his teeth and answered in as calm a voice as he could muster, "What is it you would like to know?"

Willow drew her shimmering, ever-changing colored magecloak tighter. It was a relic from a chapter of her life. An old life now vanished forever. It felt more constricting than she recalled, almost suffocating in its fit form. She questioned whether it was a mere illusion of her mind or if the stuffiness of this place could truly choke her to death.

The imposing black gates of Dragrin's loomed ahead, unchanged from the depths of her memories. Everything appeared just as meticulously arranged as she remembered. Everything in its familiar place—the fountain, the grass, and the throngs of mages who trudged about like worker ants. With just a simple magecloak, she could so seamlessly blend into this bustling enclave, becoming as inconspicuous as a bird in a flock. She was visible, yet invisible.

Purposefully, Willow navigated through the crowd, brushing off any casual remarks or inquiries that came her way. Her disguise relied entirely on remaining an anonymous part of the masses. She had not the time to dally, and she quickly reached her destination. It was a place straight from her nightmares. A place she knew all too well.

A modest desk stood outside double-doors manned by an attendant. As Willow approached, the attendant, a youthful girl with short brown hair, who seemed barely old enough to have received a ringpact, inquired, "And who are you? Do you have an appointment with the Elder?"

Willow narrowed her eyes menacingly. "No," she said. "But I think he will see me, regardless."

The attendant leveled her deep brown eyes at her, meeting her own defiant gaze. There was a spark of rebellion there, not unlike her own rebellious streak. "Appointments only," the attendant declared. She huffed to herself as if the matter was all but settled.

"Tell him Viessa wishes to speak to him."

The attendant rolled her eyes but swiftly vanished behind those double-doors. Willow leaned against the desk, but the attendant returned only a few moments later, visibly shaken.

"H-H-He'll see you now," she said.

"Excellent," Willow replied as she strode past the attendant, who now held one of the doors open for her. Leaning inside, she whispered, "And try not to pry. Believe me, you'll want to make yourself scarce for this."

The attendant swallowed hard as she whispered, "Yes, ma'am," as she let the door swing shut. She heard the quickened steps of someone retreating.

Smart girl.

Willow took two strides inside before she saw Reylar. He stood, approaching her eagerly.

"*Viessa*!" he said, not holding back his excitement. Reylar reached out to hug her, but she skipped back a step. Dejected, he coughed into his hand and added, "To what do I owe the pleasure?"

"Don't act coy," Willow replied. "Where is she?"

"You mean Willow?"

She scowled and laced her words with venom. "I mean Quistis, and you know that."

Reylar went tight-lipped, straightening his vest to emphasize the breadth of his chest and shoulders. He was a good head taller than her, and much wider at that. In the past, his size had intimidated her, but her anger burned far hotter than any past fears, like the blue blaze at the bottom of coals.

"I knew you would come," Reylar admitted. "Come, sit. We need to talk."

"We've nothing to discuss," she replied. "I'm here for Quistis, and then I'll take my leave."

Reylar sighed, scratching at his beard. Had there always been so much gray there? In her head, she saw Reylar as this bear of a man. An immortal. But this... while large still, the lines of his face and the gray of his hair suggested he was becoming an old man. Old and weak—at least weaker than he had been.

"This is your home," Reylar said. "Can you not just sit and enjoy a drink with me? For old times' sake?"

"This hasn't been my home for a long time. You know that as well as I."

"And whose fault is that?"

Willow slammed her fist against the doorframe. "It was nobody's fault! I-I grew apart from it. I saw the errors in their way of thinking. In the ways of their teachings. *Your* teachings. I couldn't ignore it any longer. Can't you see it, Reylar? See it as I see it? We are nothing but servants, born and bred to do the bidding of our elven overlords and the mages of the Spellbound Arch. We're slaves, for lack of a better term. We have little to no say in how our lives are lived. It's why I left. It's why Quistis left."

"Why *Willow* left," Reylar corrected. "You can use *his* name all you want, but I'm the one who bestowed it upon him the day he was born. And yes, I know their errors, but I disagree with your conclusion. The rules imposed on us keep us safe. Keeps the world safe. Your way would bring only war and death."

"And you would know of death and war, wouldn't you, Steelhand?"

Reylar seemed taken aback by the jab, but he did well controlling his anger, though his clenched fists betrayed him with the soft squealing of steel on steel. "You're right," he replied. "I know of death. Of war. But you—you do not. However, if you don't stop this foolishness now, you soon will."

"What foolishness?" she asked. "The pactless live within our means. We bother nobody. We even do what the mages will not: protect the Dimlight District. Without us, you'd have already had an uncanny uprising to deal with."

"And the Salvator boy? Does he 'bother nobody?'"

Willow ground her teeth. He had her there. "Salvator made a mistake," she excused weakly. "The situation has been rectified."

"'Rectified,'" Reylar gave a soft snort. "Rectified or not, your merry band of pactless are on borrowed time. You know it, I know it... It's why Willow—"

"*Quistis—*"

"*I'll call my son anything I damn well please!*"

There was a raised tension that clung to the air. Conflict. The two of them would come to blows. Nothing could stop it now. This was fate. She knew it, and, studying his movement, he most certainly knew it as well. Willow circled Reylar, drawing aethryis from the air. Unlike him, she had no ringpact to bind her. Reylar matched her stride.

"Quistis is *not* your son. Not anymore. Now where is she?" Willow said. "I will not ask again. Not nicely, anyway."

"Safe," Reylar replied. "Safe from the troubles you've brought upon yourselves."

"Against her will?"

"... I'll do anything to keep *him* safe."

Willow lunged forward, throwing a right hook towards Reylar. He shifted, her fist narrowly passing overhead as his own cold-steel fist slammed into her gut. Reylar Steelhand, the master brawler. She had to admit, his punch felt like being hit with a bludgeon. If she hadn't been expecting an attack and hadn't already used aethryis to enhance her body's defenses, she knew that he would have collapsed her with that single strike.

Willow leaped back before another one of Reylar's punches took off her head.

"Now this is bringing me back," Reylar said tauntingly. "You never could quite best me, no matter how much I taught you. You never could quite give it your all. Always holding back. Chained. Never being true to yourself. What did I tell you would happen? Do you remember?"

Willow searched for those distant memories. "You said it would be my downfall."

Reylar snapped his metal fingers together with a clang. "That's right. Still, I stand by those words. How can you protect your people when you are too afraid to protect yourself? How can you protect them when you won't even move on from here? Hells, you won't even use your own name. Pathetic." He put his finger to his head. "You should think about that, we're done here—"

Willow held her ring to the magelock on the back of her neck. "Fifty percent," she muttered, and felt a sudden flood of aethryis pour into her.

Reylar lifted his hands into a fighting stance. A brawler's stance. "Still holding back, then? Fine. Come on, let's see what you can do at half strength."

Willow surged forward, grabbing Reylar by the vest, lifting him and smashing him into a wall. There was a crash and dust fell from the beams overhead. When she tugged him back, his body left an outline in the wall. Pulling him close, she slammed a fist into his chin. He staggered, and she kept on delivering blow after blow, which would have killed any normal human, but she knew... Reylar was anything but normal. He took each blow without complaint. Stoically. Unconcerned. Keeping his eyes steadily trailed on hers all the while. In the end, she was sweating from the concerted effort; from the augmentors' aethryis, which enhanced her strength, causing a strain on her body.

"Good," Reylar muttered. "But still tempered. Still restrained. These limits you place on yourself; who do you think it helps?"

"*Everyone!*" she screamed. "*I can't—can't lose control!*"

"Control," Reylar laughed mockingly. "You think *this* is control? Limiting yourself? This is like an animal who cages itself and insists that it's still in control of its own fate. Face it, you control *nothing.*"

Anger coursed through Willow, banishing all thought and reason. She held her ring to the magelock again. "Seventy-five percent."

This time, Reylar attacked, grabbing her magecloak and slamming her body through his wooden desk. She heard the crack and crash before she felt it. Her body suddenly stopped as she collided with the floor underneath. She found herself grateful to have increased her limit, any less, and Reylar would have crippled her.

Willow kicked at Reylar's leg and when he went down to one knee, she leaned up and slammed her fist across his chin. He flew back, all the way to the edge of the room, where he knocked over a shelf and fell into a pile of books. She had forgotten what it was like to fight at this level. What it felt like to have this much aethryis available to her. It rattled her... too much; it was too much for her frail body to handle. Heat coursed through her veins. It hurt. Burned. Just as she thought of sealing it off again, Reylar rose and dusted himself off.

"Surely you can hit harder than that," he taunted. His voice betrayed himself. She could hear it—sense it. Underneath his false bravado, he was worried. Scared even. The way he carried himself told her more:

He was hurt!

Without thinking, she leaped into a barrage of punches and kicks. She missed most in her mad fury, and Reylar, ever the fighter and master of the weaponless brawl, dodged even more. But her speed, propelled by her rampaging use of augmentor aethryis, made up for the difference. Reylar had to change stances to defend, and she gave him no opportunity to counter.

Suddenly, Willow's heart plummeted as magic overwhelmed her. It was for just a moment, but in that time, her movement slowed and Reylar took his opening. His fist struck her stomach first, then her ribs, then her chin, so fast she hardly registered the blows before more came. In that instant, the fight turned, and she was on the defensive. She put her hands up to block, but it was a pitiful attempt. His strikes were too precise, too well trained. She stepped back when he reached out and grappled her. She couldn't see much other than the room rushing by as he swung her by the arm, slamming her body into the various walls and furniture around the room.

She was done. Spent. She had never, in all her years of training under him, defeated him. And today, it seemed, would be no different. The room stood still as he held her limply by the arm. Reylar leaned in close and whispered, "Still too weak." Why did he still taunt her? He had won. *Won!* Was it not enough? Why was it still not enough? Then he added in a harrowing voice, "They'll kill her, you know."

Her heart beat faster.

"Willow, my... *daughter*," he said. "They'll kill her. For what she is. For what *you* made her to be."

"Made her..."

"It's all your fault it's come to this. All your fault. And you won't even take responsibility for her inevitable death."

"Her death..."

Reylar sighed, squeezing her wrist tighter. "Still too weak," he said, dropping her to the floor. "You've always been too weak. Just. Like. Her."

Slowly, Willow reached back, pressing the ring on her finger to the magelock at her neck. *"One-hundred percent."*

Reylar smiled at her condescendingly. "Now that's more like it—"

Willow was up before she realized it, slamming a fist into Reylar's stomach. He stepped back two steps, and then doubled over, holding his stomach desperately. After a moment, he took labored and ragged breaths, but try as he might, he could no longer speak.

Good.

Willow could feel it—the entire world—as sharp and crisp as ever. Her very soul longed to drink more and more aethryis until it consumed her completely and she became one with it. Only one thought held her back from joining that infinite void. One thought: the knowledge of how the news of her death would affect Quistis, her love. Everything she did was for her. She would be anything for her. Now, looking down at her old master, she knew she would kill him to protect her, if needed.

Would she need to kill him?

Reylar suddenly threw a piece of his broken table at her and she moved on pure instinct, gliding around it. The object appeared as if moved in slow motion, and she wondered how she had lived her life up to this point so... trapped within herself. Electricity sizzled through her veins. Through her blood. The feeling was intoxicating. Dangerous. Without a thought, she stepped forward and kicked Reylar squarely in the chest, sending him flying back, crashing into a distant wall.

Electricity crackled across her body, shooting loose sparks outward that bounced and chained to the metallic items around the room. Slowly, those items levitated in the air. She tried to let it go, the aethryis, but found that she couldn't. This is what she had always feared.

She had lost control.

Reylar stood to her surprise, wiping a small dribble of blood from his lip. He straightened his vest and then took a fighter's stance. Before she could reply in kind, he was already within striking distance. When had he become so fast? So quick? She threw a jab of her own, matching his. Soon, they both were in a deadlock, throwing as many punches as the eyes could see, each matching the other's ferocity. But she—she was not made of flesh. Not anymore. She had elevated beyond the confines of her human body.

Electricity swelled through her and her punches became even faster, so fast that afterimages of her body were left in place as she moved. Even Reylar's ferocity faltered as he was pushed back. With a thought, her electricity bound him, forcing him to kneel before her. Looking down, there was now a rapier of pure electrical energy formed in her hand. When had it gotten there? She knew she could end this now. Save Quistis from her own father, once and for all. So why? Why did she hesitate? There was no reason... Reylar was but a man and she—she was something else. Something more. She reached back, the tip of her rapier aimed at his heart.

The door flung open, and Quistis stepped inside with a bewildered look plastered on her face. "What's going on here?" she asked. "What... What is this?"

Willow hesitated. "I... He... Well..."

Reylar made a grunting noise as he stretched, casually tearing the electrical binds that held him. The electricity in the air vanished and the items which floated around the room now fell to the floor. Aethryis fled from her in an instant, and she realized that she no longer had the strength to stand. As she fell, she felt a warm grasp as Quistis moved to catch her. Staring into her eyes, she said, "Thank you."

Quistis' gaze was not that of love or admiration, but of cold fury.

Reylar cracked his neck as if he had just gone through a particularly tough workout. "Now, now, don't be upset with Viessa. I taunted her into this. Pushed her, really." Looking around, he gave a full-belly laugh. "Perhaps I pushed her too far. Sellya is going to be furious with me."

Quistis' gaze fixated on Reylar, and she could feel the woman's contempt move from her to him. "Why... Why did it come to this? Why did this happen?"

Reylar scratched at his chin absently. "Because it had too. I-I had to be sure."

"Sure of what?"

Reylar drifted aimlessly towards them. "Did you get what I asked?" Quistis narrowed her eyes, but turned and pointed to the table where a decanter stood with a dark liquid inside. He smiled, turning over a side-desk and pouring three glasses which had miraculously survived the encounter, which he then set back down on the table. Quistis helped ease her over, and as she reached for the glass, she nearly dropped it, her muscles still sore from the overuse. It took nearly all her strength to hold the glass steady.

"Why?" Quistis asked again. It was clear in her voice and tone that she would not ask again. She would bring the hells upon Reylar if he didn't give it to her straight.

Reylar downed his glass, setting it back to the table with a clink. "Because... *She* needs to be ready for what's coming. Ready to lead the pactless. Ready to do whatever is necessary to survive. Regardless if that is to fight, or even to kill. She needed to stop holding back. And now—now I know she can. I know she can protect you, Willow. You both can finally stop living this lie. It's time to proclaim yourselves true and live freely."

Willow looked at Quistis, who stared back at her nervously. Was there wisdom in his words? Was it truly time to give back the name she had stolen?

CHAPTER 25

SUSPICION

Armeya glanced at Adathin, who had strolled by them, as if she were pretending he did not exist. She shook her head as she muttered, "Another time."

Another time... Kyra thought back to the first days she had spent in this place. It all started with a dead mage in the streets and Armeya as happy as a clam declaring how they would become the best of friends. She hadn't believed it then, but now she had to admit that the woman was growing on her. They all were. Those of her circle. So much had happened in such a short amount of time.

Kyra roamed the streets of Mistbreak for what felt like hours. Her legs were sore from the train, and she wished to work them out a bit before she returned. When she did finally return to Dragrin's, she decided to see Elder Reylar first. But just outside his study, she ran into Armeya as she was leaving the man's study. She opened her mouth to speak, but Armeya strolled past without a word spoken between them. She let herself into the Elder's study to find that he was as cold and calloused today as Armeya was. Still, she had a duty, and she handed him the red luminescent ore he had requested. Elder Reylar didn't even thank her as he flung it down to the floor as if he was a child throwing a tantrum. His quarters had been empty, save a single chair and a small stand desk. Although, she couldn't help but notice remnants of a few broken pieces of wood scattered about. She dismissed herself as Elder Reylar appeared to be lost in thought.

What was wrong with everyone?

Kyra attempted to visit Soren, but apparently, according to his tenders, he was busy receiving treatment. She was told that Adathin had already given the moonwillow herb to Master Aracan soon after they had returned. As she pushed past the attendees, she came face to face with a woman claiming to be Soren's own mother. She prevented her from moving past. She could hear Soren protesting in the background, as she was told in no light tone that she had to leave. That woman—those cold eyes—she had been glad to leave as soon as possible. Even away, her stare sent chills running up her spine.

Finally, she entered the study of Master Silvia Deerling. A return to her training. A return to normalcy. The woman gave her a sidelong glance as if to say, "Where have you been?"

She took a seat in the middle of the room, holding a scattering of notes close at hand. She had missed so much... In fact; she had missed more training lessons than she had attended since coming to this place. Rather than a student of aethryical arts, she felt more like a tool for the benefit of the Spellbound Arch. Perhaps this is what it meant to be a mage. That your time was no longer your own. That your education and mind were not your own either.

Armeya soon entered the study, looking rather stricken, her clothes a disheveled mess. She distinctly sat in the seat furthest from her. Even Iona showed and sat polar opposite as well. What had she done to deserve such scorn? She had been used to the solitude as an apprentice, but she had really felt like she had moved past it. Like she had gotten along with the others. Knowing now how they really felt, she held her hand close to her chest. She had been stupid to assume she could escape her past. That she could find acceptance from them.

Master Deerling suddenly slammed her hand against her lectern, calling for the attention of everyone in the room. "Today, I was going to test you on the progress you've made with attuning to your individual ringpacts.

At least, that was the plan. I've just received some grim news to share. Despite my own feelings on what information *should* be distributed to adepts, not yet masters, the Elder has decided that it is important to notify you. There have been a few more deaths. Some you may know. Some you may not. I will not say their names here for fear that some of you will launch into hysterics and I just simply cannot be bothered with such nonsense now. I'm sure the rumors will reach your ears soon enough. But, as such, we will be implementing a lockdown. The grounds themselves will be monitored by you adepts, but none shall be permitted to leave until a proper investigation by master mages is done and the culprit is captured."

A scattering of whispering assaulted her mind.

"*The Spellthief...*"

"*It has to be...*"

"*Spellthief...*"

Master Deerling narrowed her eyes, casting that gaze out in all directions until all fell silent. "Yes, the supposed *Spellthief.* Damn those shameful journalists, always sensationalizing murders and giving them titles. I've always said that if you want a copycat, give the killer a fancy name. They have no responsibility, I... Well, that's a discussion for another time. Now onto more practical matters, I want to see a demonstration from everyone regarding their aethryis. Come now, come... Yes, you first, come."

Master Deerling called each adept one by one. This went on for the remainder of the lesson until Master Deerling had eventually come upon her. She stood in front of the others and couldn't draw even a strand of light from her ringpact. Eventually, Master Deerling scolded her and demanded she sit back down. Rather harshly at that. She couldn't concentrate. Couldn't focus. *Spellthief...* that name swirled over and over in her head. Was it that pactless woman she had cornered on the rooftops? The one who had summoned lightning and fled. Was it one of the uncanny? A goblin, perhaps? The old goblin Adathin and she had met seemed like he wanted to broker peace, but what about the others? The ones she had met in the warehouse that had tried to kill them would indicate that not all the goblins were in agreement. Still so many questions, and she wasn't any closer to finding out who murdered Freed Gallok.

Then there was a hand on her shoulder. Looking up, she saw Armeya's face, cold and unreadable. "We need to talk."

Kyra's back stiffened. "Fine," she said. "Haven Teashop?"

Armeya shook her head. "Too public. And besides, we're locked inside the gates of Dragrin's for now. Meet me in my room. Give me a little time and make your way there. Knock two times and hold before knocking a third."

The woman's words felt so... constrained. So full of worry and doubt. Still, she nodded at the request and Armeya disappeared as she stepped out into the hall.

Kyra knocked on Armeya's door—twice in quick succession, followed by a pause, and then once more. There was a moment of hesitation and just as she turned to leave, the door swung open, and she was abruptly whisked inside. The door slammed behind her, plunging the room into darkness. She stumbled into a chair, immediately feeling bindings tighten around her arms and legs. A small light flickered to life as a candle was lit in the corner, casting a faint glow.

"Who are you?" Armeya's voice cut through the dimness as she materialized like a wraith in the night, cloaked in black, her normally off-colored eyes now deep red and ablaze with fear and fury.

Kyra struggled against the restraints, rocking the chair back and forth in a futile attempt to free herself. Frustrated, she drew upon her aethryis, pulling it from her ringpact, and conjuring an orb of light to dispel the shadows.

Armeya recoiled from the sudden illumination. The room was empty of others save herself and Armeya. It was clear that, whatever this was, she had concocted it alone.

"You know who I am," she spat, her voice laced with all the contempt she could muster. "Tell me what this is about. *Now!*"

Armeya's gaze was icy. "Liar," she whispered. "You're a liar. Just like those Mistwalker elves."

"'Mistwalker elves?' Adathin and Aluriel? What have they—or I—done to you?"

"*Liar!*" Flames leaped from Armeya's hands, flickering dangerously close to a stack of papers. With a flick of her wrist, she extinguished the fire, the woman's red eyes never leaving hers. "You will confess your plans. I know you're involved... you're the Spellthief. Or at least their accomplice."

"*Spellthief...*" The word sent a shiver down Kyra's spine. "I don't know who that is. Remember, I was with you when we discovered the body."

"*Exactly!*" Armeya replied, a mad smile dancing across her lips. "You were there, urging us inside. When we found the body, your calm unsettled me. I thought you were just more mature than I, or hiding how you really felt. And when that pactless woman appeared, you chased her down—perhaps to silence her. Or maybe none of this is real at all. Perhaps Adathin altered my memories. Ever since that day, I've been plagued by nightmares, and nothing seems to make sense anymore. I spoke with Iona and she felt the same way."

Armeya paced back and forth in the room, her frustration evident. Her silent mutterings to herself were tinged with doubt.

"Armeya," Kyra said calmly, "I have no idea what you're implying. Adathin and I—"

"The old goblin in the forest," Armeya interrupted, "he warned me. He spoke of the Mistwalkers—of Adathin and Aluriel—long before he heard their names from me. He knew. Damn it all, he knew."

Kyra took a deep, slow breath. "And you're basing all of this on the word of a goblin?"

Armeya's fury was palpable as she replied, "Why do you think I've kept this quiet? At first, I too dismissed the goblin's claims, but the more I pondered on it, the more plausible it seemed. When I confided in Iona, she too admitted her suspicions."

Kyra's voice was tinged with disbelief as she asked, "Who else suspects us?"

"Maxim... but not Soren. I couldn't risk alarming the others without concrete evidence. I wanted to confront you first; to give you a chance to explain. I... I want to believe you."

"And if it was Adathin and Aluriel, why would you think I'm involved?"

Armeya's voice was scornful as she replied, "Don't play the fool. Your devotion to Adathin is obvious. I mistook it for a mere infatuation at first, but now I see it for what it truly is: blind allegiance. Do you deny it?"

Kyra's defiance flared as she resisted Armeya's magic, her own light flickering against a darker force inside her. "I'm not blind, and I am nobody's pawn," she said, but even to her, the words felt forced. Armeya was right; she had unwittingly become allegiant to the man. Even now she wanted to defend him against these allegations without even considering if there was any truth to them. With a sickening realization, she had to wonder if he had used his psionics to influence her.

Suddenly, Armeya's magic flickered and in that brief moment, she broke the bindings and lunged at the woman, pinning her against the opposing wall.

"I am not what you think," Kyra insisted, pushing harder. "I'm not the Spellthief. I'm not helping the Spellthief. I... I want to find whoever did it. To prove myself. To make up for my sins!" After a tense moment, Armeya relaxed, and she stepped back, wheezing. She couldn't believe what she had just said out loud. The truth that she didn't ever want to admit, even to herself. She was still running. Still running from her past. In a calmer voice, she added, "I'm not involved, Armeya. I swear it."

"But what of Adathin?" Armeya's voice broke with emotion.

Kyra's resolve hardened. She pushed back all her pain and doubt as she replied, "Adathin is no killer. The notion that he's the same one collecting mage rings as trophies is absurd."

Armeya produced a bloodstained Augmentor's ringpact from her pocket, the woman's eyes scrutinizing her own. "The goblin, Kri'ed, gave me this as a warning. He claims the Mistwalkers are plotting against the city. Says that the Mistwalkers are tired of their bond with the Spellbound Arch. And of them fearing the rise of the pactless. That—That they offered the goblins a deal if they would attack. But Kri'ed says he seeks peace, not war."

"*Aluriel...*" Kyra's voice trailed off. "I've spoken to Adathin at length. He assured me he's not like his father. Perhaps this is what he meant. Perhaps there is truth in what you say. But Adathin—"

"Or perhaps he's manipulating you," Armeya countered, skepticism fortifying her words.

She hesitated. "I... I need time to think."

"As do I," Armeya replied. "For now, we will wait and watch. If you're still boarding with Aluriel, perhaps we can use that to our advantage."

"I admit, I remain unconvinced. Adathin truly doesn't seem the type... But I will do everything within my power to help uncover the truth. Even an uncomfortable one."

Armeya extended her hand, a tentative smile on her lips. "I needed to be sure, friend. I needed to be sure. To finding the truth."

Kyra grasped Armeya's hand firmly. "To the truth."

CHAPTER 26

PROMISES

Lhoris drank in deep of his own reflection in the silver-spun mirror. He was a beautiful specimen. A model elvish man. One who should be loved by most. Feared by all. But those fools of the Elven Enclave; they were blind, deaf, and dull. They just couldn't see what had to be done. What he could offer them.

He would make them see.

Turning, Lhoris recognized the figure in the room's corner, shrouded in black and waiting patiently for him to finish. He hadn't noticed her enter. He never seemed to these days.

"What do you want this time?" he asked, his patience waning quickly. She had cautioned him against acting for so long that he had thought they would miss their opportunity. Uppity little thing. She truly thought that he was doing this for her benefit. It took all his might not to laugh in her pretty little face.

"Are you quite finished, my preening peacock?" she asked.

Lhoris' blood boiled with anger. How dare she address him in such a way. How dare she denigrate someone of his stature. She believed him to be her ally? Well, she'll see when he was named head of the Elven Conclave. She'll see... her whole house would.

"'Preening peacock,' you say? Well, this bird is the only reason your foolhardy plan has any chance of success at all. You'll do well to remember that."

There, he had put her in her place. Not as thoroughly as he would like, but as much as he dared... for now.

The woman seemed to consider his words for a moment before stepping into the light and pushing back her hood. There she stood in her ephemeral glory: Aluriel Mistwalker. Her magecloak shimmered in its opaque multi-colored facade and her hair was spun delicately in a bun with long strands spiraling down her neck and back. He imagined that some would find her beautiful. Some. He longed to turn back to his mirror and witness true elegance. The only truly gorgeous thing left in this world. But with a hungering heart, he forced himself to stand stern.

"And you would do best to remember whose plan this was in the first place," she said. "Aye, I need you, but you need me as well. We are stuck together in this, for better or worse."

"For worse," he replied. "But I catch your meaning."

Aluriel stepped forward, running her hand across his chest and then slowly up his neck as she spun around him. He stood straighter, willing his manhood to stillness. He could no more be attracted to this wretch than a stray cat found on the streets. She was nothing but an object to him. A step to greater things for himself.

Aluriel came to stand in front of him, her eyes staring up at him quizzically, as if she didn't understand why her feminine wiles hadn't worked.

"This will be good for us," she whispered. "If neither of us can stand the other, then pretense will be all that is required. I'm sure that works for you?"

"It does," Lhoris replied, swallowing the hot bile that threatened to creep up his throat.

Aluriel spun, and a strand of hair struck his face. He knew it was a deliberate slight against him, but still he longed to rush and wash the pissant's smell from his face immediately.

"It is time," she said, stepping closer to the door. "Be ready to assume control and remember, this world is ours. *Ours!*"

Aluriel stepped out and shut the door behind her. Little Mistwalker wretch. He walked to a water basin and scrubbed his face. He scrubbed and scrubbed until his face hurt and when he turned back to his mirror, he almost looked away in disgust as he saw his reddened cheek, raw from his own touch.

"That bitch will pay," Lhoris swore under his breath. "They'll all pay." He thought back to her words. "Ours?" He forced a laugh. "This world is *mine!*"

Fall turned to winter and winter to spring, and still Kyra had no more answers than when she started. Since the lock-down at Dragrin's, mage deaths had declined fiercely. In fact, there had been only two that she could confirm. Souls stolen in the night, never to be seen again. Only the word of constables outside the gate confirmed everyone's fears.

Rumors and whispers in the dark began that there was an increase in the movements of the uncanny of Mistbreak. If the tales were to be believed, it was now the pactless above all who were keeping the peace outside the black gates. The elven had isolated themselves in the upper quadrant of the city and had apparently seen little reason to involve themselves in the happenings of those they saw beneath them; and they believed all others beneath them.

Despite that, this was all beyond her. Politics. She had made a singular pact. A promise: find Freed Gallok's killer, the dead mage whom she had accidentally stumbled upon on her first fateful day at Dragrin's. She still hadn't pondered out why she had even made the promise. It was something like fate. A destiny. A path she must follow.

Kyra had finally settled into a routine. Lessons, study and guard duty; again and again. She had managed to keep up appearances while she researched Armeya's fool hypothesis. Why would the Mistwalkers want to start a war with mages? Or want to kill mages at all. It made little sense to her. Mages served the elven, so why would they wish them dead? She had even tried to peep into Aluriel's things while the woman stepped away, apparently busy managing her house's affairs, but she was keen and suspected her of snooping right away. Soon after, Aluriel switched rooms, just as she promised she would the first day they had met.

Aluriel's parting words to her had been, "I'll see you soon." She couldn't decide if that was a threat or mere attempt at pleasantry.

Perhaps it was both.

Still, Kyra was finding it difficult to waste anymore of her time on this hapless errand. Despite what Armeya and the others may think, she *knew* Adathin couldn't be involved. He just couldn't. This... This was beginning to be too much to handle. Finding a mage killer? The Spellthief? *Ha,* how had she ever thought that she could? Why had she even wanted to? She hadn't known Freed. She certainly wasn't ordered to. She was just a mage adept. A mage in training, really. Surely this was something for the Spellbound Arch to deal with. A task for master mages. But did they even care? Why did she? *No!* She just had to keep her head low and do what was expected of her. Nothing more, nothing less.

She had tried her best, but suspicions and theories still plagued her every night. While she appreciated the solitude of having no roommate, she had to admit that it was lonely at times. Even Aluriel's sour attitude had provided a small sense of comfort. At the very least, Adathin and she were on speaking terms again, but there was now an unseen barrier between them. One that she had erected when they returned to Dragrin's and he had reinforced with his indifference. She suspected on his side that Aluriel had, once again, come between the two of them in some way.

Kyra pushed all of that aside. Tonight was guard duty for her circle—her included. She couldn't be worrying about such petty things now. She would have to remain sharp. You never know what could happen out in the dark of night.

"We need more on the Northwest gate," Gath warned.

Av'ot stepped forward. "No," he replied. "We need reinforcements in the South. That's where the bulk of the goblins are hiding. Dimlight will be overrun if they manage to break through."

Willow rubbed at her temples. The two had been arguing for the better part of the hour, and it was causing an all too familiar pain too well up at the edges of her head. Was this what Steelhand had meant when he had warned her about an upcoming danger? No, it couldn't be. If the man had known about a goblin army stomping their way up to Mistbreaks' front door, he would have done something. He would have said something... Wouldn't he? It didn't help that the mages of Dragrin's had seemingly abandoned the city. Why had the Spellbound Arch not sent reinforcements? And the elven... Well, it wasn't a surprise they wouldn't lift a finger to help. But still, there was self-preservation to consider. If the defenses of Mistbreak fell, the elven would bear the full burden of the attack alone. Perhaps they didn't fear it. Perhaps this was all according to a grander plan. A plan in which the pactless were wiped out for the cost of goblin lives.

Dark reflections gnawed at the edge of her mind, and she did her best to push them from her thoughts. It had been almost a week since the goblin warband had shown in force, peppering the outer walls with makeshift catapults and arrows. First had come the envoys that warned that if peace wasn't offered, then they would invade the city. This came not directly to her, but more as a general cry on the streets to all who would listen. Unsurprisingly, the goblins who carried that grim prophecy were ignored, and not just by her, but by the populace as well. She speculated mages would eventually come and handle the disturbance the goblins caused, but when they hadn't, she became concerned and a contact of hers warned her that Dragrins was under a strict lockdown. Lockdown... because of the Spellthief. The mage killer. Had Steelhand suspected it was one of her people? That could pose trouble for her in the future, and trouble was not what she needed now.

"Ma'am," Av'ot said, his dark eyes scanning her pityingly. It was then that she noticed that everyone in the room was staring at her.

Willow snapped back to her senses. "We must bolster both forces," she said. "Send another ten or so to the Northwest."

"And the South?"

"I'll take care of it."

Gath sputtered, "*You can't!* Who will declare orders? Who will lead us?"

Willow turned and pointed to Quistis. It was time. Her time.

"Quistis will," she said.

"Ma'am, I don't think—"

"Quistis will be obeyed as if she were speaking with my own tongue," she snapped. "I will help fend off the South, and, with any luck, figure out why the goblins are attacking. I'll find if there is peace to be had, even if temporary. Now, if that's all, make sure the sick and wounded are treated and any innocent folk of the Dimlight District are sheltered and fed. Human, mage and elven alike. Even uncanny, I care not. You have your orders. Dismissed!"

Willow breathed a heavy sigh of relief. She had never wanted this. Authority. Responsibility. It was exhausting knowing that every life revolved around the decisions she made. At the very least, she could risk her own life as well.

Quistis placed a warm hand on her shoulder. "Are you sure?" she asked. "What if the goblins make it this far? What if... What if you fall?"

Willow turned to her with sorrow in her eyes. "Then they have you, my love. Do whatever it takes to protect who you can, but, above all, yourself. Protect yourself first. *Survive!* You must survive."

Qusitis clicked her tongue and gave her a warm smile. Those eyes... those ever shifting eyes. Her heart melted upon seeing them, just as it had done the first time she had ever seen her.

"Only if you survive," Quistis said. "Promise me. *Promise!*"

"I promise," she lied.

CHAPTER 27

HIDDEN HOME

Kyra stretched as she crossed the courtyard on her way to relieve the guards at the black gate. It had been Circle Fae's turn and yet, when she approached, she found that they had already left, abandoning their post early. It seemed that the lockdown was grating on everyone's nerves, and this was just a bit of youthful defiance. Still, Circle Fae had been Norrix's circle, and, despite his flaws, she never knew the man to shirk his duty. In their place, she found a rather chipper Soren and Iona talking between each other excitedly. Strange, she was under the impression that the two didn't get along until that point.

She narrowed her eyes at the two of them, chatting so chummy together. "You two are early," she said, not hiding the bit of surprise in her voice. "That's not like you, Soren."

Soren's chilled-blue eyes went wide in false surprise. "I'll have you know that I'm always punctual. I arrive on time, every time."

"Maybe on Soren time," Iona replied.

"*Precisely!*"

A smile passed between them, but Iona's face swiftly transformed into a look of despair. Before she could ask what was the matter, Armeya and Maxim arrived, dressed unceremoniously in drab gray clothing, contrasting with their multicolored magecloak. Those two had become closer friends as well after what they had endured together in the goblin camp.

Not romantically, however. At least, she didn't think so. No... it couldn't be. Armeya's affections to Maxim were like those of an older sister for a sibling. Their time in the goblin camp... no matter how much she had asked, neither would speak to what was exactly said or what precisely happened. Armeya insisted that nothing untoward took place, and that was that. Perhaps it hadn't. Perhaps she was just being paranoid. Perhaps this change in Armeya's personality was just the shifting of the sands. A change in the dynamic of their Circle. How could it not be different? How could they not be different? They believed that Adathin, their leader, was secretly a murderer. A butcher. The Spellthief. And she could seemingly do nothing to change their minds.

"Say," Iona said suddenly, drawing all eyes to her. "You know, this lockdown... I'm tired of it. More than tired, in fact."

"Here, here," Soren agreed, pumping his hand in the air.

"So..." Armeya replied. "What is it you intend to do about it? We have our orders."

"*Orders...*" Iona spat her displeasure at the cobbled stone beneath her feet. "We're of age. And mages at that. We don't need their rules, but you know what we do need?"

Soren looked excited as he replied, "Please say tea. I could really go for some. Months without Katia's tea. *Months!* My throat is so parched. I'm a man lost in the desert with only the burning sand to drink."

"*Aye,*" Iona said. "Tea sounds lovely, in fact. Come now, it's been far too long since any of us has had any. While I don't particularly care for tea, I just want to be rid of this place, even if for a spell. I care not for the destination."

"It has been far too long," Soren said, almost giddy with elation.

"So, what, we're supposed to abandon our duty?" Armeya crossed her arms. "And for what? Tea? What would Elder Reylar think? What would he do to us?" She turned on Soren, pointing a finger at his chest. "You've been spending time with the Elder. Special training, or so I've heard. What do you think he would say?"

Soren visibly shuddered. "I... well... he would likely give me a beat down, to be completely honest." He suddenly waved his hands. "Not like he hasn't been already. It's true that ever since that incident with the goblin poison, I've been receiving private lessons with him. Sparing lessons. The man is brilliant. He's already taught me so much about my power and the ringpact. Even his style of fighting... I do think that I'm a much better fighter now." He grew a coy smile as he added, "Not that I was bad before."

Iona coughed into her hand, and she noticed the dark-rust like appearance of her ringpact. "About that tea?"

"Ah, yes," Soren said. "We'll, even Elder Reylar had been complaining of these lockdowns. Rumor is, orders came from the Elven Conclave, *not* the Spellbound Arch. *Bleh,* politics. Either way, I'm sure none will notice if we're gone for a short time. Besides, even our *leader* has better things to do than show up for this *duty,* it seems."

Armeya threw up her hands, but from the corner of her eyes, she betrayed herself. It was obvious that she too wished to get away from this place. "Fine," she said. "But only for a quick visit."

Kyra decided it was her time to chime in. "I don't think this is a good idea. What if the Spellthief infiltrates Dragrin's? Would you really be ok with that blood on your hands?"

Iona laughed. "Spellthief? You seriously want to be talking about that? We know who the likely culprit is. We *know.* And they are already safely within these walls."

Armeya nodded her agreement.

Kyra physically felt the group's dynamic shift again, as if they were pulling away. Pulling away from her specifically. She knew that if she didn't agree to go, they would leave her there... alone. Would they then think she was a part of their conspiracy theories? That she actively worked against them?

"Fine," she agreed reluctantly. "But only for a short time."

When they arrived at Haven, Kyra noticed something odd; the streets, usually so full of hawkers selling their merchandise, and citizens, both human and uncanny alike, aptly waiting to buy it, were unusually empty. Strange didn't quite cut it. The city appeared utterly abandoned, the street lights humming lonely, the only sound to accompany the fog which rolled like a low tide across the streets.

It was surreal. Uneasy.

The appearance of Haven Teashop remained unchanged, except for the dusty and neglected windows and sign, which seemed untouched by cleaning for weeks. In the corner, trash and dry leaves had bunched up as well. This seemed so unlike Katia, who normally took such pleasure and diligence in her work. She had said on numerous occasions that this place was her life, but it certainly didn't appear that way now.

Lines of worry marred Soren's face as he rapped rapidly on the wooden door. No answer. She felt a familiar sting of worry in her chest.

"*Shit...*" Soren muttered under his breath. Then he inhaled, concentrating. The air seemed to grow cold around him as he slammed his shoulder into the frame of the door, breaking the latch and sending it flying wide open.

"What are you doing?" Armeya cried out.

Iona chuckled to herself. "Effective and practical."

Soren looked regretful as he whispered, "I'm worried."

The interior was pitch black, much darker than she had ever recalled. No candles burned. No magelamps. Even the herbs that swung in little pots near the entrance appeared dilapidated, small specks of black mold growing from the wilting leaves.

"*Katia!*" Soren called out, pushing inside.

No reply came.

Kyra drew in aethryis and formed a swirling ball of light with the twist of her hand and the darkness banished around them. Upon inspection, she could see little actual damage; it truly was just neglect. If she had to guess, she would say that it had been at least a week since anyone tended to anything in here, which begged the question: Where was Katia?

"Something's wrong," Armeya spoke truth to what they all felt.. "And not just with the shop. The streets... they're so..."

"Empty," Soren said.

"Agreed," Kyra replied. "Where is everyone? The citizens? Humans, elven and uncanny? They're just... gone."

A sudden screeching of wood riled her nerves, and she spun to meet it. Moving the orb of light slowly towards where the sound had come from, she saw, on the ground, a trapdoor behind a bar table. Jumping over the table, she leaned down, gripping the looped rope which went through the wood and pulled upwards. As it lifted, specks of collected dust spit into the air and in her eyes. She wiped her face and guided the orb of light downwards, down the hatch and into the unknown below.

The staircase led down into a dark abyss. Even her orb of light couldn't illuminate everything with the current aethryis she fed it. Looking back and shrugging her shoulders, she started down, being careful to keep eyes on her surroundings at all times. Wouldn't do anyone any good if she took a knife in the back. Her least of all.

As Kyra set her feet firmly to the floor beneath the shop, she heard the others coming down the ladder as well, one at a time. Soren grumbled something about him going first, but she ignored his protest and set onwards. Her orb of light fluttered around her, spinning and revealing jars upon jars of different herbs set on makeshift light-wooden shelves. Some were set in liquid. Others dry. And even some had their own little biomes inside. It looked like a mad scientist's lab, more than a humble teashop.

Halfway down the hallway, Kyra heard the voice of a woman call out, "Who-who's there?" It was shrill and frightened... and oddly familiar.

"Katia's down this way," Kyra said, quickening her pace. She pushed a small wooden door open to reveal a sort of bed chamber. There was a bed made of some sort of red twisting vines. The ceiling had been painted with the image of the sun, not unlike Dragrin's own mural. The painting seemed to shift slowly, imitating a day-night cycle.

With her wings glowing as vibrant as ever, Katia sat huddled in the room's corner, sipping from a cup of what she could only assume was tea. Besides that, the woman appeared fine.

Soren stormed into the room, his blue eyes alight with fury. "*Katia!*" he said. Then, as he realized everything seemed fine, he calmly added, "Thank the Builders you're alright. I feared the worst when I couldn't find you. The state of the teashop upstairs... It's seen better days."

"Soren?" Katia replied, genuinely surprised. "What are you doing here? What are all of you doing here?"

"What are *you* doing down here?" Soren replied. "What's going on?"

Katia looked surprised as she set her cup on a small table. "I... do you really not know what's happening? Why aren't you defending the city?"

Soren looked frustrated as he stepped forward and said, "No, we really don't. Defending the city? What do you mean? Why are the streets barren? Why are you locked down here like a trapped rat? I've... We've been locked away in Dragrin's for some time now. Lockdown, because of the Spellthief. Why is the teashop in such disarray?"

Katia turned her head shamefully. "Uncanny," she said. "Goblins. They attacked around ten days past. They came in through the Dimlight District and seemed intent on storming up to Grayward. Rumors had it they were keen on attacking the Elven Court of Mistbreak itself. However... It seemed that the pactless of Dimlight became Mistbreaks greatest line of defense. I believe they assumed that mages would be ordered to help, but as far as I know, they never came. You lot never showed up."

Kyra's mouth hung open; was what she said true? It couldn't be. *It couldn't!* How could the masters have kept that from them? How could the Elder? Why would they?

"I-I... We..." She could think of nothing to say. There was no defense. People had suffered. Innocent people.

Armeya stepped forward, her off-colored eyes ablaze with fury. "You said the goblins are attacking the Dimlight District? Now? Right now?"

Katia shuddered, and her wings let off a colorful array of falling pollen. "I... *yes!* That's what the rumors have been, at least. I haven't been myself.

Once I heard of fighting, I hid myself down here. No customers anyway. As for the disarray upstairs, that was my doing as well. My people can age anything that grows, so I made everything appear old and untended. Far less chance of being caught if the goblins think this place long abandoned."

"Smart," Soren said. "But I'd still leave, if possible."

Katia shook her head. "No, I will not. This place is my life now. I've made it my home."

Soren nodded.

"Those damnable goblins," Armeya said, her anger so fierce she shook with it. "They lied to me. Kri'ed lied to me!"

"Kri'ed told me he wanted peace as well," Kyra replied. "I guess peace didn't work for him after all. Attacking Dimlight was the alternative."

"They never wanted peace," Armeya insisted. "It was an excuse. All an excuse. Goblins don't know anything other than pillaging and death. All uncanny are the same. *All of them!*" Armeyas' voice caught in her throat as her gaze fell upon Katia. "I... Well... I mean..."

Katia held up a hand. "Words like that have long since given me any pause. They slide off me like water on a leaf. They do nothing to my heart, nor my soul, for both are as stone in these hard times." She sighed, as if this conversation was a long time coming. "Perhaps Soren is right. Perhaps it is time I returned to my people. Abandon this place. My home. Uncanny aren't even allowed to own businesses in Mistbreak. I survive based on a lie and others' willingness to overlook the obvious. It is only a matter of time before all of this is taken from me." She looked up at the mural on the roof, the sun at its apex. "And... I miss the sun. I miss the feel of grass between my feet." Tears welled at the edge of her eyes. "Still... I cannot bring myself to abandon the gift given to me by my benefactor, Mr. Grelen."

Armeya went silent and crossed her arms, leaning on a nearby wall and staring at the floor dejectedly.

A silence lingered for a time before Soren asked, "Well, what now?"

Surprisingly, it was Iona who answered, replying, "What do you mean? *We fight!*"

Soren shook his head. "We should head back. Speak to the Elder. Rally the others."

"I can do that for us," Iona replied. "It's what I'm best at, right? Delivering messages. But you lot... people need you. Without support, the pactless will fall and next, the elven. We have a duty as mages to protect them."

In a way, Iona was right. They had a duty. A sworn charge. Kyra looked down at her ringpact, which gleamed brilliant silver back at her.

"If we do, where should we even start?" Soren asked.

Katia stood. "By finding the leader of the pactless, Willow Ashen."

Leader of the pactless... just the thought of seeing that woman again made her blood boil.

Soren scratched at his head. "This has become a lot more troublesome than a simple outing for tea."

Katia raised her hands. "Speaking of which, I have a gift. Here." She beckoned to a bundle of capped glass vials. "Made with moonwillow. My people are among the few who can manage to grow the plant. Cleanses goblin poison, remember? I suspect you may need it."

Soren held his hand to his healed wound gingerly. "Poison... right."

"I called in a few favors back when Soren... Well, I called in some favors. As I said, it's a gift. From me to you."

"I-I-I'll hold them," Maxim said.

Iona lifted the vials and handed them to Maxim. "Then it's settled. I'll go back and convince Elder Reylar to send help. Easy enough."

Kyra's chest tightened as she asked, "And what about Adathin?"

Armeya scoffed, and Iona eyed her dangerously.

"I think it's best for *him* to stay out of this," Iona replied. "Don't you?"

CHAPTER 28

ONE-HUNDRED PERCENT

Late. And for what? Nothing. Nothing at all.

Adathin stomped irritably down the hallways towards the black gate or 'The Wall', as the others had taken to calling it. Ridiculous. Mages were like spoiled children at times. Give them such a simple task, and they hemmed and hawed all the while.

Those whom he came across, likely noticing his sour demeanor, made themselves scarce from his gaze. He could hardly blame them. Aluriel, his dear sister, had mentioned she wanted to speak to him about something. Urgently, she had said. He had tried to meet her in the North Tower, but when he arrived, he found naught but the keeper of the birds. The woman had looked like a bird herself, with a sharp nose, dark eyes, and such nervous twitching. He had asked her about Aluriel, but the woman had brushed him away like a common pest. And now—now he was late for his shift at the gates. He would certainly hear an earful from the others.

As Adathin stepped into the courtyard, he noticed it to be rather empty. It seems the rumors of the Spellthief had everyone rattled still. Nobody wished to be alone at night. Not in this thick fog. Not with the looming black gates ahead. He swallowed hard; he wasn't so sure *he* wanted to be either. He pushed the thoughts aside as he approached the black gates and it surprised him that nobody was there to greet him. Had they all forgotten? No chance of that. While Soren could be lazy at times, he always showed up... eventually. And Kyra, he had never known her to abandon a duty so easily. *Kyra...* he wished he could fix the rift that had grown between them. But perhaps it was for the best. In the end, she was safer for it.

Adathin circled the black gate, finding that truly none were to be found. Just as he was about to give up and reach out for them with psionics, he heard a voice at the edge of his senses.

"Brother," Aluriel said, and he spun to find her standing a few steps behind him. When had the woman become so stealthy? He hadn't heard a single footstep from her. How had he not noticed her approach? His head suddenly felt fuzzy, but he quickly brushed that aside. It was late, and he was tired, nothing more.

"There you are," Adathin said. "You had me walk up all those stairs just to not bother showing up. Next time, I will choose the location. *Me!*"

Aluriel faked a laugh, and something pricked at him about her demeanor. It was rather odd. She stood, straight-backed and royal. She had never acted this way when they were alone before. She had always let her guard down when they spoke. What changed?

"Apologies," Aluriel said. "I just got caught up is all."

Adathin grumbled softly to himself. "Well, it seems my circle has all but abandoned their duty. Some leader I turned out to be. They've been so... distant of late. Anyway, I'll be manning the wall all alone tonight, it seems. Plenty of time to talk. So... What did you wish to discuss? Does father have more choice words about me and my behavior? Perhaps about my decision to travel to Oldrock. Oh, how he must have been furious. Wish I could have seen it myself."

Aluriel tiptoed closer, leaned in close and said in a whisper, "I know... I know who it is."

Adathin stared at her curiously, his interest piqued. "Who? Who do you know?"

"The *Spellthief!*"

Adathin's breath caught in his throat, his hands quivered and he fought, stumbling for words before replying, "That's... *That's fantastic!* Let's go tell the Elder right away. We can stop this. Everything can go back to normal. Hells, I'm sure father will allow you to return to—"

Aluriel raised a hand to stall him. "We can't speak to anyone. It is not something for the mages to know. Not yet."

Adathin got a bad feeling, like a creeping ichor rising up his spine and his head became even fuzzier. "What do you mean?" he asked.

"It would be better to show you," Aluriel suggested. "Come. Through the gate. Let's go back—back to where this all started."

"But I... we can't... I can't."

"Come, brother," Aluriel insisted. "It'll be alright. I promise."

That word... *promise.* It dropped into his mind like a soothing balm, easing his nerves and tensions. Adathin found himself nodding and suddenly he knew everything would be alright. How could it not? He could trust her emphatically. She was his sister. If he could not trust her with his life, then there was no one else he could. If not for her, he was well and truly lost.

Willow approached the entrance to the southern edge of Mistbreak, where residential housing lined the streets. Drab colors of brownish-red paint marred the structures, and every now and again, she would glimpse one of the townsfolk peeking out behind a slant of wood. Looking up, she could see even more of the scared faces of the masses as they peered helplessly from their balconies.

Salvator approached her with a few other of her pactless. An arrow had struck the boy in the arm, and the haft of it had already been broken when Enoch pulled it free. Salvator squirmed, but did not cry out. He was strong—much stronger than when she had first set eyes upon him. Was this her doing? Her teachings? Her guidance? Or had this strength always been there, hidden beneath the surface?

"What is the status?" she asked. "How many casualties?"

Salvator stood straighter, as if he were a soldier. Perhaps he now was. Perhaps they all were.

"A few," he said, with a hint of sadness in his voice. "The goblins have set up a breaching area just outside the city. The South entrance is being pummeled near continuously with arrows and catapulted rocks. The guards have performed their job admirably, holding back the largest of the waves, but the goblins are tricky. Who knows how long they've been infiltrating into the city like parasites? Small bands of them attack from shadowed corners or nearby alleyways. Some even have perched on rooftops. I—I don't think we can hold them back. We need support. We need the help of the mages and elves."

Willow took it in. All of it. The frustration. The fear. The pain of loss. She chose to feel it. She would not hide; not this time. Each strike against her people was a strike against her. Each death was like a limb torn from her own flesh. She was an animal, caught in a snare. And, like an animal, she would lash out at the ones who set to harm her and what was hers.

"Tell everyone to stand back. I'll buy us some time."

"Ma'am," Salvator replied. "I don't think that's wise. Not even you can—"

Willow held her ring to the back of her neck, pressing it against the magelock as she muttered, "One-hundred percent."

Aetherical power coursed through her, wild and free. Oh, how she had longed to feel this again. Ever since she had fought Steelhand and unleashed herself, she had felt... unburdened. The pactless were hers. This power was hers... Dimlight, as filthy and degenerate as it is, was hers.

Lightning cackled softly around her body, concentrated mostly towards her hands. She turned to stare at Salvator, who returned her look with pure, wild amazement. She saw her own face reflected in his bright eyes. Her red hair floated softly in the air behind her, and her eyes were of furious crimson.

Looking around, metallic objects, arrowheads, daggers and pieces of armor floated off the cobbled stone. She was a maelstrom of power. Why had she ever feared this? This was her, in her purest form. She had nothing to fear. Such notions were a distant thing now.

Willow heard Salvator order everyone to move, and she silently thanked him for that. While she knew she was powerful, she had little confidence in her ability to control that power. Calmly, and slowly, she walked towards one of the guard towers that overlooked the Southern Gate. Suddenly, three goblins appeared at her side, wielding gleaming daggers in the faint light. They aimed them towards her and charged. Stupid creatures. Pathetic imbeciles. With a flick of her wrist, the very breath of lightning itself eradicated all three from this plane of existence. There was little left of them but charred meat slowly smoldering on blackened stone. She had used her power to kill. It wasn't the first time, but it was the first time that she had meant it.

Why had she feared this power? Why?

Willow quickened her pace atop the towers of the Southern Gate and soon found herself staring out at the goblin horde. She warned the few remaining guards to vacate and, at first, they appeared as if they would oppose her. Try to arrest her, even. But one look at their leader, a young square-jawed and baby-faced man, made him cower and flee, the others following in tow.

Good, they could detest her and her power from a distance. A safe distance.

For some reason, the mist didn't seem as strong tonight. Strange, she had never known it to let up before. Willow glared out upon her enemy. It was a goblin warband, at least one-hundred strong, many hiding in a nearby tangle of trees from what she could tell from the dim light of the moon. They soon spotted her and began pointing and hollering nonsensical things. She didn't care. Nothing they could do would stop what was coming.

A single arrow struck the stone next to her head. It was close. Too close. It seemed one of the goblins saw her as a threat and took the opportunity presented. Smart, but the fellow should have aimed better. She recognized the goblin out of the many as he frantically tried to knock another. She snapped and a single bolt of lightning flashed through the air, leaving a small fire where a goblin had once existed.

The loud boom rocked the other goblins into action as many picked up bows and knocked arrows. Dozens of arrows flew towards her now, and she summoned a powerful gust of wind to throw them off the target. They broke against the burst of air, many failing to even reach the guard tower itself, let alone hit her.

Boredom was taking over. What could these pathetic creatures do to her? What could anyone do? She lifted both her hands to the sky, and the clouds suddenly swirled, turning black and angry. Booms of thunder brewing above caused the goblins to turn and flee back into the forest. Was this enough? Could she spare them?

Willow lowered her arms and released the aethryis that courts through her. It fled, and she breathed a sigh of relief for a moment... until it came roaring back into her, like water filling a gap. She tried to force it away, but it was as useless as swatting the ocean. She no longer controlled the aethryis. It controlled her.

Her arms lifted back into the air unwillingly and the last sight she saw before blackness filled her eyes was the blinding light of hundreds of bolts of lightning raining into the forest, igniting the trees, and burning everything to the ground.

The last thing she heard was the screams of death.

Kyra tried to hold her emotions together but was quickly overwhelmed by the gravitas of what she witnessed. Dimlight was in ruins, with humans and uncanny alike, dead or dying in the streets. She briefly saw a small child try to move her deceased mother's hand before being lifted and carried away by what she could only hope was her father. The hurt in that man's eye as he turned from his beloved gave her a shiver and a familiar pain flared through her ruined hand. It had not been so long ago that she herself was a victim. A victim of her own making, but a victim nonetheless.

Soren had taken a leadership-like position in Adathin's absence. He surveyed the scene as stoically as she had ever seen the man. He seemed completely unphased by the carnage and she was at odds with the image of a carefree Soren and this new man who now stood before her.

"We'll prioritize helping civilians," Soren said, turning to Maxim. "This is your time to shine, my friend. Look around you, there are so many in need of your skills. Your mystic aethryis. Your power to heal. Can I count on you?"

Maxim shied away from Soren's gaze, as if the man had physically struck him. He trembled slightly and tears welled at the edges of his eyes.

Soren placed a hand on Maxim's shoulder. "It's ok. I know—know how you struggle. Just... do your best. For me."

Maxim nodded, and she couldn't help but smile. Soren, it seemed, was a natural born leader. Even she felt calmer knowing he was with them. Then she felt immediate regret at how those feelings betrayed Adathin. Now was not the time to think of him, though. They had work to do.

Kyra helped the citizens in whatever ways she could. She had no healing aethryis and wasn't particularly adept at bandaging wounds, but in a pinch, precision mattered little. Eventually, she found herself helping a young man who was frantically searching for his dog. The dog was hiding in a nearby alleyway and the young man happily scooped up the small thing and whisked it away down the street. She hoped the two of them would be ok.

"Make your way towards the upper gates," Kyra shouted. "And tell them to prepare the elven guard for an attack. If possible, convince them to send forces to help."

"I will," the young man replied as he disappeared into the mist.

Kyra doubted the elven would help, but she tried to hold out a small hope that the young man would somehow persuade them. If the elven were known for anything, it certainly wasn't their compassion or empathy. All others be damned.

"Make way. *Make way!*" A group of heavily injured men and women carried a limp body up some stone stairs nearby, pushing past all others who either were trying to help the injured or were busy looting what they could. Her breath caught as she recognized the man who was calling out to everyone.

"*Salvator!*" Kyra yelled, running towards the group. She paused when the man held up a hand, a small fire sizzling on the tips of his extended fingers.

"*Get back!*" Salvator warned. "I won't let you take us."

"Take you?" she asked. "I'm here trying to help. What are you doing? And—" Just as one of the men shifted, she saw reddish hair for just a moment and then a limp arm dangling uselessly. "Who is that?"

"None of your—"

A burly man pushed Salvator aside as he said, "It's Willow Ashen. Leader of the pactless. She... she..." The man seemed to trial off, unable to finish his sentence.

Salvator looked dejectedly towards the ground. "She stopped the goblin horde at the Southern Gate, but..."

Calmly, Kyra stepped forward until the woman came into full view. Her hair was a disheveled mess, singed at the tips, leaving the red color blackened and frayed. Her hands and arms appeared burned as well, not too dissimilar to her own old injury. Yet she breathed still, if ever so slightly.

"Have you tried to heal her?" Kyra asked.

All turned their heads from her.

Salvator choked back a sob. "We... none of us know how. Healing is... difficult without a ringpact."

"*Maxim!*" Kyra called with urgency.

Maxim heard her call and rushed over as fast as his pudgy body could carry him. As he saw the wreck of the leader's body, he shuddered, stepping away as if he were in danger. Even Soren heard and had made his way over.

"What's wrong?" Soren asked, looking into Maxim's eyes. "The red-haired one needs help. Heal her."

"I-I... I can't." Maxim crouched down, holding his knees to his chest. "I can't, I can't, I can't."

Salvator cocked a flat grin. "Useless. You're all useless. We need to get her back home. I... We'll figure something out."

"*Wait!*" Maxim said, springing to his feet. He rummaged through his pockets until he found what he was looking for, pulling out a small glass vial. "Give her this. It'll help."

Salvator took the vial, but eyed the stuff as if it were poison.

"You can trust him," Kyra said.

"And can I trust you?"

Kyra breathed heavily, purposefully showing her displeasure. "Trust or not, you need us. You said she wiped out the goblin forces from the Southern Gate? What about the Western?"

Salvator ground his teeth. "Still under siege, I think. But... we're through. Done. Done bleeding for this place. Done dying for it. We've lost too many and we have too many injuries. You mages abandoned your duty and left us to die in your stead. We—"

"We didn't know," Kyra replied calmly. "But we do now. One of ours is heading to Dragrin's now to warn the others. To rally help. For now, how can *we* help?"

Willow suddenly stirred, her arm lifting up towards the sky as if she saw something up above. "Help us," she said in all but a whisper. "Defend the city." Her arm fell and her eyes rolled back. The woman was completely out, and she doubted she would recover anytime soon.

Salvator looked at Willow and her before adding, "You heard her; *help us!* Go defend the Western Gate. Show us what those precious ringpacts can do."

Kyra turned towards Soren expectantly. He seemed to be taking all the information in and stared upwards towards the sky, consideringly. It was just for a moment, but that pause felt like it lasted a lifetime.

"We're going to the gate," Soren finally said. "I know your people are injured, but can some stay and help?"

Salvator looked around at the other pactless and then some nodded in agreement.

"Good," Soren said. "Then let's put an end to this little rebellion."

CHAPTER 29

ELVEN QUEEN

Journal Entry

Year: 831 E.B

You never forget the smell of death. Never. It permeates the air, sticks to your skin and envelops your senses with its sickeningly sweet decay. No, you never forget, but you just become... accustomed.

"Look for survivors over there," Master Lu'ce had said, waving me off in no specific direction. I could see it on her face: frustration. If we had been faster—if I had been faster—we may have been able to save those people. I had nodded and walked along, checking each and every body along my way. The corpses had been bloated and stank in the humid heat. I had wrapped a cloth around my nose and mouth to block out the smell. It didn't work. Men, women and children, all human, and all very much dead. There had been no survivors from the tiny village of Millrun. None. It was as if some sort of beast had run through the streets, killing indiscriminately. But I knew it had been no beast. It had been uncanny. Goblins, specifically. I had long since recognized how the goblins attacked. Without mercy. Without hesitation. They had mostly picked the bodies clean and recovered anything they could.

But it wasn't hard to filter out the shafts of broken arrows or the cracked and jagged metal heads those same arrows had held.
In my experience, goblins were among the most savage of killers. They cared little for honor and they cared nothing for mercy.

Adathin strolled down the streets of Mistbreak with a flutter in his step and happiness in his heart. It was a bright, jubilant day, and the sun was singing lightly against his ethereal skin. Oh, how he had missed the sun. Why was it that he never felt its healing rays anymore? As he pondered the question, Aluriel's eyes met his, and he suddenly forgot what he was thinking about. He was just happy to be here with her. To be alive to witness her ascension. She gave him a queenly smile as she continued to lead him.

Oddly, he didn't see another soul along the way, and even more odd was the pristine condition in which the city found itself in. Even the Dimlight District was proud and proper, and that struck him as wrong for some reason. Had it always been this way?

"Come on, brother, hurry," Aluriel said. Then he realized that he had stopped in the middle of the street.

"Sorry, sister," he replied, his ears twitching nervously. "It's just... nevermind. You're right, we need to move quickly. *Uh...* Where are we going again?"

Aluriel sighed, exacerbated. "To meet with your circle, remember? Your friends. They are all waiting for you."

"Oh, they are?" he asked. Suddenly, he felt as helpless as a boy, and redness burned his face flush. "I'm... I'm sorry!"

"Sorry—not sorry, I don't care. *Hurry!*"

"*Sorry!*"

Adathin fell in line and kept close at heel. When had Aluriel become so persuasive? He remembered a time where the two of them could hardly get along at all, and he remembered always having a sour disposition towards her. But now—now he could see that she was someone to be followed. Revered. Someone whose integrity was beyond reproach. How had his father ever chosen him to lead their house over her? The thought clouded all in a dark miasma that threatened to consume him. The world suddenly shifted around him as the mist that he hadn't noticed before seemed to swirl like a whirlpool around him. Then all was bright again! What had upset him just a moment ago? He couldn't remember, but one look from Aluriel told him that he should move faster. He didn't want to disappoint her. He couldn't do that to her. *Never!*

"Here we are," Aluriel said, adding in a chill tone, "Finally."

Adathin recognized the place immediately. He had been here before. A few times, in fact. He faced the double-door of the familiar warehouse, and he noticed one side was already ajar. Were his friends waiting for him inside?

"Go on," Aluriel prompted.

Adathin obeyed without question, leaning in and taking a brief look around. He felt a sudden shove, and then darkness enveloped his sight.

"*Aluriel!*" he cried out. "Where are you?"

"I'm here, brother," she said, as a small light from a candle lit from the opposing end of the warehouse. "Don't worry, I'm here."

As the candle grew brighter, a metallic smell and taste assaulted his senses. He turned and held back vomit, and when his eyes fixed back on Aluriel, she sat atop a throne. Not any throne... a throne of blood and bone. Beneath her, sprawled out, were dozens of bodies, both human and elven alike. He couldn't recognize any of them, but they all had the same look plastered on their face: utter bewilderment, as if they had seen one of the Builders of old the moment they had died. They were smiling widely. Happy and smiling at their own deaths.

As disgusted as he was, he could not help himself but revere the woman who sat upon that bloody throne.

All hail Aluriel Mistwalker, Elven Queen.

Soren shushed her as he pulled her back. Kyra protested, but heard the soft pattering of goblin steps from just around the corner.

"Oy, can we kill 'em already?" the goblin said.

"*No!*" replied another in a deep, gruff voice. "We needs 'em as leverage. Those cowardly elfs hide in their towers up high. We needs 'em to come down."

Kyra turned and saw someone standing in a door leading into a building nearby. It was a woman with long black hair and she prompted her to follow her. She tapped on Soren and pointed. He nodded, and they moved away from the arguing goblins and into the house. The door shut promptly and quietly behind them.

"Close," Kyra said, taking the first full breath she dared.

"Too close," Soren agreed.

Kyra looked around at the modest room, only to be suddenly pressed aside as a bear of a man shoved a wooden dresser in front of the door.

"Never can be too careful," the man said.

Armeya clicked her tongue, giving the room a sweep of her gaze. "And who are you two?"

"I'm Mollee and this is Riral... Keats. Married. Goin on—"

"They don't care how long we've been married, woman," Riral said.

Mollee stuck out her ample chest. "Just being polite. Happened to see you lot from the window and it seemed like you needed help."

Armeya rolled her eyes as she said, "We didn't—"

"Much appreciated, ma'am," Soren interrupted. "Aye, we were in a bit of a sort. Now we have some time to plan."

"Time to plan?" Mollee looked at them questioningly. Then, as if the rising of the dawn, she noticed their magecloak and ringpacts. "You're mages? Thank the Builders you've come. I thought you never would. Are you just the first group? How many more are coming?"

"Just us," Soren replied. As the woman's face turned from exultation to hopelessness, he added, "For now."

"Where have you all been?" Riral asked, not bothering to hide his foul disposition. "We've been held up here for a few days now. We're running low on water and our children... our children are scared. Terrified. Were you lot going to do nothing?"

"I... We didn't know," Soren replied. He looked genuinely sorry. "But we do now. We've already sent for help from both our fellow mages and the elvish. It'll be alright now. We'll take back the city."

Riral gave a *humph* as he said, "We don't live in the city. *We* live in Dimlight. Mages? The elvish; you lot have never helped before, even if it is your duty. Thieves, uncanny, and others who will do us harm are left unchallenged. By the Builders, even the constables rarely head this way, unless they are looking for a little midnight fun themselves."

Mollee put a hand on the man's shoulder. "What Riral means to say is thank you."

"*Thank you?*" Riral looked startled. "I never said—"

Soren held up a hand. "It's alright, sir. You don't need to thank us. I know we don't deserve it. Yet... will you help us? What do you two know? Any information can help us."

"They caught the Sylmys," Mollee said as her husband went and sat on the floor on the opposite side of the room like a petulant child. "They are a family from across the way. Some others as well. They are keeping them as hostages as far as we can tell. Another group was defending us for a time. They called themselves pactless, I think. Mages without rings, it seems. That frightened me at first, but they weren't like the stories I've heard. They weren't savages crazed on magic. Some even fought to their own deaths. Noble, the lot of them."

Riral *harrumphed* to himself. "Far nobler than you all."

"Do you know how many?" Kyra asked.

Mollee shook her head, and then buried her face in her hands, overwhelmed by all that was happening.

Armeya's features softened as she stepped forward and placed a hand on the woman's shoulder. "We're here now," she said. "We'll do everything we can to help."

Suddenly, a scream echoed from outside. Human; female. Likely one of the captives. To be honest, Kyra was surprised it had taken so long for it to come to this. The goblins would only hold their bloodlust back for so long. They could only hold it back so long.

CHAPTER 30

CHANGES AND BETRAYAL

Kri'ed looked around at the green faces of his uncanny brethren and felt nothing but... hatred. He felt the age in his bones with every step he took. Every breath. Looking at his reflection in the broken glass strewn about the streets of Mistbreak, he could hardly recognize that old face staring back at him. How long has it been since he had felt solid, cobbled stone underfoot? How long had it been since he had slept in the well-insulated homes of a proper city?

Looking around at the goblins he now claimed to be one of, he felt nothing for them or their plight. They were savages. Bottom feeders. They killed and stole without mercy or contempt. They gave in to their base urges, never knowing of the pleasures of high-society. Oh, how he longed to once again share tea with the high-price of Xevepis. Or how he had felt when he was asked to bear witness to the birth of the prince's one and only son.

Kri'ed had been a royal merchant, once upon a time. Down to the South, in the warm sun of Xevepis, with its long desert sands that eventually gave way to a vast ocean. He could still feel it, the sun heated sand between his manicured toes. Money had bought him that pleasure—a pleasure that no other goblin had shared in before. But in the end, that money was not enough to stop him from losing favor with his prince. It had to be a goblin arrow. It had to be. One of his own kind had taken aim from high atop a roof, shooting down, aimed at taking the high-prince's life. It was he whom had shoved his prince to the side. He who had saved his life! But alas, he has not thought of the prince's son standing right beside him. The arrow had struck true, straight through the prince's son's heart. The lad had succumbed within the hour.

The prince had sought to make a point when dealing with the murdering goblin. A warning to others. The prince had strung him up from the city square for days, letting the poor sod bake in the sun, and encouraging the scavengers to feed from his flesh. His screams became a constant background of city life in Xevepis for a time. They wouldn't even allow the goblin the dignity of death; constantly treating his wounds, feeding him, giving him water only to string him up again. Kried shared a lineage with the goblin, but he cared not for his plight. He deserved it for what he had done to his prince. For what he had done to all of goblin kind.

Soon, the prince and his relationship frayed. Severed. Other merchants, ones that dabbled in the forbidden, came crawling like leeches to draw succor from the high-princes wound. In his grief, he sought a way to restore his son. To bring him back from the dead. It, of course, was an impossible task. But never tell that to a father on the brink of oblivion. Slowly, the high-prince shied away from the goods he had offered, and instead, invested in the arcane and the profound. He couldn't bring himself to do that to the prince. To feed him false hope. And because he could not, the high-prince saw fit to discard him as useless. Others of Xevepis had long since stopped using the services of goblins. Of all uncanny. The coins dried up. He was left destitute. A pauper. And when he sought the refuge of his own people, he found them to be the very thing the humans feared them to be. Savages. Monsters. And he—he was one of them.

But it wasn't he who would change. It was them. *They* had to change.

It was easy to become leader of this warband. A small slip of poison and a well-timed challenge for leadership was all it took. Even he, bound with a cane, defeated the great Brirolk easily. It was all for a chance. A chance for a new life. He would find a place that goblins could call their own. Where he could call his own. A kingdom. He would change what they were. *Who* they were. To make them worthy of it. He was all the proof anyone needed that goblins could overcome their baser instincts.

He would restore his place in this world again, no matter the cost.

"Oy, boss man," said one of his followers whose name he could not remember. "What we gonna do with the captives?"

Kri'ed gnashed his teeth irritably. Had they no sense of vision? Of propriety? Strategy? "We will use them as bargaining chips, of course."

"Bargaining... chips?"

"By the Builders—leverage. *Leverage!* They ignored us, the elves, the mages, as I feared they would. This attack was modest. Mostly structural damage. Very few casualties. They will see reason in our proposal. *They must!*"

"And... what is it we want?"

"A place to call our own," Kri'ed replied. "Somewhere civilized. Somewhere recognized. Not stuck in that forsaken forest, hidden away lest we be routed out and exterminated like rats. We can build it ourselves. We just need land. Land and recognition."

The unnamed goblin seemed to think on his words before scratching his chin like an idiot. Of course he didn't understand. None of them did. When Kri'ed had procured safety for his people, he would open schools. Bring literacy and decency to his people. Not for their sake, but for his. For his ambitions, they must change. They all needed to evolve and be more like... him.

There was a sudden scream that caught his attention. Aggravatingly, he made his way over to the source, albeit slowly, due to his bum leg. When he arrived, he was sickened by the sight of one of his own poking and prodding at a poor young human woman. This savage had taken a metal poker and placed it to the fire until it lit up in the night with a hot, white sheen. Slowly, he grazed the skin of the woman as she cried out in pain and fear. Her mate, tied right alongside her, was powerless to help, his hands and feet tied with a crude and hastily knotted rope behind his back. There was pain in his eyes. And anger. A willingness to kill. Did they not realize that they created a lifelong enemy here today? That this man, no matter what happened, would never forgive them? Would fight them until his last dying breath?

Idiots, the lot of them.

"What are you doing?" Kri'ed asked, trying to keep bitterness and frustration from his voice.

The goblin man smiled, revealing a crooked, once broken jaw complete with cracked teeth. "Teachin' 'em some manners," he said, without the slightest bit of irony.

"Perhaps you should learn some yourself." Kri'ed stepped closer and his own speed surprised him and he reached out, plucking the metal poker from the man and stabbed him in the shoulder with it.

He screamed and fell back, crawling on his hands and knees away before turning and asking, "What you do that for?"

Kri'ed threw the metal poker to the ground with a *clang*. "What did I tell you?" he asked, turning his gaze from the goblin on the floor to the others, who stared at him with disbelief. "I said that the prisoners were to be unharmed. *Unharmed!* Is that too much for you to get through your thick skulls? We need them. All of them."

"You mean *you* need them."

Kri'ed recognized that voice and tenor. Turning, he saw Lel and clenched his fist. Today of all days, and this excuse of an intelligent being dares to pay him a visit. Lel once ran his own small warband, but had been defeated by Brirolk, who—in a surprising act—spared him under the condition that they join forces. It was odd for two warbands to join; usually one just slew the other and that was that. It was the reason why he had picked this particular warband to lead. He thought that, perhaps, they had a higher capacity for reason.

So far, he had been wrong.

"I mean *us*," Kri'ed replied. "These humans could be the key to our future. To our salvation."

Lel spit on the ground. "'Salvation,'" he said. "Such a... *human* word. I's think that you's spent too much time with 'em. Are you even a proper goblin anymore? When's the last time you sunk your teeth into something raw? Or is that too 'improper' for you's? Know what I's think? I think's you's just wanna crawl back to the humans as their pet. Do ye' miss yer' master?"

Kri'ed couldn't help the scowl that crossed his face. In a low voice, he asked, "Is that a challenge?"

Lel laughed. "No," he said, pointing behind him. "That is."

Something hard and heavy struck him in the back of the head, and Kri'ed felt his cane slip from his grasp as he hit the cobbled floor. Darkness seeped into view, and the world swiftly spun away from consciousness.

Oh, how he hated them. How he hated them so.

CHAPTER 31

CHEATING DEATH

Soren pressed his back against the cool brick wall, nearing the edge that led out to a courtyard where no less than thirty goblins resided. There were human captives all in a line, strung up by rope on wooden planks. Oddly, there was also an older goblin who had been tied up as well. Curious. He could hear their boisterous, nonchalant attitudes undercut by the soft groans of their captives. It filled him with anger. Torture... he was all too familiar with that pain. The scars on his back were suddenly itchy, as if they were opened anew.

Maxim made a fearful sound from behind him. His breathing was shallow and forced, and he tapped his fingers on the stone nervously. He had to say something. Something a leader would say.

"I... are you alright, Maxim?"

Maxim gave him a nod, but he could see that the pudgy man was far from alright. There were scars beneath his exterior that ran even deeper than his own. He couldn't help but wonder what they were.

"Alright," Soren said, masking his worry with false bravado. "I'll be the spearhead. When I charge in, wait until the goblins are distracted and then rescue the captives. Heal them, if needed, but don't take long. Just enough to get them on their feet and moving. If you're attacked, save yourself first. The goblins have an incentive to keep the captives alive. You? Not so much."

Maxim swallowed heavily. "I-I... Ok."

"Good."

Soren swiveled his gaze from the courtyard to the roofs looming above them. There, he saw two figures donning multi-colored magecloaks. Armeya and Kyra. They had found their perch, just as he had instructed. They stood directly above a dead-end alleyway, waiting for his signal.

"Remember, keep yourself safe above all else," he reminded Maxim.

Maxim nodded.

Standing straight, Soren cracked his head from side to side, then his knuckles, and finally, his knees. He rolled his arms and stretched. It could prove deadly if he pulled a muscle during this. Finally, he drew in aethryis from the ringpact. Aethryis flowed into his hands and then spread out into his body. It was like a source of fuel which he could manipulate to empower different aspects of his physical form. He strengthened his muscles, increasing his speed. Made his skin tougher than iron and his bones unbreakable. It wore on him, the use of aethryis, but he pushed that aside as he stepped into the courtyard.

Soren could never know. None of them could. He was not a healer. Not a friend. Just a murderer. No, worse... he was an abomination.

Maxim nodded as Soren stretched out, preparing for his mad dash. He envied the man, so willing to sacrifice himself for the good of others. The opposite of him, really. He wondered if Soren would still consider him a friend if he knew the truth.

"Remember," Soren said. "Keep yourself safe above all else."

Safe... as if he could ever be safe. Not from others. Certainly not from himself. And besides, he didn't deserve it. The compassion of a friend.

He forced himself to nod.

Soren looked out once more upon the courtyard, seemingly planning his route. There was a determined light in the man's eyes. He loved this. Maxim could tell from just a glance. There was no fear there. No doubt. Just pure, unbridled determination.

Maxim didn't just envy Soren, he idolized him. How he wished he could have just a fraction of his competence and compassion.

Soren suddenly dashed into the middle of the courtyard, his body propelled forward by augmentor aethryis. His frost-like hair whipped around his face as he yelled, "Come, goblin scum! Let's see if any of you can take me."

The goblins, stunned at first, started hootin' and hollering at each other as they prepared weapons. Not the typical crude goblin weaponry, these looked to be proper armaments made of good wood and metal. The goblins had a wild look in their eyes at the prospect of a fight, and strangely, Soren shared a similar look. So this was what it was like. Battle fervor. He had heard others speak of it before. This bliss that came before conflict. Each breath laced with energy; your heart beating through your ears. Your mind, sharper than a tack. He had felt that way before.

He never wanted to feel it again.

One goblin, the poor soul, opted to try his luck one on one with the mage. Soren, so full of aethryis that the air around him shone with power, dispatched him with a simple backhand, sending the goblin hurdling away. He could hear the faint breaking of a bone or two as the goblin tumbled across the cobbled stone. Despite what it seemed, it was an act of mercy. Soren could have killed the goblins easily, but he suspected that he held back from such deeds when he could. He respected him for it, even though he disagreed. Death was not the worst thing in the world. Far from it, in fact.

The other goblins roared as they charged Soren. He smiled, sparing a quick glance and a nod in his direction. It was time. Time to be the mage they needed him to be. A mystic. Sworn by the ringpact and duty to heal those in need. Oh, how he wished for any other fate. Anything other than this. He set those thoughts aside. Now was not the time to dwell on past mistakes. Focus on the now. Control. Control...

Soren dashed away, heading towards an alleyway on the other side of the courtyard, just as he had planned. Looking up, he saw Kyra and Armeya perched in their respective positions. The plan was going smoothly so far. Now—Now it was his time to act.

Maxim slapped himself on the cheeks. *Act!* Act like a mage, damn you.

As soon as the final goblin cleared the courtyard, he ran as fast as he could, heading straight for the various captives. Some were propped, tied to large wooden posts and others were simply tied, hands and feet behind their back. Most were gagged, and the ones that weren't appeared injured in various ways. The smell of their blood struck his nose as he approached, and it was near enough to make him wretch. Distant, painful memories resurfaced, but he shoved them down.

No, not yet. Don't give in yet.

Maxim pressed forward, and began the easy work first, pulling a small knife from his boot. Those who still could eyed him wildly, and he could hear the soft sobs underneath their gagged mouths. One by one, he cut free those bound on the ground, and then he moved on to those bound by wooden posts.

"*Thank you!*" one man exclaimed, tears from his big brown eyes strolled down his bloody face.

"*Bless you*! By the Builders, bless you," said a woman who looked no worse for the wear.

Maxim had to admit, it felt good. The praise. The devotion. Almost, for a moment, he felt like he could wash away the sins of his past. Then the smell of blood assaulted him again as he looked upon those remaining.

Three... There were three left. Two were injured to various degrees, but one... a woman... looked to have been tortured most of all. She was limp on the ground, her hair, once brown, was singed in various places. They had burned her. Badly. A man, one he had freed, her brother or husband, he couldn't tell, wept by her side. He turned from her; the other two injured had a better chance of surviving. This... This was something he had to do.

Make calls in the field of battle. Who lived—who died. It was his choice to make. His alone. But as the man who wept for the poor woman's eyes fell upon him, he hesitated; how could he just let her die? While the goblins were most certainly culpable, how was he any different if he did nothing? And if he spent his time saving this woman, and the others perished, what then? Did their families not matter? Did their husbands, wives, daughters and sons matter less?

Maxim's heart beat faster, and his breaths came short. Too much, it was all too much. He sucked in air through his teeth, but felt darkness at the edge of his vision. He couldn't breathe, no matter how hard he tried. He felt a cold stone beneath his hands. When had he fallen? Why was he down? This wasn't the time. They needed him. They all needed him.

He grasped at his chest and found something odd. Glass vials. What were—

Katia's medicine!

Slowly, Maxim eased them out of his pocket and forced himself to stand with shaking limbs. He almost dropped the vials. While these were primarily for goblin poison, moonwillow had other healing properties, too. He had dove headfirst into studies of herbs since he received the mystic ringpact. He knew he would never be the healer his circle needed. The one they deserved. But if he knew of various herbs and healing practices, perhaps he could still be of some use.

Reaching out a hand to one of the previous captives, he said, "H-H-Here! Take T-These. G-Give them to the sick. *Hurry!*" Dazed and confused, the woman took the vials. Then, as if struck by lightning, she understood and ran to administer the potion.

Good. Even if it wouldn't heal the injured two completely, it would give him time to work on the worst of them. Perhaps he didn't need to choose. Or, more so, if he had to choose who lived or died... he chose none. None would die. He never wanted to be in that position again.

"P-please," the man who held the limp woman said. "S-save her."

Maxim nodded, his breathing and hands steadying. He fell next to them and had the man lay the woman on her back. He began by making mental notes: Woman. Around twenty to twenty-five years of age. Burns to her face and right-side torso. Broken fingers, at least three. Fractured ribs, perhaps broken. Collapsed lung. Missing teeth. Labored breathing. The more he understood, the better he could use aethryis to heal her. Many did not understand the mystic calling. Hells, he barely did himself. Aethryis, by its very nature, was chaotic. Chaos breeds chaos. Aethryis used to harm was its natural state. Aethryis used to heal was an abomination. Twisted in form from its intended purpose.

Maxim set his hands to the woman and drew aethryis through his ring-pact, into himself and then down into her. He had to target the various parts of the woman he wished to heal without doing too much. It wasn't uncommon for someone so far gone to be healed and come out of it with extra fingers, excess skin, or even a third malformed eye. Or to come back completely mindless. He had to avoid that fate at all costs. Even at the cost of the woman's life. The burns first was what he decided to start with. An infection from an untreated burn was just as likely a death as a stab wound to the heart. Slowly the woman's skin knitted over itself, fresh and new. It was a lighter shade than the surrounding skin. That was not uncommon. He lost focus and accidentally healed too much as additional layers of skin knitted over fresh skin. He pulled the aethryis away just in time.

"*A-amazing!*" the man said, hope renewing in his eyes. Hope... something that he didn't wish to see. The woman was still gravely injured.

"S-stay back," Maxim said, continuing his work. Lungs... the lungs needed to be fixed as the woman's breathing was beginning to slow. His aethryis flowed into the woman once again, traveling the roadways of her nerves and blood. He could feel it: her pain. He could sense what was wrong. As he traveled, he knew what needed to be knit. Knew what needed to be fixed. When he came to the lung, he found the damage... extensive. More... he needed more aethryis. He sucked in hard and aethryis flowed through him, bright and brilliant as a noon sky. He forced more aethryis into the woman and her body shuddered for it.

"A-A little more," Maxim whispered, not sure if she could hear him. "P-Please. Endure. You must endure!"

The woman's body shuddered violently, retching upwards and thrashing about. She was rejecting him. Rejecting the... unnaturalness of it all. The man held her down, the glimmer of hope quickly dissipating as the woman he so clearly loved writhed in agony.

So close... he was so close to saving this woman's life. Then it snapped; his connection to her. Like a thread pulled too tightly, her life frayed away. He pulled back, barely reorienting himself as death took her. Her body fell limp and Maxim forced himself to look into the man's eyes. The man looked back at him with desperation in his features, clearly on the last lines of sanity.

"I... I'm sorry," Maxim said.

I'm sorry... the words nobody ever wished to hear in this type of situation. He saw the man's face go through the series of emotions that they always did. He would blame him. Hate him. Despise him. It was the way of the world. Those who could heal had a responsibility to do so. They also had the responsibility to bear the burden of failure. He had failed.

He was a failure. Always had been.

Memories of his brother flooded back into him. He had failed him as well, but more so than the woman who lied dead before him. At least she had the dignity of death. He had denied even that to his brother. His very own brother.

Suddenly, the man reached out, gripping him by his magecloak. "Do something," he demanded. *"Heal her! Bring her back!"*

Maxim shook his head. "No," he said, his trembles disappearing against the burden of knowledge he must pass. "You cannot understand this now, but there are worse things than death in this world. Far worse."

Before Maxim knew it, the man held the pointed end of a splintered piece of wood pressed against his throat. When he agreed to this mad mission, he had hardly suspected that it would be a human that would be the one threatening him in the end. But somehow, he couldn't blame the man. He could see the hurt in his eyes. The hopelessness and agony. He would have done anything to save the woman. He will do anything. How could he blame him for that?

"No," Maxim repeated. The man pressed the wood deeper, biting into his skin. He felt the trickle of warm blood run down his neck and into his shirt. "*No!*" he repeated, more harshly this time.

The man dragged the wood across his skin, creating a small gash. Others had now noticed what was happening and rushed to his aid.

"What are you doing, Yulis?" another man asked.

A woman half cried as she shouted, "He saved us and you're trying to kill him?"

"Back off," Yulis replied frantically, waving the wood piece around in a frenzied motion. He put it back to his neck. "Last chance. I know you can. Bring her back, or you'll join her. This is all your fault, anyway. You mages. You're supposed to protect us. Supposed... to... protect..."

Maxim sighed. Yulis was right; mages were supposed to protect them. The innocent. The powerless. *He* was supposed to protect them.

"*Ok...*" Maxim relented. He knew in his heart that the man would kill him if he didn't comply with his demands. Despite his earlier notions, when faced with it directly, he did not wish for death. Not yet. He still had so much to make up for. So much. This act he was being forced to perform—this profane act—it would set him back. The scales of his sins would weigh heavily tomorrow.

Maxim drew in aethryis once again, kneeling and placing his hands against the dead woman's cooling flesh. It was easier to mend the wounds of the dead without needing to care for any discomfort or pain they felt. It only took a moment before he had healed her, both outward and inward. There was one last piece—the one thing that no mage of any age could figure out. He pumped her heart and felt the flow of blood rush back into her veins. Within a moment, her eyes flashed open, and she jumped up.

Yulis dropped the wooden stake, his arms dropping to his side and his knees quivering. "Sana... Oh my sweet Sana." He rushed to her side, taking his hand in hers.

Maxim grimaced, waiting for the inevitable. He wished he could walk away. He wished to be rid of this place. He could not. Judgment came. It always did.

"*K-K-Kill me,*" Sana whispered in a shuddering breath that sounded distinctly inhuman, like a creature mimicking human speech. Louder, she repeated, "*K-K-kill me...*"

"What—"

"*Kill me!*" Sana shrieked, attacking Yulis and ravaging his flesh with her nails. She was still only human, despite her mannerisms, and her nails broke away in his skin as he desperately tried to fend her off. Some others rushed to his aid, pulling the flailing woman back.

Maxim looked upon the horrified face of the man whose loved one he had returned. No, not returned, *animated*. Underneath the skin and bone, nothing of that woman remained. He knew it to be true, and now Yulis knew it as well.

You cannot cheat death.

Yulis' face suddenly contorted with anger as he turned back to him. "*You!*" he said. "What have you done to her? To Sana? *What have you done?*" The man came back to his feet, bloody gashes strewn across his gnarled face. He picked up the wooden stake and aimed it at his heart. His intention was clear: to strike him dead. He did not want to die, but he couldn't say that he didn't deserve it. Perhaps this was for the best.

Yulis suddenly cried out, falling to the ground and holding his knee. Behind him, he saw an odd sight: a goblin holding a cane. He was pulling it back. The goblin had struck Yulis in the back of the leg, saving him. Before Yulis could utter another word, the goblin wrapped the cane around his neck and squeezed his neck until he collapsed, unconscious. It all took just a moment, but that's when he realized he knew this goblin—Kri'ed! He had been the one he met at the goblin camp. He was the one that had been tied up. Why?

The echoing sounds of Sana's cries of 'kill me,' echoed throughout the courtyard as the once captives dragged her away and into the relative safety of a nearby home.

Kri'ed stepped forward, eyes filled with fury and regret as he said, "We need to talk."

CHAPTER 32

LINGERING HATRED

Armeya's breath caught as she witnessed Soren send a particularly rowdy goblin flying across the courtyard, leaving it injured and broken. *Exultation!* She felt alive! Finally, these beasts would get what they deserve.

Finally!

Kyra put a hand to her shoulder in an attempt to calm her, but she still wasn't sure she could completely trust the woman. Iona had made it clear that she had suspected Kyra was involved in the killings. Of maybe even being the Spellthief herself, or that she helped the Mistwalker siblings. And Iona had made such a good argument... but for some reason, she couldn't remember the exact claim that had convinced her. No matter, best to focus on the task at hand.

She seethed with fury and anger as she drew in aethryis until she felt she was about to burst. This was it. They would die. The goblins would all die.

"Armeya," Kyra said and when she turned towards her, the woman's pale face was full of worry. "Are you ok?"

"I'm fine," Armeya replied. "Better than fine, actually. Why?"

"You're shaking."

Armeya looked down at her hands. She *was* shaking; rapidly at that. Hesitation gripped at her chest. Why? Why now? She had promised her—her mother. She promised she would one day return the favor. That she would get her vengeance. So why now, when that vengeance was at hand—when the reckoning day had come—would she hesitate? It made no sense. None at all.

"I'm fine," she said, more for her own benefit. "Let's just focus on the task at hand. Let's not get distracted."

Kyra sighed wordlessly and dropped her hand, turning back to the alleyway that lay directly beneath them. If she was a traitor, why did she even care how she felt? Friend or foe, she couldn't decide which. And her blasted memory. That day—the day they had found Freed Gallok—was still shrouded, as misty as the streets of Mistbreak itself. She could still only pick out bits and pieces of it. Why had she been so weak? She had seen death before, so why did that one bother her so much?

No—No more thinking. No more contemplations. Only action. Turning back to Soren, she saw him run into the alleyway, just as he had said he would. Action... Now was the time for action.

Kyra let her hand slide off Armeya's shoulder; the woman appeared lost in thought. Dark thoughts at that. Her facial expression were those of torture and regret. She knew them all too well. She had worn them herself for years. But she also knew that there would be no talking to her now. This was something she had to handle herself.

And besides, they had a job to do.

Soren had slammed a goblin across the cobbled stone of the courtyard, and the other goblins had given chase. Maxim ran into the courtyard soon after and had untied the restraints on the captives. Good, the plan was working out smoothly. There was only one thing left to do: lure the goblins into the alleyway, seal it off, and trap them. There need be no more death today.

No more death.

Soren entered the alleyway, narrowly dodging a loose arrow that flew overhead. Luckily, the goblins hadn't noticed them yet, perched upon the rooftops above the alleyway. With any luck, it would be too late when they did.

The alleyway itself was long and narrow, winding in certain places, not simply a straight line. Soren had completed the first part of the plan, getting the goblins there. It was almost time for her part, and she drew in aethryis from her ringpact. One goblin stepped forward, speaking to Soren, but she couldn't hear the words that they shared. The goblins behind him, armed with bows, lifted them, aimed at Soren, who now had his back against the deadend of the alleyway.

It was her turn.

In the open air above the goblins, Kyra twisted and spun orbs of light. The goblins, shocked, stared up in bewilderment at her creation, but that wasn't enough. More and more she spun, until hundreds of orbs, small enough to fit in the palm of her hand, glowed above the pack of goblins. One had noticed her, wasting no time as they shot an arrow towards her. She hadn't even seen it, but felt Armeya's body as she shoved her to the side. With a thud, she saw the arrow hit a chimney top directly behind her.

"Close," Kyra muttered, forcing herself to stand again. Armeya said nothing in return. Turning back to the alleyway, she connected each orb with a strand of light. She was ready. Nodding in Soren's direction, she hoped the man saw as she ignited the thread of light from each orb with aethryis. The orbs hummed and buzzed for a split moment before exploding in a brilliant glory. She turned her eyes away and prayed it gave Soren the distraction he needed.

"I'm gonna slit yer' throat," the goblin threatened, etching an invisible dagger across his own neck menacingly.

Soren pointed to his previously injured side. "Not the first time a goblin's blade has nicked me," he said. "Death didn't take then. I don't think it will now."

The goblin seethed. Good, let him boil in his anger. It'll make him stupid. Blind. Then, as if he had willed it himself, small spinning orbs of pure white began forming above them. The goblins started fussing over each other in panicked voices.

"Oy, what is this?" one said and others mimicked his cries.

Soren hunched his shoulders as a few tried to attack the orbs, their weapons passing straight through.

Another goblin pointed to the roof above. "Up there! The mage bitch. Shoot er'."

Soren clenched his jaw as one goblin knocked an arrow and shot upwards. He heard the thud, but couldn't worry about whether it had hit. He charged forward and kicked the goblin who had threatened him squarely in the chest, sending him flying back, colliding with a few others and knocking some other archers sideways, causing their arrows to glance off the sides of buildings. He spared a look upwards and saw that Kyra had returned to her post. She looked down at him and gave a nod.

She was ready, and so was he.

Soren turned, shielding his eyes as a blinding white light, as bright as if he stood on the surface of the sun, engulfed them. In the chaos that ensued, he heard goblins screaming in agony. Any who had their eyes open form that would be blind temporarily, if not permanently. He peeked and saw the light quickly diminish. Drawing in aethryis, he propelled himself forward, launching over the top of one goblin's head, moving past a few more, jumping off the side of a building to pass even more. Soon, every goblin was behind him, trapped between him and the alleyway's entrance. It was all going according to plan.

Drawing in even more aethryis, a familiar cold enveloped him. He breathed out, placing his hands to the cobbled ground as pillars of ice began forming. This was his gift. The gift of frost. First it was just one pillar, then two others, and soon, a sheet of ice covered the entire entrance to the alleyway, blocking the goblins inside. He fortified the ice with another layer and stepped back. All Armeya had to do was draw the air from the small area until the goblins passed out. They could capture them all with little to no death or damage to the building nearby. Clean and simple.

Soren looked up and, to his horror, Armeya's dark face had not the tranquil calm of a mage, but the contorted features of a murderer. He knew that look all too well. The Cryomancer wore it often. He called out and knew his words could not reach her. Briefly, he considered releasing the sheet of ice—to save who he could. But how could he? These goblins themselves had taken captives. Tortured. Killed. He bit his lip and turned away, unable and unwilling to witness the destruction he knew was coming.

Kyra... please save Armeya from herself.

Armeya saw the goblins, trapped like rats in a cage. A frozen cage. *Good!* Rats scurried and ran, only to return later. There was only one effective way to deal with them: *extermination!* All to the last.

She drew in as much aethryis as she could hold and found that she could not help the wild fury that danced in her blood. Finally, after all this time, she could get a small payback for her mother. Finally, she could stop feeling the way she did back then. The day her powers had manifested too late. Too late to save her.

The goblins had come. They had taken and killed—like they always did. But this time—this time they had killed something that they could not know. Something they could not understand. Her mother had been a wonderful woman. So kind. So giving. A saint, if one believed anyone could be. No human could be said to be without flaws, but for the life of her, she could not think of a one her mother had possessed. That goblin, with his crudely built bow and arrow, had taken her life. It was unneeded.

Unnecessary. The goblins had already taken what they had come for. It had been given willingly. Her parents had employed these particular goblins for the harvest, but in the end, in addition to pay, they wanted the harvest as well. As much as they could carry in their filthy hands. It had been given to them, but one goblin, a young and lazy one, had called out his threats and loosed one fateful arrow. A shift in the wind fixed its trajectory, and it struck true, straight into her mother's heart. She fell to her knees and held her mother as she died. She willed with all her might the power to heal her, but it never came. Instead, another power did. The power of destruction. The wind had betrayed her, so the wind would forever be indebted to her now. The very air itself. At that moment, she ceased being a human farm girl. Now—Now she was a mage! But no matter how far she chased, the goblins were too fast for her young legs to catch up. At the end of it all, the young goblin who had killed her mother turned and sneered one last time before disappearing forever at the forest which lined her family's farm.

His name had been Graacs, and she would never forget it.

She only hoped that the goblin was in this pack. And, if not, she would just have to find more to kill.

Aethryis flowed through her ringpact as cold and crisp as the winter's chill, surging out into the world. The wind swirled, tumbling her dark curly hair around her. She glimpsed Kyra out of the corner of her eyes and the woman looked worried. Pained. She seemed to fight against the wind to get to her. No—She would not be stopped. No lofty morality would end this. Not when she was so close. With a flick of her wrist, the wind pushed Kyra away, sending the woman tumbling and slamming against the bricked rooftop. It wouldn't keep her down for long; she would need to make this quick.

Armeya stepped out into the air—onto the air itself. She had been practicing this skill, making drafts of air so powerful that she could stand on them. Directly above the goblins, she stared down and saw them begin to recover, knocking arrows and aiming their bows upwards.

Useless. The wind was hers to control. Not theirs.

The goblins loosed their weapons, but the arrows never made their way to her. She was too high, and the air was too tumultuous. She breathed out, and as if the air obeyed her every word, she said, "*Down!*" and a draft as powerful as a building slammed upon the goblins, crushing them against the stone underneath.

More. She needed more.

"Die," she muttered, and another gust broke the bodies of goblins against the stone. "*Die!*" she said again, and another. With each beckoning, the wind became more violent. She slowly lowered herself, increasing the pressure further as she did. Lower and lower she went, and the concentration became greater still. She heard the soft cries of the goblins for but a moment before the rushing of air snuffed them out. Eventually, she hovered just above them, the concentration of air so great that blood had oozed from the goblin's mouth, nose and eyes. They were dead. All of them. She knew it in her soul. In her heart. And with that, she felt just a little bit of a connection to her mother again. As if her weary soul watched her from up above and smiled.

"I love you, mother," she whispered. "Always."

The life of the goblin horde was extinguished right before Kyra's horrified gaze. Their screeching, squirming, blabbering, and curses were in vain; nothing could save them. Armeya had lost it. Fallen to madness. Floating above the alleyway, she unleashed powerful gusts of air downwards. Their bodies could not withstand the pressure and soon, all the goblins fell silent.

The wind subsided as Armeya landed back on the roof, stumbling as she did. Clearly the woman had drawn too much aethryis and was at the brink of exhaustion. But this—this could not be excused nor hand waved away. She had butchered them. Slaughtered them all like pigs before a feast day, their broken bodies littering the small space below.

Kyra stepped towards the woman and grabbed her wrist, the hand that held the ringpact. Almost she felt heat radiating from it, and she wished to rip it from the woman's finger if only she were able. She glared into the woman's eyes and was surprised to see that they were both fixed on the same color: red.

Blood red.

"What did you do?" Kyra asked, seething with fury. "*Answer me!*"

Armeya had a shocked look plastered on her wind-torn face, but soon after, she pulled her hand back with indignation. "What did I do?" she replied. "I did what needed to be done. These goblins—these uncanny—are scum! Beneath scum. They don't belong here. Not in Mistbreak. Not in this world at all. They should just die. All of them. I did everyone a favor."

"*No...*" Kyra replied. "You did *yourself* a favor."

Armeya reached out and grasped her by the magecloak, pulling her so close that she could feel the woman's labored breathing against her cheek. "And what would you have me do?" she asked. "Pretend like everything is alright? Like I'm alright? They killed her, Kyra. They killed my mother."

Kyra swatted Armeyas' hands away, stepping back as she did. Gesturing towards the broken goblins below, she asked, "Did *they*? Was it them? All of them? Do you even know the name of the goblin who did it? Do you even remember?"

Armeya gave a false, derisive laugh. "They are all the same."

Kyra shook her head. "I've heard that type of talk before," she said. "Many have said it before you, and many will after. Warlords. Tyrants and their ilk. They use such language to justify their atrocities. Is that what you're doing now? Trying to justify this?"

Armeya bit her lip. "I need no justification."

Kyra had the wherewithal to smack her, but Soren suddenly appeared, rushing towards them. Before he could open his mouth, Armeya cut him off, asking, "Are you here to chastise me as well?"

Soren looked dejected before he replied in a surprisingly disarming tone, "No. Well, not yet, anyway. It's... It's not my place. I just wanted to say that some of the townsfolk in the courtyard have been coming out of their homes. Apparently, any goblins remaining are fleeing back into the forests on the outskirts of town."

"Good," Armeya said. "Like fleeing rats."

"*Stop!*" Soren said. "Just... stop. I—I don't want to think any less of you."

That caused Armeya to step back, blushing heavily. In her eyes, Kyra could see the redness and swelling. The aethryis was fading from Armeya and her own unbridled emotions were flooding in. She would have to come to terms with what she did. Sooner rather than later.

"Enough," Kyra said. "Lets—Let's just do what we can for the towns-folk."

Soren nodded. "Maxim is already helping who he can. He's in a bad way. He attempted to heal a woman even beyond death. He succeeded... in a way."

"Beyond death?" Armeya asked.

"I've heard of that," Kyra said. "So... What's wrong with the woman? They always come back wrong."

"She's mad," Soren replied. "Not mad, but *mad!* A lunatic, attacking everything and everyone in sight. They restrained her, for now, but she'll need to be... dealt with."

Kyra ground her teeth. "Why would Maxim do that? He knows better."

"His life was threatened," Soren replied. "He tried to warn the aggres-sor—the woman's husband—against it, but in the end, Maxim followed my orders. I told him to keep himself safe above all, and if that meant defying taboo when his life was in danger, then that's on me. Whatever comes from this, I'll be the one to deal with the fallout."

Kyra breathed a sigh of relief. "It's over. Finally."

Armeya sputtered. "And no signs of other mages. Iona neither. Nor Adathin, our illustrious leader."

As if summoned, Adathin's voice rattled in her head, as clear and crisp as the night air. "Kyra," he said. "I've found the Spellthief. Come to where this all began."

Before she could reply, she felt the connection break, like the snapping of a thread. It hurt; the severing. The others watched her as though expecting answers. "It was Adathin," she said. "He wants me to meet him."

"Just you?"

"He... didn't say."

Armeya crossed her arms. "And what does he wish to meet about? Surely, he can't already know of the goblin's demise and wishes to take a crack at me as well."

Kyra held her gloved hand to her chest. "He said he found the Spellthief," she said. "I Think we should all go. Now."

Armeya and Soren's eyes went wide in shock. Wordlessly, they made their way towards the stairs which led down to the streets below. She followed with a heavy heart and the burden of knowledge.

Something was wrong. She knew it in her very heart and soul.

Once again, Kyra felt the cobblestone streets of the courtyard beneath her feet. In contrast to the sloped roofs, these were perfectly flat. It was awkward to walk on at first, but she reoriented herself before moving on.

The people of Mistbreak, human and uncanny alike, were leaving their homes to access the damage to the district. More than one shrill cry called out as they found the outsides of their homes tarnished and ruined. She couldn't blame them. The residents of the Dimlight District were not particularly reputed for their vast wealth. Like always, it was the least prominent of society who suffered most of all.

Kyra spotted Maxim doing his rounds around the courtyard and checking-in on those who left their homes. Thankfully, none seemed to be too badly injured, just a scrape here or there. Instead, she focused her attention on two other items: a woman, who flailed against haphazardly tied ropes like a wild dog, and a goblin, tied similarly, who appeared as if his entire world had come crashing down around him.

The woman she did not recognize, but the goblin... Yes, she knew him.

"Kri'ed," she said as she approached the old goblin. "It's been some time."

Kri'ed looked up and blinked awkwardly before saying, "Ah, the mage; the arcanist. Kyra, was it?" She nodded. "Despite my handsomely devilish looks, I'm getting on in my age. Names don't come as sharply as they once did. But you—I remember you. Where is your handler? The elvish boy?"

"He's *not* my handler," Kyra replied. "And what about you? If I recall, you promised you wanted peace. What does this look like to you? Peace?"

Armeya spat to the floor. "You can't trust a goblin at his word. They'd sooner slit your throat or stab you in the back than to hold up to their end. To think that I even gave your words a second thought. That I concerned myself at all."

Kri'ed frowned, looking dejected at the ground like a chastised toddler. "You're right," he said. "I was a fool. I thought—I thought I could change them. Convince them to become more civilized. I... I was wrong."

"They can never change," Armeya replied. "None of them can. It's in your blood." The last implied she included Kri'ed in her assessment as well.

"I just wanted things to be as they once were," Kri'ed said. "I was a merchant prince once. Touching elbows with Earls of the Everisles to sharing of the moondrops with the forest elves of Moonwallow. My old patron, Prince Loryn Torfiel of Xevepis, was a friend once. My best friend. Well... King Torfiel now, or so I've heard. And through circumstances beyond my control, he abandoned me. Forsook me. This—This was my final gambit. In merchantry, as well as with life, everything has risk. I risked it all to return to even a tenth of what I once had. What I once was. I failed. I lost. And now—now I have nothing. I am nothing."

Kyra listened to the poor old goblins' story and felt pity and sorrow for his woes, despite what he had done. She had understood loss and the wish to return things to the way they once were. But time—time wasn't so kind. It flowed one way, and there was no going back. You could never go back.

"You expect us to believe that load of shit," Armeya said, unphased. "As if *you* could be anything other than what you are. A smelly, worthless, pathetic—"

"*Enough!*" Kyra said. She tried her best to keep anger out of her voice as she added, "That's enough. He feels regret, and we'll gain nothing by insulting a defeated opponent."

Armeya eyed her, and then turned to Kri'ed with a dangerous glint. "We should kill him."

Kyra's breath caught in her chest at the suggestion. "Kill him?" she asked. "Why?"

"Because he deserves it," Armeya seethed. "They all do."

Kri'ed looked up at her with defiance, but it quickly fled, leaving the goblin looking even older and frailer than he ever had before.

Kyra rounded on Armeya. "Haven't you had enough killing for one day?"

Armeya stepped forward, taking a challenging stance. "Killing goblins? No, it's never enough. Not until they are all buried beneath my feet."

Soren appeared, as if he had noticed the growing tension. "What's going on?" he asked.

"Armeya suggests we kill the old goblin."

"He deserves it," Armeya repeated.

Soren put his hand to his chin and looked around. Unsurprisingly, the crowd of gathering humans agreed with Armeya, nodding to her every word. They wanted blood. Kri'ed's blood. The few other uncanny in the area, however, took meaningful steps away, not wishing the ire against the goblins to be misplaced towards them.

After a tense few moments, Soren said, "It's not our place to decide his fate."

Kyra breathed a sigh of relief.

Armeya stamped her foot. "Fine," she relented. "Then what are we still doing here? Come, let's go catch us a Spellthief."

Kyra found herself nodding. She wanted to be away from this place as well. Away from the tension. Away from that wailing woman whom had seemingly lost her mind and now begged for death. She wanted to see Adathin as well, although she hated to admit that to herself.

"*Maxim!*" Soren called. When the man appeared, he added, "Keep this goblin safe. Don't let the townsfolk have him. As for the woman, have them move her to a safe place, but keep her secure. Hopefully, other mages will arrive soon to help."

"W-W-Where are you going?"

Soren took three steps and turned back with a smile on his face. "To catch a Spellthief," he said.

CHAPTER 33

ILLUSION

It didn't take long for Kyra and her circle to walk to the place where their journey had begun: the mysterious warehouse in the heart of the Dimlight District. This place, as drab and unmentionable as it may appear, had to carry some untold significance. Something she couldn't see nor understand. So much had happened to her, from a murder to a goblin attack and now back again... There had to be something she was missing. She knew it.

"Careful," Soren warned, pressing his hand against the outer door. "I know Adathin said he would meet us here, but I—"

"You don't trust him," Kyra said, finishing the man's sentence for him. He turned away in shame. She ground her teeth, but added in a calm voice, "I'll prove that he is trustworthy. I trust him with my life, as should you all."

Armeya snorted, but she ignored it.

Soren pressed open the warehouse door and stepped inside. Immediately she heard him gasp, and she drew in aethryis, following, but what she found caused her aethryis to abandon her a mere moment later. The warehouse, it seemed, had been cleared out and in place of the half-rotted wood, boxes and rat shit, was a royal-blue carpet which led to a raised dais which held a singular throne made of silver and gems. This wasn't a warehouse, but a palace.

Armeya was the next to come in and when she noticed the change, her off-color eyes shimmered with greed and desire. Suddenly, as if appearing from the mist itself, Adathin stood in front of the stairs which led to the throne behind him. He was dressed in fanciful clothing of purples and grays. She thought her heart had stopped beating when her gaze fell upon him. He was... beautiful. Like the hero out of a storybook.

She could deny her feelings for him no more. And why would she? It was only natural that she be entranced and attracted to royalty.

"Welcome," Adathin said, his voice so full of royal rule that it set her heart ablaze.

Soren appeared aghast and at a loss for words. Painfully, the man finally squeaked out, "W-W-Where are we?"

"A palace," Adathin replied. "Is it not obvious?"

"Yes... obvious," Soren replied.

Armeya shook herself. "But weren't we just—"

A figure Kyra hadn't noticed before rose from the throne, and Adathin turned to greet them. The man kneeled, and she felt herself follow his directive, kneeling to the soft, carpeted floor. Down here, the carpet was even more vibrant, shifting between different shades of reds in an endless cacophony, like the waxing and waning of the tide. Pleasant smells of flowers overcame her as well. Well perfumed. Even the ambiance shifted as she heard a soft string instrument playing in the background, but she couldn't locate the source of the music.

A throbbing pain flared within her mind, but she pushed it aside as she stared up at the glorious figure who descended from the dais to stand among them. A god descending from on high. Braziers hung around the room suddenly flared to life, sending the darkness fleeing and that's when she could finally see who it was that approached:

Aluriel.

The elvish woman was in a dress of shimmering silver, contrasting her evenly toned ethereal body well. Not just well: *divinely!* Her golden eyes shifted and fell upon Kyra and she bowed deeper, not daring to even stare into those illustrious orbs. Glancing to the right and then the left, Soren and Armeya were bowing similarly. Tears even flowed from Soren's eyes, and Armeya wept softly to herself. She found that her vision had blurred as well. Were those tears of one graced by the presence of a god? Or was it the ramifications of the pounding headache which now plagued her? No, her head did not hurt; she felt no pain. How could she when she was blessed by the presence of a god?

"Rise," Aluriel said, and her body acted on its own, rising attentively. "You may look upon me. I will allow it."

Kyra could suddenly breathe, and when she glanced up, all was dark and drab. Startled, she blinked the tears away, and all was right again, the room bright and smelling of sweet candies. No, wait... perfumes. Flowers? *Bah,* it didn't matter. Nothing mattered but the attention of Aluriel Mistwalker, Elven Queen.

Aluriel eyed her, and for a moment, she saw contempt on that perfect face. It made her wish to gouge out her own eyes for daring to upset this godlike being.

"You must be wondering why I summoned you all here," Aluriel said. Her voice was the voice of the heavens. It's tone as musical as a songbird. "It is time for my ascension."

Ascension... Yes, of course. One such as this must ascend beyond the realm of mere mortals. Mortals like her.

"How may I be of service?" Kyra asked, disbelieving her own voice as the words gave new meaning to her life.

Aluriel smiled... she actually smiled! Kyra's heart fluttered as the goddess said, "To ascend, I must sacrifice the one I love." Aluriel frowned, looking at her own perfect and clean hands. "But I—I cannot. My hands are too pure. Too perfect. I cannot bring myself to kill one I love." She turned, looking at Adathin. "I cannot kill my own brother."

Kyra's heart stopped as her gaze fell upon Adathin. For a moment, he was a man, bound and beaten, a look of horror on his face, but then, the next, he was this perfect figure again. A perfect man, dressed in silver and gold. Or was it purple and shades of red? She dismissed the thought.

"I—I will sacrifice him for you," she said. "So that your hands remain pure."

Kyra's head throbbed, which almost sent her to the floor.

"Will you?" Aluriel replied playfully. "Very well then, Kyra *Ais* Ravenblood, I find you worthy to act in my stead."

Worthy...

Aluriel held out a long, gleaming dagger. "Take this blade and drive it into his heart. Let his blood run freely to the ground and the deed will be done. I will ascend and cast out the darkness of this world. To free all from their shackles."

Darkness...

Kyra reached out and took the dagger in hand. Turning, Soren and Armeya were gone, and nothing but a black, infinite black void laid bare at her back. She turned to Adathin with tears in her eyes; she did not wish to harm this man. She did not wish to kill him. But Aluriel... She must ascend. She must.

Kyra took a step forward.

Aluriel must have sensed her hesitation as she said, "Do not worry, child. Adathin will be reborn as part of me. All will."

Kyra took another step. Then another, until her feet would move no more.

"It's alright," Adathin said, smiling wide. "This is the punishment for my weakness. Aluriel spared me for this moment and this moment alone. So that I may die and so that she may rise. It is as it should be. As it should have always been."

Spared...

"No," Kyra said, her head pounding against every word. "*No! No, no, no, no...*"

"Kill him," Aluriel demanded. "*Now! Kill him!*"

"*No!*" Kyra screamed, but her body acted on its own. She reached out with her left hand, now ungloved, and saw that it was... perfect. She was perfect. In what world could someone as damaged as her be perfect? This wasn't real. It couldn't be.

This is all a dream.

The illusion shattered as she screamed, her head feeling as if it would split from the tremendous pain. Her eyes watered, and her ears rang and despite that, she knew—knew she had to gain control of herself. She was in danger.

They all were.

"*Adathin!*" Kyra cried as she noticed the elven man was tied, gagged, and bound in a simple wooden chair in the middle of the old and dusty warehouse. Gone was the bright, glorious palace, a fading memory in her mind. How had she ever imagined this place to be as such? Still, she could smell the lingering perfume at the edges of sense.

She pulled the gag from Adathin's mouth, and he appeared frantic as he said, "*Look out!* She isn't done."

A wave of sickening emotion hit Kyra like an avalanche. It threatened to drag her under, but she breathed steadily and drew in aethryis, summoning an orb of light and tying a string of light to it. She didn't realize why she had done this, but she knew that if she just followed the string, she could always find her way back from anything—anywhere she was sent.

Kyra opened her eyes and found she was falling, passing through ominous, thunderous clouds. As she fell, the ocean far below became a fast approaching beacon of her demise. She wanted to scream, but her mouth was suddenly full of water... No, *insects!* Bugs crawled out from beneath her tongue and throat and then her nose, ears and eyes, each skittering foot like a heated dagger drawn across bare skin. Batting them away the best she could, she suddenly found she held something firm in her hand. Glancing down, she saw the thread of light.

She pulled with all her might.

"Are you alright?" Adathin asked as she once again kneeled before him in the dim warehouse.

Coughing as if she still had a mouthful of bugs, she gasped, "I'm... alright."

"Untie me," Adathin said. "*Quick!* Before she recovers."

"You had to screw it up, didn't you? You couldn't just be a nice little cog in the greater machine. No... you choose *defiance.*"

Kyra's breath caught as a voice boomed out, once again transforming the room into something else. This time, heat licked at her skin. She stood upon a platform of stalagmite while lava danced and stewed around her, sending spitting fissures up with each boiling pop. But that was not what she focused on. She knew that voice. Knew it well.

"I... Iona?"

As if the name gave power, the woman appeared before her, clad in the same silvery dress Aluriel had worn in the previous vision. But this time, she knew what she witnessed was true to sight. Maybe not the environment itself. Maybe not even Adathin, still tied in the chair before her. Her—Iona—she was real.

She was the Spellthief.

The sulfur in the air burned at her throat as she asked the obvious, "W... Why? Why do this? Why try to kill us?"

Iona seemed to know the question was coming. She mused and rolled her head, almost playfully, as if the scenario bored her. Perhaps it did.

"Justice," Iona said simply. "Justice for my father. Justice for myself. Justice for all mages who are enslaved by the elvish lords who reign on high."

Kyra wished to ask more, but the heat was becoming unbearable. Her skin blistered and darkened as it separated from muscle. Every fiber of her being shrieked in agony and pain. She looked upon Adathin again and saw nothing but ruined, blackened flesh. He was dead. Burned to little more than ash.

"*No...*" she whispered, pulling on the thread of light once again.

The world spun and came back into focus. Adathin was still alive, gasping heavily as if he had been drowning himself. Turning, she saw Soren and Armeya sprawled out on the floor, barely conscious. What was Iona doing to them? This—This seemed like psionics. Elvish magic.

Iona suddenly laughed, her voice filling the empty air. "Of course I would have someone to face as strong as you, Kyra," she said. "An Arcanist of skill. The only order capable of defending against elvish *psionics*. It's a shame that you need to die here. Today. Now. In another life, we could have been friends, perhaps."

Kyra forced herself to stand with trembling knees. "We are friends," she said. "You are... you are part of my circle."

Iona sneered and spat at the ground. "We aren't friends," she said, pointing to Adathin. "To him. To you. To society, I am just an enchanter. A tool to be used and forgotten when my talents eventually dry out. I've seen it with my own eyes. I've lived it before, for I am not what you think." As if pulling back a mask, Iona tore at her own face until her young skin was replaced by the weathered, age-lined skin of someone much older. "My father believed in the elvish. The ways of their teachings. Believed in society and his place in it as an enchanter. My mother was a simple human seamstress in employ of the elvish, and, eventually, a relationship came between them and I was born. The union was blessed by the elvish man my father was employed for, to all's surprise. But my mother died when I was young and my father, ever devoted, was never the same. His work lacked, and he lost that favor. I—I became the tool the elvish played against him. But one day, something in him snapped. He saw an opportunity and slayed an elvish envoy from a lesser household. You see, he had been studying in the forbidden. A way to take one's power. To steal it and seal it using the very ringpact they would bind us with. With that death, he took the elvish man's psionic ability, placing it into his own ringpact. It became a part of him as strongly as if it was his own birth rite. In the end, he was caught and executed for his crime. My sentence as his daughter was stayed—if I were to become a mage and serve that elvish family for the remainder of my life as a slave." She held her hand out, and a ringpact of rusted silver adorned her middle finger, next to the newer Enchanter ringpact on her ring finger. "He passed down his ringpact—hid it from them, in a place only I would know. His power became my power and in that moment, I knew what to do."

"And so, what did you do?"

Iona laughed. "I played their game. For years—decades I played it, ever searching for my moment."

"Your moment?"

"The moment I could tip the scales. But alas, it never came... until I looked beyond the simple passions of my younger self. What if I could change everything? Fix the system at its core? Its foundations."

Kyra's legs were getting steadier by the moment. Iona peered at her as if she expected something sinister.

"Fix the system?" Kyra said. "Fix the foundations? It is awful what the elvish did to you, but you alone cannot change anything. Especially not by slaying your fellow mages. No, *you* stole power from others to feed *yourself*. So that you can have vengeance."

"*Vengeance...*" Iona seethed as she said the word. "No... *Justice!* This—all of this—is what is coming for them. What I have set in motion for them."

"And what is that?" Kyra asked, desperate to keep the woman talking while she recovered her strength. Glancing down, she noticed Adathin slowly working out the knot that tied his hands. Even Soren and Armeya looked to be recovering. She had to play for time.

"Can't you see?" Iona asked. "Aren't you an arcanist? Doesn't your light not guide the way to truth? Well, here it is: *truth!*" Iona stepped forward, and her body changed, transforming and shaping. Her skin melted, ashing away as the warehouse's roof exploded outwards, sending a spray of broken wood raining down on her like hail. In place of Iona, there was something else—something malevolent. A single horn adorned the creature's head and two elongated wings, pierced with bone and red, flayed skin and long, blackened claws. The thing that had once been Iona growled low and threatening.

"This is what a Daemon really looks like," the creature said. "I will once again light the flames of war to take this world back from the elven conquers. Your deaths will serve as a rallying cry to all the mages of the world and a warning to those of the Spellbound Arch who ignore those beneath them. I will drag them from their lofty seats and hang their worthless carcasses in pieces across the plains of battle. In the end, mages will rule this world, as they should have always been. None will be forced to serve ever again. None forced to wear the magelock. Free. Mages will be free."

Before Kyra could reply, she felt a rough tug as air embraced her, gripping her entire body. Turning, she saw Armeya standing, her hands forward, aimed towards her.

"Get help," the woman said as she flung her arms back.

Suddenly, her body whisked through the air as she crashed onto the cobbled streets outside the warehouse. Adathin landed a moment after her, the chair he was bound to breaking as he hit. The man cried out in pain, he had clearly broken something from the fall. She rushed to his aid.

"Here," Kyra said, untying the bindings as gingerly as she could. He winced with her every touch, but offered no complaint. "We've got to go back in and help. I've got to—"

"No," Adathin replied with a firm voice. "*You* need to get help. Mages... the elvish. *Anyone!* That woman, Iona, if that is what she is truly named, is a monster. I couldn't feel the power of her psionics in my mind. I couldn't counter them. I was... powerless."

"But I can," Kyra said. "I already proved it. You go for help, and I'll—"

Adathin reached up and grabbed her wrist. "I'm hurt. My leg... it's twisted and broken. I cannot move. No, it needs to be you. They'll listen to you. You have to make them listen."

Kyra ground her teeth as she heard the sounds of battle inside the warehouse, but when she stepped towards the entrance, a sheet of ice sealed it. Soren... he had shut her out to ensure she would do as she was told. Soren and Armeya were planning to sacrifice themselves to give her a chance.

Sacrifice...

CHAPTER 34

BLACK FLAME

A gruesome and horrific figure stood in front of Soren. Wearing a cloak of flame, with two large reptilian-like wings torn throughout, the creature's head had a horn, broken and protruding, and a face that was entirely shrouded in a dark veil except for two reddish orbs for eyes piercing through the shroud.

A daemon in the flesh. Here, in Mistbreak.

No... it couldn't be. It was but a trick of the mind. A psionic spell. Still, even as he tried to persuade himself of that fact, the heat protruding from the creature scalded at his skin. Flayed at his senses. Beget madness. Soren turned, and the wall of ice he had made at the entrance of the warehouse was gone now. By the Builders, the warehouse itself was gone. Only fire and brimstone surrounded him now.

Soren sucked in air and drew aethryis from his ringpact. Ice crystals formed around his hand and soon, an icy blade was in his fingers, sending a jet of steam hissing out into the unbearably hot air. He had to fight for time. He had to trust in his circle. Trust in his friends.

But as terrified as he was, it gave him a small bit of comfort to see that Armeya had remained by his side. The woman's skin showed a gleam of heavy sweat, and her magecloak looked like she had taken a dump into a river. Her black hair was twirling up, as if the wind had spun through it, fraying the ends and, with a sudden realization, he knew that it did.

Armeya had a strange affinity for the wind, odd for a thaumaturge who generally preferred more destructive practices, such as fire or earth. Yes, if he had to fight a daemon, he was glad that she was by his side. He would need to protect her the best he could. He could take the hits, steel his skin against injury, using augmentor aethryis. Reinforce muscle and tissue... She had little of those protection besides her magecloak which offered but the simplest of enchantments. He would be her shield and she, hopefully, would be his spear.

The daemon cackled, as if laughing, but no words came out. Nothing human anyway. It sounded like coals dropped into a furnace. Then, without warning, the creature that was once Iona shot forward, a cloak of pure flame whipping in the air behind them. The target: Armeya! He had to be fast; to match the creature's extreme speed. He drew in aethryis as much as he could hold and reinforced his legs as he moved to step in front of Armeya.

Soren clashed against the daemon with his aethryis-enforced skin, using his blade to block the creature's claws. He imagined himself fully clad in a gleaming silver-plated armor as he faced down his fiery enemy. The daemon pushed and pushed, but his strength would not be beaten. Would not wane. Not when he had the reason and will to fight. If Iona had thought they would bow down lightly, he was here to prove her wrong.

As Soren struggled, a gust whisked past his hair and a moment later, a gale slammed the daemon against the ground, dragging it bloody against the sharp stone and into a pit of lava nearby. The daemon screamed a guttural noise, like a thousand tortured souls all wailing at once. He wanted to hold his ears against it. He wanted to pray to whatever divine being to save them from this hell. But he knew—knew that nothing divine would intervene on his behalf. He was nothing—not even worthy of a name. *Three...* that's what he had been called most of his life. Soren, a name he picked for himself, was nothing but a hope and a dream. A wish that he could soar away, as free as the birds he so often looked upon with aspiration in his heart. Oh, how he would fly away from his problems if he could. Standing straighter, he looked down at his own hands; burned. Even with all his strength, Iona had torn through his sword of ice within a moment. He was supposed to protect Armeya, but it seemed as if he was the one in need of protection.

Soren laughed at the ridiculousness of it all. Here he was, feeling bad for himself. Feeling sorrowful for the life he had been forced to live. But this—this was not his family's wishes. He chose this. This was what he longed for. Sought for. Fought for.

Freedom!

Iona in her daemon form, ripped her way out from the pit, her claws scratching against the stone with an eerie ringing. But now when he looked upon her, he didn't feel fear; he felt... unshackled. Unburdened by what his family would make of him. They wished him to be a sword when he saw himself as a shield. But the truth was, he was neither. The truth was, he was a fist—and he would never loosen his grip on what he had earned.

What he had won.

Iona screeched again, and her wings spread out and beat furiously in the burning air. She charged, her black claws lashing forward, this time aimed at him. Soren did not move; he did not break. Drawing in aethryis, crystals formed around his hands and arms, just as Elder Reylar had shown him. Not a sword, but gauntlets of ice. Reaching forward as the daemon came within reach, he gripping the creature by the neck. Her claws dug into his flesh and ravaged him, peeling away skin, muscle, and even bone, but he ignored the torment of his own death—he had her now.

And he would not let go.

Screaming his rage out, Soren slammed Iona to the stone, her wings cracking and breaking, along with the ground beneath her. She screeched incomprehensibly, but he mounted her, using his free hand to batter downwards. With each strike, he felt a satisfying crunch as her flesh and bone gave way to him. Untethered and unbound, he swam wildly in the aethryis now. He knew blood gushed from his wound, but he couldn't bring himself to care.

Gripping the creature's single horn, he tried to slam her down again, but there was a sudden resistance. Try as he might, his strength faltered against the daemon as Iona rose.

"Enough," she seethed with the fury of a thousand forges. Then, in a whisper, she added, "That's enough."

A wave of heat struck Soren, and he rolled a few paces away. Iona was now standing in front of him, her daemon form as sinister as ever. Looking down, he saw her long blackened nail buried deep into his guts. She twisted, and he felt a bubbling pain spike up his midsection. Ah well, if he was to die today, at least he would die free.

Unbound, untethered and free... as Soren.

Armeya screamed as lava bellowed and belched its arid heat around her. Soren toppled over the daemon's hand, as if the very life had been sucked from his body. It was then that the smell of burnt flesh penetrated her senses. It was overwhelming and bile burned up her throat as she tried to stop herself from vomiting.

It was too much. It was all too much.

Iona, in her daemon form, pulled her hand back, Soren's flesh and blood dripping off the tips of her long fingers eerily, falling to the ground and striking the stone, leaving a light hiss in the air. The woman's attention turned to her now.

Strength. She must have strength.

Drawing in aethryis, she prayed to the Builders that the ringpact would obey her. She hoped that the trinket, whom she suspected more every day was sentient, would realize the danger they were in. If it did, it gave no signs of knowing, but neither did it fight her reckless use of aethryis as she drew as much as she could handle.

"It'll do you little good," Iona said in a low voice, more bereft of a beast than any human she had heard before. "You've seen what just happened to your friend."

"He was your friend too!" she replied.

Iona laughed, and it sounded like the lighting of an incinerator. "*Friend...* I reject such notions. We were never friends. I was never truly part of your circle. Don't you get it yet? It was all a lie. A ruse. I am—*was* an enchanter. Just a tool to be used and discarded. But tool no longer. No, now I am the most powerful being in this world, for my very thought becomes existence itself."

"No," Armeya replied. "You lie, just as you show me lies now. You *were* our friend. I saw it; the light in your eyes as we laughed together. The melancholy in your voice as you sang to us. You say you're powerful, but I see a coward who ran from the things that hurt them. You made it everybody else's problem. You still are."

It was at that moment that Armeya realized how much of a hypocrite she had been. She had taken her frustration and anger out of goblins that likely had nothing to do with her mother's death. Worse, she had implicated her circle in her bloodlust.

Iona seemed to sense what she was thinking as she grinned behind that daemonic visage. "Will you not submit?"

Armeya held firm to her aethryis as she prepared for the worst. "I will not," she said resolutely.

Iona flapped her wings of soot and flame, and Armeya felt the blistering heat press against her. There was no winning here. No defense she was capable of. If this wasn't real—if none of this was real—it mattered little.

"*Mother...*" she whispered to herself. "*We will meet again, sooner than I had wished.*"

Kyra slammed her fist against the sheet of ice barring the entrance to the warehouse. The sounds of battle raged inside and yet she was powerless to do anything about it. Powerless to stop it. There were grunts of frustration. Cries of rage and despair. It sounded like the throngs of war, and yet she knew that only the three battled inside.

She slammed her fist again, feeling the icy wall cut and dig into her flesh. Fresh blood dripped down the edge of the wall and she followed a single line down the wall as steam began to fume from it. Soon, the entire wall steamed and dripped until the entire thing came crashing down.

"Wait," Adathin said, still struggling with his injuries. "Don't go alone. If Soren fell, then there is truly no hope left. You're—You're just an arcanist. You have no hope of fighting against that thing Iona has become."

Kyra stood straight, reflecting on the lessons of her past. Master Lu'ce had cautioned her similarly before. "Do not endanger yourself," she would warn. "Only do what you can." She felt the familiar pain well up in her chest. Cowardice—like a vice around her lungs. Around her heart. No, not this time. Soren had shown no such cowardice. Armeya neither. They were both willing to sacrifice for her, so she must sacrifice for them. Perhaps this was it; the thing that had eluded her for so long. A willingness to sacrifice for others.

Was this... *friendship?*

Kyra stepped inside, ignoring Adathin's frantic pleas for her to flee and save herself. She could not; it was not in her capacity to run. She caught a glimmer of the drab warehouse before noticing Soren and Armeya sprawled out and unconscious to her left. She ran to them and fell to her knees. Armeya simply looked asleep, but upon closer inspection, she saw that the woman had burn scars on her neck, chest and arms. Armeya unconsciously held her left hand close to her chest. Kyra understood that pain all too well.

Soren was another matter entirely. The man had fought with everything he had. He had given too much. Far too much. His injuries were grave. Like Armeya, he had a spattering of burns across his body, but worse, he had a bleeding hole the size of a fist in his chest. It bled and bled darkened, singed blood in a pool beneath him. She would have thought the man was already dead if his chest hadn't lifted ever so slightly. Dead or not, he would be soon; of that, she was certain.

"So you've returned," Iona said as the world around Kyra shifted.

Kyra stood, drawing aethryis from her ringpact and forming the spear of light in her right hand. She had no doubts about her inability to beat Iona. The woman had bested both Soren and Armeya simultaneously. What hope did she have? What hope did anyone have? Her ringpact pulsed with untapped energy, almost as a warning. She felt something from it—something new. Almost it felt as if it tried to communicate with her. Not as much through words, but through feeling.

The warehouse faded away and in its place was something familiar to her. Very familiar. A small cottage lay atop a hill, with a field of white flowers spread out in front of it. This was once her home. Her true home. The one she had burned away to ash.

Iona knew... *she knew!*

Kyra's head pounded, and she fell to one knee, gripping her head with her free hand to ward off the pain. It did little to help.

"Familiar?" Iona said in a tauntingly sweet voice.

The woman had somehow ended up behind her, and she quickly slashed at her with the tip of the spear. It glided through the air, but the woman was gone again in an instant.

Iona chuckled. "Careful now, swinging that dangerous thing around. You know, I was surprised to learn that you, a mere arcanist, could produce a weapon such as that. So interested in fact that I began the long journey of delving into your mind whenever I could. Prying for your secrets, you see. And oh, secrets are what I've found. Secrets masking secrets. So much so that I doubt even you understand the truth."

Kyra's head pulsed again. "Secrets... What secrets?"

Iona materialized in front of her, pointing as she said, "Your hand, for starters. Shame and frustration are the reasons you hide it. But what if I revealed to you that you share no blame for what happened?"

"Explain."

"... You did not kill your family."

Kyra's breath caught in her chest. Her body froze in place. What did Iona say? She... didn't kill her family? No, this was impossible. Improbable. If not she... then who?

"I can see you're confused," Iona continued. "Here, let me show you. Let me pull back the mask of lies that has been fused to you for all these years. And remember after who it was who showed you. Remember who showed you the truth."

The world spun again, and the sky was set to a burning red. Suddenly, the flowers were blackened around her and she found herself glued to the floor; her ruined hand back in the dirt. This is exactly how she remembered it. Exactly how—the world shifted again, and what was before her cracked and broke like a mirror, falling away before her very eyes so that she could see through to another world. Another reality. Another truth.

The truth.

Kyra kneeled in the dirt, staring up at an ethereal being. There was no fire and no heat, but she could still feel a burning sensation all around her. Bright golden eyes stared down at her from a tall form with long, silverish hair and... long, sharp ears.

An elvish man!

Behind him, Kyra could see the surprised face of a woman who had not even seen the blade coming before it took her life. Still her eyes were wide open in shock as her life ebbed away. As for her father, she couldn't see him at all. Tears stung at her eyes as she craned her neck upwards in defiance of the elvish man. Instinctually she knew that the man was her enemy.

The elvish man reached down, patted her head and said, "Why did you kill them, *hmm*?"

Kyra's mind rejected the idea. *He* had killed them. Not her.

The elvish man asked again, "Why did you kill them?"

"I..." *No!* Kyra rejected the idea again.

The elvish man's fingers pressed against her chin as he pulled her neck up, asking for the last time, "Why did you kill them?"

"I... I didn't mean to." And just like that, the memory was set.

Her reality—rewritten.

Her truth—masked.

The world spun and misted away before Kyra's eyes, leaving her a small child alone in a field. Her head hurt and her heart pounded. She had done it. She had killed them. The world exploded, and she reached for the strands of light around her. She wanted it gone. All gone. The strands flowed into her and gave her the power to make her wish true as fire spilled forth, burning everything in its path.

But now—now she knew—her family was long dead before that. Slain by the unknown elvish man.

Or perhaps this was the lie. A pretty lie told by a liar to gain her favor. Was Iona playing with her? Manipulating her? So many people manipulate for their own gain: the elvish, the Spellbound Arch... Iona. Hells, even her own master had something to gain by her compliance. It made her angry. Furious. And something deep and dark, an unrealized promise, begged to reveal itself.

Today was a day of truths and today, she—she would finally live her own.

Flames bellowed out from beneath Kyra's gloved hand, sending it ashing away as the world was engulfed in her dark fury. The vision burned. It all scorched away, like a tapestry caught aflame, leaving naught but grayed verity in its place.

Iona kneeled ten paces away, her eyes wide and her face full of shock and malice, but when the woman's eyes went down, Kyra could see something was there; not a reflection, but the absence of one.

When she peered down and saw that not only was her ruined hand free for all to witness, it was covered in an ominous black flame. She recoiled, but the flames stayed firmly attached, like it was attracted to her in some way. What was it? It didn't burn; in fact, she didn't feel any heat from it at all. Not even a master thaumaturge could wield their own flame so close to their own body without damage. So why? Why could she?

"Monster," Iona said, breathless, as she sought to crawl away. For some reason, the woman's strength had all but failed her. Iona looked old now. Decrepit. Far past her years, her eyes sunken low and the wear of time plain on her pale, gaunt face.

"Liar," Kyra seethed, rounding on the woman. "*Liar!*" As she punctuated the word, the black flame leaped into the air, only to die down soon after.

Iona, perhaps sensing an opportunity, smiled softly. "No, I did not lie. Not about what I showed you. I was the only one in your entire life to show you the truth. Your truth."

Kyra reached down, gripping the woman's magecloak. The clothing did not burn, but still, Iona recoiled from her touch. "*It was me!*" she said. "I know it was. So why... Why do you show me such sweet lies?"

Iona snarled as she replied, "It is *they* who lie, not I. They lie about what mages are. They lie about what we are capable of. They lie about our place in the world. *They. Lie!*"

Kyra's anger boiled as the black flames leaped once again, washing over Iona's face. "Tell the truth!"

Iona screamed out from beneath the black flame, "*That is the truth! Nothing can change it! The elven killed them!*"

"Lies!"

The black flames engulfed Iona again. "*I swear!*" she replied, desperation clear in her voice.

"*No...*" the woman begged. "*Not again.*" Black flame washed over her. "*Not... again...*"

Again and again, Kyra denied the woman's cries of mercy. It could not be. All her life, she had blamed herself. It could not have been a lie. It could not be false. Everything she was and ever would be was based on that one simple fact: that she had killed them. That she had killed her family. Killed who she once was. Without that... Who was she?

Who was she?

Suddenly, powerful arms gripped her. Kyra snapped back to confront her new enemy, but found Adathin, clothing torn, bloody and dirty, and a makeshift tourniquet around his broken leg. He had come for her. He had come.

"Enough," he whispered through soft sobs. "Please... enough."

Kyra found herself lucid once again, and she lowered her arms from a combative stance into submission. She had no more will to fight. She could barely feel anything at all. As she stood, she turned back to Iona, and saw the horrors of what she had done. Iona face... the skin, still perfectly intact, held two smoldering orbs for eyes, and a soft plume of smoke rose from the woman's mouth and nose.

"What happened?" Kyra asked. "Who did this to her?"

Adathin stood, using her as a prop more than his own strength. "Let's just forget that for now—"

"*What happened?*" she repeated.

Adathin sighed. "Your—your black flame... it burned her, but not entirely. With each denial of her lie, your flames enveloped her, but only burning portions of her body. Her eyes and her tongue. She made you see lies, so you tore her eyesight from her. She spoke lies, so you made her forever silent."

"I... did that?"

Adathin nodded before adding, "And I would never lie to you. Never. So believe me when I tell you now that you saved me. No, you saved us. All of us."

"Saved... You?" The words felt weak in her ears; like pleasant lies. How could she save anyone when she couldn't even save her parents?

When she couldn't even save herself?

EPILOGUE

It isn't safe for us in Mistbreak anymore. It isn't safe. You must—You must leave. You must take Willow and the other pactless away. Far away. There will be a reckoning from both the Spellbound Arch and the Elven Conclave. And believe me, you do not want to be there to soak the blame when their ilk arrives.

It had been a letter from Reylar. A warning, and a gift.

Willow turned the small red crystal over and over in her hands that had come with the letter. It appeared rough, but felt as smooth as a handled diamond. Reylar had mentioned that this stone would block elven psionics. That it was his last gift to the one who would protect his daughter.

"Still pondering on his words, I see," Quistis said, running her hand across her back. "And still holding that trinket?"

"It isn't a trinket," Willow replied. "It is a marvel. A miracle."

Quistis rolled her eyes. "Don't be so dramatic."

Quistis pressed closer still, her warm body pressing against her own. She breathed heavily as pain crept into her mind.

Quistis took a sudden step back, muttering, "Sorry."

"It's alright," Willow replied. "I'm still a bit tender, is all."

"Are you sure there's nothing else I can do for you?"

Willow shook her head. "Just make sure everyone who wishes to leave with us is ready to go."

"They are," Quistis replied. "All of them. Not a single one of the pactless wants to stay in Mistbreak. None want to leave your side. You—You did that! You inspired them. Gave them hope. You're their leader, forever more. And as their leader, I believe it is time. Time to give back what you've taken and claim what has always been yours."

Willow smiled softly. "Now who's being dramatic?"

"And yet I don't hear disagreement in your tone... *Viessa.*"

Viessa... even hearing that name sent a chill up her spine. Yet, it was not a chill of dread, as she would have expected, but one of... *anticipation.* Then there was a change. A shift. Who she was fell away and who she was now stepped into the light.

"Make sure they are ready, Willow," Viessa said. "Tell them I have something to say."

Quistis'—No, *Willow's* eyes went bright with admiration and love. "I will do as you say," she replied. Then, at the doorway, she turned and added, "*Oh,* and there is a peculiar fellow wishing to speak to you. Or perhaps it's a woman—I always have such trouble with dwarves and their long beards. Should I send them in to you?"

"No," Viessa said, forcing herself to stand. It took far more effort than she was willing to admit. "Appearances are everything, especially now. I'll take them in my judgment room; one last resolution to make. One last time."

Everything had happened in a flash. I remember Adathin comforting me and then the mages appeared, with Elder Regular in tow. Adathin quickly separated from me as his sister appeared as well. Surprisingly, there seemed to be genuine worry on her face as she fussed over her brother's injuries.

I remember the burning smell; the smoldering. Glimpsing Iona, I had seen a plume of black smoke rising from her open mouth. She was on her knees, staring up towards the heavens with burnt-out, blackened eyes.

She had deserved it, and worse still.

Lhoris had soon appeared as well and as soon as his eyes fell upon Iona, it was as if her spell shattered, leaving the man with the memories of how much she had deceived him. She had preyed upon him; his hatred of mages and his ego—he had fallen headfirst into her lies. With tears in his eyes, Lhoris confessed his crimes on the spot to Elder Reylar, who subsequently had the man arrested and taken away.

As for myself, I had sent all who tried to heal me away until Maxim came. Without so much as a stutter, the man said, "Let me heal you. Please."

I did—I let Maxim heal me as best he could. It had felt the same as the healing I had received from Master Lu'ce in the past. Maxim soon moved to Adathin against Aluriel's protests that I was restored before her precious brother. Adathin spared me a pitying look. I had wondered why. He had been far worse off than myself.

Remembering Soren and Armeya, other mystics that I hadn't recognized were already healing them and they appeared barely conscious... but alive. Somehow alive. All had survived from her circle.

Even Iona, the spellthief herself.

It had been the Elders' turn to speak to me, despite my throbbing migraine and wish to sleep for eternity. "What happened?" he had asked, but when I had trouble answering, he relented, insisting that we would talk later.

Those later talks had never manifested the way he wanted. I had held back much of what I knew, although I revealed the most important thing of all: Iona had killed those mages—all of them. When I explained she enchanted her father's old ringpact using the ringpacts of the slain mages to enhance her power, and that her father had slain an elvish, giving the ringpact her psionic abilities, Elder Reylar had warned me against speaking of that ever again. He had said it was dangerous information to carry; that one utterance could plunge the world into ruin and war. I promised I wouldn't... but war was

all I could think of. War against those who would harm me. War against the
elvish man who had slain my family.

War against the elvish themselves.

I had burned at that last thought. Whenever I had resigned myself to that
fate, the thought of Adathin broke through the storm. How could I hate all
elvish when I didn't hate him? He was my living proof that not all were like
the man from my nightmares. I am an arcanist. I must speak truth; I like
Adathin.

No, I love him, in my own way.

But that love will not stop me from my vengeance. My family will be avenged.
I will find the elvish man with the strange markings upon his face and it will
be an end to my lifetime of misery.

One way or another, I will end my misery.

End

Arcanist: Spellthief

Made in the USA
Columbia, SC
25 August 2024

ac618c83-24e9-4225-8e71-c20dea748ab8R01